The Radiant Heart Awakens

Book Two

Daniel Lance Wright

Sage Publishing

Sage Publishing

Dedication

I'd like to dedicate this book to all those quiet, hard-working farm families on the South Plains of Texas. They go about the business of producing food and fiber the country cannot live without. They seek no fame but are among the most patriotic Americans.

Chapter One

The Awakening

Thanksgiving Day
Coos Bay, Oregon

Thirty-one-year-old Melissa Dane-Blakely rolled over and sat up on the side of the bed, a night's sleep having mostly eluded her. Groggy and dry-mouthed, she wondered if it finally happened. Had she become one of those annoying mouth breathers, snoring loud enough to rattle bric-a-brac on the dresser? A disgusting thought, but quickly replaced by another. *What are those odd dreams about? Why so vivid? And, for God's sake, why do they continue after I wake? Am I really awake?* She snickered lazily. *Maybe I wasn't.* She stretched stiffness from her neck with a hard side-to-side bend of the head. *That's the second time this week and the third time in two weeks—always the same, down to the tiniest detail. I'd swear I'm looking at it, not dreaming of it.*

Melissa yawned and scratched her head. Like the other times, she had no choice but dismiss it as a by-product of an over-active imagination—a quirk of the mind brought on by stress. It could be the result of things happening beyond her control at the clinic where she worked. There were a number of stressful situations popping up there all the time. What other explanation could there be? In the overall scheme of things, the dreams were unimportant. *I had to have been asleep and thought I was awake. Lucid dreaming? Yeah. I think they call it lucid dreaming.* She nodded affirmatively.

She heard her mother, Cary, clanking pots and pans downstairs in the kitchen. It was early, but her mother had already begun preparing Thanksgiving dinner. Melissa checked the over-sized and unfeminine appearing wristwatch that she loved and wore all the time. It wasn't eight o'clock yet. Although the kitchen noises were sharp, they were comforting—a home full of life—smells wafting up to this second floor bedroom divine. She tilted her head back and drew them in through flared nostrils. "Ahh." A small thing maybe, but something she missed, having lived on her own a number of years. But, she most assuredly had not missed seeing her stepfather every day. Even a passing thought of that man was enough to draw her brow into an angry knit—like now.

William Blakely was an alcohol abuser. In the past few months, he had begun consuming obscene quantities of liquor. The more he drank, the less father-like he was. Worse yet, verbal abuse of her mother was becoming louder and increasingly violent. Always over petty, senseless things. Of that, Melissa could not abide.

Melissa had a nice home of her own in Coos Bay, only a few miles from this place, her mother's house. She rented an apartment near the clinic where she worked. But it was Thanksgiving and chose to sleep over anyhow. Until recently, she preferred the single life, but alone on a holiday translated as loneliness. At these times of the year, she wanted to be around her mother, sister, and brothers.

Although enjoying her lifestyle as a single professional woman, the living alone thing was undergoing a slow, but steady, metamorphosis. A career as a nurse practitioner blessed her with income enough to live comfortably without a roommate, or a husband. Lately, the appeal of having a family of her own beckoned. Simple things, previously ignored, now grabbed and held her attention—seeing a mother with a laughing baby in her arms or a hand-in-hand couple walking the street with star-struck affection in exchanged gazes. At thirty-one, she moved to the precipice of transforming burgeoning thoughts into a goal. Melissa now looked at single men through different eyes. Although appearance and personality remained important, she realized that limiting herself to these attributes was shallow. But for years, that's how she assessed potential dates at bars, night clubs, or anywhere else. In the past few months, she had begun assessing qualities of the men she met as potential fathers and husbands—a transformation in thinking that slammed to the forefront of her thoughts overnight on her thirtieth birthday. That's the day something sprang to life inside her. Thoughts on what constituted a relationship changed, radically.

She shuffled out of the bedroom, across the hall into the bathroom, toothbrush and toothpaste tube in hand. Squaring with the vanity mirror, she ran spread fingers through her very short dark auburn hair a couple of times, then patting it into a slightly better arrangement. She turned her head side to side, checking the lay of ultra-short hair. It didn't matter or alter appearance much when she ran her hand over it, tending to spike at the crown, regardless. Plus, the plan was to don jogging gear and run for a while. She didn't need to look too chic anyhow.

Melissa inherited physical characteristics of her biological father, Kyle Dane. He had been murdered by a psychopath when she was four and before her sister, Kyra, was born. Her mother was pregnant with her younger sister at the time. Melissa was five-eight, athletically slender, skin appearing sun-kissed, even in the dead of winter with no help from a tanning booth. In the right light, her dark hair shimmered red highlights. She pasted the brush and renewed the sparkle on her teeth.

Melissa wriggled into form-fitting compression tights—her preferred running pants—topped with a snug tank top tucked in. Today's color choice was navy blue on bottom and sky-blue on top. Although the dawn boasted a clear sky, she figured it would be as chilly as yesterday. She slipped on a black zippered hoodie and pulled down a gray stocking cap over her ears. She jammed socked feet into running shoes and was tying laces into compact bows when her mother called out from downstairs, "Missy? Is that you rattling around up there?"

"Yeah, Mom. I'm up. Just getting ready to go for a run and burn a few calories before sitting down to that great dinner you're preparing." She bounced up from the edge of the bed and hurried downstairs and across the hall into the kitchen. "Good morning," she told her mother, walking straight toward her.

Cary, her mother, fingered a few strands of hair showing beneath the stocking cap on Melissa's forehead. She then hugged her oldest daughter. "Good morning, baby. Sleep well?"

"Let me say the bed was comfortable and everything else just right but...no. It was sort of a fitful night."

Cary pushed her away. "Why?" Are you coming down with something?"

"Oh no. Nothing like that. It's a recurring dream that, oddly, doesn't feel like a dream. It's like...well, like lying on my side watching a movie with no plot." She sighed. "I must have been asleep and thought I was awake. You know, like a lucid dream. Still, I don't understand why it has been the same dream three times and, each time, they're identical, absurdly clear and detailed."

Cary's face sagged into a strange expression. "What...exactly...did you see in the dream?"

Melissa pulled a knit in her brow as she marshaled thoughts. "That's part of its absurdity. You know that big ol' monstrosity of a house Uncle Jack built in Texas?"

"Yeah."

"Last night was the third time I found myself looking at the front door of the place and thinking if I stepped inside that house my life would never be the same again. I became convinced that if I took a step, I'd be there, in that place and feel a warm breeze, like a summer day just outside that big entry door. Not only that, I had no doubt what I gazed upon was a peek into the future. Strange, huh?"

"Possibly."

"Possibly?" Melissa gave a curious puppy dog head tilt, and then reared her head away to get a better look at her mother's sinking expression. "Why are you looking at me like that?"

"Missy, I think I should find out more about your dreams, but not right now. It has to do with something your Uncle Jack told me a couple of years before he died."

"Sure. How about you and I take in a little Black Friday shopping tomorrow. We can find a quiet place for a light lunch and talk?"

"Sounds wonderful. It's a date. We can..." her mother said, but then abruptly paused.

"Go ahead. Finish the thought."

"I want your sister to join us for shopping, but not sure she needs to be present for our conversation."

Melissa rolled her eyes. "Mom, Kyra's a big girl. Whatever you have to say, or whatever we discuss, I'm sure she can handle it." She licked her lips and inclined her head. "You're scaring me a little with the way you're talking. Does insanity run in the family, and you think I'm touched by it, or something like that?"

Her mother resurrected a happy face and chuckled. "Oh no. Nothing like that. In fact, you're probably the sanest one in this family." She shielded her mouth. "Just don't tell Kyra I said so."

Melissa grinned. "If I did, it would be an excellent way to start a fight. It wouldn't be Thanksgiving without the traditional family argument."

"That reminds me. When William starts going on and on about the economy, the state of politics, religion, or anything controversial, *please*, Missy, don't antagonize him like you did last Thanksgiving. For heaven's sake, roll with it. Let's have a peaceful dinner this year."

From an early age, Melissa harbored a strong dislike for her stepfather, William Blakely. Disdain for the man had begun exponentially rising. He was a strong-willed authoritarian, always had been. Heavy drinking impacted his personality, adding a violently aggressive note. No longer did he consider his rants as opinions, instead, hard facts he did not allow anyone to question. Some made no sense to anyone except him. He did not converse. It was always a profanity laced tirade that eventually turned into verbal abuse directed toward her mother. Melissa was convinced there would come a day that a line would be crossed he could never return from.

"Okay. I'll not get into any debates with him, especially if he starts gulping whiskey and that bothersome blood-shot glint appears in his eyes." I'll bite my tongue and keep my mouth shut. But, I'll be doing it for you, Mom... only you."

"Good. Now go on and get your exercise. I have cooking to do. Kyra will get off work about noon and said she would come directly from the boutique. Both your brothers will be here about then as well."

"Okay." She inserted electronic ear buds, strung from her cell phone strapped to her upper arm with a Velcro band. "I'll jog over to Pony Creek and back. I shouldn't be gone more than an hour."

She left the house and stepped into a chilled morning. The brilliant unobscured sun was now up but low in the sky, casting long shadows off the towering pines in the park across the street. The air smelled metallic and tickled Melissa's nose. Her breath puffed white. She began walking, then faster, breaking into a comfortable jogging stride. Running cleared her mind, leaving thoughts to flow freely. Some of her best problem solving and decision-making were done while jogging.

She and Kyra's half-brothers—Charlie at twenty-four and Johnny at seventeen—tried to help with their dad's growing volatility. But both boys were afraid of the man's tendency toward violence. They might beg him to calm down on occasion, but never truly confront him. All William had to do was go red-faced and start yelling. Both brothers would back down to prevent an explosive situation. Melissa had no such compunction. She was not afraid of him, only angered by him. If he should ever touch her, or anyone in the family, in a physically abusive way, she would not hesitate to grab a lamp or a fireplace poker and knock humility into him. And, if she should happen to knock out a couple of teeth... oh well. He could either be real or be unconscious. She didn't care which. Adding fuel to Melissa's low opinion of her stepfather was that he walked away from a good job at Sullivan's logging operation over five years ago and never went back to work, becoming a sloven alcoholic. He lived off Cary's seven figure inheritance left her by her ex-brother-in-law, Jack Dane. Uncle Jack had no other living family.

Their murdered father, Kyle Dane, had been Jack's younger brother and only sibling. Melissa and Kyra were Jack's sole blood relatives. William made up endless excuses for not finding other employment. It became a tiresome mantra that the owner of the logging company poisoned the job market against him. Now he was making noise about selling the mansion set in the middle of a Texas cotton farm Uncle Jack had built years ago. But Melissa's mother shared that she dreamed of moving to Texas, following William's death and living out her life there. His current pace of alcoholism indicated that day would be sooner than later. He was already beginning to look jaundiced. Cary was unhappy, trapped in a loveless marriage but her gentle soul prevented her from saying it aloud. If it had not been for Charlie and Johnny, her mother may have left William years ago. It was Melissa's opinion of what might have been and still should be. Nonetheless, she believed it. Her mother refused to consider leaving for the Texas South Plains while William was still alive, leaving her half-brothers without a father. That kind of loyalty was virtually non-existent in this world today.

At seventeen, Johnny would graduate from high school at the end of May, six months away. Charlie was employed by the same logging company his father had walked away from while throwing a blasphemous tantrum. At twenty-four, he was on his own. The maturing brothers led Melissa to believe a day would soon come when her mother would, indeed, leave William and head to Texas—an opinion, maybe—but to Melissa, a stone-cold fact. Regardless of William's frequent bluster over the issue, Melissa's mother would never sell the Texas mansion—never.

Melissa was twenty minutes into her run. She sensed the presence of a slow rolling car coming up behind her. She didn't care to turn and see who the rude driver might be. She waved for them to go around. Breathing hard, puffs of white left her nose like the constant white clouds from a nineteenth century wood fired locomotive's bell-shaped exhaust rising from the front of it, chugging down a track.

Suddenly, the car's horn blasted from close range behind her.

Startled, Melissa stumbled up and over the curb. She struggled to regain balance while awkwardly trotting over the ankle-deep grass until re-establishing equilibrium. Supremely angered, she yelled, "You son-of-a-bitch!" She ripped the earbuds out. The music of *White Snake* along with it. She spun to face the arrogant bastard, jaw set to hurl a profane diatribe, but saw her younger sister, Kyra, behind the wheel.

Her sister laughed so hard that tears streamed. Kyra regained control, easing off the guffaw. She let down her window and said, in contrived indignation, "I'll have you know, I'm *not* a son-of-a-bitch. I am the daughter of a lovely woman." She snickered again.

"Kyra! You scared me!"

"Aha. So, my nefarious, possibly ill-conceived plot worked."

Kyra Dane-Blakely was four years younger than Melissa at twenty-seven. The girls were different in looks and personality. People often refused to believe they were blood-related sisters, asking if she or Kyra might be adopted. Whereas Melissa had picked up ample Comanche traits from her biological father's side of the family, Kyra took after her mother's Gaelic roots. Kyra was five-five, fair-skinned with a freckled nose. Pale blue eyes sparkled beneath cascading strawberry blonde hair over ample cleavage.

"I thought you weren't supposed to get off work until noon," Melissa said.

"I have a wonderful boss. What can I say? She told me to go home and have a great Thanksgiving holiday. I didn't hang around long enough to ask why. You know—just in case it gave her a chance to remember things left undone and change her mind. I assumed since I worked half a day last Thanksgiving and put in a ten-hour day Black Friday last year, she was being nice. Besides, she has a couple of extra hands this year we didn't have at the dress shop last year."

"You're working for good folks."

"The best. Don't you think you've jogged enough? You're a couple of miles from home. It's a holiday, for heaven's sake. Hop in and I'll drive back."

Melissa hesitated. "Well...okay," she said, and then trotted around to the passenger side and hopped into Kyra's White Ford Taurus.

Kyra waited for a truck to pass and made a U-turn. "I hope dad keeps a lid on it today. We don't need a repeat of last year."

Melissa sighed. "You know, the older he gets, the more belligerent and foul-mouthed he becomes. His God-awful intimate relationship with a whiskey bottle seems to have accelerated and surpassed his concern and care for Mom."

"I'm well-aware how you feel about him. You won't even call him Dad."

"I remember our father, our real father, and it sure as hell isn't William. Dad was a real man."

"I understand. Still, since I was born after our father was killed, William is the only dad I've ever known."

Apologetically, "I know," Melissa replied. "I need to keep my anger in check for the sake of the rest of the family, especially for Charlie and Johnny. They're good guys and good brothers. I don't need to be antagonizing the old toot to the point of turning his anger on them. I couldn't live with myself if I did."

The drive home was quick. Kyra steered into the driveway. "Speaking of Charlie and Johnny, it looks as though they're here," Kyra said.

Melissa drank in the sight of the two-story house where she spent her formative years. "Are you ever going to move out and get your own place, Kyra?"

"I've thought about it...quite a lot actually. But every time I mention it to Mom, it's as though I tore a limb from her body and drove a stake through her heart. That pain is palpable in her responses."

Melissa laughed. "Sounds about right." She opened the car door and placed a foot on the ground. "Come on. Let's see if Mom needs help in the kitchen. It's after eleven o'clock and we're all here. If we pitch in and help things along, maybe we can eat early. I'm starving."

As Melissa led the way up the walk toward the front door, she glanced through a large bay window and saw William sitting on a sofa staring blankly at a television tuned to the local NBC affiliate, presumably watching the Thanksgiving Day Parade. He already had a high-ball glass on a table next to him nearly drained of its amber contents. She didn't need to smell-check it to know it was not apple juice. It angered her, knowing right then where this day was headed. By afternoon William wouldn't even worry about using a glass. He'd be holding a whiskey bottle by its neck and swilling it. She suddenly felt an odd chill, having nothing to do with the ambient temperature. Her white frosty breath suddenly seemed to suspend in front of her. Within it, a vivid image came into sharp focus—the front door of that Texas mansion her Uncle Jack built. It was not at all dreamlike. It was as genuine as the front door of her mom's house just ahead. She focused on the vision, scanning everything possible, picking out details, trying to determine if she was going nuts. Panic tingled the pit of her stomach.

Suddenly, the image folded in on itself and vanished.

The entire episode lasted only a second, maybe two. She turned to face Kyra in time to see her younger sister wave at Johnny and Charlie. They were tossing a football around in the side yard. "Kyra, did you see that?"

"See what?" Kyra replied, returning her attention to her older sister.

Melissa swallowed hard. The brief panic attack left her queasy. She swallowed again, this time gulping air. "Never mind." She abruptly lost her appetite.

***

William behaved exactly as Melissa expected at the dinner table yesterday bellowing on and on about everything wrong with the world and how good things would be if done his way. No other conversation was allowed traction. It was an hour-long rant from the head of the table. Numerous times, Melissa moved to the verge of attacking over nonsensical drunken crap spewing from him, sometimes accompanied by a spray cornbread dressing from between loose lips. Kyra kicked Melissa's ankle under the table several times to keep her older sister quiet.

With considerable effort, Melissa allowed Thanksgiving dinner at the Blakely's to end peacefully, earning her a grateful, "Thank you," mouthed quietly by her mother.

The following day Melissa looked forward to what her mother had to say about her dreams—if that was truly what they were. She always thought of sport shopping as too girlie to suit her, especially, Black Friday shopping. But she cherished spending time with her mother away from William. There were plenty of laughs and love to overshadow the annoyance of choking crowds.

It was almost noon. She and her mother dropped exhausted into a booth at a diner. "Whew," Cary said. "That was fun but I want no more." She laughed and held her hands above her head. "I give up."

Staring across the table at her mother, Melissa smiled. Age difference aside, her mother and Melissa's younger sister, Kyra, strongly resembled one another. The family facial and body features were nearly identical. For a woman of fifty-nine, Cary was attractive. *Mom could have any man she wants. She's beautiful.* "I'm done, too. Sport shopping is not my thing," Melissa replied. She looked around. "I know she didn't want to come with us, but is Kyra joining us for lunch?"

"She said she might, but..." She scrunched up her nose. "...I don't think she'll show. This time it's okay if she doesn't."

"Do you really think whatever we'll be discussing is so shocking that Kyra doesn't need to hear it?" Melissa noticed her mother's face go neutral and asked, "Okay, why the odd expression?"

"I have something I want to show you," Cary said. She retrieved a large manila envelope from her oversized purse and removed a thick stack of type-written pages, the outer sheets curled and smudged from years of handling.

"What is it?"

"A novel. Your Uncle Jack wrote it but died of a heart attack before having it published."

"I thought we were going to talk about my weird dreams...or whatever the heck they are?"

"We are. This is where it starts."

"I don't understand what a work of fiction has to do with it."

"Well, I called it a novel and it *is* labeled as such by Jack's own hand, but Missy, your Uncle Jack told me years before he wrote it that he would put it all on paper eventually. He was responding to my questions about why he appeared from nowhere seconds after your father was shot. I didn't believe his explanation. That's when he told me that someday he would write the entire story of his experiences. Here's the kicker: Jack said it would have to be called fiction, but it would all be true. Things happened on the day your father was murdered that I witnessed with my own eyes, making it difficult to doubt veracity," she said pecking the manuscript with a fingernail. "Still, I had no plan to share it with you or Kyra. It's too fantastical to grasp as truth. But, since you told me your story, I'm re-thinking it."

"Sounds to me like dear ol' Uncle Jack may have developed a few cranial misfires in his later years."

"Missy, honey, Jack Dane was one of the sanest people I ever met. He was also a skeptic. There were times even he didn't believe what he was capable of."

Curiosity grabbed Melissa. She snaked a hand across the table and pulled the pile of printed pages around to inspect them. She read the first couple of paragraphs. "He used his real name."

"Yes. I think he planned on changing all the names during the edit, but died before he could. As you read it, you'll see all the other names are quite genuine as well. All of them are deceased now...well, Jack and Arthur Wainwright are definitely deceased. Jack's girlfriend, Nikki Endicott vanished without a trace. She is presumed dead. Baby, I think what happened to Jack is happening to you."

Melissa's eyes grew large. "Happening?"

"I believe by virtue of Dane blood flowing in your veins, the radiant heart has been passed to you and is awakening, by virtue of your age and maturity. I'm not at all sure what those things have to do with initial manifestation. But you seem to be further proof there is truth to it."

"The radiant heart? I don't know what that is."

"Read the manuscript, Missy. As you do, remember that it is not fiction, but a detailed account of Jack Dane's life and experiences laid out in story form, according to what he told me years ago."

Chapter Two

A Glimpse into the Past

"This can't be real. Seriously? You've got to be kidding," Melissa Dane-Blakely muttered to herself. She spent Saturday into early Sunday morning, and most of Sunday afternoon reading Uncle Jack's account of events in, what he called, *The Last Radiant Heart*.

Her mother had been right about one thing. It was too fantastical to wrap her mind around as truth, more like delusions of a disturbed mind. There was no way it could have been published and labeled non-fiction. A few pages in and most serious readers of true stories would have tossed it aside. The book, at best, would have been rated one-star, if that. But as a work of fiction, it might have become recognized as a great read. Uncle Jack might have been searched for additional works to be sought after, like his little-known book about Comanche life on the plains of Texas during the westward migration of settlers in the nineteenth century. But *The Last Radiant Heart* is the one that held personal relevance for her.

She looked away from the manuscript to the large westerly facing window of her apartment. The sun had passed its daily zenith, pushing a sinking shadow line across her floor. After staring out at passing traffic on the street fronting her complex, digesting Jack Dane's writing, Melissa re-read the final sentence: *"Joining her parents in facing the light, Nikki Endicott looked back no more. Her radiant heart was born, as she stepped into eternity."*

"So, Uncle Jack's girlfriend willingly crossed over, leaving him behind. And he witnessed it? She mumbled to herself. "This book can't be a true account of events. *The Last Radiant Heart* is fascinating but give me a break," she mumbled to herself.

She mentally catalogued those parts of the book she knew to be factual. Top of mind had always been Jack's sudden and seemingly mystical appearance at her parent's neighborhood grocery store mere seconds after her father had been shot by that lunatic, Butch Johnson. Her mother had witnessed it. Minutes later, Cary watched her brother-in-law disappear with his two friends into an explosion of white light. Melissa also knew Nikki Endicott had been her uncle's college sweetheart who later became a behavioral psychologist. He reconnected with her years after the college fling. Arthur Wainwright had been a reasonably well-known psychic, easily researched to this day, on most internet search engines. It went without saying, Wainwright's fortune was huge. He left it all to Jack. Jack, in turn, left it all to her mother, Kyra, and herself.

Money her stepfather frivolously spent on booze and things the family didn't need. He should have been looking for a job and working on that pitiful attitude. She shook off the rabbit-trailing line of thinking. It had become too easy to sink into that mental muck.

One of the things she read repeatedly was her uncle's account of how each episode began: A sudden chill, with a blooming wispy cloud of white in front of his face. A picture would form in the center of it, but it was not merely a picture. Instead, according to him, it was a place—a destination beyond the space he occupied. It also could have been past or future. By his account it could as easily be a different dimension altogether—past, present, or future. The haze framing it was a portal he could pass through and physically transport himself to wherever the place happened to be, and in whatever time or dimension.

She sighed. "Okay," she said aloud, still staring out the window, now comparing her own experience. Did it mean the persistent image of that rambling mansion on a cotton farm in Texas was more than a simple mind's-eye image?

If so, why was she seeing it, and why now? Could she literally dive through and be there instantly, the next time it appeared? Was she seeing a past, present, or future version of the house? She thought it to be a vision of the future, but how could she know that? Every question coming to mind created a new one. She continued staring intently out her apartment window. Her eyes followed passing cars, but her mind was not on traffic.

Uncle Jack had Arthur Wainwright for guidance. All I have is mother. And she doesn't know much. She squeezed her burning eyes shut and wallowed balled fists into them to relieve dry discomfort from an unblinking stare. *Uncle Jack, I wish I had you to talk to about all this... this stuff.*

A shuddering chill suddenly swarmed over her. She opened her eyes and gasped.

Floating directly in front of her face was the image—the front door to the Texas mansion. "Oh...shit," she drawled. The white haze billowed again, opening the view down to the floor where she stood. She slowly turned her head. The image followed, keeping it centered in her field of vision. She turned her head back to the right. The image followed, remaining centered.

Slowly, she raised her hand and extended it hesitatingly toward the floating image. For the first time, she saw that the whitish glow was not only in front of her but surrounding her body as well. But it was not shining on her. It was emanating from her, and brighter over the left side of her chest, her heart. She continued pushing her hand toward what she saw. As her hand broke the plane, nausea washed over her. She jerked her hand back and swallowed the queasiness brought on by the shallow foray toward that door her focus was fixed upon.

She was scared. Curiosity equaled the fear. A thought came to her. Unlike previous visions of this mansion, she believed to be a glimpse into the future, this felt like the same view of the house but in a previous time.

She recalled, in the book, Wainwright told Jack that once the plane was breached by a human, the body reacted at the molecular level, causing nausea, but only for as long as it took to move all the way through the portal of light.

Melissa became concerned the image might fade, or worse, vanish altogether. She did not want that to happen—not yet. She needed to study it to understand what it was all about. Since it wasn't clear if the vision could be resurrected. She surmised that if she planned on doing something, it had better be soon.

The thought scarcely cleared her mind. She reacted before apprehension could hold her back.

She quickly stepped forward into it.

The whitish glow exploded into a brilliant all-encompassing light. She felt as though she might vomit and squeezed her eyes shut, but then realized, after a scant second, the nausea was gone.

A warm breeze brushed her face and teased her short auburn hair. Even before opening her eyes, she noticed the white light had abruptly changed intensity—still bright, just not as much.

Melissa opened her eyes to see exactly what she had seen four times in the past couple of weeks.

It was no longer a simple vision.

She stood in a different place during—she was coming to believe—a previous time. *How the hell can I know I am in the past, a couple of thousand miles from home?* Still, she had no choice but to believe her eyes and senses. She was there, standing before the front door of the mansion on what felt to be a very warm and sunny afternoon, judging by the position of the sun.

Fear sent a tingle streaking up her spine. She backed away, breathing shallow and fast, eyes bulging.

She heard a commotion to her left and snapped a look.

A young boy about six, maybe seven, came running around the corner of the house chasing a small white dog. Grime smeared the boy's face. Both knees of his jeans sported frayed holes. The youngster had clearly been playing outdoors for quite some time.

He came to a sudden stop. "Who are you?" he asked.

The child's innocence had a calming effect on her. "I'm...uh...my name is Melissa. Can I ask a question?"

"Sure."

"Is this where Jack Dane used to live?"

The kid scrunched up his nose and tilted his head to a quizzical slant. "Used to?"

"Yeah, you know, before he died."

"Mister Dane ain't dead, lady. He's inside."

Melissa reared her head. "But..." she began. She quickly closed her mouth. Anything she said would be lost on a prepubescent boy. She hardly understood it herself. But she did realize that her innate sense of time period had been correct. She just didn't know exactly when in the past she stood. "Never mind. Are you a relative of Mister Dane's?"

"Oh, no ma'am. My mama is Mister Dane's housekeeper. My name is Dwayne Logan. We live here, too."

"You think I might talk to Mister Dane?"

"I bet you can. He's a nice guy. But let me go get Mama first." With considerable effort on the little guy's part, he pushed the massive nine-foot-high door open. The architectural detail of the double doors was striking. They were massive, richly stained hardwood with intricate carvings framing over-sized and ornate brass knockers. Even the door handle was almost too big for the small boy to get his hand around. The youngster poked his head inside and shouted, "Mama. Someone's at the front door."

Melissa looked beyond the youngster, standing at the threshold. She saw a pretty woman hurry toward the boy. "Dwayne," she scolded, "what have I told you about yelling inside the house? Mister Dane has work to do and can't concentrate with you making noise." Melissa noticed the woman's striking thick, short silver hair. It was obviously premature by many years. It did not detract from her inherent attractiveness. It actually enhanced her God-given beauty. Shimmering in the sunlight streaming through the open door of the monstrous house. This woman could not have been much older than she was, if any at all.

"Sorry, Mama, but this lady came to see Mister Dane."

The lady turned her attention away from the youngster and smiled at Melissa. She extended a friendly hand. "Hi, my name is Rita Logan, and this little guy with the dirty face and loud mouth is Dwayne, my son."

Melissa took Rita's hand. "It's nice to meet you both." She smiled at the woman but held an admiring gaze on the young boy with the blondish hair and dirty face. She was enamored by the mischievous sparkle in his eyes.

"Now, run along and play Dwayne. I'll take it from here," Rita said, turning her attention back to Melissa as the boy passed her on the way outside through the open front door.

Melissa watched him run after the little white dog. The animal was clearly his best friend. "That little guy is going to be a heartbreaker someday. He's cute."

Rita chuckled. "He's a handful to keep corralled, too. Why don't you step inside and wait in air-conditioned comfort," Rita told her. "It's too warm to wait out here. I'll go upstairs and see if Mister Dane has time to visit."

Melissa smiled appreciatively as she passed by Rita to stand in the foyer. She watched Rita head up the stairs. Melissa turned a circle, surveying all within view. *How can this be? I'm standing in a mansion that is over two thousand miles from Oregon at some point in the past, and it happened in the span of a single eye blink.*

From this vantage point, the foyer matched Jack's description in the book of Wainwright's Springfield mansion. She heard a muffled conversation upstairs and then a door closed.

Rita reappeared at the top of the stairs. "He's on his way down."

"Thank you," Melissa called out.

Rita descended the stairs, smiling a final time at her guest as she went down the hall and through a door, presumably to go back to work. Melissa continued examining surroundings.

After a moment, walking into view at the top of the stairs, was a man she had only seen in photographs. Her breath hitched when she realized how young he was. She thought she would be seeing an elderly man. This was no old person. He probably wasn't even out of his forties. *Oh, my God. This is two or three decades in the past.*

"May I help you?" he asked, frowning slightly.

Still recovering from shock, she didn't know how to answer the simple question, stammering, "I...uh, sure hope I haven't come at a bad time." She offered what she figured was a goofy childish shy smile.

He continued to advance toward her. "No, no. It's fine."

Melissa wanted to approach him, but her feet felt as though nailed to the floor. She forced a smile. "I'm thinking that you very well may be able to help me...Uncle Jack," she said haltingly.

"Uncle...?" he began. She saw light of comprehension flash in his eyes. "Are you Kyle's daughter, Melissa?"

Melissa nodded rapidly, nervously. Tears welled as she realized the strong resemblance to what she remembered her father looking like. "Yes," she replied, the word almost choking off before she finally spoke.

Jack hurried down the stairs and hugged her. Still holding her, he leaned away to look into her eyes. "Since I've been through this many times, you're presence doesn't shock me." Melissa saw the wheels of his mind turning by the way he gazed into her eyes. "I flew out to see your mother last winter and you are only seven years old." Wonder took over the expression on his face. He smiled. "Clearly, you have come from a future time. You grew into a beautiful woman."

She vaguely remembered the visit he mentioned all those years ago. "This is all too unreal. That was so long ago, I'm having trouble recalling details of that visit."

"From that statement, it would seem you haven't used the radiant heart much."

"This is the first time. I'm here because I suddenly had a strong desire to talk to you about it. Everything else just...happened."

Jack smiled. "There's no bigger skeptic than me and, yes, it all does seem unreal. I suspect it will feel that way the rest of your life. After every episode of invoking the radiant heart and then returning, I could never accept it as genuine. I simply thought I was going insane. Still, it happened again and again and again, of course. It took a long time, but I finally came to accept it, and that it was not the imaginings of a demented mind. Personally, I don't want to use it anymore. It still unnerves me to know the damage I might cause unwittingly. I suggest you be very careful with it. There are still too many things I don't understand about it."

"I deeply appreciate that you're sharing a most important point first." She considered what he said for a moment. "So, if I'm seven in this time, your time, then this would have to be twenty-four years ago."

"I don't know how much you comprehend," Jack said, "but even if you already know it, it bears repeating. Once you leave to go back to your time, I'll retain absolutely no memory that you were ever here. Neither will Rita or Dwayne. The time you spend here will disappear and things will revert to the way they were before you set foot inside this house. Still, you're welcome to come back anytime." He grinned. "And I do mean any *time*. Although, you will have to introduce yourself at the onset of every visit. The only advantage you'll have is that I'll immediately assume you are a radiant heart like me when you tell me who you are. So, the introduction process will be quick on each visit. It will always be a bit surprising, but never shocking."

"Something inside me let me know this was in the past. I just didn't know how far in the past."

"Stay in tune with intuition and you will come to understand that it was no accident. You might not have realized it, but you chose this time. All I did was confirm it." He placed a contemplative finger to his lips. "How did you know what to do?"

"From your book."

"What book?"

"Oh crap. Maybe I shouldn't have told you. You won't write it for another ten, or so, years."

He smiled indulgently. "Remember, I won't retain a single memory of this visit. So, it doesn't matter that you told me. It is nice to know, if only for the duration of this brief visit, that I will write it someday." His face went serious. "In case you don't already know, you cannot alter a past event. There is nothing you can do to permanently change things that have already happened. That's the reason there will be no memory by me you were ever here. The same is true for Rita and her son. Say, as an example, as extreme as it might be, that if you pick up a gun and shoot me, I'll only be dead as long as you are in the past altering events. When you leave, time line will revert to the natural order they occurred in without your intrusion. But, more importantly, you must always remember, if *you* are harmed during a past event, it is real and lasting because you are in your personal present. That travels with you. Be careful. If anything should happen, you would be a missing person in your time, never to be seen or heard from again. You will simply have vanished, literally. Never to return."

"That's difficult to comprehend. Although, I do remember from your book that Mister Wainwright explained all that to you."

He chuckled, and then held a thoughtful smile. "Adding 'Mister' in front of Arthur's name sounds odd. The man is like an aged teenager, a hippy."

"So, Wainwright is still alive?"

"I should have said *was* an aged hippy." He sighed. "I sometimes feel as though he and Nikki Endicott are still watching over me. I'm sorry to say they are both gone." His head drooped. He stared at his feet with tightly pursed lips.

Melissa let him have the quiet moment.

"On a lighter note," he went on, "the inheritance Arthur left me financed construction of this house and the purchase of the Endicott farm it sets on."

He took a step toward the hallway and called out, "Rita, would you be so kind as to make a fresh pot of coffee?"

"Of course," came the reply.

It was easy now to understand why her mother had said Jack Dane became a recluse in later years. She recognized in his manner and by the mournful ring in his voice, he missed Arthur Wainwright and Nikki Endicott more than he could bear.

Melissa and her uncle walked out back of the house into a beautiful garden replete with statues in Roman and Greek styles, plus a plethora of cast-concrete figurines and several working fountains. It was beautiful and peaceful. It was also oddly out of place. A giant house surrounded by cotton fields in Texas. Statues of Davy Crockett and his Alamo brethren would seem much more in tune with this setting for heaven's sake.

Melissa took note of how wide open the Plains of Texas were, having grown up in the Pacific Northwest where tall trees, hills, and even high humidity had a way of obscuring the horizon in all directions. From where she sat, she could see to the curve of the earth—one cotton or grain field after another all the way to the horizon.

They enjoyed coffee and spoke at length about all things radiant heart related. Melissa was in the genesis of understanding the beauty and danger of it. All made possible by her mind and power of her heart. So enthralled with the stories told her by Jack, she had not realized how much time had passed. She glanced at her wristwatch, noticing they had been talking for over two hours. "I've got to get home and back to my time, Uncle Jack. How, exactly, do I do that?"

"Easy. Close your eyes and clear your mind. Draw a vivid mental image of where you came from and the precise moment you chose to come here. Think about your desire to be there. Your heart will do the rest."

Once you vanish from my sight, I will instantly be back upstairs working on my book about the Comanche people in this area over two hundred years ago and remember nothing of you. Tell your mother hello for me and hug her on my behalf."

Melissa became emotional. Her eyes moistened. "This has been wonderful."

They rose from their chairs at the same time, came together, and embraced. He pushed her back far enough to look into her eyes. In a low soothing voice he whispered, "Now, close your eyes and do what I told you to do and go home. Love you, kiddo."

"I love you, too," she replied. The words came out in a choking rasp as emotional tears filled her eyes. "Someday, Uncle Jack, you will be reunited with Nikki and Arthur," she said, knowing he wouldn't remember it anyhow.

Melissa closed her eyes. Things happened quickly. She envisioned her apartment. Brilliant light bloomed through closed eyelids followed by a nausea flash. She felt the temperature, smells, and light intensity change instantly. She opened her eyes to her own apartment and swiped away the tumbling tears on her cheeks. She again looked at her wristwatch and then compared it to the time on the clock next to her television. Her watch was two hours and twenty-seven minutes ahead of that clock, realizing the same amount of time had been neutralized for Uncle Jack. The difference? She had not only disappeared from his presence but from his mind as well. Melissa shuddered at the enormity of what had happened.

And then the craziest thought crossed her mind. *Jack and I shared coffee. If things reverted to the way they had been before I showed up there, it means that pot of coffee was never made. How can that be? I drank a cup. I know I did. I can still taste it.* The paradox widened her eyes and slackened her jaw. She shuddered again.

Chapter Three

Echoes of the Heart

Since no time had passed, regardless how long she spent with her uncle in Texas, it remained early, not yet four o'clock in the afternoon in Coos Bay. She virtually raced to her car and drove to her mother's house to share the story of the experience, needing to tell someone what had happened—what *she* had done. Her mother was the only one who wouldn't think she had lost her mind. Although, she wasn't ready to dismiss that possibility. To the end of his life, Jack Dane continually questioned his own sanity.

Unlike the clear warm day she encountered in the Lone Star State, the afternoon here was overcast, quite cool with high humidity. The Texas high plains' breeze she left behind was dry, light, and velvety. Markedly different than the clammy, heavy sensation on her skin here in the Pacific Northwest.

She wheeled into the driveway of her mother's house faster than necessary. Tires squealing, she bounced up the short incline off the street, and braked to a hard stop.

In the rush to talk to her mother, it had not occurred to her that she needed time to reflect on the reality of what had happened. Did it really? Or was it more like that lucid dream she thought it to be in the beginning? Maybe reading Jack Dane's book, *The Last Radiant Heart*, had intricately messed with her mind. Maybe it was a shared delusion unique to uncle and niece.

She drew a deep breath and sighed. *No. It was real. Had to be. Far too much sensory stimulation to have been a dream...of any stripe.*

She bounded out of the SUV and didn't stop to knock. Opening the front door of the house, she hurried in. "Mom," she called out as she walked. "Where are you?"

The first room she passed was William's favorite hangout. He sat in his chair in front of the television. He looked over at her, eyes heavily veined, and blandly said, "Hey." An empty highball glass set on the table next to him. She wondered how many he'd already had today.

"Hey to you, too. Where's Mom?"

"Don't know. Don't care."

She frowned. "Right." She paid him no more mind, methodically walking down the hall, looking through every open door. "Mom?"

"Back here, sweetheart," came the reply from her mother's sewing room.

Melissa rounded into the small room, a cozy nook just inside the back door across from the laundry room. It was her mother's tiny getaway space. The irony of it was that her mother owned the whole house, having paid cash for it upon inheriting Jack Dane's fortune.

"Whatcha doin'?" Melissa asked.

"Sewing a new apron. That ratty old thing I wore Thanksgiving was embarrassing." She placed the unfinished apron next to the sewing machine and turned to Melissa. "You sure seem excited about something, and I'm sure it's not my new apron."

First of all, stand up," Melissa said with a beaming grin.

"What on earth...?"

"I've been asked to give you something and I can't do it as long as you're sitting."

Cary rose tentatively. "You're scaring me."

"This is a nice thing, not a scary thing." Melissa closed the gap and embraced her, squeezing tight. "Uncle Jack asked me to hug you on his behalf. I'm keeping my promise."

Cary abruptly pushed her daughter away, back-stepping out of Melissa's embrace. She almost stumbled over her sewing chair. Her surprised lips parted. Eyes widened. "Jack has been dead for a lot of years."

Still smiling, Melissa nodded. "Yeah. I know."

"You saw him? Today? Here in Coos Bay? What are you talking about?"

"Yes, yes, and no. He didn't come here. I went there."

"There, where?"

"That big ol' house in the middle of a Texas cotton farm," she said, and then emphasized, "Twenty-four years in the past."

"Oh, hon," her mother drawled incredulously. "You read his manuscript, didn't you?"

"Yep, and then did it. I invoked the radiant heart. I can do it, like Uncle Jack could. Since I had plenty of information on the subject, vis-a-vis his book, The Last Radiant Heart, I was a bit uneasy but not at all, frightened by it. Unlike Jack who had no guide and was scared out of his mind by it. Because he had absolutely no clue what was happening to him. I went into the image I saw multiple times in those visions that I told you about, except it happened to be in the past this time, not the future, as I still believe those visions were."

"I would have been petrified and not capable of taking a step or even something as simple as lifting an arm. But you weren't scared? At all?"

"A little at first. But, after Jack's own shock and surprise faded, which happened quickly, he embraced me with open arms and we had a long talk sitting on the patio sipping coffee. All fear and apprehension went away quickly. But, Mom, if you hadn't given me that manuscript to read, and should it have happened inadvertently, I would have had a heart attack and died of fright. I have no doubt of that. It was a weird sensation."

Cary dropped back onto her sewing chair. "It's very disconcerting."

"Hey, what's the name of the guy who works that farm in Texas now?"

"Dwayne Logan and his father, Cletus. I get updates on crops and condition of the house over the phone from Dwayne a couple of times a year. Why?"

"That's what I thought. I met Dwayne." She chuckled. "He was a cute little guy with blond hair and a dirty face."

"I think he's about your age," Cary said. "I pay Dwayne a monthly retainer over and above crop-share to maintain the mansion to a livable standard." A sheepish look crossed her face. She bobbled her head. "I have Mister Logan do that just in case, you know, I get to follow through on my dream of moving to Texas someday."

"Don't give up on it, Mom. You call it a dream. I call it a plan that simply hasn't come to fruition yet."

"Dwayne fixed up the old stucco house on the property that had belonged to the Endicott's, the previous land owners. He lives there."

"Married?"

"Why would you ask that? You've never seen him...grown up that is."

"He was a very cute *little* boy. I can tell you that."

Cary laughed. "To my knowledge, he's not married." She paused and a whimsical look crossed her face. "He lives with Cletus, his father. I think they're both bachelors. Dwayne's mother, Rita, is out of the picture. But I have no idea if she's alive or dead. She doesn't live with them. I do know that."

Melissa's eyes drifted away. "Good to know about Dwayne."

"Cary," came William's gruff voice, slurring slightly. "Fix me something to eat. That crap you fixed for lunch didn't stick with me."

Melissa growled, hissing through clenched teeth, "Everything that comes out of that man's mouth irritates me."

"Calm down, sweetheart. Maybe I can talk him into taking us out to a restaurant for an early Sunday dinner."

Melissa rolled her eyes. "Good luck with that."

Cary walked down the hall and peeked around the corner. William sat in his recliner watching the Seahawks lose another game. He was mumbling curses at them. "How about we call Kyra and the boys and meet them at Rodeo Steakhouse? She asked him. We can enjoy an early dinner as a family." She smiled. "Best part is I wouldn't have to cook. It'll be my treat."

William slowly turned his head in a measured way, eyes red and puffy. Sobriety having left him hours ago. He appeared as though he was on the verge of losing consciousness. That didn't prevent exploding anger directed at his wife. "Hell no! Now, get in the damn kitchen and fix me something to eat," he slurred, slobbering over every word. He dismissed her notion in the vilest of ways and then turned back to the television, as if his attack on Cary was simply life as it should be."

Melissa marched around her mother into the living room. "Why is it you feel the need to be an absolute ass about *everything*?" she bellowed.

William clumsily sprang out of the recliner and stood, swaying side to side. "Don't you disrespect me, girl!" he shouted, blowing slobber.

"Disrespect you? Did I hear that right? From what I've seen is that you respect nothing beyond a full whiskey bottle! Mom is your wife and mother to all your children! And she's a damn good one, too! Respect her and your children, then maybe you can earn some *respect*!"

Cary grabbed her daughter's arm and attempted pulling her back in the midst of her daughter's rant. "It's okay, sweetie. Really. I'll fix him something to eat. It's not a big deal," she rattled.

Melissa yanked her arm free of her mother's grasp and continued the tirade, "You don't have a clue *what* respect is! You just disrespected your wife and my mother in the most disgusting ways imaginable. She's not your slave and personal piggy bank, you selfish idiot! Her voice ratcheted into a higher octave. "There's not a loving bone in your whole damn body for anyone but yourself!"

William's swimming eyes flashed fury. He came at her with a clenched fist. "By God, you'll never talk to me like that again. I'll make sure of that right now, you bitch!" he growled through gritted teeth. He stumbled over the corner of the coffee table, impeding the speed of his advance.

"Take your best shot, you sonofabitch!" Melissa held her ground.

Cary hurriedly came around Melissa and took a position between them. "Stop! Both of you!"

Melissa ranted in a barely controlled shout, "You're a rabid animal that should be treated like one! Dropped so far back in the woods that you'd never find your way out! Never, you bastard! Never!"

William swung a hard fist into the side of Cary's head. "Get out of my way!"

Cary spun away and fell to the floor with a whimper. She grabbed the point of impact and went limp as consciousness slipped.

Melissa's anger hit a new high. A brilliant white light exploded around her.

The image that instantly appeared was of towering trees with dense, brushy undergrowth.

William reached for and grabbed her by the arms. Melissa made a snap decision to go wherever that image happened to be and take him with her. Even as he clutched her, she grabbed wads of his shirt tail and, with all her might, pulled him into the light. The nausea lasted for only a second.

She shoved William away from her.

He happened to be so intoxicated, the nausea flash affected him to a much greater extent. He bent at the waist and vomited.

It gave her a chance to survey the area and attempt to figure out where they might be. It suddenly occurred to her, she shouted her desire to drop him deep in the woods *somewhere*, which is where they were. She had no notion as to location, or if they were even still in Oregon. As a young girl, she once lost her way in the woods and panicked before her mother and father found her. She grew up scared of being left in the woods and unable to find her way out. This forest she and her stepfather now stood in was not familiar. She glanced around and saw nothing to anchor an opinion of where she unceremoniously slung William, and herself. She couldn't figure out where or when they landed.

William regained a measure of composure along with all his anger. It clearly hadn't registered on his drunken mind he was no longer inside his house. If he was aware, he didn't care. He shouted, "I'm gonna make you bleed, girl!" He stumbled toward her.

Melissa knew how physically unfit he was and decided running uphill was the better choice. She saw a rocky path meandering up a hill where none of the spiny undergrowth had a chance to grow.

Remaining far out in front of him was easy. She reached the top of the hill and moved to the edge of a precipice. A vista opened up. She looked across a broad valley. As her eyes swept to the far side, she noticed a forest on the opposite cliff, but different—very different from the one she now stood in. Even the sky over those woods was different. The whole scene was bathed in light without shadows. Colors flashed with phenomenal vibrancy. Trees towered in a park-like setting. What she saw appeared diametrically opposite of where she stood at the moment—this warm, overly humid, and ragged, overgrown woods. Even at this distance, she clearly saw birds, deer, lambs, and all manner of docile creatures milling about among people. Interestingly, there were also predator animals among them that seemed at peace. *Could this be that dimension bridging life and death Uncle Jack wrote about in his book? His version was much bleaker—a muddy lake full of skeletons, dead trees everywhere, and very hot sunshine. This has to be my version of it, created from my own fear.* "Oh my God! This is not earth at all! It's a parallel dimension bridging life and death."

She glanced back and saw William, relentlessly stumbling up the hill with a singular purpose, to hurt her. How strange it was he had not acknowledged or wondered where he was. He couldn't be that drunk? Or could he? As she watched him come up the hill, she thought, *All I want is to go home and you to stay.*

The white glow enveloped her body. She closed her eyes. The musty smell of the moldy damp forest, the sound of William's stumbling and grunting approach over rocky ground covered in brambles, and sticky warmth vanished.

She opened her eyes and was back in the living room in her mother's home. Cary lay on the floor, addled from William's hard right fist to her head. William Blakely was no longer in the room, presumably gone forever. "Mother," Melissa said, dropping to her knees beside the woman, "Are you okay?"

Cary moaned and stirred. "I...I think so."

Melissa helped roll her over onto her back.

Cary glanced around. "Where's William?"

"I honestly don't know. In the woods somewhere is all I can tell you. But, Mom, I don't think it was anywhere on earth—at least not in this dimension."

"Did *you* do it?"

She nodded. "It must have been a radiant heart thing when I made the crack about dropping him in the woods and hoping he never found his way out. That's apparently what I did." She remembered a section of Uncle Jack's book when Wainwright explained to him, if someone accompanies a radiant heart into a time or a dimension they did not belong in and returned without the person, the only way to get them back into the appropriate time, place, and dimension was by a direct blood connection. Even then, it would be a one-shot attempt. Melissa had no such connection to William. He was not related by blood.

"Can you get him back?" her mother asked.

Melissa was silent for a moment, and then replied hesitatingly, "I'm not sure, but I don't think it's possible."

"Oh no. What have we done, Missy?"

"Not 'we'. Just me. And I'm sorry for your sake. But I don't see it as a bad thing."

Her mother pursed her lips, as if about to reply. Instead, she ran her palm over a sensitive and darkening knot on her cheek. What had been an anxious expression slowly relaxed. Her mother offered a simple nod. Although the response was unspoken and came reluctantly, the second nod was decisive.

Chapter Four

Confrontations and Consequences

Together, Melissa and her mother decided to handle William's sudden absence by explaining to Kyra, Johnny, and Charlie that, in a fit of drunken rage, he left and vowed never to come back. Although the vow was a lie, Cary did have the swollen bruise on the side of her face making the story credible. Melissa could look her siblings straight in the eye and tell them truthfully she had no clue where he went, but was certain he was not coming back. Her mother remained eerily calm, as if she had known all along this day would come, just not how or when. Cary accepted it and, in fact, seemed relieved.

Cary picked up the phone and called Johnny and Charlie. She explained that she had important family news and asked them to come over right away. Lastly, she called Kyra. "Sweetheart," she began in dour tone, "I must tell you something and I can't do it on the phone. Can you drop by the house for a short while?"

"Right now?"

"Yes."

"What's the matter? Has something happened to Melissa, Johnny, or Charlie?"

"No. It's nothing like that. William...left us. He won't be coming back."

"Say no more. I'm on my way."

Melissa's three siblings came through the front door bunched together, talking, topping one another, and speculating. The three came around and walked into the living room where Melissa and her mother stood. Kyra went directly to her mother and embraced her.

"Mom, what is this I'm hearing about Dad. What in the world is going on?" Charlie asked.

"Yeah. What happened?" Johnny chimed in.

Kyra stepped away from the embrace and examined her mother's face. "Did Dad do that to you?"

Cary sighed. Her show of despair carefully measured. "Afraid so." She turned away from her four adult children and approached the large bay window framing a view of majestic pines in the park across the street. "Melissa, would you explain what happened? I'm not sure I can do it adequately.

"You were here when it happened?" Kyra asked.

Melissa nodded. "Yeah. I was." She drew a breath, held it briefly, and then huffed it away. "William demanded Mom cook him something to eat, complaining how awful lunch had been. Mom thought it would be a good idea for us all to get together and go out to dinner. So, she asked him if that would be okay. Of course, he was drunk as usual and became belligerent and profanely abusive, also *as usual.*"

Melissa could not contain resurging anger as she relived the episode. "I refused to allow him to talk to Mom that way. I confronted him. He came after me, believing I was disrespecting him by shutting down his despicable rant. Mom stepped between us, trying to keep him away from me. He punched her in the side of the head, knocking her to the floor to get her out of his way."

Melissa paused. The rest of this story had to be framed just right. Her siblings needed the truth, but not the absolute truth. She decided to shift the account and move into broader generalities. "I cursed him. He cursed me. And then...he...disappeared."

"Just like that?" Johnny asked. He was clearly the only one of the four siblings shocked and saddened. As the youngest, all he saw was that his father had abandoned him.

"I'm so sorry, Johnny. But yes...just like that."

Johnny's face tightened. "Do you think he'll come back?" he asked, heart-broken.

Cary faced her youngest child. "No, Johnny. I don't think any of us will ever see him again." Mother and son came together and hugged.

Melissa checked faces, assessing how Kyra and Charlie handled the information. They displayed no overt signs of sadness. Their faces were bland. Lack of expressiveness matched her mother's at hearing the news. Johnny, the youngest, was the only one having a tough time with the revelation.

Charlie, in a very adult move, approached Melissa. As he walked by Kyra, he grabbed her hand and the three came together in a huddle. He said, "Look, guys, we have to pull together for Mom's sake. We need to do everything we can to help her make this transition. They may have had problems, but it will still take time for her to learn to live without him."

Melissa smiled. "You're right. Thanks for saying it."

Kyra glanced at Cary. "What do you think Mom will do, now that Dad is out of the picture?"

Out of the picture is an understatement, Melissa thought. "Some time ago, Mom said to me that it was a dream of hers to, someday, move to Texas and live out her life in that big ol' mansion Uncle Jack built. Although, I'm sure she would not consider it until Johnny graduates from high school. So, it probably would not happen until sometime in May at the earliest."

"You really think she would move to Texas?" Charlie asked.

"I think a day will come she will. Yes," Melissa replied.

We all grew up here in Coos Bay," Charlie said. "I have friends and a life here. We all do. I don't want to move out there. How about you, Kyra?"

"I'm open to it. I can get a job in retail anywhere. It would be an adventure, more or less."

"I have enough experience as a nurse practitioner. I'm confident of finding employment in Texas. I sort of like the idea of a change, too." *And I really like the idea of seeing what kind of a man Dwayne Logan grew into.* "Other than family and a few friends, I have no deep ties to this town or this area."

Charlie looked back over his shoulder at his mother and younger brother sitting closely on the sofa, involved in a whispered conversation. While his gaze remained fixed on the pair, "Once Johnny is out of high school, if Mom truly wants to, I'll support the decision. It doesn't take a psychiatrist to see a change would benefit her. She has endured too much heartache for one lifetime, the loss of your dad and now the loss of ours." He then breathed, "Dad turned into a real jerk. I hope I never see him again."

Melissa sighed. "I don't think you have to worry about that."

Chapter Five

Reflections in the Dark

Cary lay in bed staring at the barely visible ceiling in her darkened bedroom, a fluffy comforter pulled up to her armpits. She glanced at the clock on her nightstand.

Two-thirty.

Her eyes shifted to the double window. The moon wore a hazy ring. In this part of the Pacific Northwest, it often did. The light was adequate to cast a silver shadow of window and mullion framed light across her blanketed body. She questioned the clock's accuracy, feeling as though she had lain with her fingers laced together behind her head for more than the few hours that it actually had been. Sleep was not coming easily. Even that passing thought spawned questions anew. Her mind raced. *How does one define reality?*

The awakening of the radiant heart in her oldest daughter gave the word "reality" new context—put on another plane altogether. After Jack explained it to her many years ago, she never truly believed it, any more than she would have any other science fiction writer. But now...

Her life had turned upside down in a single day once again. Over the years the tragedy of losing her first husband, Kyle, Melissa's and Kyra's biological father, eased its suffocating grip on her heart. Thanks in large measure to the early years with William. Unfortunately, that was a different William in a different time. He hadn't always been an abusive alcoholic. The instant her eldest daughter,

Melissa, had told her William would never return, Cary's mind slipped into the angst of missing Kyle, not William. It was disturbing how easily she dismissed a twenty-year marriage to her second husband—a frown-worthy conundrum. For heaven's sake, he was the father of two young men she loved and admired beyond words.

That wasn't the most shocking revelation Sunday offered. What about that radiant heart thing Melissa discovered she could do with her mind and the power generated by her heart? Was it dangerous? It appeared to be life ending for William in an odd way, gone but not necessarily dead. He wasn't really dead, was he? How does one define death? William ceased to exist, but only in this plane of existence. Cary considered spiritual implications. She was Christian and believed upon death the soul, or life force, is released, consciousness living on unencumbered by the confines of flesh, blood, and bone. But, what about William's soul? If he no longer existed, as if he were never born, what then? Or was he still wandering, lost and alone, in that place Melissa had thrust him, and then left behind? Maybe this was William's hell sanctioned as appropriate punishment by God himself. Did he still need nourishment and other bodily necessities? It was so confusing to contemplate these things. In the universal scheme of things, did his time on this earth account for nothing? She shivered and pulled the covers up to below her chin. The veracity of Melissa's weird talent did not seem at all plausible.

She remembered Jack Dane, brother of her first husband, Kyle, attempting to explain it twenty-four years ago. According to Arthur Wainwright, his advisor and psychic, if anything a radiant heart did happened to fall outside a divinely inspired master plan then it simply would not be allowed, like altering historical events. It was not possible. Since Melissa left her stepfather behind—somewhere and possibly in some other time or dimension—it must mean the action was indeed divinely approved. But for what reason, and to what end? What purpose did it serve? Maybe it's supposed to be the nexus for a series of future events serving the master plan, like the butterfly effect. At this point, all she could do was wait and see what the future held for her family.

Jack Dane's recitation of events he endured was such a fantastic tale, Cary worried at the time he might be delusional and dangerous. The last thing he told her was to keep an eye on Melissa and younger sister Kyra, because they were in his and Kyle's bloodline. He could not say for sure but thought one, or both, girls might possess the power of the radiant heart. After Jack's death, she finally took time to read his unpublished manuscript. He told her a few weeks before his death *The Last Radiant Heart* was a factual account but was being written as a novel.

After reading it, she hid it in her closet until Melissa began having visions. Everything Jack told her suddenly came back to her with shocking clarity. Now, she had no choice but to believe.

Although it was her hometown, Coos Bay had become a noose tightening around her neck for decades—now frighteningly claustrophobic. She visited the mansion Jack built in Texas one time, when she and William flew to Lubbock for her brother-in-law's funeral and the reading of his will, and to put the more valuable possessions in the mansion into long-term storage. The wide-open spaces of the Texas South Plains seemed as though it would be a great way to start over. Breathe deeply a new life, in a new place, with new friends, and leave a sad past where it belonged, in Oregon.

As Texas beckoned, Cary's mind eased. She relaxed. A smile curled the corners of her mouth, remembering Melissa's attraction to a dirty-faced little boy by the name of Dwayne Logan, the son of Jack's live-in housekeeper and a man she now had begun to remember fondly, Cletus Logan, Dwayne's father. She looked forward to seeing the elder Logan again. Melissa and Dwayne had to be about the same age. Melissa wondered aloud several times if the adult version of Dwayne would still be as charming with that boyish twinkle in his eyes as he had been as a youngster.

Cary had an advantage. She saw the boy as a young teen at Jack's funeral in Lubbock. Even then, he was a fine-looking young man and would definitely be a handsome adult, based on her memory of that lanky teenager scrubbed clean with neatly trimmed light brown hair. Taller than his mother and youthfully slender, the boy was good-looking. He had been standing near his mother, Rita Logan, a woman with short silver hair, strikingly young and beautiful—not in spite of, but because of, the premature hair color. Young Dwayne stood next to her at the graveside service.

Cary now shared her daughter's fascination with this guy. But her captivation was not limited to Dwayne. Standing on the other side of Dwayne at the funeral was his father, Cletus. He was charming and handsome in his own rugged way. She remembered fondly how easily the elder Logan captured her eye and then held it. Seeds of imagination were planted in that instant as she surreptitiously watched him. *I wonder, of course, what kind of man Dwayne has become. And now, I wonder if the years have been kind to Cletus. Maybe we'll have the opportunity to get answers to all these questions very soon.*

As Cary's thoughts eased over onto pleasant things, Texas things, her eyelids became heavy. She rolled over onto her side and barely remembered thinking, *It's going to be a short night. And then, I must plan a one-way trip to Texas.*

Chapter Six

Mysteries and Family Ties

Monday morning. Twenty-seven-year-old Kyra Dane-Blakely began her daily ritual, getting ready to go to work at Bonnie's Boutique. She dressed, showered, and was putting on makeup in front of the bathroom mirror, wondering why her stepdad left without saying goodbye. A ranting, raving departure would have been expected and in character. Simply walking out the door made no sense. He always had to have the last word. Why not this time? Why did her sister and mother seem so calculating in their description of events leading up to his sudden departure?

Missy's and Mom's exchanged glances told a story and I want to know what it is. She thought. *It's as if they were seeking unspoken permission from one another to speak. Something's going on.*

Kyra and Melissa shared a strong intuitive connection. It was no different this time. Kyra's red flags went up, waving at full mast. Mother and sister were hiding something.

Kyra carefully applied lipstick and pressed her lips together. She wasn't delusional. She knew her stepfather's behavior had become dangerously untenable toward her mother.

If he didn't love Mom any longer, that would explain the argument, even the punch in the face and storming out the door but leaving without saying goodbye to his children is not logical. I don't care if he was blind drunk. When he sobered, he would have contacted me or the boys.

As Kyra considered the circumstances, she realized moods had been so chill the past few months, it might be better if her dad did begin a new life elsewhere. There could be an upside. A chance to get his act together and stop drinking. It had become obvious, neither he nor her mother had been happy for a long time. Unhappiness spread like sticky tentacles throughout the family, her father at the center of it.

She assessed her makeup job in the mirror. Being fairer of skin than Melissa, light colored hair gave her a washed out appearance in the absence of makeup. Kyra inherited the physical characteristics of her mother's side of the family, whereas her sister leaned heavily to the Dane side. Kyra darkened her eyebrows and applied a liberal amount of eyeliner and added color around her eyes. She had always been jealous of her older sibling needing hardly any makeup. With those few drops of Comanche blood flowing through her veins, Melissa was beautiful without makeup, always appearing to have a light, sun-kissed tan with dark auburn hair and gorgeous dark eyebrows. Missy's hair was short enough to spike at the crown but she left a long sweeping bang across one side of her forehead as a style preference. It worked well on her sister giving her the appearance she could have been a runway model, if her desire leaned that way which, of course, did not. Kyra sighed and presented one profile then the other to the mirror for a final check. *Well, this is as good as it gets.* A mischievous smile sprouted. *And it's not a bad look at all, if I do say so myself.* She kissed the air, directed at her reflection.

As she poured granola cereal into an open container of vanilla Greek yogurt, she thought about the developing plan to move to Texas. *Are Melissa and Mom serious or was it simply conversation to lessen emotional impact of a drama-filled afternoon?* "Humph," she wondered as she crunched a bit of granola from between her fingers.

She picked up a spoon and scooped up yogurt with ample cereal over it and shoved it into her mouth. Lazily crunching, she stared across the kitchen bar through the window over the sink to the backyard of the house she had grown up in. She saw her mom beyond the patio with gardening gloves on, loading potted plants onto a four-wheel dolly. Going about her business as she normally would any other day seemed a bit odd, considering her husband left home in a huff just yesterday. Her mother was moving potted plants to a place better protected from the weather. Another cold front was forecast. This time, a frigid blast of Arctic air barreling down from Alaska and then southward across Canada, expected to slam into the Pacific Northwest soon. Temperatures would drop dramatically in the next day or so. Her mother was an early riser, always had been. Before Kyra got out of bed in the morning, her mother had usually put in a couple of busy hours doing household chores.

Her mind reeled back over the years, suddenly realizing how often she had watched similar monotony play out. She straightened and scoped her surroundings with fresh insight. She had never lived anywhere except in this house. It never bothered her before. Now it did. It came upon her abruptly. She poked another spoonful in her mouth and crunched.

I'm twenty-seven years old, for Christ's sake. She thought. *That puts me on a fast downhill slide to thirty. Blink a couple of times and there I'll be, and probably still unmarried. I don't have a steady boyfriend. And geez! I'm still living with my parents.* She bobbled her head. *Well...parent. Singular now.*

The more Kyra thought about her situation, moving into a huge mansion set in the Texas countryside suddenly seemed like an embraceable adventure. A chance to look at life from another angle. "Humph." *Doesn't sound bad. Not bad at all.*

Kyra quickly finished breakfast and drove to the boutique. She arrived at eight-thirty to prepare for a nine o'clock opening, like always. She saw Bonnie Crandall, the owner, moving about through the street-side display window next to the sidewalk. The shop was of modest size and only one in a strip of five connected store fronts in an older section of Coos Bay near downtown. Bonnie was a wonderful person. Over the course of Kyra's four years working here, Bonnie had become more than an employer. She was a friend, her best friend. Walking away from the boutique might be difficult for that reason. Sure, she had acquaintances—lots of them. How could she not? She grew up in this town. But, none of them were as close as Bonnie, a divorcée with no children and almost twice her age.

"Good morning, Bon-bon," Kyra called out as she came through the door into the dress shop, still devoid of customers.

"Hey, kiddo," Bonnie replied. "How was your weekend?"

The question struck Kyra as odd. Any other Monday morning, it would have simply been a benign pleasantry. "Well...Thanksgiving dinner Thursday was nice... sort of. And Saturday was okay. But then, Sunday came."

Bonnie snapped a sideways glance. Her hands abruptly stopped sliding dresses up and down a rack, sorting by size. "Sounds ominous."

Kyra drew deep the cool clean aroma of new clothing. "Without putting too a fine a point on it, my stepdad left my mother and did not look back, and I mean that in the most literal way. According to Mom and Missy, he won't be coming back either. They both seem quite certain of that...," she frowned, "...for some reason."

"Oh, Kyra. I'm so sorry."

"It's okay. Really. Dad has not been...well, he just hasn't been a good husband or father for quite a while. He's an alcoholic and his liquor consumption increased dramatically over the past year, or so. He had become verbally abusive to everyone, especially Mom. It finally came to a head when verbal turned physical. He hit Mom hard enough to give her a black eye."

Bonnie's face drooped to a saddened slant. She then offered a knowing nod. "That's horrible."

"Yeah. It is."

"My brother was the same way," Bonnie offered. "Except in his case, his wife left him. I'm familiar with such situations. I'm also aware that it throws the family into a quandary. It messes up everything for a time, even though it may be for the best in the long-haul."

"That's for sure. I've been thinking about it all morning. I was so lost in thought for a while I'm surprised I made it to work on time. My head has been swirling over what we, Mom and my three siblings, are going to do now."

"Did you come to any conclusions?"

"Maybe. But it does involve you and the boutique."

"Oh?"

"Mom and Missy are talking about moving to Texas. They asked my brothers and me if we wanted to move with them. Charlie and my youngest brother, Johnny summarily kicked the idea out. The want to stay here in Coos Bay. But I've been considering it."

"Why Texas?"

"Remember when I told you Mom inherited a large sum of money from my uncle?"

"Yeah. He was that Midwestern newspaper guy that fell into a fortune. Right?"

"That's him. Jack Dane. He built a large mansion in north Texas above the caprock, in an area they call the South Plains, near Lubbock. It was where Jack's girlfriend grew up on a farm. He developed an affection for the place after her parents died and she disappeared. So, when it came up for sale, he jumped on it and built an oddly out of place mansion on a cotton farm, patterned after a large house his close friend had lived in back in Springfield, Missouri. Mom inherited the farm and that big ol' house, too. She wants to make a new life out there. She has endured too much in this town, too many painful memories. Losing my biological father to murder. And then, my stepfather punches her with a tightly packed fist, rendering her unconscious and then walks out on her. That Texas property is a place for a fresh start. And it's move-in ready."

"You may be right." Bonnie sighed. "But the thought of running this place without you saddens me."

"Aw, Bon-bon, you do realize you're my best friend in this whole freakin' world, don't you?"

Bonnie's eyes glossed. "You are my *only* friend," she muttered.

"Even if many miles separate us, it won't matter. You will always be the greatest friend a girl could have." She tilted her head trying to get Bonnie to look at her. "Look at it this way. You'll have a great vacation destination that will cost you nothing and you would, of course, be welcome any time you choose to come see us. Maybe I'll meet a boot-scootin' cowboy with a good-looking friend for you. Heck, I might even learn to say y'all." She snickered.

Bonnie finally smiled and looked at her. She whisked away a dribbling tear and playfully slapped Kyra on the arm. "Oh, you..." Bonnie then pulled Kyra close and hugged her. She whispered directly into Kyra's ear, "I will be a hundred percent behind you, however you choose to play it." They cried together.

At no point during the day did Kyra's distraction end. Bonnie had to direct her to every necessary task. She had a head full of Texas thoughts. Bonnie understood.

The boutique normally closed at seven during the week. It was now five-thirty. Bonnie stepped behind Kyra and put a hand on her shoulder.

Kyra flinched.

"Sorry. Didn't mean to startle you," Bonnie said.

"I apologize for being such a do-nothing today. "My head hasn't been in this game all day."

Bonnie offered a knowing smile. "I've noticed. Don't worry. I know you have a life-changing decision to make." Bonnie looked around, spreading her arms wide. "Not a customer in the store and I don't anticipate business picking up before seven. Why don't you go ahead and bail. I'll look after things until closing." She grinned wryly. "I don't think I need fear a last minute inundation of customers."

Kyra felt a warm surge of emotion. She embraced her friend and employer. "Bon-bon, you're the greatest." Her words almost would not come, choking back another round of tears.

"I know, I know." She fluttered her fingers toward the door. "Go on. Get out of here."

Kyra hurried to her car and got in, but then hesitated and did not start the car. She sat unmoving and thinking. *I want to know right now how serious Missy is about moving.*

She pulled a cell phone from her purse and hit her sister's quick dial number. "Missy?"

"Hey, Kyra, what's up? Anything wrong?"

"Everything's fine. You still at work?"

"Yeah, for another hour. I have one more patient. Why?"

"I just didn't want to bother you in the middle of something."

"I have a few spare minutes. Speak."

"How serious are you about moving to Texas?

"Very. The lease on my apartment is up in thirty-five days. That means I only have five days to renew it for another year or lose my deposit for not giving the landlord thirty days' notice. And I want that deposit back. I made up my mind only hours ago to tell the apartment manager this evening that I'm not renewing the lease. So, you see, I've given myself a bit of time pressure with my decision. Otherwise known as make a boom-boom or get off the pot."

"How about Mom?"

"Oh, she's just as serious. But her situation is different. She plans on staying until Johnny graduates high school. Then she'll move. So, for her, it'll be late May or June before she makes the leap. When Johnny graduates, he and Charlie will move into Mom's house. Johnny is planning on getting a job with Sullivan's Logging Company, where Charlie works. If Johnny goes to college, it will be later."

"When are you moving?"

"I started filling boxes last night. Does that give you an idea?"

"So, I suppose you'll be on the road to Texas soon."

I'm hoping before next week is over," Melissa replied. "And, if my landlord can get my apartment rented quickly, I might get a little refund on the unused portion of next month's rent that was paid in advance." She paused. "Where do you stand on the idea of moving, Sis?"

Kyra watched Bonnie through the display window of the store moving about inside. She didn't reply, just sat thinking."

"Kyra?"

"I think I'll go back inside the boutique and put in my notice right now," she finally replied. "This going to be difficult. I love Bonnie."

"I know. Give her my love, too. She's a good person with a huge heart." She paused and then sighed. Tell ya what, meet me at Mom's at seven and let's firm it all up."

"Sure." Kyra ended the call. The burden of decision lifted, she felt lighter. A smile stretched her cheeks, thinking of wide-open spaces, picture-perfect sunrises and sunsets—and, of course, tall good-looking cowboys in tight jeans.

Chapter Seven

The Texas Dreams

As Melissa came through the door of her mother's house, she heard a conversation down the hall. Rounding into the kitchen, Kyra and their mother sat on stools at the center island sipping margaritas and munching tortilla chips dipped in salsa, chatting about Texas and the mansion. "You two can do whatever you want," Melissa announced abruptly, "but I'm reserving the easterly facing bedroom on the second floor as my own." She snatched a chip from the bowl and bit off the corner. "That way, I can see those gorgeous sunrises. And later each day, I'll go out to the patio and watch equally beautiful and romantic sunsets." She dropped her purse on the bar, noticing Kyra staring oddly. "What's that look for?" She grinned and popped another chip in her mouth.

"Aside from a few nondescript photographs of the exterior, you've seen the inside of that house the same number of times I have...*zero*. How come you're talking as if you know how it's laid out on the inside?" Kyra asked.

Gravity had its way with Melissa's grin. It dropped fast. She froze, mouth open, realizing she screwed up by mentioning the interior of the mansion. After an awkward second, she shot her mother a what-do-I-say-now look. "Uh... "

"I told Missy about the layout from memory when I visited there the day of Jack's funeral," her mother interrupted, rattling the response quickly.

Melissa was aware her mother had been inside it almost a quarter century ago. She and her mother never discussed the interior beyond generalized terms of elegance and size. "That's right, Kyra. I'm guessing," she lied.

Kyra's eyes narrowed to suspicious slits. She glanced from Melissa to her mother and then back again. "You two are hiding something. I got this same feeling yesterday when you and Mom were explaining Dad's sudden departure. What is it the two of you don't want me to know?"

Her mother shrugged her shoulders nonchalantly. "It's nothing. Really."

"Why don't you let me be the judge? It might be something to me?" She pulled a sardonic half-grin. "I'm pretty much all grown up. In case you haven't noticed."

"Oh really?" Melissa blurted. "I don't see that 'all grown up' thing often." Her reply was propelled by a twinge of anger at her sister's disrespectful sarcasm. "We haven't told you because you wouldn't believe it anyhow, and I'm not certain you have the intellectual wherewithal to handle such information if we did tell you."

"Are you saying I'm too stupid to understand basic principles of something? Kyra blustered.

Melissa took her tone down a notch. "Oh, I assure you there's nothing elementary about it? In fact, it is quite complex. Even a lifetime of study might not reveal all its aspects." Although Melissa spoke down to her sister to end the sarcasm, she remained painfully aware that, aside from what was in her uncle's book, she knew little about the radiant heart herself.

"I have no idea what you're talking about, but you definitely captured my curiosity. Okay, spill it," Kyra said. "Come on. Tell me."

"Please don't, Missy," her mother said. "Anything you say will only—"

"I think we should tell Kyra, even if she doesn't believe what we say. Maybe, at some point in the future, if it happens in front of her, she will have had a heads-up and not keel over dead from heart failure." She poked a stiffened finger into the air as an additional thought struck her. "It's possible my darling baby sister can do it, too, and hasn't realized it yet."

"There you go again," Kyra whined. "You two are carrying on a conversation about *me* and, for heaven's sake, I'm sitting right here."

Cary sat, saying nothing. After a long, thoughtful pause, she finally nodded resignation. "Okay, sweetheart, if you insist. But, Kyra, I suggest you keep a wide-open mind." She backed off the stool and put a hand on Melissa's shoulder. "I'll get Jack's manuscript. Go ahead, Missy, tell Kyra your story."

As her mother walked away, Melissa replied, "Sooner or later, I think we'll have to tell her anyhow. We might as well make it sooner."

Cary never broke stride while walking away to get the manuscript. Melissa figured that, unto itself, was a strong suggestion of tacit agreement with the hastily formed plan to explain it to Kyra.

* * *

Kyra was confused by the cloak and dagger attitudes. *What in the world is so important they think I should be shielded from it? Mom thinks so, anyhow.* "Okay, Missy, the floor is yours. What's so important you guys feel the need to tip-toe around me?"

"First of all," Melissa began, "when are Charlie and Johnny coming home?"

"Not for a while. Johnny is at Butch's house...you know, that goofy friend of his, and Charlie has to work late. Why?"

"I don't want to be in the middle of this and one, the other, or both walk in."

"There you go with the secretive stuff again." She paused, rolled her eyes, and then added, "Like me, they're just about all grown up, too."

Melissa's stare down to the countertop intensified. "Do you remember those odd dreams I was having about that big ol' Texas house of Uncle Jack's?"

"Yeah. So?"

"They weren't dreams."

Kyra guffawed sarcastically. "So, my sister is having prophetic visions. Is that about right? Or is it some other form of nonsense." She snickered.

Melissa lowered her chin to chest, drew a breath, and sighed long.

Kyra saw her sister becoming frustrated.

"Don't be flip about this, Kyra!" she barked, "Or you may soon get a shock that your system cannot tolerate." She closed her eyes and drew another breath. "What I was looking at was not an imagining, it was a portal *I created*, and then looked through to the other side. It began with the thought but intensified by the power of my heart, vibrating powerfully, creating a glowing white aura around my entire body, enabling me to, not only see the house, but to breach time and space to go there *physically* as well. I mean it in the most literal sense. Flesh, bone, and blood. I...was...there. That's how I know what the inside of it looks like and how it's laid out. That's not even the strangest part. It was twenty-four years in the past. I assume it was because I wished I could have known Uncle Jack better before he died. So, that's the destination and timeframe I unwittingly created."

Kyra's smirk remained fixed, distrustful of every word coming out of Melissa's mouth. Still, she allowed her sister to finish with no interruption. "Missy, I swear. You do have a flair for the dramatic. You're quite the storyteller."

Melissa suddenly turned sideways on the tall stool to fully face Kyra. She grabbed her younger sister by the upper arms.

"Hey," Kyra protested. "You don't have to get angry."

"Oh, I'm not angry. I'm determined to make you understand."

Kyra was unnerved over Melissa's sudden passion. "You're hurting my arms."

Melissa loosened her grip but continued clutching her. She closed her eyes and began breathing deep and even.

"What are you doing?"

"I'm going to try something," Melissa whispered. "And you're going to sit quietly while I do."

After a scant second Kyra thought she noticed a halo develop around Melissa. She blinked her eyes and then clenched the lids for a second, thinking her eyes may have filmed over. The barely noticeable glow brightened. "What the hell...?"

Melissa did not respond, continuing to sit with her eyes closed, breathing deep and even.

Curiosity and fear began to mingle. The still brightening and downward flowing glow surrounding Melissa formed a white wall of light between them. What appeared to be a beam of brighter light shot from the left side of Melissa's chest and caused a billowing cloud of brilliance between them. It seemed to wrinkle and then distort at its center. There, a picture appeared. It was the Texas mansion she had only seen in old photographs. Kyra watched the white glow growing brighter around Melissa. The light appeared to create a bubble of sorts, containing the vision and her sister's entire body. The glow came at her from the vision like brilliant misty tendrils, surrounding her as well.

"Get off the stool and stand," Melissa whispered, still holding Kyra's arms.

"I don't know what's happening, but you're scarin' hell out of me, Missy." Hesitatingly, she did as ordered and slid awkwardly off the stool.

Melissa stepped around Kyra and stood behind her. The vision projected in front of them both. "Here we go." Melissa gently pushed her forward a couple of steps.

Kyra's face heated with a nausea flash. An abrupt chill washed over her. "I think I'm going to puke."

"No, you're not," Melissa replied, her voice soft and soothing.

Kyra closed her eyes. The feel of the air abruptly changed. It was chilly. The light changed from white to a yellow tint. Even before she opened her eyes, she realized she and Melissa were no longer in their home but out of doors somewhere. She heard birds singing and felt a breeze brush her skin. She opened her eyes. "Oh, my God," she whispered, as if worried someone besides Melissa might hear her. "Is...that Uncle Jack's mansion in front of us?" She looked up and down, then side to side.

Melissa huffed away a deep sigh. "That's it."

Kyra turned her back to the house to survey the area. Fields were bare but it was obviously a farm. The landscape was void of trees with the exception of those around the few rural homes within sight and two rows of large Poplar trees lining both sides of a long driveway. "But...that would mean we're no longer in Oregon. Are you telling me, within the span of a second, maybe two, we have come to Texas?"

"You shouldn't need to ask. For heaven's sake, girl, you're looking at it. Touch it. Feel it. It's the real deal," Melissa said, flipping a palm-up hand toward the front door. "I'm hoping we're not in some other time, like twenty-four years ago, again. I don't know. I can't be certain. I'm still learning about this stuff."

"What?"

"The last time I was here, it was a hot summer day twenty-four years ago. Kyra, if you think what we just accomplished is phenomenal, chew on this. I met Uncle Jack as a younger man. I sat and talked with him for two solid hours. He was a wonderful man and terribly concerned about potential consequences of the power he possessed. After all his adventures using his talent, he remained uncertain and fearful of the width, breadth, and depth of its true potential." Melissa took a turn, scanning the area, making her own inspection. An old, dirty, and dented pickup truck set parked at the end of the sidewalk leading to the front door. Otherwise, things looked as they did the last time she was here, except the trees lining the driveway had grown much taller. "This time, I directed my thoughts to the present. Our time, I mean, but to the same spot as before. The air is cool and the fields are bare, so it would seem the season is right."

Kyra, wide-eyed and loose-lipped, "I—uh... Maybe I should—"

"Don't hit me with a barrage of questions until you've read Uncle Jack's novel, *The Last Radiant Heart*. When you do, understand that it is *not* fiction, but is written in the form of a novel. It's my guidebook and, possibly, for you, too. That's the manuscript Mom was talking about. It will answer most of the questions swirling around inside your head right now."

"Why would it be a guide book for *me*?"

"It's a bloodline thing, unique to the Dane family. I think. It's called the radiant heart."

"Did our father have it, too?"

"Don't know. If so, he was murdered before its power manifested. The one thing I must tell you is not to wander off. To get you home, you'll need to be standing within my aura when I make it happen. Or, God forbid, I'll leave you behind." Melissa's expression froze. "Hey, I just realized something. If we are in the present, as I envisioned before coming here, then if I leave you behind, you can fly home. No big deal."

Kyra reared her head. "That's not funny! Besides, you don't need to worry about me getting too far away from you. This...all this, goes way beyond overwhelming and is, frankly, scary as hell."

"I didn't mean for it to be funny. I was speaking of something that needed exploring some day. That's all." Melissa finally smiled, the first time since beginning the conversation on all the strangeness. "I was scared, too, at first. Once Uncle Jack realized who I was, he made me comfortable with my sudden appearance in his life. M y apprehension melted away around him. I wish he was still alive."

"Hey, look," Kyra said, pointing at the front door. "It's ajar."

"I suppose whoever owns that old truck is inside right now. Come on."

Upon entering, it was clear at a glance the house was vacant and had been for some time, probably years. Still, it was clean and did not smell dank. Only basic furnishings remained. Melissa guessed all items that would be attractive to thieves had been removed. She and her sister gawked at everything.

Suddenly, a loud metallic clank came from down the hall.

"What was that?" Kyra asked.

"Don't know. Sounded like it came from the kitchen. It's just down the hall to the left."

"Do you think we should be in here?"

Melissa shrugged her shoulders. "Why not? It's our house."

"True enough, I suppose," Kyra said. She began ambling in the direction Melissa had indicated.

"Hold up. Let's not be too bold. It may be someone up to no good," Melissa whispered.

As they introduced stealth to their approach, they stopped to the side of the door into the kitchen. Kyra poked her head around the jamb. She saw slender jean clad legs of a man on his back lying under the kitchen sink. He had on well-worn western boots with scuffed and curled toes and holes in both soles. Oddly, his faded Wrangler jeans were neatly pressed and the legs creased. Also, it appeared the jeans were starched stiff and seemed out of place on a guy working on plumbing. "Excuse me," Kyra called out.

The guy snapped his head up and banged his forehead on the sink trap. "Shit," he hissed. "Who's here?" he asked as he worked his way out from under the sink, rubbing the red spot on his forehead.

"Sorry. Didn't mean to startle you."

He sat up. The white western shirt with pearl snap buttons he wore was neatly tucked into those boot cut jeans behind an ornately tooled belt, fastened with a large silver buckle sporting a brass bucking bronc centered. Kyra took a quiet second to admire the view.

Kyra fully entered the kitchen. Melissa at her side. "Hi. My name is Kyra Dane-Blakely and this is my sister, Melissa Dane-Blakely." Kyra glanced sideways at her sister to see a starry look on Melissa's face.

"You must be Dwayne Logan," Melissa mused.

He looked puzzled for a moment, then awareness flashed across his face. "Oh yeah. Certainly. You two must be Cary's daughters. She didn't tell me y'all were comin' for a visit."

"Oh, she didn't know," Kyra blurted.

Melissa elbowed her. Kyra realized too late she shouldn't have said anything that might lead to questions about how they came to be here.

"I hope she's all right," he replied with appropriate concern. "She seems like a really wonderful lady." He rolled over and came to his feet, and then pulled a red bandanna from his hip pocket and wiped his hands.

"She's fine," Melissa said. "And thanks for saying that. I'll pass along your well wishes. We wanted to tell you personally we'll be moving into this house soon and, since neither one of us has been here before," she lied, "we thought we'd take a look at it for ourselves."

Dwayne smiled. "Well, it'll be a hoot havin' y'all as neighbors."

Kyra snickered. "Yeah, a hoot." She looked to Melissa's profile. It didn't take a psychic to see her older sister was smitten with the easy country manner of this good-looking cowboy. No. Not merely good-looking but freakin' gorgeous. Dwayne was over six feet tall. He was slender, but not skinny. Inside that long-sleeved western shirt, she could easily tell he was well-muscled. He sported a clean-shaven face with light brown hair barely long enough to part and comb. "Would you mind showing us around?" Kyra asked.

"Oh, yes ma'am. I'd be more 'n happy to."

"Thanks," Kyra replied. "And, for future reference, I'm not a ma'am, just a Kyra." She grinned.

"May I call you Dwayne?" Melissa asked.

"Sure thing. Or, *hey you*, will work just as well if you forget my name. Shoot-fire, I even answer to shrill whistles. You can ask my dad." He laughed. But, as the laugh faded, he began to stare quizzically at Melissa. "How come I have this spooky little feelin' I've seen you somewhere before. Like I've known you my whole life some such fool thing. I know darn well this is the first time I've ever seen you."

"Who knows," Melissa said, "maybe in another life, we did know one another, she cooed, and then smiled demurely.

Dwayne pretended a shudder. "Ooh. Just had a little déjà vu chill. Come on. Let me give you girls the nickel tour."

As Dwayne turned his back to lead them away, Kyra looked over at her sister and mouthed, "What's that about?"

Melissa gave her a knowing smile, yet still shrugged her shoulders.

Kyra stared a moment longer at her sister with a raised eyebrow, as they fell in behind Dwayne, who had begun chattering about growing up in and around the Dane mansion. The tour Dwayne gave them came complete with colorful explanations of architectural advantages, disadvantages, and funny or unusual things that happened to him as a child in the house. The tour took nearly two hours.

If this was the nickel tour, what might a grander tour entail, examining electrical and plumbing with a magnifying glass? She glanced over at Melissa, who had become unusually quiet. It seemed obvious her sister was interested in Dwayne Logan the man, more so than Dwayne the tour guide. It occurred to Kyra, over the course of two hours, she had developed a measure of comfort with the absolute weirdness of their circumstances. *Now, how, exactly, is it we get home?* She wondered.

The thought barely cleared her mind when Melissa leaned in and whispered in her ear, "We have to separate ourselves from Dwayne."

"Why?" She glanced to Dwayne whose back was to them, pointing out architectural features in the large library—the giant arched windows, the fifteen-foot floor to ceiling bookshelves with rolling ladders, and the massive reading table centered in the room. It had the feel and size of a public library.

Melissa leaned back in and whispered, "It would be impossible to explain why we don't have a car here and we certainly can't let him see us disappear."

The wrinkle in Kyra's brow relaxed. "Oh. Yeah. It might scar him for life," she whispered, and then turned to Dwayne. "Thanks for the tour. But I guess we'd better get back to Lubbock to catch the plane home. Would you mind getting me a drink of water before we leave?"

"You betcha. Be back in flash." He headed for the massive oak door that separated the library from the hallway.

* * *

Melissa casually followed Dwayne as far as the library door and closed it behind him, and then hurried back to join Kyra. "Okay, stand next to me until our shoulders touch, close your eyes, and don't move."

"How are we—?"

"Hush. I have to concentrate." Through closed eyelids, Melissa saw the white light develop and then came the chill and flash of nausea, followed by an obvious change in temperature and the general feel of ambient air. They were back in their mother's home in Coos Bay.

"Oh God," Kyra exclaimed. "What a rush."

"That's my feeling about it, too." Melissa saw her mother, manuscript in hand, standing at the kitchen door. "I saw the light from down the hall and thought you were about to disappear."

"What are you talking about?" Kyra asked, shocked. "We were gone for over two hours."

Surprise splashed over their mother's face. "That can't be true. I came in to see you both surrounded by a white glowing haze, but it faded away, and you both are still right there where you were."

"Okay, you two. Here's what you both need to understand," Melissa said. "Look at the clock on the wall."

The clock on the wall showed ten minutes after seven.

"And, what time was it when I got here after work?"

"I guess it was a few minutes after seven. Let's say three minutes," Kyra said hesitatingly.

"We talked for about seven minutes. Right?"

"I guess so."

"Now, look at your wristwatch. Tell me what it shows," Melissa said.

As Kyra lifted her wrist, her mother hurried around to look at the watch with her. The watch showed nine-seventeen. Kyra and her mother looked at one another. "Oh my God," Cary murmured.

"Not a single second has passed from the time we left until the time we returned," Melissa explained. "But, Kyra, you and I are over two hours older than when we left, because we carried our personal time streams with us. Mom, you're not crazy. From the instant Kyra and I disappeared until our return, the passage of time was nonexistent for Kyra and me in *this time line*. So, it appeared to you, Mom, we remained right where we had been."

"I'm going to the living room. I have to sit down," Kyra muttered. "I can't process this. It's too much."

Her mother followed. "For me, too."

"Kyra?" Melissa called out as her sister and mother disappeared into the living room.

"What?"

"If you're having trouble processing the time thing, then it'll be interesting for you when I explain why Dwayne had such a strong sense of déjà vu about me."

Melissa thought about the sense Dwayne mentioned of having known her. *If there is no memory of a radiant heart left behind after visiting the past, why would Dwayne sense such a thing about me? Isn't that a memory, or something similar? Is it possible that having a soul mate is a real thing? Could that be a reason for a connection over time, even though he can't remember why?* "Humph. That deserves more thought," she mumbled to herself. As she headed toward the living room to join her mother and sister, it occurred to her she might learn more about this radiant heart thing than even her uncle Jack or Arthur Wainwright had been aware of.

Chapter Eight

Confronting the Past

Dwayne stood at the open library door of the Dane mansion holding a glass of water. "Hey, where'd y'all go?" he called out. He walked to the front door and looked out. No vehicle out front, other than his badly dinged and dirty twenty-five-year-old Ford pickup truck parked at the end of the sidewalk. "Humph." He scratched his head and looked up and down the gravel road at the end of the long driveway in front of the house. No cars in sight, coming or going. *Wow, they weren't kidding when they said they had to get back to Lubbock. They bolted out of here like lightning. Oh well, best get that plumbing chore taken care of.* He turned and headed for the kitchen, drinking the water meant for Kyra. *If they were truthful, they'll be back soon enough. Both those girls are pretty, but there's something about Melissa that sets this ol' heart o' mine to flutterin'.* He smiled.

Kitchen faucet replaced, Dwayne got in his old pickup. After wriggling to find that sweet spot of comfort on the badly worn seat upholstery, he turned the key. The vehicle belched gray smoke but quickly settled into a rumbling idle, loose muffler rattling. He let down his window, rolled his tongue between his lips, and loosed a shrill whistle. From around the corner of the house, a chocolate Labrador retriever came running, tongue wagging. Without slowing, the dog went airborne, sailing into the bed of the pickup, skidding on flared claws to the cab. "Let's go home, Hotshot," Dwayne called out to his canine pal. The dog woofed a happy reply.

Dwayne lived in the stucco house the original owners of this farm, the Endicotts, had lived in. It was only a couple hundred yards up the gravel road from the mansion. He lived with his single father who came back for his mother's funeral and never left. It pleased Dwayne that his dad chose to stay. Although his parents' marriage disintegrated, his father remained in Dwayne's life the whole time. He was the caretaker for the mansion in the early years, before Dwayne took over the job, keeping him in close proximity, visiting often. Although the elder Logan moved from one house or apartment to another frequently in those years, he was never over an hour's drive back to see his only son, or to take care of odd jobs around the mansion. Unfortunately, Cletus Logan had had a contentious relationship with Dwayne's mother, Rita, refusing to be around her and, when he was, it was usually family business concerning Dwayne. It had been a true love-hate relationship. They both said they never stopped loving one another, yet arguments erupted as dependably as sunrises and sunsets. Some verbal battles made it to the precipice of physical violence. It saddened Dwayne, but he understood the need in their case for permanent separation. He witnessed many arguments and, even at a young age, realized any one of them had the potential to reel violently out of control. Although, toward the end of the marriage, there had been a flashpoint that neither his father, Cletus, nor his mother, Rita, ever talked about. Dwayne never knew what had happened. But whatever it was had been the coup de grâce, the final disconnecting thread in the flimsy marital fabric. Dwayne never questioned either of them, believing it was none of his business. They had divorced. That was all he needed to know.

Father and son now made their livelihood raising cotton, grain, and cattle on this six-hundred acre farm on a crop-share basis with Cary Dane-Blakely, living rent-free in the old Endicott house. And, on this chilly December day, there were cows and horses to be fed. They also kept hogs and chickens for slaughter and eggs. In the spring, they grew a large vegetable garden. But, usually, ended up giving most of the produce away. Neither of them cared anything about canning or preserving whatever bounty a garden made, just enjoyed it while it was producing. In fact, cooking was an undesirable chore kicked back and forth between father and son. Neither liked doing it.

Dwayne steered onto the long driveway up to the small three-bedroom house that he called home since shortly after Jack Dane died of a sudden and massive heart attack over ten years ago. Cary Dane-Blakely, Melissa's and Kyra's mother, seemed like a really nice woman. She offered to allow him to live there rent-free in that monstrous house and pay him an equal share of all crop income once he agreed to continue the farming operation and to continue on as caretaker of the mansion. The agreement, at Dwayne's request, was modified to change the language from the mansion to the small stucco house. All else remained the same. Dwayne believed it to be more than generous and accepted those terms. All he wanted was to live a simple country life. Residing in a twelve-thousand-square-foot mansion did not fit into that desired lifestyle. His father, Cletus, questioned the wisdom of passing up such an opportunity. But now that the Dane girls, and eventually their mother, Cary, would be moving to Texas, his decision was obviously the smarter choice. Otherwise, he would be clearing out his own stuff and forced to find a place to live, pronto. If he would have accepted the original offer, the stucco house would have likely been rented to someone else. That would have been about as popular as losing a coin-toss to become the permanent cook in the family.

As he stopped in front of his home, worn brakes squealing, he saw his dad carrying a bucket of feed to the hog pens. He threw open the door of the pickup and dropped to the ground. He called out across the bed of the pickup, "Hey, Dad, how's feedin' goin'?" Hotshot, the chocolate-colored labrador retriever, dove out of the pickup bed to stand at Dwayne's side, tail and tongue dancing side to side. Dwayne jostled the old dog's ears.

Cletus set the bucket on the ground and approached. Cletus was fifty-nine, a couple of inches shorter than Dwayne, thinning hair, with a ruddy complexion common to farmers, complete with a deeply wrinkled and sun-reddened neck. He was the epitome of the phrase, ruggedly handsome redneck. "I'm about to get them all fed," Cletus replied, pulling the corduroy collar of his blue denim coat higher to cover his neck against the dry chill of this early December morning.

"I'll crank the tractor and spike a round bale of hay for those ol' mother cows in a few minutes," Dwayne said.

Cletus pulled off his leather work gloves and ran spread fingers through his mussed and thinning hair. "We're runnin' low on dry corn mash for the hogs and chickens."

"I'll run into town after lunch and pick up some," Dwayne replied. "Those two Dane girls dropped by the mansion for a visit and a quick tour a while ago."

"Dane girls? Are you talkin' about the owner's daughters?"

"Yeah. They left a few minutes ago, headin' back to Lubbock, presumably to catch a plane back to Oregon. You should've seen their car race by." Dwayne snickered. "And I do mean 'race'. They split out so fast I didn't have a chance to say goodbye."

His father looked confused. "I've been putterin' around the yard for over an hour and I haven't seen any cars, comin' or goin'. In fact, I haven't seen any of the neighbors so far this mornin', no vehicles whatsoever."

"That's odd. I was replacing a leaky faucet in the kitchen and had left the front door open and they walked right on in. I didn't look out the front door until they were gone. So, I never saw a car. I don't know what they were driving, a rented vehicle of some sort, I'm sure." He paused, frowned, and chewed the inside of his cheek for a moment. "Still, it's like they just vanished."

His dad laughed. "Yeah. Poof!"

Dwayne joined him in a laugh.

Chapter Nine

A Family's New Path

Kyra bombarded her older sister with questions. Melissa didn't have a problem with it until she went to work the day after their instantaneous Texas visit. Kyra's persistent inquiries about the radiant heart became a nuisance once Melissa returned to the daily due diligence of working with patients as a nurse practitioner at a local clinic. Besides, she didn't know any more about it than what Uncle Jack had written in his book. "Look, Kyra, I'll tell it to you one more time, but then you have to wait until after work to discuss it further. Deal?"

Kyra sighed melodramatically. "Okay," she drawled. "It's a deal. Bonnie has been looking at me suspiciously. I've let her take care of all the customers here at the boutique so far this morning. But, Missy, I'm having trouble understanding. Or, even believing it, for that matter. Are you sure your newfound talent isn't mind control? That would be easier to wrap a belief system around."

"Kyra. For heaven's sake, girl. That sense of déjà vu Dwayne was talking about is because I met him as an eight-year-old boy, when I went to visit Texas the first time. It was twenty-four years ago. When I transport myself, and anyone with me, to a previous time, we carry our personal present time with us. That's why our wristwatches kept right on ticking and time advanced, but for us only. It is divinely forbidden—I don't know why—for a radiant heart to change the course of history. So, once I left that place, in that time, everything reverted back to the original sequence of events without me. In fact, the way I understand it, Dwayne should have no memory whatsoever of my visit. I cannot explain why he was struck with déjà vu about me. Unless it was something simple, like a pick-up line he uses on girls at bars all the time. But, if true, it sounds like a type of memory to me." She paused. "Are you with me so far?" A nurse approached, wanting her attention. Melissa lifted a finger, quietly requesting one more minute to her clinic colleague.

"I think I understand," Kyra replied.

Melissa turned away from the persistent nurse and whispered through cupped hand, "That means Dwayne could not possibly have a true memory of my presence during that time, but it must have left an odd sense of having seen or known me before. Yet, the rational part of him was saying, loud and clear, he had never seen or talked to me before. Now, when you and I went, our time was synchronized with the rest of the world. We were in the present. We just happened to be a couple of thousand miles from home. So, if Dwayne should have seen us vanish, he most certainly would have remembered it and would likely think he was losing his mind. We had to leave the way we did, for his sake." Melissa glanced back over her shoulder and saw the nurse expressing frustration. "Look, Kyra, I have to get back to work."

"But, what if—?"

"Kyra," Melissa whined, "read the book. Jack and Arthur Wainwright explain almost everything you're asking me. I certainly cannot add anything to their explanation, not at this point in time." She abruptly ended the call and turned to face the nurse. "I apologize." She smiled sheepishly. "Family stuff."

"It doesn't bother me," the nurse replied, "but the woman with a possible sinus infection in examining room four might be upset. She's sick and miserable."

"I'm on it." Melissa scurried toward the room.

Kyra didn't bother her the rest of the day. Maybe she had finally taken the pointed cue to read the book. Melissa envisioned her sister crouched behind a rack of clothes reading the manuscript, while letting poor Bonnie handle all the customers. Kyra, she believed, took advantage of that woman's good nature too often.

She saw her last patient about five-thirty. Shortly afterward, she was out the clinic door on her way back to her apartment. It felt good to be in the quiet and private surroundings of her own space. But she was on a mission to get to her mother's house, leaving her little time to enjoy it. She showered and changed clothes.

Arriving at her mother's house, she saw both brothers' cars in the driveway. That was bothersome. That is, if a discussion of the radiant heart with her sister and mother was to take place. That happened to be the reason for hurrying over. *Maybe I can close myself in one of the bedrooms and call Dwayne. I need to apologize to him for leaving so suddenly.*

When she came into the house, Charlie and Johnny were sprawled in the front room watching television. The older brother, Charlie, lay on his side on the sofa. While Johnny lay stretched out on the recliner. Hey, guys. What's up?"

Charlie yawned. "I'm thinking about going back to my apartment, showering, and getting more rack time than usual. It was a long hard day at work. I'm still not used to working fulltime. On top of that, a couple of the guys didn't show up and all their duties fell on me, making the day even longer."

Johnny snickered. "My big brother is my personal poster boy for stamping out any possible notion of not going to college. No other encouragement is necessary. All I have to do is see him exhausted from a fifteen-hour workday. That does it for me."

Melissa frowned at Johnny's idiotic remark. "I hope you do go to college, baby brother, but I also hope you realize, regardless what your chosen profession is, you'll have long hard days on occasion," Melissa glared at the boy, head tilted aggressively forward with one eyebrow jacked.

"Aw, Missy. Now, don't go and burst my bubble. Leave me with my dream," Johnny replied.

Charlie rolled off the sofa and sluggishly came to his feet. "That's my cue to cut out and head back to my place." He trudged past Melissa, yawning again. "I'll probably see you guys tomorrow evening, if you're around."

As he passed her, Melissa patted him on the shoulder. "Go home and get some sleep and don't doze off on the way."

Charlie did not reply. He offered a one-finger salute as he walked through the front door into the dimming light of early evening.

Melissa turned back to her youngest brother. "Where's Mom and Kyra?"

"Kitchen," Johnny replied, never tearing his eyes away from a replay of the Seahawks last football game.

"Mom?" Melissa said as she entered the room.

"Hi, sweetheart. How was work?"

Melissa scowled at Kyra who was helping her mother measure ingredients to make a pie. "Aside from unwanted interruptions that had nothing to do with my job, it was fine. Where do you keep Dwayne Logan's phone number?"

The busy hands of both women came to an abrupt halt. Her mom and younger sister grinned at one another.

"Come on now. I want to call and apologize for not saying goodbye yesterday."

"Of course you do," Kyra said.

"You'll find his number in that address book by the lamp on the table next to my bed," her mother said.

Melissa had already turned to leave the kitchen. "Thanks. I'll call him from up there." She stopped, turned her head, and shielded her mouth with the back of her hand. She whispered, "I don't want to take a chance that Johnny hears a conversation that places me a couple of thousand miles from Coos Bay yesterday. If I thought Kyra was a nuisance with questions, I can only imagine the bombardment I'd be getting from my seventeen-year-old brother. My answers have to be mostly lies. I really hate it when I have to manipulate the truth, regardless how noble the cause."

She took the stairs two at a time up to her mother's bedroom. She found Dwayne's number in a neatly organized address book and dialed it on the land-line next to her mother's bed.

"Hello," came a raspy greeting.

"Dwayne?"

"Nah. This is his ol' man, Cletus. Ya need to talk to him?"

"If you don't mind."

"Want me to tell him who's calling," Cletus said, "or shall we just surprise him?"

Melissa laughed. "You're funny. I didn't know you lived with him."

"Unless you're a neighbor, how would you know...whoever-you-are. And that opens the door to my next question. Who are you?"

"Oh, I'm sorry. My name is Melissa Dane-Blakely."

"Right. Right. You and your sis dropped by yesterday. I hear y'all might be movin' into that big ol' house up the road."

"There's no 'might' about it. I'll be moving there within a couple of weeks, maybe sooner. My sister, Kyra, will probably join me soon after and my mom, Cary, will be here in the spring, after my youngest brother graduates from high school."

"Well then, I'll be lookin' forward to it. Hang on. I'll go get the boy. It may take a minute. I saw him headin' toward the chicken coop with a rifle in his hand. Those ol' hens were carryin' on like there may be a coyote lurkin' about." He paused. "Oh, by the way, tell your mom hello for me."

"Uh...okay. Sure. No rush. Take your time." *Why would he want me to tell Mom hello for him?* As she waited, Melissa wondered what Cletus looked like. Would he be an older version of Dwayne, or radically different, like she and her sister were? Her mind took the question and built a suppositional picture of Cletus Logan. Suddenly, a chill tingled up her spine. The small hairs on the back of her neck prickled and rose. A billowy white glow formed at the end of a beam emanating from the left side of her chest a few feet from her. A scene formed within it. She saw a truck with tall wooden sideboards backed up to the high end of a concrete ramp, inclined to meet the truck bed. Her view was from a vantage point nearby but up in the air, as if floating over it. Dwayne was inside a substantial fenced corral attempting to coax a large white bull up the ramp lined on both sides with a stout pipe railing, ending at the truck bed. A physically fit older man that must be Cletus Logan, stood outside the chest-high barrier of the incline about half-way up. He had something in his hand—some type of wand or club. With the other hand, he clutched the pipe rail. It was about four and a half feet high, to funnel animals in a straight line up the ramp.

The bull was obstinate. Dwayne attempted herding the animal up the incline multiple times, but it kept backing down off it. He finally coaxed it to climb.

The older man clung to the partition rail as the bull hesitated next to him. The skittish animal stepped backwards. The older man touched the neck of the huge horned bovine with that wand. It must be a cattle prod because when it touched the bull, blue sparks arced from the end of it to the bull's neck. It must have sent a strong jolt of electricity into the animal.

The bull reacted, throwing its head to the side.

A horn gored the older man in the neck.

The bull slung its head the other direction, tearing a gaping hole in the guy's throat. He fell off the ramp onto his back. The carotid clearly torn, blood pumped in a geyser from the wound. The man grabbed for his throat but his frantic movement quickly slowed as life pumped away, fueled by his racing heart.

Melissa gasped. Breathing hard and fast, she said aloud, "No, no. I don't want to see any more." She clenched her eyes tight. The chill vanished, along with the vision.

"Melissa, were you sayin' somethin' when I picked up the phone?" Dwayne asked.

Melissa swallowed, trying to get her breathing under control. "Just talking to my sister," she lied.

"It's good to hear from ya. Especially since you didn't give me a chance to say goodbye yesterday."

"Sorry about that. Had to catch a plane. Say, do you have a bull?"

"That's an odd question."

"You're a farmer that raises cows. Why would it be an odd question?"

"I guess it's not so odd. But it's surely an interesting one, coming from you. It just so happens I bought one today. Dad and I are going to load it up and bring it home tomorrow. Got a great deal on it. The guy said if I took care of the loading and transport, plus dehorn it myself, that he'd knock a couple of hundred dollars off the price. I couldn't pass it up."

"Is it white?"

"Uh, yeah. Good guess. It's a big ol' Charolaise. Why are you so interested? Are you thinkin' about raising cows yourself?"

"No. That's not it at all. Dwayne, I'm going to tell you something and you must listen. It's a matter of life and death. I'll explain another time how I know this but not right now."

"Are you all right?"

"I'm fine. It's not about me. I have no choice but to lay it out there for your own good, more specifically, the well-being of your father. Please trust me on this. Tomorrow, when you go to load that bull, your dad will climb up on the side of a loading ramp with an electric cattle prod. When the animal tries to back down the chute, your dad will shock it behind the ear. The bull will react violently and fatally injure your dad. Do not, I repeat, *do not* let your dad put himself in that situation."

"I don't know how you think you know this, but Dad and I have been working cattle for years. We know what we're doin'."

"Please Dwayne, pay close attention to your dad as you two are loading that animal. That's all I'm saying."

"I will," he replied. "I'm going to hold you to that explanation of why you think you know this."

"I'll explain it. I promise, just not now. Honestly, the original reason I called was to apologize for popping out on you yesterday. I realize that's not a neighborly thing to do and a poor way to start a friendship."

"Aw heck. No apology necessary. Don't give it a second thought."

Melissa felt a heart-thumping surge of emotion. She liked Dwayne—a lot. The chemistry she felt was genuine. He was unpretentious and seemed to be a great guy. "Please remember what I told you. I'll be in touch soon," she said, and then ended the call. Melissa figured she'd be chewing a few fingernails off between now and tomorrow afternoon, praying Dwayne took her warning seriously.

***

Dwayne, holding a steaming cup of coffee, gazed out the large picture window fronting the living room in his house, curtains fully open to let in the morning light. The streaming brilliance was powerful, spotlighting lazily floating dust motes within the rays inside the house. He stared across the early morning view of bare cotton stalks in that part of the field beyond the front yard out to the gravel road fronting the property. The stalks were like gnarled sticks standing upright in straight east/west quarter-mile rows. It had been harvested a few weeks before. He didn't look forward to the chore, but those stalks needed to be shredded and turned under or, at least, ground into the soil by a disc plow, to get the field ready for another crop year starting in the spring.

He sipped his coffee and looked back to the east. The sun had fully risen, but the bottom of the fiery orb still kissed the horizon, casting long, stark shadows across the front yard and field beyond. Frost, coating the brown dormant grass in the yard, sparkled in the pristine Texas air. He sighed contentedly, took another sip from his mug and called out, "Come on, Dad. We'd better go get that bull before ol' Mister Hadley decides he made a bad deal and backs out." He turned up his mug and gulped the last swallow of coffee, enjoying the sensation of the hot liquid on his throat.

Dwayne stepped into the frigid morning. Every warm breath turned white as it hit the cold dry South Plains air. He pulled up the collar of his heavy fleece-lined coat to block the wind from his neck. The green John Deere cap he wore was not meant to keep his head warm, but it was his favorite and worth the sacrifice.

He climbed into the borrowed dually pickup truck outfitted with tall wooden sideboards and a rear gate to transport an animal as large as an adult Charolaise bull. Although the animal was viable, it was young, but would likely weigh over a ton, sporting ten-inch horns. It should give years of good breeding service. Dwayne cranked the truck's diesel engine. It roared to life, belching gray smoke, settling into a clattering idle.

Cletus came trotting out the front door of the house, carrying the remnant of a slice of toast. He chewed as he hurried to the truck and climbed in, pulling the door shut. He poked the last bite of toasted bread in his mouth and spoke around it. "Get that heater goin'."

"Engine must warm up first. You know that."

Cletus brushed bread crumbs from his jeans. What's the big rush?" he asked.

"I just want to get it done early. That's all. Besides the sooner we can get that animal in with our cows, the sooner he can get to work on givin' us a calf crop next year. If we're lucky, some of those ol' mother cows will be dropping calves by Labor Day, just in time for fall rains. That, of course, would be perfect to get 'em strong and healthy before bitterly cold northers blow through next winter."

Dwayne's dog, Hotshot, came running. "Sorry, buddy, you can't go this time."

The dog stopped and danced in a circle, pawing at the ground, not understanding why he couldn't go. He always did before.

Dwayne put the truck in gear and began rolling away. He cranked his window down. "Can't have you spookin' the bull while we're trying to load it. Sorry, pal." He rolled the window up and accelerated down the driveway.

"Let's get on with it," Cletus replied, as he slapped away bread crumbs from around his mouth.

During the ten-mile drive, Dwayne glanced sideways at his dad and wondered about the warning the Dane woman had given him on the phone. A modicum of disappointment shaded his thoughts. He hoped she might become more than just another neighbor up the road. He liked what he saw. Melissa Dane-Blakely was quite a woman. Now, he was forced to consider that the woman might be insane.

The truck's heater warmed. It felt nice. He relaxed. After a few minutes, the thinking game became tiresome. Still, it was difficult to set aside. *What if that woman is certifiably nuts? And, if so, why is she running loose? I'd be thrown in the same loony bin for trying to justify dating her anyway.* "I guess I'll know soon enough, one way or the other," he mumbled, and then clucked his tongue.

"What'd ya say?" Cletus asked.

"Nothin' important. Just thinkin' out loud."

Ten minutes later, he steered down a rutted private road next to old Mister Hadley's house. A holding pen came into view with a concrete loading ramp rising to about four feet behind a big barn covered in rust-streaked corrugated sheet metal. The ramp was lined on both sides with welded pipe rails. The bull was the only animal in the pen. Dwayne backed up to the high end of the ramp. The truck bed mated it perfectly, as he gingerly closed the gap until the end of the ramp came into contact with the truck's bumper. Killing the engine, he flung the truck door open and dropped to the ground. "Let's get this chore done."

He heard the squawk of a screen door and turned to see grizzled old man Hadley step out onto the back porch of his house. He only had on a strap undershirt and white undershorts that were once briefs, but on old man Hadley looked more boxers. He didn't seem to care who saw him in that state of undress or that he was scratching his crotch with one hand while waving at them with the other. "How you boys doin' this mornin'?" the old man shouted.

"Great, Mister Hadley, just great," Dwayne called back.

"Y'all go ahead and get your business done." He grinned. "I'm going back inside where it's warm and finish my breakfast."

Dwayne did not reply, simply waved and climbed up to the second rail of the corral fence to check out the situation. It looked straightforward enough—open the holding gate at the bottom of the ramp, and close it and latch it, once the bull moved far enough up the ramp so that he could. He would then herd the animal on up into the truck bed. The only problem he saw was the possibility of the bull turning on him and charging before he could get the big fella onto the ramp. Melissa's warning crossed his mind. "Dad, I want you back here helping me guide the bull up the ramp from behind. I don't want you standing anywhere on that ramp outside the rail. That bull has some long horns and he might not like us forcin' our intentions on him."

"Why not? If you can get his head turned up the ramp, it would only take a shock or two on his backside with this prod to get him all the way up into the truck."

"Please, Dad, do what I ask." Dwayne walked over to the older man and took possession of the high voltage prod.

"All right, all right. If that's the way you wanna do it, then that's the way it'll be."

Dwayne felt he had cause now to dismiss Melissa's warning. His dad would remain some distance from the ramp, plus he had control of the prod. He climbed over the fence followed by his dad. Dwayne waited for Cletus to take up a position opposite him so they might funnel the animal to the ramp. "Here we go." As Dwayne approached the bull, the animal sensed something was about to change and it involved him. He snorted and turned to walk in the opposite direction. Dwayne did not rush. So as not to spook the animal, he simply followed the big bovine across the pen until it turned and faced the loading ramp of its own accord. Dwayne touched the rump of the animal and gave it a shock. It bolted forward, straight for the bottom of the ramp. The big animal actually got on the ramp on the first try but had not moved up it high enough for Dwayne to close the holding gate behind him to prevent it from backing down and off the ramp. With the electric wand in his hand, Dwayne grabbed the gate and tried using it to coax the bull a little farther up so he could close and latch the gate behind him.

Suddenly, Cletus hurried over and snatched the cattle prod from Dwayne's hand. "Gimme that thing. You keep pushing the gate, I'll give the ol' boy another jolt on the butt."

"No, Dad! Stay off the side of the ramp. Don't get near it," he exclaimed, still feeling the need to man the gate with both hands.

"Don't be a nervous Nellie," Cletus said as he continued walking toward the side of the ramp.

"Damn it, Dad! Don't do it!"

"You just keep your hands on the gate, boy." Cletus grabbed the pipe rail about halfway up the concrete incline and leaped up to stand on its edge.

The bull startled and took a step back down the ramp, forcing the gate open, despite Dwayne's meager attempt to hold it.

Cletus lifted the prod.

Melissa's warning was coming to life before Dwayne's eyes. He let go of the gate and raced the few steps to where his dad stood up off the ground on the edge of that inclined concrete loading chute.

Cletus positioned the prod to touch and shock the bull's neck, since the animal's backside had moved out of his reach.

As the prod made contact with the fleshy area behind the bovine's ear, Dwayne grabbed a handful of his dad's coat collar and yanked as hard as he could. But not before the prod had already shocked the animal.

As Cletus flew backwards, the huge animal slung its head to the left. A horn nicked the old man's neck.

Cletus fell onto his butt in the well-pummeled and crap-covered dirt of the pen enclosure.

"Damn it, boy! You could've broken my back, yanking me like that."

"Yeah, well, that blood on your neck could've easily been your whole throat ripped out. I don't care how mad at me you get. I'm gonna call this a win."

Cletus pulled his fingers across his neck. He examined his blood covered fingertips, just then realizing that his son had spoken a truth. "Oh...well...I guess I should be thankin' ya, not cussin' ya."

The big animal snorted and trotted on up the ramp and stepped onto the truck bed, as if the monstrous animal simply did not want to be forced into something he wanted to do anyway. Dwayne pulled off his green John Deere cap and scratched the side of his head. "Well, I'll be darn." He hurried over and closed the gate on the back of the truck, penning the animal in, now ready for transport. He looked back at his dad, still sitting on the ground, legs splayed in front of him. The full impact of what surely would have been a disastrous tragedy without Melissa's warning struck home full force. Dwayne shivered mightily. The early December air only played a small part.

Chapter Ten

Leaving It All Behind

Melissa gave notice of her planned departure at the clinic the day after her tense conversation with Dwayne. Administrators told her a week's notice was sufficient, as long as all her patients' records were up to date and attending physicians apprised of all contingencies. She accepted the terms appreciatively, eager to get the Texas adventure underway. She hired movers and vacated her apartment during her final week at the clinic. The plan took shape and was getting real quickly. The required week of notice ended.

It was happening. She stood next to her little blue Chevrolet SUV, looking back over the top of it at her mother and sister, Kyra. The two waved at her from the open front door of her mother's house. Melissa offered a heartfelt and enthusiastic return wave, shouting, "I love you, Mom. And I'll see you soon, Sis."

"Be careful driving, Missy," her mother shouted through cupped hands. "If you get tired, stop for heaven's sake. You don't need to be in a rush, you hear?"

"Yeah, keep your road rage in check," Kyra called out, and then laughed.

"Oh hush," Melissa replied and offered a final smile and wave as she got into her sport utility vehicle.

It would be several more days before Kyra joined her. Bonnie Crandall hired her younger sister's replacement at the boutique, but Kyra promised to train the new girl before joining Melissa in Texas. So, her remaining days of work were left open-ended. Still, Melissa expected her sister to follow within a week. Since Kyra never moved out of their mother's house, all she had to be concerned with moving were clothes and precious few personal items. Melissa already had those few boxes loaded with her things in the moving van. All that remained for Kyra to do was toss a suitcase in the trunk of that white Ford Taurus of hers, get behind the steering wheel, and head southeast to Texas.

All week, leading up to her departure, Melissa wondered if Dwayne heeded her warning about his dad. She sensed everything had turned out okay. She recalled a specific part of Uncle Jack's book, *The Last Radiant Heart*, where Arthur Wainwright told him to never disregard intuitive feelings, because to a radiant heart, it went beyond mere faith in an outcome. Although, psychical intuition may have been a lesser part of the gift, it was an important one. She knew it had turned out well and tragedy had been averted. Still, it didn't prevent her from wondering. Full trust in her radiant heart would come in time. Of that, she was confident. She just wasn't there yet.

Twice in three days, she went to answer her phone but the caller hung up on both occasions. The number in the display was a Texas area code. It was Dwayne. She knew it even before seeing the area code. He could not, or would not, talk to her. But he wanted to. That was bothersome. First thing upon arrival in Texas, Melissa vowed to arrange a conversation with Dwayne. She agonized over how much to share with him. He, obviously, was aware she had a psychic ability of sorts. He could not know though that it went much farther than seeing potential future events. She hoped a relationship might develop. She really liked the guy. But it would never happen if she handled an explanation badly and inadvertently frightened the bejesus out of him. There were many ways it could go, but only two were likely, depending on how she handled it. Scare him so badly he would want nothing to do with her, disbelieve it, or consider her mentally unstable. The best-case scenario would be that he would have enough faith in her that he would be patient, learn, and then come to believe it in time. Even then, it would take persistent tolerance on his part. Could he? Would he?

It was now clear to Melissa why Jack Dane was so fearful of people knowing what he was capable of. Thanks to her uncle, she was not as skittish as he had been about this thing called the radiant heart. In fact, she was in the early stage of embracing it. It piqued her curiosity and she was eager to learn more. She realized, though, caution must rule, confining knowledge of it to a small circle of people. It seemed prudent. If widely known, the government would lock her up and study her, to weaponize her. Unscrupulous people would want to use her for money and fame. The more she considered the ins and outs of it all, she understood with increasing clarity about her uncle's hesitance in the use of his own radiant heart.

She considered her attitude toward it. *Am I foolish for not being more fearful of this talent, curse, or however it should be labeled? After all, I left my stepfather deep in the woods, and I know neither where nor when. Bastard as he was, he might not have deserved being blasted into sub-atomic particles that can never be retrieved. If that is, in fact, what I did.* The notion spawned another, more philosophical question. *William Blakely disappeared by an action I precipitated, but I didn't touch him once we landed in that place. All I did was keep him from hitting me without laying a hand on him again. Does that make me a murderer because I went home without him? I did not plan to leave him behind. I just didn't know he would not come back like I did. Can he even be considered dead? I wonder where those deep woods were anyhow.* She had always been directionally challenged in the woods, or anywhere the horizon could not be readily visible from any direction. She would invariably panic about finding her way. She had been that way her whole life. Even now, safely inside a car with a clear direction of travel, the thought of becoming lost among tall trees far from civilization was disconcerting. She gripped the steering wheel tighter as she left Coos Bay. The lifelong fear hovered near phobic proportion. A tiny shiver vibrated her body. She abruptly realized it was possible to do it to anyone. Inadvertently or purposely, it could happen. For God's sake, she could do it to Kyra or Dwayne or her mother or anyone else. *What then? Would I be able to get them back?* It happened to her Uncle Jack's girlfriend, Nikki Endicott. But he and Arthur Wainwright managed to get her back. It began to burn inside her that, if it ever happened, she would have one shot at a retrieval from a future time. Theoretically, she could get Kyra back because of the Dane blood connection, but what about her mother or Dwayne? As she understood it, no matter where or when she was in time, alternate dimension, or geographic location, she would be traveling carrying her personal present with her. That meant if she ever tried and failed, she would not get a second chance because a failure would put the attempt in her personal past and she was divinely forbidden to change history, even her own. On the other hand, if she traveled to the past and left someone behind when she returned, there would not even be a one-shot chance. That person would cease to have ever existed. No memory of them by anyone, save for herself, would exist, or any knowledge at all the person ever set foot on planet earth. Frightening paradoxes mounted as the miles clicked off.

Melissa's southeasterly trek across the states from Oregon gave her time to think, concluding she needed a partner that understood her and the perils she faced. Kyra and her mother were all she had. Kyra was too impetuous to be a moderating factor or a steady hand in a perilous situation. Her mother, Cary, God love her, was the polar opposite of Kyra. She would oppose anything she deemed dangerous. Which, Melissa was certain, would be almost everything. She needed a steady hand and a cool head by her side, like Jack's sidekick, Arthur Wainwright. *What about Dwayne Logan? Could that be a possibility?* "Hmm. I wonder...?" she muttered.

***

After a much-needed night's sleep at a motel in Las Vegas and sixty-five gallons of gasoline later, Melissa passed the Lubbock, Texas city limit sign, arriving just as the glare from the setting sun worried her tired eyes. As annoying as the brilliance could be, she appreciated the unobstructed view. She witnessed an explosion of color created by ultra clean air between her and wispy clouds invading the setting sun's space far in the distance. She glanced often at the artful mix of colors on the western horizon—hues of orange, pink, blue, white, gray, and everything between. Clear as the sky was, she figured those clouds responsible for the gorgeous colors were probably located high above the eastern plains of New Mexico a couple hundred miles away, across the border from Texas.

She considered getting another motel room and drive out to the farm in the morning. She whimsically wondered if the radiant heart worked on large inanimate objects, her SUV as an example. She was exhausted and tired of driving. It would be nice to zap herself and her ride instantly to a parked position in front of the Dane mansion.

She snickered.

But the grin melted away, as the pragmatic underpinning of that thought kicked in. *Wait a minute. When I transported here the last two times, I didn't arrive naked as a newborn. I still had on clothing, shoes, and jewelry.* The more she thought about this space-time thing, the more fearful and confused she became about the rules of it all. It was disconcertingly clear why Jack Dane told her even after all his adventures using the radiant heart, he had precious little knowledge about the extent of his capability and why things were possible yet other, similar things, were not. There was one time he inadvertently transported himself while in the midst of a traffic accident, a car rollover. He went to his radiant heart destination without his vehicle, yet his shoes and clothes were on him, as they had been. *That's all I need is another freakin' conundrum.* She was too exhausted to dwell on it.

Before she had time to decide about getting motel room for the night, she found herself on the south side of Lubbock exiting the loop onto a south bound highway, only fifteen or twenty minutes from the farm. *Might as well gut it out and put this tiresome trip entirely behind me.*

Although the artwork and expensive pieces of furniture had gone into storage, and had been untouched for years, Melissa remembered basic pieces, like beds, remained in the mansion. She glanced over her shoulder to the blanket and pillow she carried in case she needed to pull off the highway to rest. *That should be good enough for a night until I can get things set up.*

She turned east off the highway onto a gravel road between the small towns of Ropesville and Meadow. After another mile, the stucco house Dwayne and Cletus Logan lived in came into view. That had to be her first stop. She needed the key to the mansion. The sun had set, now just a glowing ember on the western horizon as darkness encroached on the light of day. She turned onto the gravel driveway and rolled to a stop beyond the front yard, gravel crunching beneath her tires.

She knocked on the door.

An older man opened it. She noticed the bandage on his neck below his jaw. "Hi," Melissa said. "You must be Cletus."

"Yep. Can I help you?"

"I'm Melissa Dane-Blakely."

"Aw yeah. You're the one I spoke to on the phone." He opened the screen door and stuck out a friendly hand. "Nice to meet ya, young lady."

She took his hand. "Nice to meet you, too, Cletus."

"Come on in. Dwayne's in the kitchen fixin' supper."

"Really? So, he can cook, huh?"

Cletus smiled. "Let me put it this way. The boy knows his way around a can opener." He snickered. "Expertly, I might add."

Melissa laughed. "I like you, Cletus."

"Well, if I ever give you cause not to, let me know and don't brood about it."

"I think you'll find me fairly straight forward."

"Hey, son, look who's here," he said, leading Melissa into the kitchen.

Melissa saw what Cletus had said was as much truth as joke. Dwayne was opening a family size can of Spaghetti-Os. Her smile grew wider.

"Sure nice to see ya again, Melissa," Dwayne said as he turned the crank on the can opener.

"Your dad told me you were the cook."

Dwayne glared at the elder Logan. "Funny. Real funny." He turned his attention back to Melissa. "Truth is, by the time we put in a twelve to fifteen hour day around the farm, we're both too doggone exhausted to care much about serious cookin'. Are ya here to stay this time?"

She sighed. "I am for a fact. And, I'm exhausted. Can I borrow your key to the mansion? I'll get one made for myself tomorrow."

"You plannin' on stayin' there tonight?"

"I thought I would, yeah."

"Look, it gets chilly in there overnight and the gas hasn't been turned on. So, there's no heat. Why don't ya spend the night here? We have another bedroom back there. It hardly ever gets used and the sheets on the bed are clean. Whaddaya say?"

Melissa hesitated, but finally said, "Are you sure I wouldn't be an imposition? I did just pop in unannounced, after all."

Dwayne smiled and jacked one eyebrow. "Yeah, you do seem to pop in and out quite suddenly. Ya think a pattern might be developin'?"

Melissa felt her face flush. "I'm so sorry. I'm leaving you the impression I'm flighty and undependable."

"Don't give it a second thought. I was just havin' a bit 'o fun with ya. How about it? Want to use that bed back there tonight?"

She nodded shyly. "If you don't mind. I'm really tired."

He clapped his hands. "Great! Dad, why don't you set out a couple of fresh towels in the bathroom? Melissa, you bring in your things. And, while y'all are takin' care of that stuff, I'll heat up this giant can of Spaghetti-Os and we'll share 'em. It'll be like a picnic."

Before she could react to the plan, Cletus took off down the hall toward the bathroom and Dwayne took a couple of steps toward her. He leaned in and whispered in her ear, "I need to thank you. Your warnin' about Dad is responsible for him being here and alive tonight. If I had not reacted, he would have been killed. I have a truckload of questions for ya. I just don't know how to get started with 'em."

She nodded. "I know you do. And, you deserve a truckload of answers, just not tonight." She yawned.

Chapter Eleven

Into the Unknown

Dwayne opened his eyes. He lay on his side, a pillow between his knees, another beneath his propped elbow, hugging it like a teddy bear. He opened his eyes and glanced through his bedroom window without raising his head. It was dark but instinct told him it was time to get up and out of bed to begin the day. The glance out his window shifted to the glowing hands of his wristwatch. Suspicion confirmed. It was a few minutes after five. He rolled onto his back and extended into a shuddering full body stretch and yawned.

A beautiful woman he met only a few days ago, lay asleep in the bedroom the other side of the wall behind his head. He placed a hand on the cool, rough texture of the wall surface, comforted by perceived closeness to that gorgeous creature. She was worth a lingering thought. Although only an acquaintance, he strongly sensed sophistication, intelligence, and grace behind those beautiful, almost exotic, brown eyes. Every move, everything she said, everything she did, spoke of a confident woman with purpose.

Purpose? Admiration abruptly became convoluted with the strangeness surrounding Melissa's warning that saved his father's life. *What is her purpose? Heck, I don't even know what she does for a living, or if she works at all. Does she? If so, doing what?* He yawned again. *Maybe she has a little fortune-telling business, crystal ball and all.* He snickered lazily, stretching a final time. He needed to pee and tossed the covers off, reason enough to stop being so darn lazy and get out of bed. He reeled in his rabbit-trailing thoughts and stood.

As he lazily walked out of his bedroom and started down the hall toward the bathroom, he stopped by Melissa's bedroom door. He again thought about the magnificent woman the other side of the door, spending the night in his house, right here in this very house. *How wonderful is that, for God's sake?* In that bedroom lay a woman that had been a stranger to him mere days ago. It had all happened so suddenly. He couldn't be happier about it. Dwayne loved his dad, but he was lonely, desiring another type of companionship—one that only a woman can provide.

The bedroom door swung open. There stood Melissa, fully dressed in blue jeans, running shoes, and a snug-fitting tank top, sporting an unbuttoned flannel shirt over it. It was the sexiest thing he'd ever seen and worthy of lingering over, until he remembered his own state of undress. A big smile stretched her face tight, as her eyes met his, and then traveled down the length of his body. "Well, that's quite a greeting for so early in the morning."

Only then did he realize the only clothing he wore were his boxers, the crotch bulging a little. "Oh, crap," he muttered, and then said, "I'm so sorry. I'm not accustomed to havin' anyone other than Dad in the house." He fanned the fingers of both hands and covered the suspicious crotch protrusion. A fig leaf would have covered more. He turned toward his bedroom, but then realized he still needed to pee, badly now, thanks to the shock of Melissa suddenly appearing in front of him and the natural morning chill in the old house. He stopped, turned, and stuttered a step in the opposite direction. Heat of embarrassment flushed his face as his eyes again met Melissa's. She was still grinning, still unmoving. "Sorry," he said, as he glided by, "but I have to go to the bathroom. No choice. Can't wait."

"Please don't apologize. I've lived alone a few years. I know what it's like to fall into habits of moving around wearing little, sometimes nothing."

Dwayne bounced a weak smile, nodded, and hurried on toward the bathroom. That comment only exacerbated his problem. He couldn't prevent the visual image of her casually walking around nude from popping into his head.

"By the way, good morning," she said to his back.

"You, too," he replied as he closed the bathroom door behind him. He stopped just inside the door and considered how casually she took his faux pas. He smiled and tilted his head thoughtfully, liking her even more.

"Dwayne?" she said through the door.

"Yeah?"

"Where do you keep the coffee? I'll get a pot going."

"Sure. There's a can and filters in the cabinet above the maker."

"I realize that you, ahem, still have to get dressed," she said.

"Sure glad to hear you have sense of humor about it. And, yeah, I do need to cover up a little more of this ol' body o' mine."

***

Cletus joined Dwayne at the dining table which, in the style of country living, was located in the center of a large, square kitchen. It happened to be a popular style of construction in the fifties when the house was built. Even the dining table and chairs seemed to be from the same era with chrome legs and soft plastic-like seat coverings that, amazingly, were in reasonably good shape, considering the many butts that sat on them over many decades. Dwayne appeared dressed in the manner which she had come to expect, crisply starched and creased but faded Wrangler jeans cinched by a wide belt with a large silver buckle and a worn western shirt. But, even the shirt, with frayed elbows, had been neatly pressed. She sipped her coffee and offered him a smile equal to the one earlier.

He responded with a head bobble and an eye roll.

Cletus noticed. He pointed a flicking finger between them. "What's goin' on with you two? What're those looks for?"

Without pulling her eyes from Dwayne, Melissa replied, "Oh, it's nothing really. Dwayne let me know what bachelor life is like. And, he didn't need to say much at all to get the story told."

"True enough." Dwayne poured two cups of coffee and handed one to his dad. He went to the front door, opened it, and whistled. "Where are ya, Hotshot?" he shouted.

Curious, Melissa rose and walked to the doorway separating kitchen from living room. A large chocolate brown Labrador retriever took a flying leap right over the front porch, through the open door, directly into the living room, sliding to a stop on the hardwood floor. The dog's exuberance startled Melissa. "Wow! This is a seriously motivated dog."

"It's breakfast time," Dwayne replied. "And ol' Hotshot knows it."

The dog, she now knew by the name Hotshot, ran past Dwayne, nails clicking on the floor, and stopped in front of her, tail and tongue wagging. "Looks like you have another new friend," Dwayne told her.

"Seems so." She patted him between the ears and the dog lifted his head tight against her hand, as if he was petting her hand, not the other way around. "He really is friendly."

"If he likes you he is. But I've seen ol' Hotshot take out after a Rottweiler that laid angry eyes on me. It was growling and stalking me. Believe it or not, it wasn't Hotshot that backed down."

"Isn't that unusual? For a Labrador retriever, I mean?"

"Extremely unusual." Dwayne came over and affectionately patted the dog's side. "That's exactly why I love this guy so much. He's the only protective one of this breed I've ever known. As a rule, Labradors live most of their lives with their tails between their legs and would rather lick you than bite you. Hotshot's equally capable of both."

Discussing the dog brought her and Dwayne closer together. Only the dog stood between them. Once dog talk ended, it became awkwardly quiet. "Do either of you want more coffee? I'm pouring," she blurted.

"I'll take a warmup," Cletus replied.

"One cup's my limit," Dwayne said. "What's your plan for the day?"

"I want to find out where the storage facility is located that holds Uncle Jack's things."

"Aw, sure. It's in Brownfield. That's only a few minutes south of here. I'd be happy to take you."

"I don't want to pull you away from things you have to do today. I'm sure it's a lot."

"Hey, Dad, mind takin' care of feedin' the livestock this mornin'?"

Cletus slowly twisted around in his chair and looked over his shoulder at his son, grinning wryly. "Don't I always?"

"Well...not *always*."

The exchange tickled Melissa. It also let her know Dwayne wanted to spend time with her and this was a way to make it happen. She wanted it, too. "That would be nice," she said. "Thanks so much...to both of you."

On the way to town in Dwayne's pickup, Melissa took note of a thick layer of dust on the dashboard, the dried mud on the rubber floor mats, and the frayed seat covers. "Your truck looks like it works as hard as you do."

"It's my work truck, all right."

"Oh, so you have another vehicle somewhere?"

"Uh...no. This ol' pickup is all I've got," he deadpanned.

Melissa blushed. "I'm sorry. I didn't mean to—"

He laughed. "Aw, I was just havin' some fun with ya."

"You sure like to do that. Do you think a pattern might be developing?"

He grinned sideways. "Touché."

She turned to watch the powerline poles zip by as Dwayne rumbled down the highway. She couldn't wipe the smile from her face, feeling the fast friendly warmth developing between them.

"Melissa?"

"Why don't you call me Missy? It's less formal."

"Okay. Missy it is. What is it you do?"

"I'm a nurse practitioner."

"Ah, almost a doctor, huh?"

"I think doctors depend on us a little too much sometimes. But I do love the work. Speaking of jobs, any ideas where I might look for work?"

Lubbock would be your best bet. It's certainly close enough to commute and opportunities would be better there, I think."

"Thanks. I'll check it out after I get moved in. The moving van should be here tomorrow. I need to hire some guys to help me get things set up to a livable condition. Any ideas?"

"I sure do. First thing is to forget hiring people."

"What are you talking about?"

"You're in Texas now. Here, you call on your neighbors."

"I can't do that. I don't know anyone here, aside from you and your dad. And I barely know you two. I'm not about to burden you guys with it."

"Well, ya see, I have a problem with that statement. It's not a burden. It's my pleasure to offer my help. Besides, I betcha I can have ten to fifteen guys and maybe a few women on your doorstep, more than willin' to lend a hand, on the day of your choosin'."

A sudden rush of emotion glossed her eyes. "You would do that for me?"

"For you? Absolutely. For anyone else..." He shrugged his shoulders. "...maybe."

She reached across and placed a hand on his forearm. "I hardly know you, but I couldn't ask for a better friend."

He grinned. "I sure do like the sound o' that."

After a minute, she noticed him staring down the highway with unblinking intensity. "Something on your mind?"

"Yep, and I'm pretty sure you know what it is."

"I think I do. I knew it was coming and I suppose this is as good a time as any to talk about it."

He glanced sideways. "I want to thank you for the heads-up about my dad. If you hadn't warned me to watch him closely, I don't think he would be alive today."

Melissa sighed. "Dwayne, had I not warned you, I can say to you, definitively, he *would* have died. I saw it happen as clearly as I'm seeing you right now. It robbed my breath and it was painful to watch. Had you not intervened he would have been killed."

"Missy, my first question is a given. Are you psychic?"

"Yes...sort of, among other things."

He snapped his head around to face her. "'Other things?' Whaddaya mean by that?"

The conversation hit the first speed bump. *How much should I share?* She thought, and then hesitated. Maybe her psychical intuition should be the extent of his knowledge about her—at least for a while—give him time to digest information slowly, before moving on to those other things more difficult to believe. After all, how she came to see the episode unfold had nothing whatsoever, to do with intuition or psychical ability. She was literally looking across space and time. She remained silent for a few fat seconds. She wasn't certain of the extent of her talent anyhow.

He continued stealing glances her way, waiting for a response. "Well?"

"Dwayne, there's so much I want to tell you, but speeding down the highway is probably not the best venue for such a discussion. I know how it would go if I dumped a lot of information on you all at once."

He chuckled, and then, sarcastically, "Oh, so you know what I'll be thinking before I think it."

Melissa silently stared at him, until she saw the light of realization widen his eyes. She offered an understanding smile and nod. "That's exactly what I'm saying."

"Oh, sweet Jesus, have I thought anything unflattering or mean that you've picked up on?"

She smiled warmly. "No, Dwayne. Every vibe I get from you is very, very nice. Incidentally, I'm new at this. I had no knowledge of this talent a couple of weeks ago. Why it did not appear until the age of thirty-one, I have no idea and no understanding on that point. I do wonder why it waited till adulthood to make its presence known. I can't fathom why I wasn't aware of it many years ago. Now, my mind has opened to many things. But I'll say no more about it, for now. I can't have you thinking of me as a delusional twit."

"I may be thinking a lot of things, but after what you did for my dad, I'm certain *delusional* is not a word I'll be usin' to describe you."

"That's sweet, but I don't know how you can believe it, having known me such a short time. Heck, even I have trouble believing it. Anyhow, be patient, be my friend, and maybe I'll never give you reason to change that opinion. We'll get there...given time."

Dwayne drove through town and pulled into a storage facility with four long rows of cubicles, each one clad with an orange nine-foot roll-up door. He turned down one of the rows and rolled along slowly, coming to a stop in front of units that did not appear the same as all the others.

"Which one is it?" Melissa asked.

He laughed. "One? There are six twelve-by-twenty units filled front to back and floor to ceiling with Jack Dane's stuff."

"Seriously?"

"Yep. Anything that ya might call thief bait and there's a bunch of it, mostly artworks, rugs, seriously valuable antiques, and all manner of things. If you'll notice the difference in these units versus all the others. These are fitted with triple padlocked diagonal bars over double thick iron doors for added security.

The interiors are fitted with iron bars and heavy gauge expanded metal. If someone did happen to penetrate the outer sheet metal siding, they still couldn't get in or pull anything out. I don't know how much all the stuff is worth but I'm thinkin' well into the millions."

"Whew! It would seem after we pick through and take what we can use, there'll be plenty left over for a Sotheby's caliber auction and an estate sale." She paused, and then asked, "How come you haven't stolen it? You probably could have, and we would have been none the wiser."

Dwayne frowned and reared his head, shocked by the question. "Shoot, girl, I don't need or want my life complicated by that much money. Besides, even if you never found out, I would always know what I did and would not be able to live with myself. Not only that, I'd carry the baggage of guilt my entire life. So, nah. I'll leave that mischief for the crooks. There has always been and will always be plenty of them. I'll save my interest in such things to movies, television shows and novels. As long as I can afford the family-sized cans of Sphegetti-Os I'll be just fine. Thank ya very much."

"Here's an idea. Maybe we can use some of the proceeds to make a few improvements around the farm, or the house you're living in, if you wish."

"Well now, that's the horse of a different color we've always heard about. I sure like the way you think, Missy. By the way, you need to know that I'm an expert picture hanger?"

"I'm willing to let you show me just how good you are," she said in sultry tone, double entendre intended. She smiled, not attempting to conceal an amorous expression.

Dwayne's cheeks flushed. "Uh... " It was obvious he did not know how to respond, nervously twisting in his seat, finally getting out of the old pickup truck to get on with it. He stared back through the open window at Melissa for a moment, appearing as though he wanted to speak.

"Something on your mind, Mister Logan?"

"Yeah. But I'd better keep my fool mouth shut."

Melissa laughed.

He quickly added, "You and I need to go about the business of why we're here." He hesitated a moment longer, but then turned and walked toward one of the bays while searching his laden key ring. Still walking away, and without turning back, he announced loudly, "Don't you dare be readin' my mind. Ya hear me, girl?"

She laughed and laughed again, louder yet. "Oh, I don't need to be a mind reader to know what you're thinking. You're a guy."

"Yeah...well...let's get to work before all my thoughts that you're *not* reading right now reel totally outa control."

Chapter Twelve

The Family's Secret

Kyra's excitement swelled with each passing day after her older sister left her behind in Coos Bay and headed for Texas to begin setting up housekeeping. Now it was her turn. The thought of new adventures beckoned her to a new state far from the Pacific Northwest, although reluctant to leave her mother behind. After all, it was her mother's dream to move to Texas. She and Melissa had coat-tailed the desire spawned by her mother, adopting it as their own. And they, somewhat unfairly, were making it happen before their mother.

Kyra's wait ended, and so did her tiresome southeasterly trek to the Texas South Plains. She pulled onto the long driveway to the Dane mansion, stopping to take it all in. She drew a deep breath. *I'm finally here. Man-oh-man. That was a long drive.*

On either side of the driveway at its end near the main road were two tall brick columns with a massively arched header over it. It matched the color and style of the mansion. Set into the over-arch in cast concrete was the single word, *Dane*. The driveway was asphalt paved with neatly cut ditches on both sides. The driveway was so straight it would put an arrow to shame. Beyond the ditches on both sides were rows of towering Poplar trees parallel to the approach, plainly multiple decades old, judging by their size. Beyond that, open cropland but currently void of vegetation. She suddenly accelerated, now ready to get out of the car after such a long, tiring drive.

Melissa had kept her apprised of the goings-on and a blow-by-blow of the move-in process. Kyra was aware Dwayne Logan had been playing an instrumental role, working closely with her sister. She impishly wondered what other process dear Mister Logan was involved in with her sister. She did not need to be watching to realize over the past two weeks that, since Melissa's arrival, he had been spending much time and energy trying to please her. Melissa did not hide the fact she was more than happy to let him. *Surely, the man has a farm to take care of. Doesn't he?*

Kyra got out of her car and performed a few stretches, loosening the stiffness of sitting for most of two days. As she eyed the big house, a surge of optimism flowed through her. She marched through the open front door. "Missy," she shouted. "Where are you?"

"Up here," came the muffled reply.

Kyra started up the stairs, noticing it seemed Melissa and Dwayne had the house furnished and ready to live in, at least the part within view. At the top of the stairs, she stopped. "Where are you?"

"In here," Melissa replied.

Kyra turned left and walked along a narrow mezzanine walkway above a hallway. It created an elegant view of the staircase and spacious foyer beyond the ornately carved rail on the left. She opened a door into the easterly facing bedroom her sister had called dibs on. Kyra stopped inside and took a moment to examine it. It was set up and ready to be used. "Wow! Nice."

"It really is," Melissa said, and then sighed, dropping her hands onto her hips. "How was the drive down?"

"Long and tiring." She approached Dwayne, hand extended. "Hi Dwayne. I hear sis has been keeping you busy."

He took her hand. "Nice to see ya again, Kyra. Believe me, I haven't done a single thing more than I wanted to. It's been more fun than a small car full of rodeo clowns."

"That was certainly a color full explanation. And thanks for saying so," Melissa said.

"You're quite the gentleman, Dwayne. In a southern kind of way, of course." She turned her attention to her sister. "You'd better hang on to this one, Missy."

Judging by the smug expression, Kyra had achieved mission success. Melissa was duly embarrassed. To quickly put the moment behind her, she gestured to the window she and Dwayne had been looking through when Kyra opened the door. "Dwayne was telling me Uncle Jack did all his writing at this desk facing the window." She pecked the desktop with her fingernail. "He had a clunky old-fashioned word processor and printer setting right here, so he could look out and see the house Dwayne and his dad, Cletus, now live in. That's where his girlfriend, Nikki Endicott grew up. I'm sure Dwayne's house kept gentle memories of Nikki at the forefront of his thoughts. And why he bought the farm and built this house. He had a strong emotional attachment. I believe love had become deeply rooted in them both but stymied from blossoming by all their adventures that included Arthur Wainwright." She picked up a hardbound book lying next to her laptop on the desk and handed it to Kyra. "This is the first book he wrote, while still living in Springfield."

Kyra took it. It was titled *A Truly Brave Child*. "Oh yeah. Mom told us about this book long before she showed us the other one, the unpublished manuscript. It's an interesting bit of family trivia," Kyra replied.

"What manuscript is that?" Dwayne asked.

Melissa placed a hand on his arm. "That's another one of those things I intend explaining...someday. Patience, dear friend."

He sighed and scratched the side of his head. He shrugged his shoulders. "Okay," he drawled. "I'll keep on bein' patient," he replied while taking a step away. Then stopped and turned back, adding, "...but not forever."

She smiled and again faced her sister. "Not only that," Melissa continued, "nearly everything in this house, Uncle Jack did not buy. It was inherited from Arthur Wainwright. That eccentric old guy he loved so much. That's the reason he duplicated Wainwright's mansion in Springfield, Missouri on this farm. Uncle Jack knew everything would fit as it did there. It was another one of those strong emotional attachments."

"It's difficult to imagine love and friendship so strong."

Melissa glanced at Dwayne. "I can imagine it."

Kyra rolled her eyes. "Right." She shifted attention to Dwayne. "Don't you have a farm to tend?"

"Sure do. But it's the dormant season. Aside from feeding livestock, I have leeway with my time. I do need to get out and shred cotton and sorghum stalks. Or, if we get rain anytime soon, I'll just disc it all down and forego the shreddin'. Either way, them ol' stalks will still be there and dead when I get around to it."

Kyra snickered. "I don't have a clue what you're talking about, but I like your sense of responsible attitude about it."

"But then along comes the month of April," He continued. "The latter part of that month, things change. My personal time shrinks dramatically. This farm will own me until harvest time in October/November and maybe later than that."

"I'd like to learn more about farming," Melissa said. "It sounds fascinating."

"I don't know about 'fascinating.' The jury is still out on that, but it's a good life."

***

Every word out of Dwayne Logan's mouth made Melissa like him more. The man was earthy and unpretentious. He seemed to exude truth from every pore. She had only known him a few days but felt as though he could be trusted implicitly. She had never met a guy like him.

"Missy, do you mind if I borrow Dwayne for a while?" Kyra asked. "Since I'm new to Texas, I thought he might drive me around and show me a few of the sights."

"That's not up to me," Melissa said. She thumbed Dwayne's direction. "Ask him."

"What about it Dwayne?" Kyra asked.

"It just so happens Missy and I were wondering what we should do next and nothing was coming to mind, so, sure. I don't mind at all. Fair warnin' though, there's not much to see unless you have some odd attraction for barren fields."

"Are you telling me that nickel tour this time is not worth a full five cents."

He snickered. "That's about the size of it."

"Take her over to Rich Lake," Melissa said, and then turned to Kyra and held up the book, *A Truly Brave Child*. "This book centers on that place and this farm. Our distant relative and his tribe, a sect of the Comanche known as the Quahadi, stayed there most of the year, hunting buffalo and curing hides and meat with the briny crust covering the shallow water of the lakebed."

"Sounds like a plan," Dwayne said. "Come on, Kyra. Let's take a drive."

"Take your time. I think I'll put my feet up for a while," Melissa said.

After Dwayne and Kyra walked out, Melissa remained in the bedroom. She sat on a love seat across the room from that desk facing the window. It was quiet. Having been so busy, it was nice to sit, stare, and allow her mind to wander without pressure of things left undone.

She focused on the back of that empty chair in front of the desk. It was fascinating to think Jack Dane, her uncle, had sat in that very chair to do his writing, looking out the window in front of the desk for inspiration. But there was an unsettling shadow surrounding the thought. This was also the room where he suffered the heart attack that took his life sixteen years ago. She shuddered. A chill raised tiny hairs on the back of her neck. *How can that be? It's not at all cool.* She had been perspiring only moments ago while removing clothing from large cardboard wardrobes provided by the moving company, arranging garments in the closet.

Her first instinct was to look for a place a draft might come from. That's when she noticed her body emitted the familiar, whitish glow. *I'm invoking the radiant heart and not even trying.*

The glow grew and the heart beam billowed into an odd little cloud close to her body, as she rose to her feet. The luminance intensified, casting its light throughout the bedroom. It then rippled before her eyes and a picture revealed as the light parted at its center. The image followed her line of sight. Whatever direction she chose to look, it remained directly in front of her eyes. What she saw was identical to the view she had at this very moment—the chair, the desk, and the window beyond it, but with two major exceptions. What she witnessed was a gray day outside that window with large snowflakes flying by and, secondly, Jack Dane sat with his back to her, hammering away on the keyboard of an old-style personal computer. He paid strict attention to the words flowing from his fingertips onto the screen of a bulky monitor.

Melissa took one step forward. The flash of nausea came and went as she stepped into the past. The ambient odors and the feel of the air changed abruptly. Light in the room shifted to a dimmer but warmer shade of yellow, now dependent on the lamps inside the room and not the light of late afternoon streaming through the window, as it had been in her own time.

She stepped backward and took a seat, noticing it was no longer a love seat but a button-tufted oxblood leather wingback chair with a small round table next to it. Quietly, she lowered her body onto the chair. She took quiet moments to simply stare in awe at the back of her uncle's head. His hair was totally gray now, but no thinner than it had been as a younger man. She swallowed apprehension. In a voice barely above a whisper, "Jack?"

He stopped typing but did not turn around. "Sorry, I didn't hear you come in, Rita. Since you are here, would you mind terribly fixing a nice hot cup of coffee for a tired old man?"

Melissa smiled. I'd be happy to, but I'm not Rita Logan."

Jack swiveled around in his chair, plainly alarmed.

His general appearance shocked Melissa. His face sagged—his coloring not good—skin grayish with dark circles beneath sunken eyes.

"Good Lord! Who are you and where did you come from?" he asked.

"Please don't be shocked, Uncle Jack."

"Uncle?"

"Don't you recognize me? I'm Kyle's oldest daughter, Melissa."

His eyes darted around as he examined her face. "But you're a skinny little girl barely in your teens."

Her smile widened. "Yes, I was at one time, but that was over a decade ago."

Jack slowly rose as shock remained frozen on his face.

Age progression was not only on his face, but also in his mannerisms. He pushed himself up using both hands on the arm rests, coming to his feet slowly, and then pushing off the chair with shaky elbows. Even after standing, he wobbled.

His expression softened as he realized what was going on. "I knew it. I damn well knew it. You're a radiant heart. Aren't you?"

"Yes, Uncle Jack. I am."

His eyes moistened. "Get over here and give your old uncle a hug."

Embracing him, she held tight for several seconds. The man was withered—emaciated. She felt protrusion of bones in his upper back and ribs.

"It saddens me," he whispered in her ear, "but I must tell you I won't remember anything of this visit."

She backed away from his embrace. "I know. You've already told me."

"How many times have you come to see me?"

"Just one other. It was about fifteen years ago, in your time stream. But even when you told me then, I already knew it."

"How?"

She pointed over his shoulder to the computer monitor. "I read your book before I came to see you the first time. Thank you for making all this less scary for me."

"So, I do finish writing it, huh?"

"Sure. It's my guide-book into all this radiant heart stuff."

"I must say, it has been a terribly difficult project to complete. Too much sensitive emotion involved." His eyes fell away as he stared at the floor for a moment. After a time, he again smiled and re-established eye contact. "Did the book sell well? How many copies do you think it sold?" he asked.

Uh-oh. Should I tell him it was never published because he died before it could be? She stood awkwardly quiet, wondering what, if anything, she should tell him.

"Why are you hesitating to answer?" he asked.

I don't guess it matters. He won't remember it anyhow. "I'm sorry to say it was never published. You—you died right after you finished writing it."

Jack slowly lowered himself back onto his chair. "Well, under the circumstances, I suppose it's a good thing I won't remember your visit. Otherwise, I'd stop writing right now." He momentarily stared at his feet. "Would you do something for me?"

"If it's within my power, sure."

"Get it published, even if you have to self-publish."

"I can probably get that done. Why?"

"I owe it to the memory of three people no longer alive that meant everything to me. Your father, Kyle, my dear friend Arthur Wainwright, and most assuredly, my sweet Nikki, Nikki Endicott. God, I miss that girl so much. We never had the chance for a real relationship. She was too busy keeping up with me and my adventures. I would have eventually married her. I'm sure of it. But I'm not at all certain she knew it. I still feel stupid for never having told her how deeply I loved her." Tears spilled from his watery heavily veined eyes, trickling down his cheeks. He sat down awkwardly emphasizing his advanced age.

To Melissa, it was obvious. The emotion he was feeling streamed directly into her own heart. She felt his sorrow. It was quite literal and palpable within her, as her own tears welled. "I promise. I'll get it published." She whisk away a dribbling tear. "Would you do me the great honor of holding my hands as I shift back to my own time?"

He extended his hands. She approached him. He turned his hands palms up on the arms of his chair. "I love you, sweet little Missy."

She took his hands into hers and squeezed them tightly. "And I love you." She closed her eyes and drew a deep slow breath. When she opened them again, Jack was gone and she found herself holding only the two arms of the chair. Once again, the light of day, not lamps, provided illumination in the room. It was a terribly emotional visit, because Jack died later that very day she had just returned from. She felt it, therefore, she knew it to be true. Her mother told her his heart attack occurred just as he finished writing *The Last Radiant Heart* and was found crumpled on the floor the next morning by his housekeeper, and Dwayne's mother, Rita Logan. Melissa had seen he was working on the final chapter.

It didn't matter that Jack would not remember the visit because she would, knowing for the rest of her life she was granted the great privilege of seeing and visiting him in the final minutes of his life. She looked skyward and mumbled, "You are with them now. Love to you and your true soulmates forever." She kissed the tips of her fingers, tapped her heart and pointed toward the ceiling. Melissa drew a deep jagged breath and cried.

It dropped her into a funk. She sat on the love seat. Time spun by as many things ran through her mind.

Suddenly, Kyra's voice broke the silence. "You sure seem to be deep in thought."

Startled, Melissa straightened. "How long were you guys gone?"

"Not long. It doesn't take much time to look at a crusty ol' lake bottom," Dwayne replied.

"What time is it?" Melissa asked.

Kyra rolled her eyes. "You've got a watch. Read it for yourself."

Melissa raised her eyebrows and inclined her head, giving her sister a you-know-what-I-mean look. She then saw the light come on in Kyra's eyes.

Snapping her wristwatch up to a readable height, "It's a couple of minutes after four," Kyra said.

Without saying a word, Melissa showed Kyra her watch. It read four-thirty-seven.

"Seriously?" Kyra asked, knowing now what Melissa had been doing, just not when or where.

Chapter Thirteen

Morning Glory

Monday morning and dawn had already lit the eastern sky. The sun was inching above the eastern horizon beyond Melissa's bedroom window. Making up her bed, she glanced frequently out the window, enjoying old Sol's entrance to the new day and the new week. The sunrise spread tentacle rays of color through finely textured clouds lining the horizon in exquisite slow motion. It seemed, with each glance, a new color variation was revealed. She smoothed the burgundy and white spread over the bed and walked to the window. Crossing her arms beneath her breasts, she sighed contentedly wanting nothing more at the moment than to enjoy the sunrise. Life was good. She wanted it to stay that way.

Melissa had begun thinking of the Dane Mansion as home after four days living in it. Not working at furnishing, not arranging, and certainly not trifling over decorating details. Simply cloaking herself in the comforting warmth of a new life.

Friday had been a day of job hunting in Lubbock. Now blessed with callbacks for interviews from three clinics after dropping off résumés. She was confident it was only a matter of a day, maybe two, before she would be commuting to one of those clinics in Lubbock daily.

Her eyes drifted away from nature's reverential show in the east to a big green tractor pulling a broad disc plow, followed by a boiling cloud of dust and a bevy of darting and diving birds searching for breakfast turned up in the fertile loam. They frolicked, swooped, and snatched whatever insect or worm surfaced. The tractor moved from north to south at a monotonously slow pace along the entire half-mile depth of the farm. She saw Dwayne in the tractor's cab. After a moment, he noticed her standing in her bedroom window. He took off his John Deere cap and waved it heartily out the cab window, seeking her attention. He didn't realize he already had it. In fact, Dwayne Logan had her attention from the first moment she met him as a grimy-faced eight-year-old kid. He just didn't know it. *Rita, I know you're looking down from heaven right now. I want you to know you raised Dwayne just right. Thank you for that.*

She smiled at him and waved both hands over her head to let him know she indeed saw him. What he could not know, was how much she appreciated the view. The first time she met him as a youngster, she felt an inexplicable tug of affection. When he banged his head on the drain trap beneath the kitchen sink, and then crawled out, she not only got her first grown up view of him, but that tug of affection turned into something entirely different, a heart stuttering moment, complete with breath-robbing rush.

Dwayne had asked her out to dinner Friday, but she declined, fatigued after a day of job hunting. *I hope he didn't get the wrong impression. I sure hope he asks again.* Worrisome. She frowned. *I hope he didn't think I was pushing him away.* She watched Dwayne plow out to near the road and then turn the monstrous tractor around to head back, cutting a fresh swath of turned earth in the opposite direction. *Wait a doggone minute. This is the twenty-first century. I don't need to wait for him to ask me anything.*

Now with a mission, she shed her pajamas and put on a pair of sweat bottoms and a large floppy sweatshirt, hanging loosely off one shoulder. After lacing up her running shoes, she stepped to the mirror and made sure her hair was presentable. It was a vain gesture because she grabbed a knit stocking cap on her way out the bedroom door. The long sweeping bang of black hair revealed itself from beneath the cap partially covering her left eye making for quite a seductive look. Good enough.

She hurried downstairs and into the kitchen. She made a pot of coffee and filled two large insulated metal mugs to the brim, holding most of the pot's content. Before stepping into the morning chill, she snugged the stocking cap down over her ears. It was a chilly morning, but for mid-December, not bad—more bracing than annoying. Still, it put a spring in her step as she made her way along the ditch separating field from road to where Dwayne was turning the big tractor to make yet another round which, to Melissa, seemed like a monotonous task of back and forth all day.

He noticed and waved her over, killing the noisy diesel engine. "Get on up here," he called out. "It's too chilly to be standin' around out there."

"Aye, Cap'n." She realized the tractor was huge but didn't fully appreciate its size until coming to stand next to it. The tires were higher than her head with three steps attached to the frame for climbing into the cab. She held up the mugs of coffee to the extent of her reach to hand Dwayne both mugs. "I thought you might like some coffee."

"I surely would," he said, bending far over to take the mugs from her.

She climbed the ladder and stepped into the cozy cab, closing the door behind her.

Dwayne flipped up both armrests on the single pedestal seat. "It might be a little tight, but I think we can both sit here...long enough for a coffee break anyhow." He took his first sip. "Ah, it doesn't get any better than this. This is good."

"Thanks." She looked around the interior of the comfortably warm cab. "Nice tractor. Big, too."

"It's how I make my livin'. No choice. It has to be powerful and dependable. I don't need an appraiser to tell me this machine is worth more than my house, pickup truck, and all those outbuildings behind our house."

"Seriously?"

"Yep."

"Wow." Melissa sipped her own coffee quietly for a moment. "Dwayne, I had an ulterior motive for coming out here this morning."

"Oh? Nothin' serious, I hope."

She smiled. "That would depend entirely on your answer."

"Well, don't keep me in suspense. Lay it on me, girl."

"First, I want to apologize for declining your invitation to dinner Friday."

"Aw shoot, you don't need to be apologizin'."

"Sure I do, because I want to make it up to you later today. How about you and I go to that steakhouse in Brownfield you mentioned Friday. My treat."

"That sounds great, but I did promise Dad we'd go to town and eat this evenin'." He wrinkled his nose and added, whispering, "I think the old guy is gettin' a little tired of my version of cookin'."

"That's not a problem. Not for me. We can all go together. Why don't I invite Kyra along, too?"

A smile stretched Dwayne's face tight. "That sounds like a wonderful plan. All of us have been doin' nothin' but workin' since you came to Texas. We should all be ready for a little down-time. Did Kyra find a job?"

She laughed. "It took my baby sister about two hours to find a job in a dress shop there in Brownfield. It's all because of a glowing recommendation given to the shop owner by her former employer and good friend, Bonnie Crandall back in Coos Bay. She gets off at five-thirty. I'll call and tell her to meet us at the steakhouse."

Dwayne stopped sipping and started gulping the lukewarm coffee. "Well then, Missy, the plan is set. I'd better keep this ol' tractor rollin' if I want to be finished in time to spiffy up late this afternoon." He turned up the metal mug, downing the final swallow.

Melissa climbed down and dropped to the ground. "I'll be at your place about five-fifteen. We can take my little SUV," she said, taking the mugs handed down to her.

He fired up the big green tractor. It rumbled to life belching a streamer of black smoke. It roared when he throttled up and rolled away.

Melissa stood watching the tractor generate a cloud of dust as the large serrated disks cut into the sandy earth. She didn't notice the morning chill, as she looked on. Her thoughts kept her warm. *It's so easy to envision a life with that man, complete with children.* She headed back to the big house about a hundred yards away, glancing back often, smiling.

***

Kyra's new job at a small dress shop in Brownfield, aptly called *A Matter of Style*, was not only new to her but also for the owner, Lisa Rivera. Lisa was a beautiful forty-six year old Latina. Her husband, Oscar, a vice president at a local bank just a few blocks away, helped her establish the shop. Lisa had no business experience, which did not deter Kyra whatsoever. It intrigued her. A chance to help a business from the ground up seemed as though it would be an enjoyable challenge. She enthusiastically accepted employment as Lisa's first hire. Kyra saw relief in Lisa's face when she revealed that she had experience in retail clothing. Her new boss didn't have to endure growing pains alone. Lisa now had a partner to face the wolves together.

The first impression of Lisa was good. Kyra was confident from her experience with *Bonnie's Boutique*, she could and would provide valuable assistance to Lisa every step of the way. Kyra's developing bond with Lisa Rivera ticked up each time the pretty lady opened her mouth. Never did she use unflattering language about anyone, yet had several opportunities and justifications just in the short time Kyra had known her. Kyra's opinion of Lisa as a wonderful human being quickly became fact. Kyra's sense of obligation to the dress shop, *A Matter of Style*, encouraged her to keep a protective eye on Lisa because of her skittish nature. Lisa continually questioned her own ability to succeed, and the doors had not even opened to the public. Kyra realized, for the near future, she would have to be Lisa's calm in the storm, as the wheels of this enterprise began turning.

"I hope I'm not putting too much on you," Lisa said, as she wheeled in a rack of clothes to be sorted by size and displayed on circular racks near the front of the free-standing store.

"Heavens no," Kyra replied with a smile. "I'm happy you gave me the chance to help you get this business going, and then grow it. You took a chance on me. Now, I'll give all I can for the opportunity."

"Thanks for that. I'm nervous about it all. My husband didn't exactly give me a rousing vote of confidence, although he did put up the money to get it started." She bobbled her head shyly. "I think he just wanted to keep me busy. Even my younger brother said, 'Well, good luck with that.' And then he laughed. Can you believe that? He laughed…very sarcastically. It hurt my feelings and did *nothing* for my confidence."

"Don't listen to naysayers, Lisa. We'll work our business plan methodically and I'll bet this store will be profitable within six months."

"I love your optimism."

"You have a brother?"

"Actually, I have two, both younger, and one older sister. Delia, my big sister, died of breast cancer several years ago. She was far too young."

"I'm so sorry."

"I've come to terms with it. Richard, we call him Ricky, he's the youngest brother, and the one that laughed at me. Robert is the older brother, Robert Castillo. He's forty this year and he's my rock. You'd like him. He's good looking, too."

"Is he single?"

"Sure is. Divorced. Wife left him because she hated Texas."

"Sounds like the marriage would not have worked wherever they lived."

"You got that right. They couldn't agree on anything."

"I really would like to meet him."

"I'll make it happen. He manages a hardware store right here in town. We see one another several times a week." After transferring the dresses, Lisa wheeled the empty rack toward the back of the store. She suddenly stopped and looked through the front display window into the parking lot. "Speak of the devil, there's Robert now. He's pulling into the parking lot."

Kyra abandoned her dress sorting project and drifted toward the front window to get a better look at Lisa's brother, Robert Castillo. When he got out of his car, she saw that her new friend and employer had not exaggerated. *Damn. That man is gorgeous.* As he came toward the shop door, Kyra swallowed hard and exhaled a breathy whistle. Robert stood over six feet tall, smooth swarthy skin was graced with almost delicate features, and a thick crop of jet-black hair, neatly cut and combed. He was slender and strode with the bearing of a man who knew what he wanted from life. The bell over the door tinkled as he came inside.

"Hey, Robert," Lisa called out. "I have someone I want you to meet."

Kyra circled around a clothes rack to stand at Lisa's side near the center of the store.

"Kyra, this is my brother, Robert Castillo." She then turned to her brother. "And, Robert, this is my new friend and employee, Kyra Dane-Blakely." She smiled at Kyra, adding, "She has been a Godsend."

"Wow," Kyra replied, "I couldn't ask for a better introduction. Thanks, Lisa."

Robert extended a friendly hand and for the first time in her life, Kyra abruptly lost her power of speech. She lifted a shaky hand. All the while, her unblinking stare remained on his beautiful face. "I—uh..." she stammered.

Robert took her hand. He held it, sandwiching it between both his hands. "It's my pleasure, Kyra. I love the name. It's certainly worth remembering and repeating often. Kyra," he repeated, emphasizing both syllables.

She bobbled her head shyly. "Thanks." Loose lipped, Kyra looked sideways at Lisa, who was also a lovely creature. She found her voice and declared, "Damn! Your Momma and Daddy grew some beautiful children." The words were out of her mouth before she could stop them. "I'm sorry. That was crude. I should not have said it…at least not that way. I hope—"

"It's okay," Lisa said, chuckling. "You said it just right."

"You sure did," Robert chimed in. He shifted attention to his sister. "Hey, could I have a minute. I need to talk over a little family business with you."

"Sure," Lisa replied. "Let's go to the stock room." She looked to Kyra. "Please, excuse us for a minute."

"Not a problem," Kyra replied. As they walked away, her cell phone rang. She walked to the counter and retrieved it from next to the cash register. "Hello."

"Hey, Kyra."

"Hey, Missy. What's up?"

"Dwayne, his dad, and I are going to dinner together at that steakhouse down the street from where you're working this evening. Want to meet us over there after you get off work?"

Kyra glanced through the open door to the storage room and saw Robert and Lisa talking. They were smiling and laughing. Whatever family business they were discussing appeared not to be a serious matter.

"Well? What do you say? Are you joining us, or not?" Melissa asked.

"If I can make it happen, would you mind if I bring a guy with me?"

"You're kidding."

"No, I'm not."

"You found someone already?"

Kyra continued looking at Robert who apparently felt her gaze. He looked at her and smiled. She returned his smile. "I think I may have."

***

"I hope Kyra and her new friend show up soon. I'm getting hungry," Melissa said, glancing frequently toward the entrance to the steakhouse from their table.

"I could say that, too," Cletus said. "Then again, I'm always hungry," he said while chewing on a slice of buttered Texas toast. "Meaning it doesn't, and shouldn't, carry equal weight with your comment, Missy."

"That's true," Dwayne offered. "I suppose, though, I should take a teensy bit of blame for that. Dad never wants seconds from the stuff I put on the table."

Melissa laughed.

Who's Kyra's new friend?" Dwayne asked.

"Not sure. I think it's a relative of Lisa Rivera's, her employer."

Cletus blew a breathy whistle. "That Lisa is one beautiful woman. If her husband, Oscar, ever walks out on her, I'll be first in line at her door, wearing my best puppy dog eyes," Cletus said.

"Dad," Dwayne whined, "you said that like a dirty old man."

"Hey, I may be gettin' a little older, but I'm not dead, boy." The elder Logan turned back to Melissa. "Kyra only has two choices. It has to be either Ricky or Robert Castillo."

"You know them?"

Dwayne grinned, and then chuckled. "Hey, this is Brownfield, Texas. Everyone knows everyone else. Be careful who you gossip about. There's a high probability you'll be spreadin' rumors about a sister, brother, mother, father, cousin, or best friend of whomever it is you're talkin' to."

"Good to know."

"The Castillo family are fine folks, all of them. Kyra couldn't go wrong with either one of the Castillo brothers," Cletus added, and then sipped his iced tea. "Although, Ricky, the younger brother, is a bit on the wild side, sort of brash, lots of tattoos, long hair. You know the type."

"I sure do," Melissa replied.

Light suddenly flooded the interior of the restaurant as the door at the front opened.

"It looks as though I won't wonder about it much longer," Melissa said, nodding toward the steakhouse entrance."

Dwayne followed her nod. "That's Robert. He's the older brother."

As Kyra and her new friend headed to the table, it became obvious, what Dwayne said about familiarities among people around town was true. Robert walked straight for Dwayne and his dad.

"Hi, Dwayne," Robert said as he stopped at the table and shook Dwayne's hand.

"How's it goin' down at the hardware store, Robert?"

"Great." He looked over at Cletus. "Good to see you, too, Mister Logan." Robert reached across the table and shook his hand. He turned his attention to Melissa.

"This is my sister, Melissa," Kyra told him. "Missy, this is Robert Castillo."

"Nice to meet you," Melissa said, "and do call me Missy." She looked at everyone in turn and added, "Now, for heaven's sake, everyone sit and let's order. I'm starving." She noticed Robert looking at Kyra with an appraising look and then at her. "See something you like?" Melissa quipped.

"Sure do. But that's not why I'm staring," Robert replied. "If you had not been introduced as Kyra's sister, I would have never believed it. Kyra, with her strawberry blond hair, fair complexion, and pale blue eyes, while you, Melissa, come closer to my skin tone with eyes the color of toasted almonds."

"Wow. I sure like your description of my eyes, sort of poetic." She glanced at Kyra. "Hang on to this one, Sis."

"Stop stealing my lines," Kyra groused.

"We are sisters though. Same father, same mother. I just picked up the traits of the Comanche in us from my father's side and Kyra seems to have gotten more of our mother's genetic traits, the European side." Melissa grinned. "And, believe me, Robert, we are as different in personality as we are in appearance." She turned her nose up to a slightly indignant angle. "I, of course, have more common sense."

Robert snickered, but Dwayne and Cletus exploded in laughter.

"Oh hush," Kyra shot back, frowning. Once levity ran its course, it quietened, and Kyra added, "But, one thing I can add. As different as we are in many ways, we are sisters all the way and there will always be unbreakable love between us and we'll always have one another's back...always."

"Touché, Sis...touché."

Chapter Fourteen

Family and Faith

Five-forty Tuesday evening. Melissa sat in the library of Dane mansion, her bare feet propped on an ottoman. She sipped a glass of chardonnay, idly flipping through one of hundreds of books lining shelves on both sides of the room.

She took a break from reading, dropping the book in her lap, and replacing it in her hand with the wine glass. She scanned the library, giving the space due respect. She understood why Uncle Jack and Arthur Wainwright spent most of their time in the library of the Wainwright mansion in Springfield that this one was patterned after. There was something about the environment in this room. It called to her. Is it possible, as is supposed about the Great Pyramids of Egypt, this space has been imbued with a certain mystical energy by architectural design? Or, does the radiant heart leave a signature trail, of sorts? Perhaps, it is residual psychical energy left behind by Jack Dane, or, perhaps, the combined energies of her uncle and Arthur Wainwright. The kitchen may entice her when her body needed nourishment, but this room beckoned when troubled or simply in need of a quiet inspiring place to think. Other than her bedroom, this was her favorite room in the rambling two story house.

"So, how was your first full day at your new job?" Kyra asked as she came into the library taking off her earrings.

Melissa snuggled down into the squeaky leather of the over-stuffed wingback chair and smiled lazily at her sister. "It was good. I think I'll enjoy working at that clinic." She closed the book and set it on a small table next to her chair. She cradled the wine glass in both hands. "People in this area seem extremely cordial and friendly."

"I've noticed it, too," Kyra replied.

"At first, I thought it was because of Dwayne and Cletus and the people they introduced me to, but it's not...not entirely anyhow. It's *everyone* I meet. It's nice to be openly invited into people's lives and not just tolerated, out of some odd sense of obligation."

Kyra shielded her mouth, as if an out-of-towner might overhear. She whispered, "I hate to say this, but I think people are nicer around here than on the west coast."

"I wonder about that, too, but I don't know. It's a different style of living, for sure." Melissa set her wine glass back on the table next to her and slapped her thighs as a thought struck her. "Say, speaking of different living style. There's probably an hour of daylight left. Why don't we bundle up and take a brisk walk down to the big hump that looks like a terrace on steroids, get on the little road atop it, and walk for awhile? I'll tell you all about my day and you can tell me about yours."

Kyra scrunched her nose up. "What big hump?"

"You know. That big mound of dirt that's probably twenty feet wide and eight or nine feet high with a rutted road on top of it. You know what I'm talking about, right? It extends in a straight line to the back side of the farm."

"Oh, that thing. What is it? Does it have a purpose?"

"It looks like some kind of dam, but I can't see that it holds anything in or out. I honestly don't know. I'll have to ask Dwayne. He probably does."

Kyra agreed to the walk. The sisters went behind the house and kept walking until the backyard turned into a plowed field continuing on until they came to the long, straight mound of dirt. They climbed the side and walked along the top of it. They followed the rutted path Dwayne and his dad used as a direct route to the backside of the property in the pickup or on the tractor.

The sun had set, the sky darkening. The brightest stars were already making themselves a visible fixture in the eastern sky. "We'd better not walk far. It's already getting dark," Kyra said.

Melissa drew deep and then exhaled into the chill of dusk, watching her white breath. "You're probably right. But look around. It's magnificent out here." She turned a full circle. "You can see lights of towns all around. It's as though you can see forever." Again, she closed her eyes and pulled in all the early evening air her lungs could hold and exhaled. She walked a few more yards, but abruptly stopped.

Kyra backed up to where her sister suddenly came to a halt. "What's the matter?"

"Not sure. I had a sudden chill."

"Yeah, it is getting colder out here."

"No, no. It's not that kind of chill. I have a feeling that I'm about to—"

"Oh crap," Kyra muttered. She stepped behind Melissa and watched.

The white glow enveloped Melissa and then extended billowy white tentacles to include Kyra. The center of the misty glow at the end of the heart beam opened to reveal a vision. The scene was of a tractor, Dwayne's tractor, pulling that big disc plow along the steep side of this very mound they stood atop. But, as quickly as it all appeared, it disappeared along with the glow around her body.

"Why would you get a vision of Dwayne plowing? Furthermore, why did you see it now, in this particular spot?" Kyra asked.

"I have no idea. I've watched scenes like that many times. Not once, until now, has the radiant heart come over me because of where I happen to be standing, thinking nothing of the location specifically. Until now. I wonder why." She studied the area around where they stood and saw nothing different or unusual about the spot. Aside from a dead tumbleweed still rooted to the earth, the spot appeared identical to every other place along the hump. The spiny weed stood alone, apparently missed the last time the little road had been plowed.

"Wait a minute. I thought a radiant heart could only connect with someone in their bloodline," Kyra wondered.

"I think there's a bit of difference between simply seeing things about someone's future, a psychic connection I mean, and joining them physically in that setting," Melissa replied.

"But what about our leap from Coos Bay to that mansion? Dwayne was the only human around at the time."

"First of all, keep in mind that I'm still learning about all this stuff. I figured it had more to do with the house belonging to Uncle Jack, also a radiant heart."

"Oh. That makes sense, I suppose," Kyra said, and then paused. "Maybe your mind is fatigued and a bit too receptive from a busy first day of work at the clinic," she added. "Like a mind that races as random thoughts swirl just before falling asleep."

"Maybe. I sure can't think of a better explanation."

Let's get back to the house," Kyra said. "I want a glass of wine and put my own feet up for a while. I made so many laps inside the dress shop today that I'm surprised I didn't create a rutted trail."

"Sure." They turned and began the walk back, but it was unhurried. The scenario she witnessed was peaceful enough. But why, deep in her gut, did she sense something dark and tragic from such a serene picture of the man she was coming to admire, going about a mundane farm chore?

***

As had become part of her early morning ritual, Melissa stood at the easterly facing bedroom window, steaming coffee mug in hand, watching the sunrise. She was dressed and ready to go to work at the clinic. These final quiet minutes she reserved for herself to mentally prepare for the day without external pressures from other things or intrusive people. She had on salmon scrubs beneath a white smock. Outside, a strong breeze blew from the west and she noticed a stream of dust come into view from the field behind the house. She sauntered over to a northerly facing window, suspecting where the dust came from. She saw Dwayne in the cab of the big John Deere tractor dragging that disc plow along the inclined side of the same hump she and Kyra walked last evening. She sipped her coffee and smiled. *I wouldn't want him to be a jerk about it, but I wish Dwayne would be a wee bit more aggressive with me. He's so nice and polite, he's almost too laid-back.* She chuckled as she put the coffee mug to her lips.

Without warning, a massive shudder racked her body. She sloshed coffee onto her shoes.

She drew a fast panicked breath.

A veil of terror dropped over her, and then pummeled her, as if caught in a hydro-swirl of a huge wave crashing on a beach.

She dropped the coffee mug and steadied herself with a hand on each side of the window frame.

The sensation of abject horror intensified. She massaged her chest. Her heart hammered beneath her hand.

What the hell is going on?

This time there was no slow growing glow developing around her body. Brilliant white light flared. She saw the same scene she and Kyra witnessed last evening, an ethereal scene overlaid what she saw in real time out her window, both happening simultaneously.

But wait.

There was a difference. A minor one, but a difference. It had to do with the location of that big tumbleweed she had taken note of the evening before.

The vision produced by her mind and heart, showed Dwayne plowing the side of that hump parallel to the little road atop it, the tractor already at an ominous tilt. When he passed by that big weed, the outside rear tire suddenly dropped into a hole. The massively heavy tractor rolled, tearing the cab entirely off. Melissa saw Dwayne's mangled body appear pressed into the soil from beneath the monstrous tumbling machine.

Melissa realized she was witnessing a future event, but it could not be more than a minute into the future. Looking through the vision to Dwayne's tractor in real time, she saw the tumbleweed, and visually marked it. The big dead weed was only about fifty yards ahead of where he was right now, steadily rolling toward it. He was heading straight for his death, unaware.

"No! No! No!" she yelled in fast rising crescendo.

With the weed firmly in her sight, the vision did not disappear but did reset to the present, with only seconds to go before Dwayne's outside rear tractor tire would tumble into that hole. With the single thought of saving his life, she leaped into the vision. Within the span of a single heartbeat, she found herself standing next to the weed. She threw her hands into the air for him to stop, just as Dwayne rolled to within a few feet of her.

He stomped the clutch of the big machine and the drag of the disc plow stopped his forward momentum instantly. He slammed open the cab door and leaped to the ground. "Good God, Missy! Where the hell did you come from? You...you appeared from thin air."

She looked at Dwayne. He stood, mouth wide open, having become utterly speechless. She bounced a shoulder shrug and bobbled her head like an embarrassed child caught taking money from Momma's purse. "I know you're in shock and, maybe, a little scared of me right now."

"I'm a damn sight more than 'a *little* scared' of you right now." He closed the gap between them.

"Rightfully so, I suppose. Does it help if I told you I just saved your life?"

"What are you, some kind o' witch? Someone who practices black magic, or some such?"

She reared her head surprised by the supposition. "Surely, you don't believe in that stuff. I don't."

He put his hands together and yanked them apart, as a magician might during a sleight of hand. "Poof! You magically appear in front of my tractor, yet you don't believe in witchcraft? Somethin's not right with that logic."

"Well. Okay. I see your point. Let me say, I don't believe in *that* kind of witch-craft." She dropped her hands onto her hips and looked down for a second, and then reconnected with him. "Look, Dwayne, I've put off a full explanation of my, so-called, talents. It would seem I, now, have hit the wall on procrastinating. I'd rather have you leery of me, maybe even scared, before seeing you crushed to death, mangled beneath that behemoth machine you're driving."

"What are you talkin' about, girl? I've plowed this ol' hump hundreds of times with no problems."

She sighed, realizing out here in the early morning chill, nothing could be explained satisfactorily at the moment. And she didn't want to be late to work on her second day of employment. "Look, I'll make you a solemn promise, I'll explain everything this evening. Meet me at the mansion about six o'clock. I should be home from work by then. Deal?"

He pulled off the John Deere cap and scratched the side of his head. "All right," he drawled, "but my head's gonna be in a tizzy all day until you do."

Melissa again huffed a sigh. "I know. I'm concerned you'll be in *more* than a tizzy after I explain it all to you. I'm truly sorry I was forced to shock you, but I had no choice." She looked behind her, working a quick positioning calculation of where she stood compared to what she had seen in the vision. "Follow me." She walked to a specific spot and pointed to the ground, which looked like the ground everywhere else around them. "There is a hole right here, a big one. If you passed over it, the rear wheel of the tractor would have dropped into it. The tractor would have rolled and crushed you. It's not a guess. It would have happened. I saw it. And I'll not go into any more detail of the gruesomeness than I've already shared. It was too horrid to watch. I just want to forget what I saw. I pray it never does happen, or anything similar."

Dwayne walked to the spot she pointed to. He tamped his booted foot in selected locations, until he hit a point that felt springy beneath his boot in the sandy loam soil. He stomped it harder and his foot went right through it, snagging his boot. "Well, I'll be damned." He dropped to his knees and gazed down into the hole he created. "It's the rusted roof of an old car."

"Why would anyone want to bury a car?"

"I think I know what happened. No one *purposely* buried a car." He rose and dusted his hands. "Ya see, back in the thirties, during the Depression and the Dust Bowl years, this had been a barbed wire fence. Resulting from all those sandstorms, the fence trapped a bunch of them ol' tumbleweeds along its entire length. Then blowing sand drifted against the weeds. At some point, someone likely towed an old car out here that didn't run anymore and left it. In those days, the final years of the Great Depression, nobody had money to buy parts, and such. If they couldn't improvise a repair, then they did what they had to do. In this case, simply tow it out of the way and abandon it. As the drought continued, along with sandstorms, the mound of dirt grew higher and higher. Grasses and weeds began growing through it and held it in place while more sand would layer it higher still. When more frequent rains began again, this area turned into crop land, no longer fenced pasture land. I can only assume the original owners, the Endicotts, didn't see a need to work this big ol' mound down, as it made for clear demarcation between their property and the Smith's farm over yonder. But, in my spare time, I've been keepin' the weeds off it, so that, in time, it will eventually blow flat once again. Who knows what else we may find beneath all this sand besides, of course, one old car and a lot of rusty barbed wire."

"So, you almost fell through the roof of a car, not a hole, per se?"

"Yep. That's about the size of it." Dwayne looked at the hole and back to the tractor. "Ooh, boy. You say it would've killed me, huh?"

Melissa nodded. "Afraid so."

"It looks as though, if you hadn't come into my life, both Dad and I would be dead and you would have had no neighbors at all in that stucco house of ours." He snapped a stern finger up and pointed toward her. "But you still scared hell outa me."

"I'd be concerned if you weren't scared of me right now." She smiled. But her pleasant demeanor vanished as she checked her wristwatch. "Crap. I'm going to be late for work. Not good anytime, but unforgiveable on the second day at a new job."

Climb up into the cab and I'll take you back up to the house. Or do you just pop yourself over there?"

"I honestly don't think I can do that."

"This just keeps getting' weirder."

"I can handle you thinking what I can *do* is weird, but I never want to do anything that makes you believe I *am* weird."

Dwayne had already turned to walk back to the tractor. He glanced over his shoulder at her but said nothing, his expression bland and unreadable. His mind must have been in overdrive with wonder. It was disconcerting to think that his head at the moment was probably filled with more negative thoughts than positive.

As Melissa followed Dwayne back to the tractor, she realized, for the first time since appearing out here, how cold it was. Aside from the lightweight white smock, she had no coat on. "Brr!" A realization hit her quite suddenly. *I made a radiant heart leap to join Dwayne in his space and he's not of my blood. Geez! What else am I going to learn about this—this radiant heart stuff? Does it mean my talent runs deeper than Jack's did? I need to re-read that part of "The Last Radiant Heart" that talks about that Asian fellow, Maigo. He didn't need to be blood related to anyone either, I think.*

Chapter Fifteen

Preparing for the Future

Driven by a notion, Melissa raced home after work. She must find her copy of her uncle's manuscript, *The Last Radiant Heart*, and see it again with her own eyes. She would not be able to believe it until her eyes, again, flowed over Jack Dane's own words on the subject. She had to know before the upcoming discussion with Dwayne. Driving south, she braked hard and turned off the highway onto the gravel road, taking her the mile and a half to her new home. Driving fast, a dusty rooster-tail shot up behind her little SUV. Tires picked up gravel from the road, pelting the wheel wells, clattering like pennies in a washing machine.

All afternoon, she mulled ways to handle an explanation of the radiant heart that would bring Dwayne Logan fully onboard. Explain it in such a way as to expedite acceptance of what she had to tell him. He had become too important to lose now, moving ever closer to a time she would finally admit to herself how deep her feelings for the man were. She wanted nothing more than to have him at her side as a believer and partner. But the epiphany she had, following the near fatal accident earlier, shook her confidence. How could she explain it to him in a believable way, if she didn't fully understand it herself? Melissa's appreciation of Jack Dane's fear and reluctance of things he was capable of doing hit a new height.

She steered onto the paved Poplar-lined driveway ending at the two-story house. Coming to a hard stop, the SUV dipped on the front and, before it settled back, she had killed the engine and was out of the vehicle hurrying for the front door. It was unlocked. Kyra apparently home from her job at the dress shop in Brownfield.

Melissa didn't slow, hurrying down the hall next to the staircase and across from the kitchen toward the library, near the rear of the sprawling first floor.

"Is that you, Missy?" Kyra called out from the kitchen as Melissa breezed by.

"Yeah. Say, is our copy of Uncle Jack's manuscript in the library?"

"I put it in the far left drawer of that big central reading table, the drawer nearest the window," Kyra replied. "Why are you sounding rushed?"

"Oh, Sis, I think I've discovered something extraordinary about my radiant heart."

Seconds later, Kyra poked her head around the door into the library. "Say what?" She fully entered and approached Melissa. "What are you talking about?"

Melissa jerked open the drawer, and then poked a finger into the air. "Hold on. I have to re-read something Jack wrote." She pulled out the thick pile of typed pages bound with brass brads and thumbed through it. After a couple of minutes skimming over several pages, she sat back hard in her chair.

"That's all the quiet I can take," Kyra said. "What's the deal? What's so important?"

Melissa remained quiet a few more seconds, but then finally said, "I can do something even Uncle Jack could not. In fact, I can do what that Asian guy, Maigo *could* do. And, he, apparently, was some kind of radiant heart giant... so to speak."

"Maigo?"

"That man Wainwright introduced Jack to with extraordinary radiant heart abilities."

"Oh, yeah, him. So, what is it? What can you do?"

"I can join *anyone* I visualize in the future, the past, and, I suppose, other dimensions altogether, and they do not have to be in my bloodline to make it happen."

"What about Dad? You did it to him and he was not a direct blood relative."

"That was different. I dragged him into my vision. I didn't travel through time and space to join him in some other place and time he already inhabited. But this morning something happened that showed me something new."

"What?"

Melissa explained the near fatal accident she averted by moving mere seconds into the future to a point in front of Dwayne's tractor to stop him from falling through the top of an old car and rolling the tractor. She concluded by adding, "Dwayne is not a blood relative."

As Melissa ended the explanation, Kyra tipped her head, displaying an obvious expression of suspicion.

"What?" Melissa asked. "Why are you looking at me like that? Don't you understand how important this can be?"

"Surely, you haven't overlooked an obvious question you should ask Dwayne, have you?"

Melissa searched her sister's face for clues to what the heck she meant. "What question?"

"Your affection for the very handsome Mister Logan is blinding you to a possibility. Remember, Jack thought the same thing about Nikki Endicott, until he discovered she was a distant cousin."

Melissa's face sagged. "Oh...crap."

"That's right. You have no choice. You have to ask Dwayne if Cletus Logan is his biological father. If he says yes, I think I might still find a way to see if he has a familial match to Cletus, or, if you're unlucky, to Jack Dane. I'm assuming you don't know how Rita Logan came to be Jack's housekeeper, for how long, or, whether there was anything romantic between them before Dwayne was born. You know how these things are. It's all about timing. When exactly did the

Logan's marriage fall apart? Yep, Sis. There's a few things you need to find out, possibly while holding a calendar, before you can be certain of that, so-called, newly discovered ability of yours."

Melissa drew a deep breath, building courage to do what needed to be done. "This is exactly why I need confidants, level-headed people that can help me see things, things like that. Now, an unsavory question has been thrown into the mix. God help me, I pray Dwayne is my soul mate and not my cousin."

Kyra grinned. "I suppose a cousin could be a soul mate."

Throaty bongs of door chimes sounded.

"This is no time for that warped sense of humor," Melissa grumbled, as she sprang to her feet. "That's probably Dwayne. Look, Kyra, I promised to tell him everything about me this evening. Sit in with us. You can help me if I falter and maybe learn a few more things yourself. I hope it turns into a thoughtful discussion and not a reason for Dwayne to run screaming in terror across a plowed field."

"If he does, I might join him. You're kind of scary sometimes, Sis."

"Stop it! Not funny, not funny at all." Melissa headed for the library door, but suddenly halted. "I'll explain everything except, of course, what I did to our stepfather. I don't think I ever want him to know about that. Please, don't say anything about it to him...or anyone else...ever. Okay?"

"You really didn't need to ask," Kyra replied.

"I really don't want to get into a philosophical discussion of the exact definition of death or if what I did could be considered murder, since I could conceivably retrieve him someday."

The door chimes sounded again.

"I'd better hurry and get that. He's likely jumpy about all this radiant heart stuff and might walk away if I tarry," Melissa said. She continued down the hallway, crossing the foyer. She yanked on the massive front door. It opened with a whoosh of cold dry air in her face and as expected, there stood Dwayne Logan, handsome as ever. But the bland expression she last saw on his face early in the day, he still wore. "Dwayne, you're right on time. Please come in," she said, attempting a pleasant expression and demeanor. She stepped aside, gesturing inward. "Are you hungry? Would you like Kyra and me to fix us something to eat?"

"Thanks, but no."

"Oh. Okay. I just thought you had probably been working hard all day and...well, never mind. Why don't we join Kyra in the library? That's a good place to talk."

Dwayne followed. "My mind and my stomach have been churnin' all day. I haven't been hungry. I haven't even thought about food, not once. Missy, you have single-handedly turned everything I've ever believed upside down."

"I know and I'm sorry." She stopped and glanced back over her shoulder at him. "But I'm sure glad you're alive this afternoon," she added, offering a quick nervous smile, and then continued on to the library. "If I had it to decide all over again, I'd still do it. I'm just sorry I had to shock you in the process. I really want the chance to know you better. There would have been no chance if I had chosen to do nothing, simply for the sake of guarding a secret."

As she and Dwayne walked into the library, Kyra looked up from perusing her uncle's unpublished manuscript. "Hey, Dwayne."

"Howdy, girl," he replied, but then paused and chewed the inside of his cheek for a moment. "Would I be correct in assuming you already know about all this hocus pocus stuff?"

"Honestly, Dwayne, I know very little about it," Kyra said. "Although, since I've experienced it with her, I now believe it's not sleight of hand or mind control. It is real. Of course, it depends entirely on how you define the word *real*."

"Dwayne, are you sure you wouldn't like something to eat or drink? This might take a while," Melissa said.

"Drink? Got any bourbon?"

"No, but now that I know you like it, I'll make sure I have some the next time you come over. I do have a one-and-a-half liter bottle of Chardonnay that I'll be happy to pop the cork on."

"Sure. That'll work. As a matter of fact, you might as well just bring the whole bottle. I may need more than one glass, maybe a lot more."

"I can do that," Melissa replied. Her heart lightened, having noticed for the first time since he arrived the glimmer of a smile on his lips. "Please, sit down," she said, pointing to a chair on the opposite side of the reading table from Kyra. "I'll be back in a jiff with an uncorked bottle and glasses."

When Melissa returned, Kyra and Dwayne were chatting about the weather and their respective jobs. It was clear he was simply being courteous. She set the glasses down and poured Dwayne's near the brim, less for Kyra and herself.

As she sat next to him, Dwayne kicked off the discussion. "Are you human? I mean fully human and not some hybrid from another planet?" he asked in all seriousness.

Kyra guffawed.

Melissa snickered, too. "This is *not* how I envisioned this conversation beginning."

"Well...are you fully human or not?"

"Absolutely. And so is Kyra."

Dwayne took a not so dainty pull on his wine glass, downing a third of it in one swig. "Okay, are you the only one of your kind? And, is Kyra capable of doing what you can do? Also, what all *can* you do?"

Melissa held out an open hand at him. "Whoa, Cowboy. I think we need to change how we handle this discussion. If I keep allowing you to ask questions, every one of them will only create several new ones and we'll wind up all over the road and you'll still be confused. You just asked one I can't answer. I have no idea if I am the only one, currently living, that is. Kyra and I both don't know if she is capable of it, since it seems to manifest later in adulthood. Enjoy your wine and let me explain what I know about it, which is not much. I'm still learning, too."

Dwayne turned his chair to face her directly, and then settled back. He gulped his wine and said, "Go for it. The floor is yours."

Melissa mimicked the move so she might face him straight on, their knees nearly touching. "The ability I possess is called the radiant heart. It's born in the mind, and then executed by the power of my heart. The reason I know what it's called is thanks to the original owner of this house."

Dwayne sat straight. "You mean Jack Dane knew about it? This stuff called the radiant heart?"

"Oh, he did more than know about it. He was a radiant heart, too. But he was much more fearful of it than I am. He certainly never flaunted it.

"God almighty. I had no idea," he drawled.

Truthfully, though, the more I learn, the more I'm becoming skittish about using it willy-nilly. There are simply too many things I don't understand or how dangerous it could be, in some cases."

"Judging by what he said in his book, the one Kyra is reading over there, his friends had to force him on most occasions to use it and he always did so with great reluctance."

"I wonder if Mama knew what Jack could do?" he asked.

Melissa shrugged her shoulders. "I can't answer that question, but I probably could find out if you really wanted to know." The question reminded her she still had one big important thing to ask Dwayne. She became uncomfortable and fidgeted.

"How could you possibly find that out? They're both dead."

Melissa offered a comforting smile. "Dwayne, here's where it really begins to get strange, especially to someone, as yourself, who has never experienced it. I have visited Uncle Jack on two separate occasions in just the past month."

"How? Do you commune with his spirit?"

"No."

He scratched the side of his head. "You're confusin' hell outa me, Missy. How, on God's green earth, could you possibly visit with him, if you're not talkin' to his ghost?"

"Well, you see, it's like this…I can move physically to the past or to the future, and even shift dimensions within any of those chosen timeframes."

"Aw, now, you're just bullshittin' me," he replied with an edge.

"No, Dwayne. I'm not. I'm serious."

His suspicious eyes drifted toward Kyra.

Kyra pursed her lips and nodded, confirming her sister's comment.

"Seriously?" he asked, now wanting a verbal reply.

"Afraid so," Kyra affirmed.

"So, you're tellin' me you've leaped around in time and to different dimensions?"

What she had done to her stepfather, William Blakely, crossed her mind. "The dimension shifting thing only happened once and I'm not sure how I did it. Therefore, I won't talk about it." She paused to get off the subject and back on point. "Look, Dwayne, have you read that book about the Comanche in this area titled *A Truly Brave Child* that Jack wrote?"

"Sure. It's an interesting piece o' history and seems extremely well researched."

"What if I told you the entire part of the book about the young Quahadi Comanche named Brave Child was *not* the result of research, or even hypothesis, but, instead, first-hand knowledge?"

"You mean he went back to that time?"

"Uh-huh. He sure did. But that's not how it began. Brave Child, with the help of an old Comanche shaman, made a connection with Jack first and traveled *forward* in time to seek help. In the process of helping the boy, he learned things you read about by witnessing and, sometimes, experiencing them up close and personal. I can only assume Brave Child was the radiant heart power but was too young to use it. The shaman must have sensed, or known of, the boy's ability and used the boy's own undeveloped power to make the connection, because the boy was a distant relative of Jack's. They were of the same bloodline, which is important." Melissa glanced at her sister.

Dwayne finished the glass of wine and poured another. He waggled the bottle at her. "As you can see, I'm workin' hard at opening up my mind to what you're sayin', but I ain't there yet."

Melissa reached across the table and retrieved the manuscript, placing it in front of Dwayne. "Over the next couple of days, read this. As you do, keep in mind, it actually happened. This has been my guide book and the reason I've been able to retain my sanity. Otherwise, I would have had the same mindset as my uncle and assumed I was going insane. Still, I wish I had someone living that is knowledgeable about the radiant heart I could talk things over with as I explore the width, depth, and breadth of my abilities." She paused and sighed. "If not, at least I do have Mom and Kyra. They don't understand it at all either, but they are aware of it. So, I have them to confide in." She pulled her chair a few inches closer to him. She placed her hands on his knees. "I was hoping I might count on you in this small but very select group of intimates. May I?"

Dwayne's eyes drifted down to Melissa's hands upon his knees, clearly thinking about what he had learned so far.

"Look at it this way, Dwayne," Kyra blurted, "if you're nice, Missy might take you to some super-cool place and time in the past *or* in the future."

Dwayne's head snapped up. He looked at Kyra.

Melissa shook her head vigorously, glaring at her sister. *Damn it, Kyra, I didn't want to take the conversation there. I didn't want to get into it at all tonight.*

"What's she talkin' about, Missy?"

Melissa read the irritation in Dwayne's question. His patience wearing thin as apprehension, maybe all-out fear, rose exponentially. She picked up the half-emptied wine bottle and topped off his glass. "Okay, I'll not lie to you, but take another couple of drinks first." Lips tightly pursed, she glared at her sister through eyelids narrowed to slits. "Thanks to my dear sister, it looks as though easing into this over a period of time just isn't going to work like I planned."

Kyra cringed as her cheeks flushed. "Sorry, Sis."

Melissa slowly tore her angry eyes away from Kyra and, again, looked to Dwayne. She sighed and relaxed, realizing the inevitability of what needed to be said, a full-boat explanation of the technical aspects of the radiant heart, as much as she could.

Dwayne set the nearly emptied wine glass on the table. "With this rosy glow, I think I can deal with about anything you have to say, *now*. So, go ahead, speak."

Melissa began, "When I set my mind on a particular time, place, *and* person...and really concentrate on it to the exclusion of anything else on my mind, then the power of my heart takes over. A vibration begins in a frequency range high enough to create a white glowing aura around my body. Keep in mind there is a huge gap in the difference between the speed of light and the speed of time as I explain this, because the white glow develops only after vibrations of my heart exceed the speed of light and *equal* the speed of time itself. Uncle Jack's mentor and friend, Arthur Wainwright, told him that once the light reaches that level of brilliance, divine intervention is at play. Why some humans, like Jack and I can do it and no one else, well then that becomes a question only God can answer. I have no clue. Neither did Jack or Arthur. Still, that's only the beginning. The vibration continues to increase until the *barriers* of time and space melt away, becoming an open highway for me that I can travel back or forward in time. The vision I create in my mind becomes genuine and directly in front of me. It, too, is surrounded by the light, becoming integrated with my aura. It brightens, depending on my intent or emotions at the moment. I have the option of simply witnessing what transpires, or I can literally step into it and join that time and space physically. I can move into alternate dimensions as well. The way Arthur Wainwright explained it to Jack made it easier to visualize destination capability. It is like looking at an eroded cliff face where stratified layers are visible. If you pick a point on one of those layers anywhere up or down the face, we can call that line the present time and present dimension in which we live. The time stream, as it were. Now, as you move up each layer, the horizontal line crossing the vertical line I just described, would be points in time in the future, or every layer down from that point would be the past. And, of course, *every* horizontal stratum runs in both directions meaning that creates dimensional considerations; past, present, or future. "Make sense?"

"Oddly, it does," he replied. "It's a good way to visualize it."

"Dwayne, what Kyra said would be frivolous and possibly dangerous. I don't know. I need to learn more about it myself before I consider doing something offhanded. But, yes, if you are standing near me, my aura becomes your aura, along with the vision. At that point, you can go wherever, and whenever, I go."

Even as he slipped deeper into inebriation, the information Dwayne was fed kept him wide-eyed and on the edge of his chair. He occasionally jerked his head side to side abruptly, as if attempting to make sure he wasn't dreaming and what was discussed was actually happening.

"Are you understanding what I'm saying?" Melissa asked.

"Understand? Yes. Believe? I don't know. Confused? Absolutely."

"It's difficult for me to believe, too, but I *have* to believe it, because I'm the one doing it. You saw an example of it this morning, right?"

"Yeah?"

"What you saw me do, Dwayne, was to shift about a minute into the future, transporting my body to the spot you saw me appear. I didn't attempt to use the radiant heart to go back to my time and space, since the future jump this morning only amounted to about a minute, maybe less. It didn't seem necessary for such a brief jump forward in time and so close to the house. But it's worth pointing out that you and I are about that same length of time younger than we would have been had I not taken that one minute leap forward. Kyra, on the other hand is about a minute behind us." Melissa smiled slightly. "My sister has always been a little behind anyhow."

"Hey!" Kyra snapped. "That was uncalled for."

Dwayne dipped his chin and shook his head, plainly having a difficult time buying it. "That is awfully difficult to follow, Missy. As well as you're explaining it, it's still darn confusing."

"Yeah. I know. But, if you think you're confused now, I have something else to tell you that I don't at all understand myself."

"Oh?"

"Uncle Jack's ability to travel back and forth in time and space was directly linked to making a connection to someone in his bloodline. They had to be family before he could invoke the radiant heart to the point of traveling in time and space. I assumed I had the same limitation, but now that has been called into question."

"Hey, wait a doggone minute. You appeared before me this morning and I'm not in your bloodline."

Melissa exchanged a glance with Kyra. "Dwayne I have to ask a hard question you might find offensive, so I'll go ahead and apologize before I ask." She closed her eyes and drew a breath. "Here goes. Are you absolutely certain Cletus is your biological father?"

"Of course he is," Dwayne replied without hesitation.

"Did your mother know Jack Dane before you were born?"

"Are you insinuating that my mother and—" Dwayne abruptly cut himself off. His eyes drifted away and fixed on a spot above and behind her. "Holy...crap," he drawled. "It looks as though I need to have a come-to-Jesus meeting with Dad, because I can't be certain enough to answer your question truthfully."

Melissa placed a comforting hand on his forearm. "Dwayne, I like you. I like you a lot. But I sure don't want to find out you're a first cousin. I don't care how knotted your gut is right now, it's no more so than mine."

Dwayne snatched up the wine bottle and emptied it into his glass, muttering once again, "Holy...crap."

Chapter Sixteen

New Beginnings

What is that horrid smell? The first thought to cross Dwayne's awakening mind, eyelids fluttering apart. An unfamiliar sight blurred into view. Focus was slow to follow. *Where am I?* He drew a breath and exhaled noisily. He screwed up his face, realizing the repulsive smell came from his open mouth. He swirled a dry tongue around, noticing a wet spot on a sofa cushion below his loose lips. It was probably the entire saliva content of his open mouth overnight. *Sofa?* He lifted his head and looked around. *Why was I asleep on a sofa?* The large bay window at the front of the room finally wheeled into clear focus. He recognized it. He must have fallen asleep in a seldom used first floor living area of the Dane mansion.

With both hands, he pushed himself to a sitting position. A sliver of sunlight streaked at a severe angle left to right with laser-like clarity, as it beamed in through the southerly facing bay window. A pain in his head throbbed, feeling every beat of his heart in his temples. A crow swooped across his field of vision outside the big window. His eyes followed its flight path. He moaned. *Doesn't that damn bird realize it hurts my head to move my eyes so fast?* All the wine he consumed the night before wasn't leaving his body without a warning never to drink so much, or that fast, ever again. He moaned. "Oh...God," he muttered, holding his head.

Melissa came into the room holding two steaming cups. "Good morning, starshine."

"What time is it?"

"Almost nine." She held out one of the cups to him. "Coffee?"

"Thanks." He took the cup and put it to his lips. He sipped. "Ahh. Good. I don't think I'm in good enough shape to have made it for myself." He abruptly sat straighter. "Nearly nine, you say?"

"Eight-fifty-seven to be exact, according to my wristwatch, which I seem to be resetting frequently these days."

He placed the cup on a low table in front of the sofa. "Crap. Dad'll probably have the sheriff out lookin' for me. I'd better get home."

She sat beside him and placed a hand on his knee. "Relax. Kyra called him last night after you fell asleep." She grinned. "Sis told him you and I had been playing word games and you had a bit too much wine to drink and wouldn't be home until sometime this morning."

"You coulda shoved my drunken butt out the door. Even snockered, I could have found my way home. It's only a hundred yards up the road."

"With my luck, there would only be one car on the road all night and it would be the one to run you down in the dark," she said.

Dwayne snickered lazily. "Word games, huh? I suppose that's about as truthful a lie as I've ever heard." He picked up his cup and took another sip. "As long as he doesn't worry about me, I'd rather sit and drink coffee before I take off anyhow."

"Good." Melissa's pleasant expression mellowed. Her facial expression told the tale of a mind having drifted from the present. She stared pensively at a small oil painting on the wall.

"Okay, somethin' is on your mind, Missy. What is it?"

"I realize you probably don't want to talk anymore about the things we discussed last night but let me just leave you with a couple of thoughts to mull for a few days. First, have a talk with your dad about paternity. I mean...you don't *have* to. Cletus will always be your dad, no matter what. But I would consider it a personal favor." A faint smile came back. "I know you'd make a great cousin. Although, I would prefer it if you weren't."

"You don't need to remind me. I'll do it soon, maybe today. Depends on this headache and how fast I can rid myself of it. I kind of like you, too, Missy. And I sure don't mean as a cousin."

Melissa scooted nearer, surrounded his arm with hers, pressing her cheek into his upper arm. "Thanks for saying so. I needed to hear it."

"Shoot girl, I thought you already knew it."

"I suspected it, but this is the first time you've said it." She playfully slapped him on the arm. "Guys. I swear. What is about men? If they're thinking it, they seem to believe everyone around them should be able to hear their thoughts."

Dewayne reared his head. "You can. Can't you?"

"Oh yeah. Right. I forgot." She grinned mischievously. "Look, if it becomes necessary, I'm pretty sure I can get a DNA test done, if you can get me samples from both of you."

"Good to know," he replied. He gulped the final swallow of cooling coffee. "I guess I'd better get on with my day. I've got things need tending to around the farm." He stood and swayed slightly. "Oh man. I'd better take it slow for a while. The ol' head keeps reminding me I shouldn't have over-indulged on the wine. It'll take twice as long to do all those chores. I'm sure of it. If I stay bent over too long, I'm sure whatever is in my stomach will be on the ground shortly afterward."

"Oh, before you go, the other thing I wanted to mention was to read Uncle Jack's unpublished book as soon as you have time." She retrieved it from the low table in front of the sofa and handed to him. "Read it. As you do, remember everything in it is true. And, please, handle it with care. It's the only one I have. Never electronically filed. I promised Jack I'd try to get it published. So, I'll be driving to Austin soon."

"Do I need to go out to the barn and read it, to keep it away from Dad?"

"No, I don't think that's necessary. Although, I do believe it might *not* be a good idea we share the truthfulness of it. If word of this became too widely known, there would be some who'd want to commit me to a mental institution. The government might want to lock me up and study me to see if they could weaponize it. Or, worst of all, tabloid reporters lurking about day and night like jackals sniffing out fresh meat. Tell your dad it's a novel Jack Dane wrote. He knows Uncle Jack was a writer. And, it is written in the style of a novel after all. Although, he did use real names of all the players. I assume he died before fictionalizing the names. Still, that explanation will work. So, don't worry about Cletus seeing it, or reading it for that matter. Heck, he might enjoy it."

Book in hand, Dwayne pulled his green John Deere cap on and snugged it down. "Thanks for puttin' me up for the night, Missy."

"Anytime," she cooed then slowly pushed the long, black sweeping bang farther to the side. She took a gliding step slowly toward him. "Some day we'll have to do this when we're both sober and see just how much fun a sleepover can really be."

Dwayne said nothing, backstepping sheepishly toward the front door. He smiled and stepped out the door into the morning chill, squinting against the unfettered and brilliant sunshine. From around the sunny end of the house, his chocolate Labrador retriever came running at him. "Hey, Hotshot. You knew where I was last night. Didn't ya?" He jostled the pooch's ears. "Thanks for comin' to greet me. Let's get on back up to our place. You and I have things to do, pal." He patted the side of the pickup bed on his old truck.

That was prompt enough. Hotshot ran and leaped into the bed of the pickup.

Before getting into the driver's side of the truck, Dwayne looked back at Melissa standing in the open doorway, her head resting against the door jamb waiting for him to drive away. Even after all the weirdness discussed last night, he didn't back up a single step. Melissa Dane-Blakely had a definite place in his future. *Dang, I hope I don't find out she's my first cousin.*

***

Dwayne's day was filled with the usual—feeding livestock, plowing, repairing and maintaining tractor and equipment, plus other chores to facilitate all the farm work that lay ahead during the upcoming growing season. It had been just another day on the farm, with one notable exception weighing on him. It was that necessary conversation with his dad, probably over the supper table.

The sun had set. The light of day dimming quickly. After completing his final chore of the day, changing the oil in the big tractor, Dwayne stood at the open barn door wiping his hands with a dirty rag. He stared at the back of the house. He saw light switch on through the kitchen window. It wasn't late but days were short this time of year. *I guess I'll go find us something to eat before I dive into it with Dad.*

Coming through the back door, Dwayne let the screen door slam behind him. The cozy warmth of the house's interior pulled him in. "What's for supper, Dad?" he called out, as he gently pushed the door shut.

Without hesitation, Cletus said, "Hey, I had to feed the animals this morning while you were sleeping off too much wine in the presence of two lovely ladies. That sounds a heck of lot more fun than the evening I had here last night. Supper should be your chore. Of course, I suppose I can operate a can opener as well as you. Especially, if you're still suffering from the lingering effects of guzzlin' fermented juice of the grape. Or, as I prefer calling it, the wine bender."

"Wine bender?"

"Well, yeah. That's what it was."

"I guess you're right," He paused. "I'll tell ya what. I bought breaded steak fingers the other day. I'll fry 'em up, make a few mashed potatoes, and a bit of gravy. How does that sound?"

Cletus stepped into the kitchen as Dwayne opened the refrigerator. "Not the healthiest meal I'm sure, but it sounds good, a heap better than Spaghetti-Os. You're gonna make a *fine* wife someday." He laughed.

Dwayne grinned. "Right." He retrieved things he needed from the refrigerator and set them on the counter. "Dad? Missy, Kyra, and I were talking last night. I realized over the course of the conversation I knew very little about you and Mom before I came along."

Cletus pulled out a chair and sat at the table centered in the kitchen. "If you have questions, ask 'em. Lord knows, Rita and I were havin' trouble gettin' along in those months before you were conceived."

"Was the Dane mansion already built when I was born?"

"Not quite, but almost. It took about two years to build that behemoth."

"Did Mom go to work for Mister Dane before it was finished?"

"I don't think so, but I'm not sure. She did tell me one time she met him when she worked part-time at the courthouse in Brownfield, before she and I started havin' so much trouble stayin' out of arguments. Dane was in the process of surveying and legally splitting off a couple of acres to build the house on, in case he ever wanted to sell the house separately from the farm."

As Cletus spoke, Dwayne went about the business of cooking supper, wanting to keep the conversation light and non-judgmental. As he quizzed his dad in an easy conversational tone, he never turned to face him. "So, Mom worked at the courthouse a while, huh?"

"She never liked it. Always said it was confining, monotonous, and didn't pay enough."

Dwayne nodded understanding. "I suppose, at some point, during her employment at the courthouse she must've told Mister Dane about her dislike of the job and that could have been when talk started about her going to work for him. Does that sound about right?"

"I suppose it does."

"When was it you and Mom finally decided y'all would rather live apart?"

Cletus raked the stubble below his chin with the backs of his fingers. "Well, let me think. It was in the summer. Awfully hot that year, as I recall. I believe it was July, maybe early August."

"Mom went to work for Mister Dane sometime the following year, after I was born. Is that right?"

"I believe so, yes, late in the year."

"During the year prior, did Mom date any after you left home?"

"I'd heard from friends she was dating some, not much. It was only one guy for a while and no one after that. That's the story I got."

The timeline tightened to a frightening degree. It had begun to seem possible. Cletus might not be his biological father. If true, his dad might not be aware of it either.

Dwayne finished peeling and cutting potatoes, dropping them into boiling water and placed frozen steak fingers into a skillet of hot oil to sizzle. He wiped his hands on a cup towel and finally faced his dad. The kitchen began filling with mouth-watering smells. "Dad, would Jack Dane happen to have been the man that dated Mom after you left home?"

"You seem mighty interested in asking—" Cletus abruptly stopped talking.

Dwayne saw it in his dad's widening eyes. The elder Logan figured out why Dwayne was asking questions in such a way as to bring Jack Dane into the mix so much. "You're wondering if I'm your real father, aren't ya?"

Dwayne nodded slowly. "It would have never been an issue if Missy hadn't sashayed into my life. But, now that she has, I need to know."

Cletus's eyes drifted down to the red and white checkered oil cloth over the table. "I understand."

Dwayne saw the possibility of it bothered his dad, a lot. "Look, Dad, nothin' is gonna change between you and me...regardless how it turns out. Okay? You were always my dad and always will be. Regardless of the problems you and Mom had with one another, you were always there for me. That's all that matters. I love you..." He grinned. "...Old man."

Cletus smiled, but his eyes remained focused on the tablecloth. After a couple more seconds, he finally looked up and said, "I suppose it's possible Dane is your real father. Can't be certain, now that it's an issue needin' resolution. The timing sure seems to match up. Although, I don't know if it was Dane that Rita dated. I never gave it any thought, but her live-in arrangement with Dane may have been a cover for a deeper relationship to, you know, keep gossip mongers in the community from talkin'. And there are plenty of those."

"Maybe."

Cletus tilted his head questioningly. "But ya know what? If true, I don't understand why they didn't just get married?"

"I think I have an answer. Jack lost a girlfriend he dearly loved. I don't think he ever got over her and couldn't share his heart with another woman. He was a good man and probably didn't want a marriage founded on shifting loyalties. His heart and his love would always be split. I remember as a kid he talked about Nikki Endicott all the time, as if she were still alive. But I do know beyond doubt that he cared deeply for Mom. I saw that in everything he said to her and did for the both of us."

Cletus heaved a sigh. "Well, how do you think we ought to proceed?"

"Dad, I think I may be falling in love with Missy and I sure don't want to find out later she's a first cousin. Would you mind if I gave her samples from both of us for DNA testing?"

Cletus stood, walked over, and embraced Dwayne, patting him on the back. "Not at all, son."

The unselfish act touched Dwayne. His eyes moistened. He patted his dad on the back, too, and pushed him away. He turned, not wanting Cletus to see his leaking eyes. "I'd better make some gravy, if we want all this to be hot at the same time."

Chapter Seventeen

The Wedding

A Matter of Style, Lisa Rivera's dress shop, had only been open a week and receipts indicated the store was on course to break even. Lisa was ecstatic, but Kyra had assumed from day one that whatever eventually happen with receipts in later weeks and months, the first week would draw good sampling traffic and adequate sales with minimal promotion. Consumers gravitate to a grand opening, plus, local customers don't want to be rude and walk away without buying something, even it's just a scarf or pair of earrings. But, once everyone checks out the new place in town, then the shop had better continue to offer quality, value, and affordable prices. And, of course, don't anger anyone. Brownfield was too small for even one bad review that would poison a large percentage of potential customers. Although a consideration, Kyra was not overly concerned on the final point. Texas folks were nice. That made it easier. She realized snippy customers seemed to know which of her buttons to punch to receive a quick response in kind. At *Bonnie's Boutique* in Coos Bay, Kyra singlehandedly lost a few overly demanding customers because of her quick acerbic retorts.

Red pen in hand, Kyra worked down a line of gaudy Christmas sweaters slashing prices to barely above cost. The uglier ones, she arbitrarily marked at or below wholesale to clear them out. The sweaters didn't sell well before Christmas. No reason to believe cutting prices would improve prospects after the holiday. When Lisa asked Kyra what they should do with the colorful sweaters that did not sell. Kyra didn't have to think about it. "Donate them to the homeless."

She said it in a joking manner but was quite serious. She then requested to play a role before holiday sweaters were ordered next time. The storeroom was compact and could not handle even a box or two of the ugly outerwear till the next Christmas season. There would be plenty of other merchandise deserving of storage, to be pulled out for clearance sales later on.

"Kyra?"

Kyra glanced up from her price cutting chore, as Lisa approached. "Whatcha need?"

"Robert said he would buy our lunch, but he's too busy at the hardware store to pick it up right now. I'll watch the store, if you'll run downtown, get some cash from him, and go pick up burgers."

"Sure. Consider it done." Kyra grabbed her purse from beneath the cash register and out the door in a matter of seconds. It was nice to be out of the store for a while. Even nicer to have a reason to see Robert in the middle of a work day. She or Lisa could have paid for lunch and then be reimbursed by Robert. But where's the fun in that?

Her mind gravitated to something different. In the past few days, Kyra had been thinking about the conversation between Dwayne and Melissa a couple of weeks ago. It was great the DNA test proved Cletus Logan was, indeed, Dwayne's biological father. Kyra ached for Melissa as they waited together for an agonizing week, wondering. When the news came, Dwayne and Melissa celebrated by having their first formal date. When Dwayne came to pick her up, Kyra opened the door and giggled. His toothy smile boyishly bunched against freshly shaven and rosy cheeks. He wore a new corduroy sport coat, spiffy for sure—the Texas version of a fashion statement. It was the first time she had seen him in blue jeans that weren't faded. If he were sixteen with a few pimples, he would have looked like a teen picking up his date for the prom. Instead, he was the country version of Prince Charming, an ecstatically happy Prince Charming. "Hey, Dwayne. Where's the green John Deere cap that usually seems surgically attached to your skull?" Kyra giggled. "Come on in, cowboy. Your timing is great." He needed no more prompt.

Melissa's head had been rutted so deeply in the paternity issue, she thought of little else. After scrutinizing the test results, it opened a whole new line of thinking, and ponder she did. It also proved that her original assumption was correct. Her radiant heart was, indeed, capable of connecting to, and then physically joining someone in space and time not in her bloodline. There simply had to exist a strong emotional attachment. Jack Dane's talent fell short of that ability.

Kyra could read it in how her older sister spoke. Melissa was becoming almost as reluctant as their uncle had been about this awesome power. Fear sparked and bubbled ever higher in her older sister. In the beginning, Melissa had grandiose plans for experimenting and discovering her limitations. Not so much anymore. She now feared potential blind corners, wondering if she would ever fully understand it—where it came from and why the Danes were, by default, among the rarest families on earth. Or could it be the Danes had been selected for some unknown reason by God? Maybe Dwayne was right after all. *Could it be possible that, somewhere up the line in the Dane lineage, there had been extra-terrestrial cross breeding?* Kyra thought. It was a fascinating possibility and, frankly, made as much sense as anything else.

Although Melissa spoke little of what she had done to their stepfather by leaving him stranded in that forest, lost to the sands of dimensional time, assuming it was forever and irreversible. Kyra saw it bothered Melissa more than ever, once she learned it might be possible to invoke the radiant heart beyond blood relatives. Melissa now realized she could possibly retrieve him from that place—wherever, and whenever, it happened to be. Kyra warned her to leave it be, because it might create a new set of problems if she tried and succeeded—maybe even a chain reaction of negative consequences. Melissa hesitatingly agreed. Kyra understood it was a moral issue her sister grappled with.

As happy as it was after the DNA news came out, that was not why Kyra now considered that awkward conversation with Dwayne. It had to do with genetics as it related to the ability. Maybe there were markers important to the process that went beyond simply being blood related. She and Melissa were quite different in appearance and temperament. Maybe Melissa carried genetic markers that she did not. *Is it possible being blood related to Missy and Uncle Jack is not enough?*

She had not made up her mind whether she wanted the, so-called, talent. One minute she'd be intrigued, but the next, she would think negatively. Kyra did not care for the burden of responsibility that would come with it. Her happy-go-lucky attitude toward life would forever be changed. It was not an appealing thought.

This mental back-and-forth on the subject was almost non-stop since the night Dwayne drank a whole one-and-a-half liter bottle of Chardonnay in less than an hour. She smiled, remembering his antics. Dwayne was a good guy. Melissa deserved someone like him in her life. It was the first time she or Melissa had seen him inebriated. By nature, Kyra was carefree, having no desire to change. After watching Melissa agonize over their stepfather, William Blakely, her desire toppled rapidly in favor of never wanting the power, even if she did happen to inherit it. *Heck, Missy's the responsible one. I sure wouldn't want to take that title from her.* As she pulled into an angled parking space downtown in front of the hardware store, she smiled. *Missy can be the superhero in the family.*

Stepping inside the store, she scanned across rows of shelving loaded with products and spotted Robert straightening bottles of herbicide on an endcap. "Hey, Mister," she called out in the most ominous tone she could, and then pretended to spit on the floor. "I'm here for the contents of your wallet, partner. Hand it over. Or it's gonna get nasty," her voice lowering to an ominous tone.

"What the hell...?" came a gravelly voice from down an aisle out of sight. A deeply tanned, cigar chomping, rotund man, bald with an unkempt curly fringe in overalls, stepped into the cross-aisle next to Robert. Kyra didn't recognize him. He eyed her up and down. He then looked at Robert. "Want me to get an ax? I believe we can take care of this little problem without much trouble." That cigar went in a circle, as the man chewed the slimy end of it. He watched Kyra appraisingly.

"It's okay, Froggy. I know her," Robert replied.

"Oops. Sorry," Kyra said. "I didn't know anyone else was here."

"All right," the man said. "In that case, I'll just go 'bout my business." One of his overall straps hung loose down the front of the grimy denim that was stretched tight over a bulging belly. Both cuffs lay haphazardly over the tops of his short work boots. It was clearly a workday. His appearance didn't seem to matter at all to him.

Kyra hurried over to Robert. "Did I hear you right? His name is Froggy?" she whispered.

"It's what everyone calls him. That's Froggy Burton. He farms about five miles west of town." Robert retrieved his wallet from his hip pocket, pulled out a twenty, and handed it to her. "I don't know what his real name is, but I sure hope his parents didn't give him a name like that. It would be a cruel thing to do to a helpless newborn." He chuckled.

"It looked like he was serious about getting an ax."

"He was. Just because farmers live several miles apart, as a rule, it doesn't mean we're not a close-knit bunch. You attack one, you attack us all. We will always rally around one another."

"You talk as though you farm, too. Do you own a farm?"

"Nah. But I certainly identify with them. I couldn't survive without farmers."

She looked beyond Robert to where Froggy was putting bolts, washers, and nuts in individual little bags. He paid her no mind. She grabbed Robert by the green work vest he wore and pulled him to her. She kissed him and took a moment to stare into his eyes. "Well?" she asked.

"Well, what?"

"Sorry. I thought I was obvious. I'm giving you an opportunity to ask me out."

Robert smiled. "Well, aren't you the little pistol? Did you learn that in Oregon?"

"Be nice and I may show you lots of things I learned in Oregon."

"I sure like the sound of that." He paused and thought for a second. "Okay. How about a movie later and a fried shrimp basket afterwards?"

"Perfect. We can take in the first feature after work. That way you don't have to drive all the way out to my house and pick me up." She kissed him again and turned to leave. "You *are* going to meet Lisa and me over at the dress shop for lunch, right?"

He nodded. "In about thirty minutes. I have to wait for my part-timer to cover while I'm out. She hasn't come in yet."

As Kyra walked away, she waggled a warning finger back at him. "Keep in mind, I will be requiring a large bucket of popcorn at the theater later."

A laugh was his only reply.

Kyra went about the business of picking up lunch. *If I was capable of doing what Missy can do, I wonder how Robert would handle such a revelation. He acts more mature than Dwayne. But who knows? He might turn into a quivering lump of jelly. Dwayne may be more of an emotional rock than I'm giving him credit for.* She drew a breath and huffed a sigh. *Oh well. It probably will never be an issue, if I'm right about that genetic marker thing. More specifically, my lack of it.*

Chapter Eighteen

Resonance of the Past

Melissa lay on her side facing Dwayne. They shared a pillow. She watched his eyes move around her face. "I hope you're seeing something you like," she said.

He smiled. "You're the prettiest cousin a guy could ask for."

She jerked her head off the pillow. "Hey, don't joke about that. The DNA test could've easily gone that way."

His smile didn't waver. "Yeah, So what? We could've been kissin' cousins." He yawned and stretched.

"Oh hush." She flipped the covers off and sat up on the side of the bed. Snatching jeans from the floor next to the bed, she pulled them on. She had just had her hair trimmed, returning it to a super short style on top but with that sweeping bang decorating her forehead to just above her right eyebrow. All she had to do was shake her head and she was good to go. She loved the style. "I'm sure glad it's Saturday. I have no desire to be at the clinic. Anything you want to do today? We can spend the day together."

"I'd rather lie in bed all day with you. But like I told ya when we first met, my time is not my own come the latter part of April. And since we had good rains recently, I think I'll try to plant cotton a little earlier this year. The ground is warm enough and certainly moist enough. It should germinate well."

"That's okay. I *have* been monopolizing your time since the DNA test came back in our favor in January." She grinned and winked at him. "I won't be apologizing for it though."

"Missy, you're welcome to monopolize me anytime. In fact, you can monopolize me over and over, all night long."

She laughed. "I like the euphemism. Perfectly suited for use around the more genteel." She stood, buttoned her jeans, and picked up a ratty t-shirt with a few holes in it and slipped it over her head. "I talked to Mom yesterday. She'll get on a plane and head for Texas the same day my little brother, Johnny, graduates from high school. That day is coming soon. I hate to say it, but when Mom moves in, you can't sleep over anymore."

His fingers suddenly stopped as he was buttoning his blue chambray work shirt. "Say what?"

"Sorry. I know I shouldn't feel guilty. I'm not a teenager anymore, but she is my mother. I wouldn't feel right about it."

"Is your little brother coming with her?"

"Nah. Johnny and his older brother, Charlie, will move into Mom's house and share expenses. Charlie works at a local logging and lumber operation and, after graduation, Johnny will work there part-time and go to school. He enrolled in Southwestern Oregon Community College right there in Coos Bay. He'll be going for a degree in business administration with a minor in marketing. I think he would like to own a business someday."

Dwayne sat up and pulled his boots on. "So, it'll just be you, Kyra, and your mom in this big ol' house?"

"Yep. That will be the full complement of residents."

After thinking on it for a minute, I understand your hesitance with sleepovers when your mom moves in. I'd be equally uncomfortable with you sharing my bed while Dad is in the house."

Melissa walked around the bed, wrapped her arms around him and gave Dwayne a long deep kiss. "We'll work something out. I promise."

Dwayne pulled on his green John Deere cap and headed out the door on his way to get spring planting underway.

Melissa followed him down the stairs fantasizing about marriage. She didn't want to talk about it with Dwayne yet, but it floated in and out of her thoughts since realizing the day that her mother would be moving in rapidly approached. Still, she didn't want to pressure Dwayne into making a hasty proposal. She wasn't a hundred per cent certain, yet, that she wanted him to propose. It was early in the relationship. She wanted to know him better. Although, it didn't prevent her desire for marriage. If he did propose, she wanted him fully committed to a lifetime of togetherness and not the result of a single aspect, sexual desire.

An unplanned routine developed. Kyra spent a couple of nights a week with Robert Castillo in his house in Brownfield. On those nights, Dwayne came over and would not go home until the next morning. It became a comfortable situation for everyone involved, without the need for surreptitious plotting.

Kyra seemed infatuated with Robert, although the word *love* had not been used when talking about him. There was one little kink in Kyra's relationship that worried Melissa, and it had nothing to do with Robert. It was a persistent problem with his younger brother, Ricky Castillo. He had been lewdly propositioning Kyra and had been overly aggressive on a couple of occasions. Kyra had not told Robert or Lisa about it. Melissa advised her repeatedly to share it with both Ricky's siblings, to get their support in stopping it before it reeled out of control. Kyra surely had sense enough to find a way to put the kibosh on it before Ricky could do something foolish. Still, Kyra was hesitant to say anything about Ricky to his siblings. She liked Robert and Lisa and didn't want to be the wrench thrown into their family gears.

Melissa stood in the open doorway, admiring the few tufted patches of bluebonnets that had begun to appear. That view beautifully framed a scene she was becoming enamored with, Dwayne standing with the door of his old pickup truck open and whistling for his pal, Hotshot. The dog came bounding around the mansion, leaping through the open window on the passenger side of the cab. Dwayne laughed and she heard him tell the dog, "All right, Hotshot, I guess you can ride up here with me."

She waved at him and shouted, "See you later today."

He poked his arm out the window and returned the wave as he and Hotshot ambled down the long driveway to the road fronting the property past those gorgeous bluebonnets in the ditches and edges of the plowed field beyond.

*****

Dwayne glanced over at the dog. "I suppose since Missy moved in, I've sort of been ignoring you. Haven't I?"

Hotshot sucked his wet tongue back into his mouth and slammed his mouth shut. He may not have understood the question, but it was clear he was aware it was a question. Sitting on his haunches facing Dwayne, he responded by dancing his front paws on the seat.

"Tell ya what, old friend, I'll make a point to start spending more time with you. It's the nature of what we do. I'll be spending much less time during the day with Missy and more with you and Dad over the next couple of months. But you gotta know, old son, I'm not promisin' you anything when the sun goes down." Dwayne jostled Hotshot's head between his ears and laughed.

"That Missy is really somethin', Hotshot. She's beautiful, sexy, damn smart, and, yes, a little scary, too." He glanced at the dog. "I still don't know what to think about that radiant heart stuff. Although, I do understand why she would not want it widely known. Man oh man, can you imagine all the people who would be banging on her door if word got out what she could do?" He fixed a stare straight ahead giving that some thought. "Oh well. That's Missy's business and none o' mine. No matter how close she and I become, I don't want it to *ever* be any of my business. Yep, I'll keep her secret. It's too spooky for this ol' country boy to think on much anyhow."

He pulled his old pickup to a spot near the monstrous John Deere tractor he had already hitched the wide planter to and parked the truck. Stacked on the ground beside the rig were two wooden pallets of fifty-pound sacks of cotton seed. Dwayne pulled his cap off and ran his fingers through his hair. He snugged the hat back down on his head. "Well, are we ready to get another crop year underway?"

Hotshot gave his pal the affirmation sought. A quick dance of the front paws and then woofed and jumped out the passenger side window to join his best friend, Dwayne, on the ground.

***

It had been such a wonderful night with Dwayne, Melissa hadn't considered how she would fill her Saturday until he walked out the door. She felt flat and somewhat lost. *Now what?* Aimlessly, she wandered through the mansion, coffee cup in hand. As she moved about, another sensation set in. It was an unwelcome, but familiar sense something was about to happen, an uneasy tingle in the pit of her stomach.

She looked down, expecting to see a milky aura emanating from her body. There was nothing. Still, she intuited things to come, not good things.

Melissa continued strolling through the house, attempting to formulate a plan for her day off. She sauntered toward the large patio at the rear of the house. It was a nice morning. Somewhat cool perhaps, but pleasant enough to sit outside and drink coffee. As she opened one side of the French doors and stepped into the morning air, an odd instinctual awareness within her hit hard, stopping her suddenly, as if she had walked into a frost-encrusted chilled wall. It robbed her of breath.

This time, she didn't need to look for the white aura, it had abruptly exploded around her and lit her up like a giant white street light. She briefly wondered why her uncle, Jack Dane, needed a strong emotional event to trigger the radiant heart and she did not. Why?

The vision revealed was that of the interior of *A Matter of Style*, Lisa Rivera's dress shop where Kyra worked. *Why am I seeing this?*

Staying calm, she examined everything within view in the vision suspended in front of her eyes. She saw Lisa standing behind the cash register. A daily calendar next to the register showed today's date. As Melissa watched, Lisa turned and checked the clock on the wall. It was ten after twelve. *Okay, I'm seeing the inside of the store a little after noon today. Why? What does it mean?*

Lisa said something and Kyra appeared from the stockroom in the back of the store. Kyra smiled and waved at Lisa. Lisa walked out of the store, leaving Kyra alone inside. There were no customers.

Melissa's point of view on the ethereal appearing scene floating before her eyes changed to the inside of the stockroom as her sister re-entered it and resumed marking boxes on a shelf with a black marker.

Suddenly, Lisa and Robert's younger brother, Ricky Castillo, came in. He said something to Kyra. Melissa could hear none of it. She would have had to step into, and join, what she witnessed to hear it, but actions spoke volumes.

Kyra angrily confronted him. She shoved him back with one hand while vigorously pointing at the door with the other.

He shoved her back hard.

She stumbled over a box and fell onto her butt.

Ricky locked the only door into the stockroom and hurried back toward Kyra, still on the floor, scooting backwards, rising fear slathered across her face. It wasn't difficult to lip-read that Kyra was shouting, "Stop!" and "Get away from me!"

Ricky straddled her and ripped open her blouse.

"Oh, hell no!" Melissa shouted. She began to step into the vision and go to Kyra's aid when better judgment told her she could not physically stand up to Ricky Castillo. He was too big and clearly too strong. The guy was a little shorter than Dwayne but more muscular. Remembering what she witnessed would not happen for about four more hours, she realized she needed a plan, not a knee-jerk reaction. If used wisely, she had time.

Before closing her eyes in disgust to break the vision, Melissa saw Ricky slap, then backhand, Kyra across the face, solidly enough to snap Kyra's head sideways. Kyra's nose and lip bled. He pulled her dress above her waist.

Closing her eyes tightly against the gruesomeness of what would happen next, Melissa chanted in a whining whisper, "No more, no more, no more. I don't want to see anymore!"

The chill and brilliance of the aura went away as quickly as it had initially washed over her. She breathed hard, drawing deep for one solid recuperating breath of air, as if she were the one who had been attacked. On weak knees, she backed up to the outside wall of the house and leaned against the brick, not trusting her legs to support her weight. Her mind raced. *What am I going to do? What? What?*

She looked to her right into the rising sun and saw Dwayne's tractor silhouetted at the center of its brilliance, dust boiling up from beneath plow points cutting into the sandy loam. The sight showed her the way to a plan. *Dwayne Logan, I need you. I need your strength.*

Melissa raced back through the house and out the front door to her small SUV. She had to talk to Dwayne.

She hurried down the road and stopped at the end of the rows where Dwayne would be ending the current round he worked. It was the spot where he would turn the tractor around and do it all over again and again until the entire field had been planted. She had driven so fast she was already out of her vehicle when the trailing dust cloud arrived to engulf her. She ignored it and jogged out into the field toward the tractor slowly coming toward her, too eager to wait for him to finish the run.

Dwayne stopped. She arrived out of breath. He shoved open the cab door and shouted over the engine noise, "Missy, what on earth is goin' on, girl?"

"I need your help and I need it right now," she shouted.

Dwayne shut off the engine and climbed down out of the cab. He approached her. "Help with what?"

"Ricky Castillo is going to rape Kyra, violently rape her. He's going to hurt her, Dwayne. We have to stop it before it happens."

"Come on." He grabbed Melissa's hand and pulled her in tow. "Let's get in your car and head to town."

Melissa dug her heels into the soft soil and pulled him to a standstill. "Wait. We don't have to do that. It would do no good to confront Kyra or Ricky right now. It won't happen for a few hours. You and I need to flash forward and stop it as it's developing, but before he can do anything. It's imperative we catch him in the attempt. I don't have the strength to control Ricky. He's a big guy. That's why I need you."

"Flash forward? How does that work?"

Melissa threaded her arm around his. "I'm going to take you with me. You'll feel a pang of nausea, but it will go away quickly. When we get there, be very quiet. I will attempt putting us in a concealed place so Ricky doesn't see us appear from thin air. You ready?"

"Oh, Lord..." he stammered.

"I have to concentrate for a moment." Melissa closed her eyes and drew a mind's-eye image of the clock on the wall of the dress shop. She mentally mapped the interior of the stock room in the rear of the store from memory and picked out a spot near tall industrial-type shelving loaded with boxes. The location should provide adequate concealment for them both. Visualizing it clearly, she then thought, *Right there. That's where we need to be and the time we need to arrive and we need to be there...now.*

That was all it took for the glow to bloom and surround them both. "Remember, don't talk once we get there," she whispered. Without saying another word, she shoved Dwayne backward into the vision she watched.

She heard a low guttural sound from him. *It's just a little nausea. Hang in there.*

All Melissa had time to do was blink and, when she opened her eyes, they were in position behind the shelves she saw in the vision. She looked to Dwayne. He was expelling a breath through rounded lips. She put a finger to her lips, wanting him to remain quiet.

He nodded affirmation.

Melissa peeked around the shelved boxes and saw her sister checking off a list on a clipboard at the opposite end of the room, about twenty feet away. She heard a noise. The stockroom door was opening. She backstepped into the shadows of this poorly lit end of the storeroom.

Kyra turned in response to the opening door and saw Ricky Castillo coming in. Ricky was as tall as his brother, Robert, but had broader shoulders and clearly more muscular than his older sibling. Unlike his clean-cut brother, he had a scruffy beard and long hair down over his ears. He also sported various tattoos on both arms that disappeared up under his short-sleeved shirt, indicating the ink continued out of sight up his arms. "If you're looking for Lisa, she went to meet her husband for lunch," Kyra said casually and returned her attention to the clipboard in her hands.

Ricky did not respond.

Kyra looked at him again, quizzically this time.

"I'm not looking for my sister. I see her too much already. But I don't get to see you often enough. I thought it was time to change that." He closed the stockroom door and locked it behind him.

Kyra dropped the clipboard to her side and fully faced him. "What are you doing, Ricky?" Fear in her voice pushed it to a higher octave. Her eyes fixed on him, unblinking. She tossed the clipboard atop one of the boxes, freeing both hands.

Melissa felt Dwayne's body brush hers as he began to step around into full view. She stopped him with an open palm against his chest, mouthing, "Not yet."

Ricky advanced on Kyra.

"Don't do anything foolish, Ricky." She took backward steps, trying to maintain a neutral buffer between them. "If you do, I won't have any choice but tell Lisa and Robert. I haven't said anything to either one of them about your behavior. That's not to say I won't, if you continue this stalking game you're hell-bent on playing." Tall shelves behind her stopped her retreat. She held out a stiffened arm, preventing him from coming any closer. "Please, don't make me change my mind."

He leaned into her extended palm, saying nothing.

She shoved him and pointed to the door. "Get out of here!"

Although Kyra clearly pushed as hard as she could, Ricky did not take a single backward step. The opposite happened. He took another step towards Kyra. "Oh, I think if you were going to tell them about my plans for you and me, it would have already happened." He grabbed her arm.

"Let go of me and get the hell out of here!" Kyra demanded. She wrenched her arm free of his grasp, yanking it away.

Ricky's face went from odd smile to a lip curling in anger. He shoved her.

She stumbled over boxes and fell sideways.

He raised his hand to hit her.

"Now!" Melissa shouted at Dwayne in a voice for all to hear. She removed her hand from Dwayne's chest and pushed him into plain view.

"You better be dropping that hand back to your side, Ricky," Dwayne said, in calm but authoritative tone.

Ricky jerked his head around, shocked by Dwayne Logan's sudden presence. He glanced toward the door. It was locked. "Logan? Where did you come from?"

"Don't you be worryin' about such details. You need to be worryin' about the part of your anatomy you're thinkin' with right now and stop what you're doin', because it looks to me like you're about to do somethin' stupid. I'm talkin' prison-time-stupid."

Ricky spun to fully face Dwayne. "Go on. Get out of here. This is none of your business," he demanded in a thinly controlled shout.

Melissa stepped into plain view. "I say it is his business, and I damn well know it's mine," she told him.

Clearly befuddled, Ricky glared at Melissa, but his anger did not seem to be abating.

Melissa saw Kyra looking at her mouthing, "Radiant heart?"

Melissa nodded.

"Just walk away," Dwayne said. "This can all end right here, right now."

"Bullshit, Logan!" Ricky growled. He doubled his fist. The intention became clear in an instant, as he took one large step toward Dwayne.

Dwayne kicked him very hard between the legs.

Ricky pitched forward but stumbled backwards.

"Ricky," Dwayne drawled, "you may have some size on me, buddy, but I have a few more fights under my belt than you do. I assure you, ol' friend, you won't come out on top of this one. So, please, don't try."

Ricky recuperated, anger exploding to white hot. He came at Dwayne growling.

Dwayne snatched a wooden coat hanger from the shelf next to where he stood and slapped Ricky hard on the side of the face with it.

Ricky's head went with the blow.

With a hard-packed fist, Dwayne swung at Ricky's head from the opposite direction.

Ricky spun away, dazed. He stumbled and fell.

"Doggone it, Ricky," Dwayne begged, "leave. Just...*leave*, for Christ's sake. Think about your family. Think about the trouble you're causing for yourself.

It'll devastate Robert and Lisa if you wind up in prison, simply because you couldn't control yourself."

Dwayne's not-so-gentle persuasion worked. Holding his jaw, Ricky's aggression subsided and seemed to be ending altogether. He did not respond, only glared at Dwayne. He staggered to his feet and stumbled out of the stockroom.

Melissa hugged Dwayne. "You were magnificent." She kissed him and pressed her cheek into his chest.

Kyra joined them. "I'm thinking that the word *magnificent* is not adequate. She came up on the tips of her toes and kissed him on the cheek. "Thanks Dwayne. You saved me."

Melissa pulled away from Dwayne, turning to Kyra. "Ricky would have raped and beaten you badly. I saw it happen. The boy has true anger issues that need to be dealt with. It may not be because of you, but I believe he will, someday, end up in prison."

"I sort of figured you had seen something by the tone of the conversation," Kyra replied. "Where did you come from? I mean from what time?"

"From only about four hours ago," Melissa replied. "Look, Kyra, Dwayne and I are going back the same way we came. In that timeline you will have no memory of this until the exact moment it occurred in this timeline. But the second the clock passes the time this confrontation began, you will suddenly begin a real-time unfolding memory of these few minutes, but it will never have actually taken place because of what we did to prevent it in this timeline. Can you understand that?"

"I think so."

"You will also remember this conversation. Although, I can't be sure but I sense you're going feel very weird, maybe dizzy. Not sure. Anyhow, try not to be surprised by a memory of something that did not happen...because it will not have, now that Dwayne prevented it. The only residue of this entire episode will be reduced to your, seemingly, false memory of it. Understand?"

"Spooky stuff, but, yeah, I understand," Kyra replied.

"As for Ricky, well, the same thing will happen to him, and probably will scare the bejesus out of him when he suddenly, and vividly, remembers something he knows did not happen, but has obviously wanted to do for some time. Let's hope that's the only incentive he'll need to stop stalking you." She grinned impishly. "I bet he'll suddenly develop a ghost pain where Dwayne hit him and wonder why his face hurts. His false memory should be that vivid." Melissa turned to step back toward Dwayne, but then hesitated and retrained her attention on her sister. "You'll have to tell me what that sensation is like at the end of this day, because I will likely never experience it myself, since I'm the one initiating the time jumps," she added.

"Oh, I'm sure I will," Kyra replied.

Melissa turned to Dwayne. "Are you ready to go home, my sweet knight?"

He smiled. "Sure."

She embraced him as the white glow enveloped them both. The vibration of her radiant heart escalated slowly. It warmed her. It was usually a sudden chill, but not this time. She figured it had to do with the appreciation and love she felt for Dwayne at this moment. In a blink, they were standing next to his tractor in the field, the still-rising sun sending out radiant warmth into the remnants of cool night air being overtaken by old Sol. The feel of the air was strikingly different in an instant.

"Well, that was weirdly interesting," Dwayne said. He looked at the tractor, pulled off his green cap, and ran the fingers of his right hand over the top of his hair. He flexed the fingers a couple of times, probably still stinging a bit from the smashing blow to Ricky Castillo's head. He then snugged the cap back down. "I'd better get back to work. I've lost enough time."

"You've lost no time whatsoever. We returned to the exact time we left. Although you are a little older than you were."

"Oh? Okay."

Melissa chuckled. "How in the world can you be so nonchalant about everything? Your mind should be spinning, maybe afraid, and you're not at all. Why?"

He kissed her on the forehead, and replied, "I have a good answer for ya. It's because I trust you, my little witchy woman."

"Don't talk like that. I'm not a witch."

He bounced his eyebrows, grinned, and began climbing up into the tractor cab. "Somehow, I knew, I just damn well knew from the moment we met, that knowing you would be an adventure."

Melissa blew him a kiss and watched him take his seat in the tractor cab and close the door.

He fired up the big diesel engine and it blew a sudden black jet of smoke before settling into a noisy idle.

I sure love that man.

The remainder of the day was blissfully uneventful, although Melissa was anxious to hear Kyra's experience when the false memory hit her. As it turned out, Kyra was equally anxious to share it.

"Missy, where are you?" Kyra shouted as she came through the front door of the mansion.

"In the library," Melissa replied.

Kyra began talking before she appeared through the door of the library. "You were right. That memory raised goose bumps all over my arms. I was minding my own business, doing inventory in the stockroom when I suddenly had a vision of Ricky Castillo coming into the stockroom. It was so vivid, I actually looked to the door, but he wasn't there. It wasn't at all like any memory I ever had. It was like...well, like watching a movie in my mind's-eye that was eerily clear and detailed."

"So, you didn't abruptly remember the entire event?"

"No. It unfolded, just like you said it would. It seemed like a movie. As the vision progressed, I was feeling the surprise, the fear, the pain, and finally the relief when you and Dwayne showed up. I suppose what I was experiencing was the event in real time, as you suspected. Although, when it was over, I knew it had never happened. Now, here's the weirder part. I stepped out of the stockroom to find Ricky leaning against the counter next to the cash register. He was holding the side of his head. I asked him what the matter was and he said, "I don't know. A sudden sharp pain hit me on the side of my head. Now I have a horrible headache."

"Keep in mind, he had just had the exact same vision that you did, only from his perspective. I'm sure he'll never share that with you," Melissa said.

Kyra laughed. "Judging by how oddly he was looking at me, I have a feeling he won't be stalking me anymore."

Melissa nodded and smiled. "I think you might be right. Let's hope."

Chapter Nineteen

The Final Goodbye

"**B**oys, are you sure you'll be okay?" Cary Dane-Blakely asked again.

"Mom," Johnny whined, "would you please stop worrying." Johnny celebrated his eighteenth birthday in September. Now, high school diploma earned, he worked at Sullivan's logging operation up the highway from Coos Bay. The plan was for him to work fulltime June through August and then go part-time at Sullivan's and attend college.

His older brother, Charlie, now twenty-five, piped in, "Yeah, Mom. Johnny and I will be fine. You've left us the house, so we have no rent or mortgage payments and, between the two of us, we can cover utilities, necessary items, and food, plus have a little play money left over every month. We'll be living our dream. Go live yours...*please*." Charlie kissed her on the cheek.

Cary looked at both her sons in turn, realizing she had not considered how difficult leaving them would be, until this moment. The day had come to move to Texas. This empty-nest sensation was of her own making, leaving her adult sons by her second marriage to make it on their own. Their father, William, was out of the picture. Misgivings she harbored about the circumstances of his departure had moved to the fringes of consciousness. She hardly ever thought about those circumstances, or him, anymore. But she would be thinking about these two precious young men often.

"Okay. I'll try to worry about you boys as little as possible. Still, I'm your mother. That makes it impossible to stop worrying altogether. Always know if one, or both of you, want to visit me and your sisters in Texas, I'll spring for airfare or gasoline, ever how you choose to travel."

Charlie and Johnny simply smiled and nodded.

Two blasts from a car horn blared beyond the yard in front of the house.

"Oh, my goodness, my taxi is already here. That was quick. I thought we'd have more time to say our good-byes."

Charlie hugged her. "Go on, Mom, have an adventure. You've deserved this for a long, long time."

Johnny pushed Charlie aside and embraced his mother. "There's a whole big world waiting for you out there. In fact, I hear it's almost as big as Texas." He chuckled.

The car horn blew again.

"I'd better scoot. I don't want to miss my connecting flight to Lubbock." Cary grabbed her purse and headed out the front door but stopped to take a last look at the house she had called home for many years. The separation anxiety was more than she bargained for. She thought it would be easier to leave Coos Bay. Although she had grown up in this town and lived, to this point, her entire life here, she did not want the balance of her years to be spent here. *I know he was trying to be funny, but Johnny was right. There is a whole big world out there and I would like to experience at least one more part of it before my days are done.*

Her sons carried her luggage to the waiting taxi. "Tell Missy and Kyra we love them," Charlie said, as he placed her cases in the open trunk. He slammed it shut.

Cary got in the back seat and let down her window. "I love you boys."

The taxi began pulling away. "Call me often," she shouted. "Keep me up with how you guys are doing. If you need anything, anything at all, pick up the phone and call, you hear?"

As the taxi wheeled out onto the street, she heard Johnny shout, "Have a safe trip."

The taxi approached Southwest Oregon Regional Airport. Cary's anxiety eased. She began the transformation of looking ahead to the future, and not flounder in the past. There was a charge of excitement about it.

When she thought about past versus future, it amused her, knowing Melissa's talent to see and physically move between the two, to travel over great distances instantly at any point in time she chose, or shift dimensionally in time and space. As thoughts deepened into her eldest daughter's inherited capability, amusement faded. Melissa was comfortable, even captivated, with the radiant heart ability in the beginning. But lately, she seemed apprehensive. Cary had believed Melissa was taking it all too lackadaisically, but that was changing. Knowing her daughter now took it seriously, comforted. Genuine possibilities existed for serious and permanent consequences, not all of them good. Unlike the rest of the world, time flow was not an inescapable prison for her. Judging by phone conversations with her daughter, Melissa was comfortably conversant about the radiant heart, thanks to information left behind by her deceased brother-in-law, and Melissa's uncle, Jack Dane. Melissa had no reservations about going back to visit Jack when questions arose. It was an odd relationship between Melissa and Jack. One that seemed to be growing stronger. Cary wasn't sure how to feel about it. Since Melissa could not change the past, each time she popped in for a visit, he had no memory of her ever having been there before. Her daughter grew weary of re-introducing herself over and over. Yet, she had no intention of stopping the visits. Cary could hear it in Melissa's voice, she was becoming attached to her deceased uncle and dependent on their conversations. Maybe even seeing Jack as a father figure. *Is a relationship like that healthy? It might be cause for psychological damage.* Cary could not say, but worried that Melissa's growing affection for a man dead for many years, might damage Melissa's mental health, somehow. *She and I will be having a conversation about that in the coming days.*

***

Melissa felt her cell phone vibrating in the large side pocket of her white smock and retrieved it. "Excuse me. I'll just be a moment," she told the patient she examined, as she stepped out of the examination room into the corridor. The display on the phone showed Kyra's name. Melissa figured it had to do with their mother flying in today. She hit the icon and sent the call directly to voice mail. Melissa went back into the room and refocused on her patient. "I'll send a prescription over to your pharmacy. I think an occasional Xanax will take care of your sporadic anxiety issues."

The elderly lady slid off the examination bed to her feet. "Thanks so much. I thought I was going crazy."

Melissa smiled. "Anxiety is more of a problem these days than most people realize. Call the clinic if you have any other issues, or if anything changes for the worse."

The woman shuffled out of the room, assisted by a four-prong cane.

Melissa closed the door and returned Kyra's call. "Hey, Sis, got your message."

"I was wondering what time you were picking Mom up from the airport."

Melissa chuckled. "Why? Ya miss her?"

"Of course I do. But I was asking because I thought I'd cook dinner and wanted to time it so it would be fresh and hot when you got here."

Melissa checked her wristwatch. Four-forty-five. "I understand her plane arrives at five-thirty, which means I should leave for the airport soon."

"I'll plan on dinner at seven-ish. Is that okay?"

"Good enough. See you then." Melissa ended the call and hurried into the corridor, and walked briskly to the reception desk. "I have to meet my mother at the airport," she told the middle-aged receptionist. "I have no more patients, so, I won't be back to work today. See you in the morning," she added as she breezed by the front desk, heading toward the exit.

It was the middle of the first week in June. The airport seemed sedate for a travel hub. Mostly business people in dark suits carrying briefcases and satchels, likely returning from day trips to places too far to drive, and then return from in a single day. She saw no couples or families.

Melissa heard the roaring whine and rumble of a landing jet, realizing she walked through the terminal door at the perfect time. She checked the digital board overhead for the correct gate and sauntered in that direction. There was time. She was in no rush. It would take a few minutes for the jet to taxi to a stop, and then allow passengers to deplane.

She took an interest in every traveler who passed by. It was a game, guessing by their appearance and luggage where their destination might be, or where they were returning from. Although, she never actually asked anyone to substantiate a guess, it was fun, nonetheless.

Melissa had always been a novice student of the habits of men and women. Over years of casual observation, she came to the conclusion that humans of all creeds, colors, and countries of origin are much more alike than different when it came to the daily business of living.

People coming off the plane filed through the gate off the tarmac. She saw her mother, pretty as she always had been, about mid-way up the line. Melissa waved enthusiastically, and continued waving until Cary saw her and reciprocated. The returned wave was accompanied by a beaming smile. They hurried toward one another and embraced.

"I'm so glad you were here when I arrived," Cary said, and then pulled her eyebrows down into a knit, and whispered, "You didn't pop over here, did you?"

"Oh, Mom. I don't abuse the ability. I only use it when necessary."

"Whew! That's good. I have no desire to be whisked here to there...or anywhere, for that matter."

Melissa pulled her mother back in for another hug, and kissed her on the cheek. "Good to know. I'll make a point of leaving you behind."

"Ha-ha. Real funny."

The drive through Lubbock proved the ideal opportunity to get her mother caught up on what living in this part of northwest Texas was like for herself and her sister. She exited the Loop and onto the southbound highway toward the Dane mansion. Melissa shared stark differences in climate, people, and lifestyles. It kept her mother busy asking questions.

As Melissa turned off the highway onto the gravel road to their home, she drove by the old stucco house where Dwayne and his father lived, Cary's eyes locked onto it. "Is that where Cletus lives?"

Melissa glanced quizzically at her. The question was odd. "Personally, I believe there's a better way to phrase the question. As an example: is it where Dwayne Logan lives with his father?" She wondered. Her head tilted sideways. "I don't remember talking about his father much. How come his was the first name that came to mind?"

"Oh, it's nothing, really. I was remembering having met Cletus the week William and I spent here after your Uncle Jack's funeral twenty-five years ago. That's all. He and I spoke at the cemetery, and we saw each other a couple of times during the week afterward before your stepfather and I went back to Coos Bay. As you know, that was a long time ago."

Melissa thought she noticed her mother's cheeks flush. If that wasn't the case, there was a clear expression of something. Embarrassment, maybe? Melissa dismissed it as a travel fatigue thing. She steered onto the driveway up to the mansion and snatched a couple of quick glances at her mother, who continued looking back toward the Logan home. "Is that a twinkle I see in your eye?" she joked.

Cary's cheeks flushed. "Oh hush." Her mother turned her head away and sat quietly for a moment. She then mumbled, "He *was* quite a handsome guy though."

No guessing this time. Mom is blushing. Melissa chuckled. "Yeah. I sort of got that from the tone of this conversation." She cut her little SUV perpendicular to the end of the sidewalk in front of the house and stopped. "Here we are."

"Other than the size of the trees around the house and all those huge Poplar trees lining the drive, the place looks exactly the way I remember it," Cary said.

"The first thing for you to do is stop calling it 'the place' and start calling it home."

***

Dwayne and Cletus Logan sat, eating bologna sandwiches and chips. Washing them down with sweet iced tea. The sun had set and daylight faded slowly. From where Dwayne sat in the kitchen, he looked back through the doorway, through the living room, and out the large picture window at the front of the house. He was thinking, while absently tossing bologna bits down to his faithful companion, Hotshot. The dog sat on his haunches next to him, eagerly awaiting each morsel. Front paws dancing, nails clicking on the worn vinyl-covered floor. No tossed bit of bologna ever hit the floor. Dwayne was exhausted from another long day of work. He needed a shower. His chambray shirt retained dampened sweat streaks on the collar and in the armpits. His tired mind flit from one thought to the next. He was thankful this day was coming to an end, and a shower would put the perfect punctuation on it. About eleven hours of sleep sure wouldn't hurt anything either.

"What are ya so intently thinkin' 'bout?" Cletus asked.

Dwayne's mind grazed in a different pasture and didn't hear his father.

"Hey, you."

Dwayne startled to attention. "Sorry. What'd ya say?"

"Just wonderin' what subject has you thinkin' so hard."

"I was thinkin' the weeds seem to be coming up faster than the cotton out yonder."

"Farm life. Ain't it wonderful?" Cletus chuckled. "I suppose we have to take the good with the bad. We were blessed with ample and well-timed spring rains. Every seed in the dirt out there germinated, good and bad." He took a bite of sandwich and pushed it into his cheek. "Well, my thinkin' has gone in a different direction," Cletus said. "I'm tired of bologna sandwiches. And, sadly, I've noticed we still have plenty of the dadgum stuff in the fridge."

Dwayne brightened. "That reminds me. Kyra called earlier while you were feeding the hogs. She invited us to dinner at the mansion tomorrow evenin'. Missy picked her mother up from the airport this afternoon and thought it would be nice if we got re-acquainted with her. I was what...twelve or thirteen the last time I saw her? Back then, you were about my age now. Isn't that right?"

"Yep, about right." Cletus broke eye contact and slowly chewed his sandwich. He nodded slowly, and then finally added, "I suppose that's as good a way as any to get variety in my diet."

"You do remember Cary, Jack Dane's sister-in-law, don't you?"

Again, Cletus nodded. He slowly turned back to look directly at his son. "Oh yeah. I remember."

"Your expression indicated you may not have remembered her."

"What you saw, boy, was me having a sudden vivid memory." Cletus stared at Dwayne for a moment. His lips pursed, as if about to form a word. It seemed he wanted to say something. But nothing came out, not a single word.

"Come on now. What're ya not sayin'?"

Cletus remained quiet a few more seconds, but finally broke his silence. "Thanks to your paternity questions, I'm sure you got the gist of it. For about a quarter century I kept it to myself. I'm thinkin' Cary didn't talk to her kids about it either. So...yeah...I'm looking forward to dinner over in the Dane mansion tomorrow evening, as much as you I'd bet. Gettin' re-acquainted sounds good...very good." He shoved the remaining bite of the bologna sandwich in his mouth and mauled it, pushing it from cheek to cheek as he chewed. "I wonder if she's as cute as I remember?" he muttered.

Dwayne saw that his dad stared at the wall. He wondered what images his old man conjured. He drew a slow grin at his own assumptions of what they might be.

Chapter Twenty

Family Ties

After a couple of hard raps of the brass door knocker on the mansion's front door, Dwayne and Cletus waited for a response. Dwayne eyed his father up and down. "It's been a long while since I've seen you lookin' so darn spiffy. You didn't look this good the last time we went to church."

The older Logan's brow sank to the center. "Put a sock in it, boy. I simply thought a little extra effort on my appearance was called for, since we'll be in a fancy mansion with three lovely ladies. Nothin' more to it than that."

Dwayne grinned and snickered. "I might believe it if you had expended the same effort when we went to the steakhouse with Missy and Kyra. I sure believe you're specifically referring to *one* lovely lady. Now, ain't that right, old man?" Dwayne continued the attention on his father, smiling.

Cletus stared at the brass door knocker on the massive oak door in front of him, as Dwayne noticed a slight smile crease his father's face.

The sound of echoing footfalls grew louder from the other side of the door, and then stopped. The door whooshed open and Melissa welcomed them in with a beaming smile. "I'm so happy you two could get away from farm work long enough to join us for dinner," she said, leading the way to the semi-formal sitting area to the left in the front corner of the house. "Kyra and Robert are in the kitchen. They volunteered to team up and do the cooking. My only job is to annoy them and make numerous unwanted suggestions." She laughed, as she stepped through the door into the living area.

Dwayne saw Cary Dane-Blakely sitting primly on the same sofa he woke up on after the night of Melissa's radiant heart revelation and too much wine.

"Cletus...Dwayne...you remember my mother, Cary, right?"

Cletus walked around his son, shouldering him aside with both hands extended toward Cary. "Of course we do." He took Cary's hands and held them. "For heaven's sake, you are as beautiful as you were the last time I saw you, twenty-five years ago."

Cary blushed. "You're not so bad yourself, Cletus."

Dwayne took Melissa's hand and pulled her back a few feet. He whispered in her ear, "You see what I'm seein'?"

"Yep. It's something...definitely something," Melissa replied."

"Good food with a gorgeous woman, and a mystery to solve. I couldn't ask for a more entertaining way to spend a Saturday evening."

"It's not that much of a mystery anymore," she replied, and then tugged on his hand. "Come on. Let's go open a bottle of wine and visit with Kyra and Robert, while Cletus and Mom get reacquainted."

Dwayne was fascinated and wanted to hang around and watch the reacquainting ritual. He couldn't prevent his hesitance, feet remaining planted. He pulled Melissa to a standstill. "Aw, can't we wait a few minutes? We might hear somethin' good."

Melissa yanked his arm harder. "I'm not sure I'm old enough, or mature enough, to hear what they might say to one another. Come on. Let's go the kitchen."

She pulled his arm until he had no choice but to follow her or to trip and fall. Those were the only choices. No other. As he clumsily yielded, his eyes remained on what appeared to be the developing intimate conversation between his father and Melissa's mother.

He finally gave in and followed Melissa down the hall. After years of maintaining this huge rambling house to a habitable standard, Dwayne noticed it was no longer a large empty structure with sound bouncing off every wall. Thanks to the Dane girls, the transformation was complete. It was a home in every sense of the word. Wonderful smells of good things to eat wafted down the hall toward them. Laughter came from the kitchen and the unmistakable warm ambience of a house filled with love. It touched him. It also sparked memories of his mother and his childhood, growing up in this house.

As he and Melissa entered the kitchen, she said, "Good grief, Dwayne, life must be boring at your house, if you wanted to hear what our parents had to say."

Kyra was handing Robert a couple of oven mitts and he, apparently, had said something funny. She had been laughing, but cut it short when Dwayne and her older sister came into the kitchen. Kyra looked away from Robert. "What're you guys talking about, Missy?"

"Well, it would seem a twenty-five-year absence hasn't dampened whatever Mom and Cletus have in common. They fell into a quiet conversation almost immediately. It was obvious they didn't want Dwayne and me hearing what they had to say."

"She speaks the truth," Dwayne added.

"What do *you* think's going on?" Robert asked, as he set a hot casserole dish on a porcelain trivet.

"I'm certain the chemistry between those two a quarter century ago apparently hasn't withered in the slightest," Kyra said. "I wonder if they have anything in common, besides heat."

Dwayne watched Melissa's response with interest.

She turned to Dwayne, but her blurted response was directed at Kyra without hesitation. "Sis, let's not go down that road. It's none of our business."

"Hmm. Sort of makes me wonder what Mom's true motivation was for moving to Texas," Kyra said.

Melissa turned full attention to her younger sister, nodding slowly, as her eyebrows lifted in tacit agreement.

Kyra and Robert did a magnificent job with dinner. Robert used a Castillo family recipe for chicken enchilada casserole, each serving ringed by a bed of finely shredded lettuce and cherry tomatoes. Every plate also received a generous dollop of guacamole. Robert had also brought a quart of his mother's home-made salsa verde and a quart of chunky homemade picante sauce.

By the time dinner had been consumed, so had most of four bottles of good dry red wine from a local family-owned vintner. Dwayne explained that grapes and wine had become a good money-making venture on the Texas plains. The rich sandy loam soil produced stronger, healthy vines.

Laughter was coming easy for everyone at the table. Humorous stories were swapped about farm mishaps by Dwayne and Cletus, plus, funny things happening at the hardware store as told by Robert. Kyra shared the funny side of her and Lisa's struggles to make the dress shop profitable, and Melissa had a couple of stories about patients at the clinic.

Dwayne noticed the only one without a story to tell was Melissa's mother. "Cary, surely you brought some funny stories from Oregon," he said.

Although the elder Dane woman had been laughing along with everyone else, the sparkle in her smile sagged. She seemed to become embarrassed. "I... well, I can't think of—"

"The last few years in Coos Bay hasn't been much fun for Mom..." Melissa interrupted, coming to her mother's rescue. "...for any of our family."

Cary smiled appreciatively at her oldest daughter.

The moment broke the mood. It became awkwardly quiet.

"I'll personally guarantee ya this, Cary. We will all be givin' you reasons to smile, however long you choose to live around here," Cletus said.

"Thank you for saying that, Cletus," Cary said, as she shyly ringed the top of her wine glass with a fingertip.

"Dwayne looked from her to his father. "Speaking of reasons to smile, you two seem to have really warmed up to one another in record time."

"Anything you two want to share with the group?" Kyra asked, grinning mischievously.

Cletus glared at Kyra and slowly pulled a toothpick from his mouth and sucked air between his teeth. He turned to Cary. "Ya think we should tell 'em it's none of their business?"

"I think, for now, *yes*," Cary replied.

If Missy wanted to, she could zap herself back twenty-five years and find out what happened. I wonder if she would consider such a thing, Dwayne thought.

***

Dwayne, Cletus, and Robert left at the same time, just after ten o'clock. Standing in the open doorway, the three Dane women waved goodbye. Melissa closed the door. The door bolt had barely passed the striker plate when she turned to her mother. "Okay, they're gone. I want to hear the Cletus and Cary story."

"So do I," Kyra chimed in.

Cary said nothing. She simply smiled and walked away toward the living room.

"Come on, Mom," Kyra said, "if you believe the air around you two wasn't charged with noticeable romantic energy, then you're seriously mistaken. The magnetism between you two was on display. I not only saw it, I felt it. Right, Missy?"

Melissa followed her mother to the sofa. They sat at the same time. "She's right, Mom."

Cary bobbled her head. "Okay, girls. Here's the deal. Cletus and I had...chemistry. It would seem the passing years have not dampened it."

Melissa huffed impatience. "We already know that. But it plainly goes deeper," she said. "Care to explain?"

"Not really. But...I assume this interrogation will not stop until you two know the story."

"Details. I want details," Kyra said as she settled onto the edge of a chair facing the sofa from the other side of the coffee table.

Cary sighed. "When William and I came to Texas for Jack's funeral, I was introduced to Cletus and Dwayne at the cemetery. I even met his ex-wife, Dwayne's mother, Rita. Although, she and Cletus were hardly ever in the same space at the same time. She was a lovely woman."

"I don't see how an attraction could develop at a funeral," Melissa said.

"Oh, there was a spark, but it was during the following week that events drew us closer."

Kyra wrinkled her nose. "I thought you and dad only came down for the funeral. How long were you here?"

"Almost two weeks."

"Why?" Melissa asked.

"There were legal things that needed attention to settle Jack's estate. Rita moved out of the house and took Dwayne with her. They moved to Brownfield. After lengthy conversations with Cletus, he accepted responsibility as first caretaker of this house. Dwayne was a gangly eleven-year-old boy. Of course, he waited until Rita and Dwayne had moved out before he came around much. He wanted to respect their space. Besides, there was always tension when Cletus and Rita were in close proximity. That was the oddest relationship I ever saw. They loved each other, but couldn't be together. The few times I saw them together, an argument erupted within seconds. I didn't need to be told they were divorced. It was obvious."

Was there something that triggered it, or a specific moment that defined your attraction to him?" Kyra asked.

"Yes. William wasn't aware of it, but he provided the 'something' and the 'moment'."

"Dad? Seriously?" Kyra said, suddenly sitting straighter. "How so?"

"William was drinking too much even back then. As I was going about the business of settling Jack's estate, William found the liquor cabinet next to the pantry in the kitchen. Prior to his death, Jack kept it well-stocked. William spent time alone in this rambling house and began drinking heavily. I came back one afternoon and he was already showing signs of his abusive nature, making profane, rude, and snide remarks. He accused me of paying more attention to a dead brother-in-law than to him. We argued. Cletus happened to knock on the door to give me a set of padlock keys to the storage bays in Brownfield that had been loaded with the valuable contents of this house. He heard the commotion and became concerned. He used the door key I had given him and came in to hear William's barrage of profanity."

"What did Cletus do, punch him? I would have," Melissa said.

"No. Cletus never raised a hand to William, but managed to talk him down from his over-the-top angry tirade. He was magnificent, a real gentleman, but he had an air about him. William was intimidated. That was clear enough. I feel, though, if William had done something stupid, like take a swing at him, Cletus would have doubled a fist and hit him...drunk or not. And that, girls, was the genesis of my affection for Cletus Logan.

Kyra looked at Melissa then back to her mother. "That's all there was to it? It seems so anti-climactic. There's bound to be more to this story."

Cary snapped up a belligerent palm and stiff-armed the air toward both her girls. "Stop right there! I'll be answering no more questions. What Cletus and I had, what we...shared...is none of your business, either one of you."

Melissa's mouth sagged open, as did Kyra's. They exchanged glances. "I believe we can infer from that comment and the tone of it, what happened." A smile stretched Melissa's face tight. "Good for you, Mom. Bravo."

Chapter Twenty-One

Shadows of the Past

Melissa woke and got out of bed Sunday morning. Quietly, she went down to the kitchen and turned on the coffee maker. The house was noiseless except for the gurgle and hiss of the coffee maker. As it dripped into the carafe, sending out its inviting aroma, she thought about the conversation with her mother the night before. Her stepfather had only instigated the brief romantic liaison between her mother and Cletus Logan twenty-five years ago, remaining a secret for years. Mention of Logan by her mother over the years had been brief and casual—never a hint of the emotion that must have been simmering in the recesses of Cary's mind during all that time. Now that her mother's feelings for Cletus were known, William Blakely was suddenly thrust into the spotlight of Melissa's growing remorse over what she had done to him. Deep resentment for the man had softened with the passage of time. For Melissa, the absence of her stepfather had grown to a festering concern. Love nor respect for the man had anything to do with it. She wanted her mother and Dwayne's father to hit it off—romantically and permanently. She hoped nothing would interfere. But the conversation had rekindled a growing crisis of conscience over leaving William suspended in time in another dimension of existence, or non-existence. She couldn't be sure which.

Passing time lessened her rage toward the man, realizing William was not a bad guy, but the victim of a disease he had lost control of. It was a horrible addiction to alcohol that created the angry and belligerent man he became, lashing out at loved ones. All the while, hating himself because he couldn't control it and knew it. *If he had sought professional help and rehabilitation, would it have turned out differently? Would he and Mom still be together?* She glanced at the coffee maker—almost done.

Although Melissa had not killed her stepfather, she did leave him in a place he was unable to return from on his own. In the absence of her intervention, he might as well be dead. That place, she came to realize, was a dimension thinly separating life from death. Out of those woods and across the valley lay eternity—true death. Under the circumstances, he likely could not make that crossing without her presence. She had been, after all, his host there. He would have to die in a natural way in this time and space to make that crossing without her assistance. The concept sounded simple to think about or speak of, but the truth was that she, a flesh and blood human, had the awesomely terrifying power to expel a human from this existence to another not of this earthly dimension into a prison of souls. She was mortal and should not be divinely allowed to possess such power and responsibility. Her mind was becoming a swirl of extremes that no human should have to contend with.

Now she had arrived at the genesis of the notion that she might be able to retrieve William. The alternative would be that if drunken curiosity overtook him and he was able to cross without her presence, there would be no returning and no way to bring him back. It was divinely forbidden to cross over and then return. She would be unable to penetrate it and retrieve him under any circumstances. She would be in that place eternally as well. It lay far beyond the simple bounds of time, space, and dimension.

Simple? The word gave her pause. Here she stood, staring at a slowly filling coffee carafe, thinking of moving through time, space, and dimension as simple concepts. Amazing. Life had certainly taken an abrupt turn the past few months.

Melissa felt a hand brush over her shoulder. It startled her. She turned to see her mother in a robe.

"Didn't mean to shake you from ponderous thought," Cary said.

Melissa's expression settled quickly. She smiled. "Actually, you're right. I was working through something." The coffee maker gave its final gasp and dripped its last. Melissa retrieved a cup from the cabinet and poured it brim full. She handed it to her mother and poured one for herself.

"Is it anything I might be able to help you with, Missy?"

"I don't know if you can help, but I'm certain you'd have a firm opinion on it."

"Oh?"

Melissa sipped her steaming coffee. "I've been thinking about what I did to William. Our talk last night put it right back on my mind. When I shoved him into that dimension, although I didn't mean to do it, I figured he deserved what he got. I was angry. I felt no remorse...at the time. As conscience now dictates, regret has weaseled in. I didn't have a right to remove him from this realm of existence. I only wanted him to stop abusing you."

Cary placed a gentle hand on Melissa's forearm. "I can't claim to be any less of a troll. My opinion of him grew very dark in those last days. I wanted him to disappear from my life, our lives...just not the way in which it happened. I think I would have left him in a matter of days anyhow. What you did beat me to it."

"So, it sounds like you understand why I've begun to re-think my actions."

"Of course," Cary replied. "In the early years, William was a good man who helped me more than you'll ever know to get over your father's violent death. He was kind and loving. That's the man I fell in love with, but I didn't love the man he became."

Melissa cradled the steaming mug in both hands. She turned and paced away, but suddenly turned back. "Let me throw out an idea. What if it were possible to get him back, would you want me to?"

"Not for my sake. But if you try and succeed, I'd hope that he would stay in Coos Bay and live with Charlie and Johnny, then...maybe so," she said haltingly, but quickly added, "Although, I'd immediately file for divorce, which I should have already done anyhow. I'm not moving back to Oregon, under any circumstances, especially for him. But the boys would probably get along with him fine. They're old enough now, it's possible they could play an active role in keeping him sober." She smiled sheepishly. "As for me...well, I want to explore things here, and I'm not talking about the scenery."

Melissa could not control the tiny smile that sprouted. She nodded and kept on as she paced in a tight circle, thinking it through. "Okay, I'll work on it, but I need to be honest about the possibility of making it happen. Once I transport to that place, if William should enter that valley, for whatever reason, and walk toward the other side for only a short distance, he would not have the wherewithal to turn away and would continue on, drawn to it, until he reaches the other side, crossing into eternity. My presence would likely allow that to happen. Since he was inebriated, he would have less willpower to prevent it than he normally would. It seems like a plausible scenario. If so, I wouldn't be able to do anything about it. I remember Uncle Jack recounting the episode of swimming after Dad, trying to catch him before he crossed over."

"I remember that part of his book, *The Last Radiant Heart*, too," Cary said. "Jack wrote that after he swam a short distance, he began losing control, propelled by some power not of his making, forcibly shoved through the water by unseen hands. He was drawn to it and had to fight to return to where he started."

"That's right. No one would be able to resist it. And, I assume that inhibition to stop would melt away the closer the opposite side came."

"I have a question," Cary said. "If William was angrily, and drunkenly, chasing you through those woods, wouldn't he still be angry, still drunk, and still be chasing after you, bent on hurting you?"

"Good point. Although time keeps marching on this dimension, maybe the time flow is not the same there. I tend to believe that the passage of time totally stopped for William, because he, unlike me, was not traveling by his own standard of time. It became irrelevant and ceased to pass, for him—not me. And, one indisputable fact is, I don't remember what time it was when crap hit the fan that day he hit you."

Melissa's eyes drifted toward the ceiling. She contemplated the complexity of what awaited her if she retrieved William and returned him to the house in Coos Bay. The only difference would be a fast-forward to the present time. William's timeline would have to match theirs. He couldn't be returned to the instant he was thrust into that dimension. That, now, is a past event and history cannot be changed. He would only be there as long as she was. He would have to be re-introduced to the world in the present. *If that all goes as planned, what will happen to William when he sobers up and discovers he has no memory of the past seven months? To him, mere seconds will have passed, not a fraction more,* she thought. As she contemplated the ins and outs of it, an upside crossed her mind. *Maybe it will serve to scare him into a rehabilitation program, if he thought his brain had fried to the point of a memory lapse of such gargantuan proportion.* All legitimate concerns but getting him back had to be the first step.

"You know, I think you're right, Mom. If I join William in that dimension, it would likely be at or near the same time I left him there. So, yeah. He would be drunk and angry, wanting desperately to punch me in the face. Even drunk, I couldn't control him long enough to concentrate on the time and place to end the jump while holding onto him. I simply couldn't do it alone."

"Sorry, dear, but if you decide to follow through on this, I'm not volunteering to go with you and be his punching bag again."

Melissa waved off her concern. "That didn't even cross my mind, nor did asking Kyra for help. I need strength. I need Dwayne."

***

Dwayne stood, one booted foot perched on the weathered bottom rail board of a low fence. Scuffed and old, the dried mud-encrusted sides and soles of his western boots had curled the worn pointed toes of the footwear. He watched three gilts and four barrow pigs, plus an old mother sow eating corn mash he'd dumped into a trough. By mid-summer, all the barrows and two of the gilts would be heading to the auction ring. "Well boys and girls," he said to the swine, "you may not realize it now, but by the end of July y'all will miraculously be transformed into Christmas money."

"Hey, Doctor Doolittle. Do you always talk to your animals?" a familiar feminine voice asked from behind.

Dwayne spun to face Melissa. The shock of her sudden appearance melted into an adoring gaze. "Not always. Only when I have something I think they need to hear."

Melissa snickered. She flicked her chin toward the open field beyond the yard. "And all this time, I thought it was only Hotshot out there that received such personal attention."

His eyes followed her prompt to see Hotshot running flat-out chasing a jackrabbit across plowed ground. "As a rule, that's probably true. Ol' Hotshot and I do have regular philosophical debates, for sure." He paused and looked about for her car. "I didn't hear you drive up."

"I didn't drive. I walked over, right across that plowed field from our place. All the cotton you planted is up and looking good row after row of little leafy soldiers."

"It is for a fact. I was thinkin' about puttin' in a big garden. That's really what was on my mind when you caught me conversing with Porky Pig and his siblings. I'll be gettin' a late start on plantin' it this year. But rains have been good. I think it'll be okay." He dipped his head seductively, looked around for prying eyes and ears, and whispered, "I'm a little behind this year. I have a new lady friend that has kept me kind of busy this spring."

Melissa raised a suspicious eyebrow. "I hope you're talking about me."

Dwayne stepped nearer to her, leaned in and kissed her lightly on the lips. "Maybe I shouldn't be jokin' about it. Don't want to be on your bad side."

Melissa's smile sagged. "Speaking of my 'bad side', I need to tell you something that might put *me* on *your* bad side."

"Oh?"

"I did something I'm not proud of. And I may need your help correcting it."

"Walk with me. I have to go to the barn and get Festus ready to help me plant the garden. You can tell me on the way."

"Festus? Who's Festus?"

"It's not a *who*. It's a *what*. A 1948 Ford 8N tractor."

"Why did you give it a name...more specifically, the name Festus?"

"Well, I'll tell ya. Festus Haggen was a scruffy old squinty-eyed character that wasn't handsome at all, but the old boy had the heart of a lion and loyal. So is *my* Festus," he said as he slid a large barn door on rollers open to reveal the small gray tractor sporting one broken headlight and a layer of dust. Two sparrows flew, darting and diving, out the opening door along with settling dust and a few feathers. He pointed to the empty light socket on the little tractor. "Ya see. Squinty-eyed. This is my gardenin' tractor." He patted it on the radiator grill. "Festus, here, never lets me down. I'm going to change the oil, put the battery on charge, and gas it up. While I'm doin' that, tell me your story."

As Melissa followed him to a work bench where cans of oil set stacked inside a drain pan, she said, "As I've already told you, I had lost all respect for my stepfather, William Blakely. He was a verbally abusive alcoholic. One day, I became fed up with the string of obscenities he hurled at Mom. I confronted him, giving as good as I got, throwing it back at him in equal measure. I refused to allow his tirade to go unanswered."

"Heck, I would've gotten in his face, too. You were just defendin' your sweet mother," Dwayne replied, as he carried the shallow pan and a wrench back to the tractor. He squatted beside it and began unscrewing the oil pan plug.

"Mom, ever the pacifist, stepped between us, as William was coming at me. I held my ground. She tried to stop him, but all she got for her effort was a backhanded fist to the side of her head that sent her spinning to the floor, dazed."

Dwayne glanced up at her. "Damn. The man must have been insane."

"He was. Alcohol abuse had deeply impaired his reasoning ability. Knowing this didn't help. In that moment, my over-top-anger at him reeled out of control. As did his toward me."

Dwayne scooted away a couple of feet to prevent oil from splattering on his jeans. "From what you've told me so far, it seems that you didn't have a choice. You had to act. You had to do something."

"Even if I hadn't become so angry, I probably would have still slapped the bastard for hitting Mom. But, Dwayne, here's where the story becomes harder to tell and much weirder to hear or understand," she continued. "But, I suppose, since you've already gone through a similar experience, maybe not so much for you."

Dwayne positioned the pan beneath the plug and removed it to drain the crankcase. Thick black oil gushed out. "Go on. Keep talkin'. I'm listenin'."

Melissa drew a breath and huffed it out. "This is more difficult to tell than I thought it would be."

From his crouched position, sitting on his heels, he twisted around, offering visual proof she had his full attention. "Whatever it is you have to say, Missy, I won't be judging you."

"Again, I was angry, too angry. William was far too sloshed to realize what he had done. I can't be certain he was even aware he'd hit Mom. In that moment I was out of control as much as he was. Without burying you in minutiae, the radiant heart kicked in and I yanked him to the scariest place I could think of...deep woods. At first, I didn't know where I had transported to while holding on to him. Later, with Uncle Jack's help, I came to understand I had not made a time jump. Instead, it was a dimension shift. It was my mind's literal manifestation of a realm between life and death."

Dwayne finished replacing the plug in the oil pan and came to his feet. He pulled a rag from his hip pocket and wiped the grime from his hands. "Gawd all mighty, girl. Did you leave him there? Is that what you're trying to tell me?"

Melissa was hesitant to affirm his guess with a positive nod. But did.

"Does that mean he's dead?"

"I don't think so. He's just stuck there."

"When did this happen?"

"Not long after Thanksgiving last year."

"That was nearly seven months ago. He probably starved to death within a couple of weeks," he said.

"Well, you see, that's where the facts of the situation become murky for me. Since it was a dimension shift and not a time jump. Mom and I have concluded it's possible his time stream froze when I broke with that place and returned home. That would mean, if true, William will be exactly as he was when I returned to Mom's house in Coos Bay without him."

"Okay," he drawled, drawing out the word. His head tilted to a quizzical slant.

"In other words, if I should succeed in going back to attempt a retrieval, it will be as though no time has passed for him at all. He'll still be nearly blind drunk and he'll still be chasing me up a hill with the sole intent of hitting me like he did Mom. As far as I could discern, William had no clue that he was no longer in the living room. He never stopped to look around. I had no problem avoiding him because he was extremely inebriated and very out of shape. Thinking back, he was so drunk, I don't understand how he remained conscious." She stopped talking, taking a moment to give that some thought. She finally waved off contemplation. "But that's neither here nor there. The fact is, he *was* conscious. Dwayne, William is strong and I wouldn't be able to control him long enough to concentrate on getting him back to the current time and our dimension of existence because, as you know, he would have to be very close to me as part of my aura long enough to invoke the radiant heart. That's why I'm confessing this now. I need your help. As time goes on, my conscience is wreaking havoc on me. I can no longer live with myself, knowing what I did. He may not be dead in the strictest sense, but he might as well be."

Dwayne blew a breathy whistle. "Wow." He pulled off his cap and palmed away perspiration on his forehead. "You were right about it being weird. This ol' country boy is havin' a difficult time undertandin' it."

"Well, you can do like me and believe it without full understanding."

"Don't get me wrong. I believe you. I surely do. It's just a little bit difficult to get my mind around."

"Hah! Tell me about it, stud."

Dwayne chewed the inside of his cheek, looking beyond Melissa toward the work bench. Hat in one hand and the other on his hip, he stared, thinking it through as he quietly walked back to the work bench and picked up a can of oil and a can spout. He shoved the piercing point into the top of the can and sauntered back to the tractor, then turning the can upside down into the open port to the crankcase.

"Do you need more time to think about it?" Melissa asked. "I want your help, but I wouldn't think less of you if you chose not to. It might be dangerous, but it's something I need to do."

"Oh, this quiet moment is not me being reluctant. It's me being fascinated. I can't think of very many challenges in my life that I've walked away from. And, since you're the one doin' the askin', it only makes it a foregone conclusion that I'll give you a hand with it. Of course, I'll help get your ol' stepdaddy back and, maybe, offer an assist in sobering him up, too. When do we leave?"

Melissa smiled warmly at his willingness to join her on this adventure that might become problematic, possessing dangers she hadn't yet considered. Something unexpected could fly out of the cosmos and hit her, or Dwayne, directly between the eyes before they noticed it was coming. Not a far-fetched notion, believing something coming at them like that could be literal. "We can leave anytime. It's not like we need to pack a suitcase. I just make it happen...if I can. Remember how time passage will be affected. For example, if we should leave right now, we'd be back..." she said, nodding toward the tractor, "... before that can of oil draining into the tractor is empty, regardless how long you and I are in that place," she said. The upside down can was burping out its contents as it drained into the crankcase. "That is, of course, if all goes well while we're there."

Chapter Twenty-Two

Facing New Realities

Cary walked away from *A Matter of Style*, across the parking lot to her car. She was impressed with the progress that Lisa Rivera and Kyra had made in the short time the little dress shop had been open for business. She saw how much Lisa depended on Kyra's expertise. Cary was proud of her youngest daughter's modest, yet efficient, approach to offering assistance that went beyond a simple relationship between employer and employee. Lisa treated Kyra as an equal and Cary thought it was only a matter of time until Lisa officially offered Kyra a chance to buy in as a full partner. Cary hoped so and would be more than willing to give Kyra the money to do it if she ever asked for it.

Cary got into her car and pulled out onto the street. Earlier, when she hit town, her destination was the grocery store. But she had an alternate notion and came over to the dress shop, offering to buy lunch for Kyra and Lisa. It was a busy day at the shop and the girls declined the invitation. It appeared as though her outing would be confined to a quick grocery buying trip and then go right back home.

As she pulled off the street onto the grocery store parking lot, she saw Cletus Logan getting out of the dinged and dirty old pickup truck he and Dwayne shared. She was struck with a sudden rush of excitement. She felt her cheeks heat with embarrassment. School girl thoughts running through her head. She didn't need the aid of a mirror to know she blushed.

Cletus was not a big man—of average height and probably weighed less than a hundred-eighty pounds. He strode with the confident gait of a man half his age. Tie the swagger in with the heavily tanned face and arms, Cletus presented quite a fetching sight. Years of daily sun exposure had deepened the lines on his face, but that only added to his appeal. His hair was brown, slightly darker than Dwayne's, with ample gray in the sideburns and over his ears. The farm lifestyle had obviously been kind to his well-being and health.

Cary sped across the parking lot and rolled up next to him as he walked toward the front of the store. "Hey, cowboy, you planning on doing some cooking?"

He laughed. "Heck, no. I'm heading straight for the deli in the back of the store. I had to come to town to buy garden seed and thought I'd pick up something for supper this evenin'."

"Can you put it off for a while?"

Cletus stopped walking.

Cary braked to a full stop next to him.

He leaned against the window opening. "What do you have in mind?" he asked.

"You like Chinese food?"

"You bet. I can always go for a plate of Kung Pao somethin' or other."

Cary giggled. "Well, if you can put off the deli visit a while, I'd be happy buy your lunch at that little Chinese place on the corner."

Cletus stroked the whisker stubble beneath his chin with the backs of his fingers and stared off into space, as if giving it serious consideration. "Well, I'll tell ya." His eyes came back down to connect with hers. "You have just brightened my day by a factor of ten, or thereabouts. I think that's a dandy idea... thoughtful, too."

"Great. Hop in. I'll drive. It's only a few blocks."

Cletus hurried around the car and got in.

"Thanks for accepting the invitation. I thought I was doomed to spend the entire day alone. This makes a nice respite."

"I'll enjoy it as much as you... maybe more." He paused. "So, are you feeling settled in yet, and getting the hang of life on the South Plains?" he asked.

"Absolutely," she replied. Since Missy and Kyra have full-time careers, my job is taking care of that big house and doing the cooking."

He fixed a gaze on her and grinned.

She glanced, and then again. "What?"

"So, you're sayin' you're goin' to keep right on bein' a momma. Is that about right?"

She bounced a shoulder shrug. "We all do what we're good at and I happen to be *very* good at 'bein' a momma.' "

"I'll certainly not argue the point. You have two of the sweetest daughters I've ever known. I figure they didn't get that way all by themselves."

She pulled off the street and parked in front of the restaurant. "Let's go eat. I'm hungry."

True to his word, Cletus ordered the large portion of the Kung Pao chicken and cleaned his plate. Cary noticed him stealing glances at her almost every time she looked up from her meal. She relished the attention.

"How was your lunch?" she asked.

He pushed his plate back. "It was a great change of pace. All Dwayne ever wants when we come to town is some kind of steak—chicken fried, grilled, or broiled. Makes no difference to that boy, as long as it's beef."

"Meat and potatoes kind of guy, huh?"

"Somethin' like that. Still, he'll eat whatever I bring home for tonight, or he can chew on his tongue."

She snickered. "You're funny."

"The way I see it, with the way I look, I'd better have a sense of humor, especially in the presence of someone as beautiful as you."

Cary's smile remained but her eyes softened as her head drifted to a thought-ful slant. "Cletus, you have no reason whatsoever to question your appearance. You're very handsome, ruggedly so. And, just so you know. You are definitely the type I prefer."

She saw that her words had captured his attention, and the twinkle in his eye indicated a fantasy might be swimming around in that head of his. "Something on your mind?" she asked.

"As a matter of fact, yes. Would you care to go out on a real date with me?"

"I'm flattered you asked. I'd love to."

Once again, a smile stretched his face. "It would be nice to have a reason to use some of that cologne gathering dust in my bathroom and, girl, I can't think of a better reason than you." He suddenly frowned. "One little thing though; could we take your car? That old pickup truck of ours isn't exactly fit for datin'."

She laughed. "You are so funny."

Chapter Twenty-Three

A Mother's Love

Late afternoon daylight dimmed rapidly. Dwayne checked the seed boxes on the planter attached to the garden tractor he dubbed Festus. He came to the end of the final set of rows of his long garden. The last of the seeds had dropped through the chute into the soil at the same time. *Perfect.*

The sun slowly sank behind a billowing thunderhead in the western sky. The top on the cloud towered upward to at least forty thousand feet, taking on an anvil shape—never a good sign, usually indicating hail and high winds. In this part of Texas, particularly spring and early summer, storms came and went quickly, doing their worst in squall lines preceding fast moving Pacific fronts. But Dwayne heard a weather report earlier stating this front was expected to stall. It appeared that it might happen directly overhead. If so, they might be in for stormy weather until midnight or later. He refused to worry or complain about it, even considering stormy conditions. Getting a soaking rain after all those garden seeds had been planted would be needed and well-timed. He should get a quick stand of corn, black-eye peas, squash, watermelons, and cantaloupe. Dwayne looked across his cotton crop as he drove the little tractor toward the barn. Row after row of tender young cotton plants stood proud in quarter-mile rows and putting on occasional adult-size leaves. He turned eyes upward. *A little rain would be nice, Lord. But, if you see fit to do so, please hold the hail. Amen.*

Dwayne parked the tractor in the barn and walked toward the backdoor of the house. Cooler air from the approaching thunderstorms began mixing with sun-warmed air farther east, causing winds to pick up and gust, whipping loose sand, blowing it in streamers low to the ground. The chickens instinctively took the hint and returned to the coop. Each fresh wind gust was progressively cooler than the ambient air. The stark temperature difference caused Dwayne to shiver. *Dadgummit! I bet we do get hail out of this storm.*

He leaped up onto to the back porch of the house and slung open the screen door, closing the other door behind him. "Dad, are you home?"

"I'm in the bathroom."

Dwayne sniffed the air, noticing a pine and cedar wood scent filling the house. "What'd you do, bathe in cologne?"

"Well...sort of. I have a good reason to wear it now."

"Oh?"

"I have a date."

Dwayne hurried down the hall and stopped at the open bathroom door. His dad was examining his freshly shaven face while combing his hair. Dwayne grinned. "Well, Casanova, who's the lucky lady?"

"Cary," he said, flashing a toothy smile at the mirror while checking his brushing job, making sure they sparkled.

"Makes sense. I think we all saw this coming. But ya know what, Dad?"

"What?"

"A storm is on its way and getting close. I don't know what your plan is, but you may want to re-think the timing. You might not want to be on the road when that cloud gets here."

Dwayne suddenly had Cletus's full attention. "I haven't looked outside in a while. Does it really look that bad?"

Dwayne nodded. "Afraid so. The western sky is gettin' blacker now. It'll totally blot out the late afternoon sun in a matter of only a few more minutes."

Cletus pursed his lips and snorted. "Damn."

"Sorry. I didn't mean to pop that romantic bubble you've been inflating." He pulled off the green cap and scratched his temple. "Look, I promised Missy I'd go over to her place and help her with a project this evenin'. Why don't you go with me? You and Cary can stay in and go out another time. You two can have all the privacy you want. Heck, that house is huge. Besides, Missy and I would like to be left alone, too."

Cletus lifted an eyebrow. "Got some intimate plans, do ya?"

"Get your mind out of the gutter, old man. It's nothin' like that. Missy just has a problem she needs help with. That's all. And we don't want you or her mother barging in on us while we're figuring some things out."

Cletus grinned. "Yeah, right. *'Figurin'* things out,'" he said, clearly disbelieving Dwayne's motivation for privacy.

"Oh, for heaven's sake. That's enough of that. What do you say, goin' with me or not?"

"Sure. Why not? I can't think of a better way to sit out a storm. Cary and I can go to Lubbock another time."

***

Melissa hurried to answer the door and opened it to see Dwayne and his dad huddled together beneath a single raincoat as a shared umbrella. Strong wind and driving rain swirled around them. "Hurry. Come in," she said.

Cletus dragged spread fingers over his head as he followed Dwayne through the door and Melissa hastily closed it behind them. "Well, taking time to comb my hair was a waste of precious seconds," he said.

"I heard on the radio driving over that a strong cell west of Levelland with golf-ball size hail in it was on a southeasterly trek," Dwayne said. "It looks like that one might make it here."

Cary was descending the stairs toward the front door. "Cletus, it might be best if we stayed in this evening," she called out.

"Dwayne has already talked me into it. If it's okay with you, we can go out to dinner and a movie another time."

Relieved by the answer, Cary sighed. "My thoughts precisely."

"Dwayne," Melissa said, "why don't we let Mom and Cletus have the run of the house while you and I monopolize the library to work on that...problem."

"That sounds like a good idea," Cary said with a wink directed at Melissa, knowing what her daughter was about to attempt. "Cletus and I can put together something for dinner in the meantime."

"Sounds like a plan," Dwayne added. "Where's Kyra?"

"She had a date with Robert," Melissa replied. "I'm sure they're doing the same thing we are...staying in at his house in Brownfield," she added, walking toward the library door. She and Dwayne stepped through it into the library. Melissa closed the door securely behind them.

"So...are we ready to do this thing?" Dwayne asked.

Melissa drew a courage-building breath. "I'm about as ready as I'll ever be, I suppose."

Dwayne implied a smile. "It's certainly one way to create a little adventure on a dark and stormy night."

Melissa took his hand. She guided him to the center of the large room, then turned to fully face him. She took his other hand. Holding them both, she stared into his eyes and pulled him closer. She put her lips to his and kissed him—a deeply romantic kiss. "Thank you for agreeing to help me with this. It bears repeating, everything I've told you has been assumptions and snippets I picked up from conversations with Uncle Jack. I'm not sure what dangers we might encounter. Still want to help?"

"At your side is where I plan on stayin'. I don't care where or when it is." He gave her another quick kiss.

"Great answer."

"Get your engine started and let's do this."

She smiled. "You and your jokes...." She drew a deep breath and closed her eyes, concentrating on the memory of the place where she last saw William stumbling up that hill toward her, gasping for a good breath, bent on beating her, and probably with tightly packed fists. Through closed eyelids she detected the change of light in the library from soft amber to bright white. Her radiant heart awakened, as she developed a clear mental image of that place in that dimension.

"And there it is," Dwayne whispered while looking over his shoulder behind him, connected to her and seeing what she saw behind closed eyelids.

Melissa opened her eyes. The remembrance she had constructed in her mind was clearly visible, framed by the light. "Are you ready," she asked.

"Let's do it," Dwayne replied.

She wrapped her arms around his waist and walked him backwards.

Feeling the nausea flash herself, she heard Dwayne emit a faint groan, obviously feeling it at the same time.

The white light bloomed and then disappeared. The air texture instantly transformed. It was uncomfortably warm and humid. The flora appeared temperate; the air was calm, heavy with humidity. It felt tropical. It was her original conception of a horrible place to be lost in. The trees were tall, blocking the sun, if there was even a sun in the sky somewhere. A steamy haze hung below the lofty canopy, further blocking any view of the sky beyond. Virtually the entire forest floor was covered with a variety of tangled, thorny vines—not a hospitable environment—void of birds and wildlife. The only unencumbered path was the rocky ascent up the hill ending where she and Dwayne stood.

She detected movement. Her eyes shifted. There he was. William stumbled drunkenly up the hill toward her, cursing between gasps for breath, just as she had left him seven months ago, by her reckoning of time. That part of her assumption had been accurate. She had returned to the exact instant she exited this disgusting place to return to her own time and space. One major difference; this time she did not attempt to run or even step away.

Dwayne took a position in front of Melissa as her stepfather closed in on them.

William came to a stop a few feet down the hill from them. Gasping for a breath, he looked at Dwayne and blinked a few times, clearly uncertain of who or what he saw. "Who are you? And where the hell did you come from?" he slurred.

"My name is Dwayne. I'm Missy's friend and I'm here to help get you out of this place.

An awkward silence followed as William finally realized he had no idea where he was or how he had come to be here. Although his eyes floated in drunken pools, and appeared independent one from the other, enough lucidity returned that he finally took time to examine his surroundings, attempting to process what he saw. When she had shoved him into this dimension, William had been so intoxicated, and so intently focused on hurting her, he did not take time to realize he wasn't in his living room at home any longer. The presence of Dwayne shocked a modicum of rationality into him. Although inebriated almost to the point of blacking out, he clearly realized he had no clue where he was.

In an over-the-top gesture of friendliness, Dwayne closed the gap between them with an outstretched hand. "I am truly pleased to meet you Mister Blakely."

William's anger returned. "Get out of my way! That girl disrespected me, and I plan on disciplining her. I don't give a tinker's damn how old she is. She's not too big for a whipping." He shoved Dwayne's hand aside and began to continue up the hill toward Melissa.

Dwayne grabbed his arm and spun William around to face him. "Now, doggone it, Mister Blakely. When you sober, you'll see that it's the booze causing you to go off the rails like this. Don't do something you'll regret later."

"Let me go!" He rolled his hand into a tightly packed fist and swung a wide, arcing haymaker punch that missed Dwayne's face handily.

"Oh, for heaven's sake," Dwayne said. "You shouldn't have done that." In a fast move, he plowed a fist into William's jaw.

William's eyes rolled to white and he crumpled to the ground.

Dwayne looked back at Melissa. "Dang. I hope I didn't hit him too hard."

"You had no choice. His anger was alcohol driven and he would not have stopped otherwise."

Dwayne dropped onto his knee next to William's unconscious body. He rolled him over onto his back so that he would be in a more comfortable position when he regained consciousness. Dwayne removed his green John Deere cap, ran his fingers over the top of his hair, and replaced the cap, snugging it down. He sighed and shook his head. "I'm sure sorry I had to put you down like that, Mister Blakely. I was hopin' for a less vigorous solution."

"Between the alcohol and the punch, I think it's safe to say he'll be out for a while," Melissa said, as she turned to look farther up the hill. "Come up here. I want to show you something."

Dwayne came to his feet, dusted his blue denim clad knees, and walked up the hill to rejoin Melissa at her side. They stepped to a cliff's edge a few feet away.

She pointed. "See that beautiful scene the other side of the valley?"

"My goodness. It sure is colorful. The trees look healthier and the air clearer. What am I lookin' at?"

"Uncle Jack told me that we all have personal ideas of what we will see when we die. You are standing in a physical manifestation of *my* interpretation. On the day of your passing, which I hope is far, far in the future, you will see your own construct of how this place should appear. It is my opinion that since you are here in my version, yours will be similar when the time comes. Now, to answer your question; what you see the other side of the valley on that ridge is the edge of paradise, the gateway to permanent death. If you and I walked down into the valley and began crossing over to that side, we would hit a point of no return and neither of us would ever be able to come back to this side, the side of living. We would be in that place eternally."

Dwayne blew a breathy whistle. "That takes more brain power to contemplate than this ol' country boy possesses. I can't get my mind wrapped around it."

"That makes two of us and I'm the one that brought you here. I still have trouble grasping the magnitude of what I'm capable of or what we're looking at right now."

"Speaking of your capability, what are you going to do with your ol' stepdaddy?"

Melissa drew a long, slow breath, and went silent. She stared across the valley. Finally, "I still need to work out the logistics. First, I need to keep in mind William will remember having been here, although he won't have a clue where *here* is. Secondly, I need to get him back to Coos Bay but I don't think I can return him to his time because of my brothers. As far as they were concerned, there father left Mom and fell off the grid after Thanksgiving last year. I can't change their past. So, it would seem I will have created a paradox should I attempt it. It would be William's present but my brothers' past, which I cannot change. I have a feeling William would simply pop out of that scenario and end up right back here once you and I leave and go home. He would only exist in that previous time as long as I am there making his presence happen." She paced away, thinking about the situation, uncertain how to handle it.

"Let's look at this logically," Dwayne offered. "He's nearly blind drunk and unconscious. That's a stone-cold fact. Your brothers believe he ran away from home, abandoning your mother. How about you drop him on the streets of a large city, Seattle for example, in the present time—our time. Maybe near a homeless shelter, so he would have a place to sleep and be able to get something to eat. He will have no idea how he got there, but he is drunk after all."

"That might work. I can call Charlie and Johnny and tell them that we were contacted and notified he was found wandering the streets, lost. And, then I can tell them he has no idea what he had been doing for the past seven months. That would serve two purposes. It would encourage my brothers to get him into rehab *and* make William believe his brain had finally fried from years of heavy drinking. I can't think of a better way to shock sense into the man than make him believe he lost seven months of his life and all he has is a nightmarish memory of chasing me in a hot, humid forest in a fit of anger."

"Seattle?"

"Sure. That's as good a choice as any. It's about four hundred miles up the coast. That would be about right. Why not?"

"Can you conjure a location to take us?"

"Let me say it will be interesting to try. Although I have been to Seattle a few times, it was never in search of a homeless shelter. So, I don't have a memory I can recall to create a useful image."

"How about the center of the city, downtown?"

"I'll give that a shot, and...well, we'll have to wait and see how it goes."

Melissa stood on one side of William lying unconscious on the ground. Dwayne faced her standing on the other side of him. She reached across and held both of Dwayne's hands. "Let's try it," she said. Closing her eyes, she relaxed her mind and thought of her last visit to Seattle a few years ago. It was easy enough to see a mind's-eye image of the downtown area. With that image fixed in her mind, she thought about a homeless shelter, silently questioning where one might be in the downtown area, or nearby. Suddenly, as if the universe knew her wishes, a broad alley appeared. Next to a dumpster, mounted to a brick wall and extending perpendicular to it, a faded sign hung like a tin shingle and moved gently back and forth, responding to a breeze. It hung over a plain, rust-streaked metal door. The sign read:

SIDESTREET OUTREACH CENTER

Helping the indigent since 1979

Donations Welcome

"And there it is," she whispered. "Exactly what we need and we need it synchronized with our time." She noticed the whitish glow develop. In a measured way, the glow enveloped the three of them and brightened. "Stay close to me.

I need you to drag William as we move toward that image, so we all arrive together."

He bent and tucked his fingers inside the waistband of William's pants and grabbed his arm with his free hand. "Let's go."

They only moved a couple of steps and the white light flared then disappeared. The air was blessedly drier and cooler—the sky brilliantly clear overhead between tall buildings on both sides. They stood in the shadow of those buildings.

"Okay, we need to work fast. I don't want William regaining consciousness and see us here," she said. She turned and hurried toward the door into the outreach center and went in.

She stepped inside and saw two men facing one another at a small, heavily scarred table, both holding spoons and hunks of bread, eating soup. A checkerboard lay between them. It appeared they had stopped mid-game to eat. She saw another man standing farther back. He did not appear homeless—clean shaven and wearing khaki pants, a shirt tucked neatly into them. "Excuse me, sir. Are you in charge here?"

"Yes. I'm Artie. I manage this outreach center. Can I help you?"

"I wanted to let you know there is a man lying unconscious just outside your door. He's the one in need of help."

"Thanks for the heads-up. I'll take care of him. God bless you."

Melissa smiled warmly. "Have a wonderful day."

She hurried outside and over to Dwayne, still standing over William. She grabbed him by the hand and yanked him into a trot behind her. "Come on. Let's get out of sight and go home."

Moving swiftly down the alley, Melissa slowed and glanced back.

William was stirring.

Artie, the outreach manager, stepped outside and knelt next to him to check him over.

Seeing William was in good hands, she again began to trot, coming upon a recessed door set back into the brick wall. "Here. This is good enough." She pulled Dwayne into the alcove behind her and out of sight. She wrapped her arms around him and hugged him affectionately. "You are magnificent. If it weren't for you, I'd still be wondering how to handle the situation and probably be petrified of doing the wrong thing. But I think this is the best of all possible solutions. Thanks so much for the idea." She smiled. "You're a pretty smart cookie. Did you know that?"

He snickered. "I suspected it."

She pressed the side of her head onto his chest and thought about home and the library in the Dane mansion. In the blink of an eye, they were back.

Melissa looked up into Dwayne's eyes. "I'm hungry. How about you?"

"Oh yeah."

They stepped into the hall in time to see Cletus and Cary walking toward the kitchen. Cletus reared his head, surprised. "I thought y'all had a problem that needed working out."

Dwayne blurted, "Shoot, we already—"

"We already decided it could wait until another time," Melissa said, interrupting.

Dwayne cringed as he realized that no appreciable time had passed—only seconds, maybe a minute, since they walked into the library and closed the door. Although, he and Melissa had been away for more than half of an hour and he came back with bruised knuckles on his right hand.

Melissa looked at her mother and winked.

Cary offered a questioning eyebrow lift.

Melissa nodded affirmation. "Mom, could I have a quick word with you in private?"

"Sure. Cletus, why don't you and Dwayne go on to the kitchen? We'll be right behind you in a minute."

Melissa and her mother watched the men turn into the kitchen.

"Well?" Cary asked.

Melissa detailed what she and Dwayne had done. "Now, it would be best if you called Charlie and Johnny and tell them we were notified by authorities their father has been identified and found wandering the streets of Seattle in a stupor. And, maybe, advise them to take him back to Coos Bay and get him into rehab. I have a strong feeling that a perceived seven-month gap in his memory will make him amenable to the plan without argument."

"I'll do it," Cary said. "And then, before I even set the phone down, I'll be calling an attorney and filing for divorce which, honestly, I should have taken care of months ago." She looked toward the kitchen door, adding, "I want to see where this thing with Cletus might go and I don't need a failed marriage hovering over me like that storm cloud outside."

Lightning flashed followed by rumbling thunder.

"Let's go cook something," Melissa said. "I'm starving."

Chapter Twenty-Four

A Sister's Secret

Cary's phone call to her boys had the desired effect. Within the week Charlie went to Seattle, picked up William, and returned him to Coos Bay. According to Charlie, William indeed had no memory of what he had been doing for seven months and, frankly, it took considerable convincing to make him believe the time had passed. But once he had no choice but believe, it was easy to get him to agree to a detoxification clinic for rehabilitation. Apparently, William was scared, very scared by the memory lapse. When Cary heard this, she couldn't prevent, or want to stop, the smile of satisfaction that spread across her face upon hearing the news.

The older brother became convinced William needed serious psychiatric care. It was added to the rehab stint. Cary covered the expenses for the sake of her sons.

Cary sat on the patio at the rear of the big house, enjoying the morning sunshine sipping a cup of coffee when the cell phone on the small, round table next to her sounded off. She snatched it up and saw Charlie's name in the display. They exchanged pleasantries. Then the conversation turned to William.

"How is Johnny handling your father's condition?" Cary asked.

Charlie sighed. "Not well. He can't understand how Dad could have simply lost seven months of his life. Frankly, Mom, I can't either. There are so many questions. How did he survive on the streets of Seattle for that long before

"

anyone noticed? How did he buy food? He had no money. Heck, he didn't even have identification on him. His clothes showed no signs of deterioration and mostly clean. His shirt and pants should have been in tatters...at least filthy. They weren't. Why not? This situation, the whole thing, is weird."

"I don't know the answers to those questions," she lied. "I suspect it's a form of alcohol induced amnesia. He may have been lucid and functioning up until the bender that wrecked his mind, which might have been recently. He may recall it all someday during the course of psychiatric therapy and prolonged sobriety. That's as close to an answer as I can get, and it's only a guess at that. Try not to worry too much about it. You have him back now. And that's what counts."

"You sure sound calm about it all."

"He's yours and Johnny's father and I love him for giving you boys to me, but I do not miss him or his abuse at all. The love I once had for him as a husband and partner in life is totally depleted. That's probably why you're hearing a lack of concern in my voice. I wish him well and hope he can get his life together, with you and Johnny in it. As for me, I want no more to do with him and will be fine never having to see him again."

"Do you still want me to keep you up with his progress?"

"For the sake of you boys, yes."

"Love you, Mom."

"Love you, too. Tell Johnny to hang in there and that I love him."

"I will. Talk to you soon." He hung up.

Cary continued holding the phone a moment longer, tapping her teeth with it, concerned about the conundrum she was creating for herself. She wanted her boys to maintain the relationship with their father and she wanted to stay in close touch, but not at all with William. There would be no way around it. William would always be at the periphery of her life—not an appealing thought.

She heard the rustling of a bush at the corner of the house and turned to see Cletus walking toward her. "Good morning, Cletus." She held up her coffee mug as a gesture. "Care for a cup? I'd be happy to pour you one."

"Thanks, but no. I have too much work to do, but it does sound a heap better than sloppin' hogs and choppin' weeds out of the garden. I had attached a little cultivator to Festus and was plowing out the middles in the garden. Since I was working so close and saw you sitting here, I thought I'd walk over and say good morning."

Her smile beamed. "You have no idea how happy it makes me that you would take the time."

"The way I see it, you're worth makin' time for." He grinned. "But not too much time. I still better pass on the coffee. Say, have you ever done any canning or other types of food preservation?"

"Jams and jellies a few times but, otherwise, no."

He tossed a thumb over his shoulder back towards the garden. "Well, that patch still has a couple of months to go, but I'd say that you and I have a date with some canning jars in our future. Never enjoyed pickin' and preservin' vegetables. Usually, we would eat fresh out of the garden and let the rest of it go at the end of the season. But now, I have a reason to spend time with you and end up with good garden veggies for the cold months."

"That actually sounds fun."

"Now that you'll be joining me this year, it sounds fun to me, too."

"I'll be looking forward to it. You still owe me dinner and a movie, you know."

"Hey, lovely lady, far as I'm concerned, we can do that every weekend till the beans are ready to pick. I'll be bangin' on your front door about six o'clock Saturday. If that's okay with you."

"Absolutely."

He lifted her hand and kissed the back of it. "Well, I need to get back to work, if I plan on finishin' that chore today." He turned and sauntered away.

As Cary stared at his back, a tingling shudder of joy coursed through her when she realized that, finally, unrealized happiness may be in her future.

213

Chapter Twenty-Five

A New Day

"**I** don't know where he is, Mom," Charlie said, "But Johnny is freaking out."

Holding the phone tight to her ear, Cary pinched the bridge of her nose. She struggled to prevent lack of interest to shade her tone. She sighed. "Tell Johnny not to worry. Your dad probably got tired of confinement in that rehab center and took a break for a few days. I'm sure he'll be back."

"He should have at least filled us in on his plan if a few days away was his intent. He didn't...not a word. That's why Johnny thinks something bad may have happened. And, frankly, I'm sort of wondering about that, too."

"Remember, the detoxification stint in rehab and the psychiatric care were all voluntary. William didn't have to stay if he didn't want to. Apparently, he didn't want to." Cary paused. "Are you sure he didn't give clues that would have indicated why he suddenly left, or where he may have gone?"

"Not that I can think of. Since he sobered up, all he's been talking about is feeling terrible for having treated us so badly, especially you, Mom. Sometimes, when Johnny and I would go see him, all he could talk about was wanting to apologize and beg for forgiveness."

"It's nice to hear he feels that way. When he comes back, tell him I've already forgiven him, but that doesn't change anything. Our life together is over. I've moved on. He should, too. I hope he continues therapy. And, although he's been sober for six weeks, he could relapse any time. That's the most worrisome thing. He walked away and left his support system behind. The man may be strong as a bull physically, but he's weak-willed, and would fall into old habits quickly. I know him too well."

Buried within a sign, "You're right. You always are." He paused. "Well, I'd better get to work. It's getting late. I'll call and let you know when he comes home."

"Thanks, kiddo. I appreciate that. Love you."

"Love you, too, Mom."

The comment of appreciation was for Charlie's benefit. She didn't care if the boys ever saw the man again. To her way of thinking, if he disappeared of his own volition this time, it would just be William showing his usual lack of concern for anyone's feelings but his own. Drunk or sober, she didn't believe he would, or could, change. Personality quirks hardened over decades. She believed firmly that quirks had burrowed in like irretrievable ticks. The boys would hurt for a time but would be better off without his presence.

Cary turned thoughts to planning the day. It was easier to think about such things outside. She poured another cup of coffee and headed back to the patio. As she walked through the French doors at the rear of the house, she automatically looked toward Cletus's house. Rekindled feelings for the man were deepening. It was now the end of the first week in July—the weather warm, but not unseasonably so. She and Cletus had gone out every Saturday evening for five consecutive weekends, although there still had been no intimacy. She didn't mind. Simply having a man close who truly cared for her was enough for now. A man she could depend on—a guy who would love her for who she was and not what she could do for him.

They had been blessed with regular rains, which she didn't see as unusual because of where she had come from. But Cletus informed her regular summer rains on the South Plains only happened in unusual years. The corn was tall and loaded with ears in the milk stage. The stalks had grown to six feet or more—tall enough to partially block a view of Cletus's stucco house and surrounding yard. Still, she searched the area behind that house, trying to catch a glimpse of him. She didn't have to search long. Cletus was walking down a row in the garden.

With a light heart and a big smile, Cary took off walking across the cotton rows toward the garden next to the Logan house. She was in the garden when Cletus finally noticed.

"Hey, Cary. Good morning," he said.

"Mornin', Cletus," she drawled in her idea of a Texas accent. It amused her that the suffix *ing* seemed to have been banished from the local lingo. A pleasant rush of good feelings created a rosy glow for this ruggedly handsome farmer. "Anything ready to pick yet?"

"You betcha. We have green beans, yellow squash, cucumbers, and, I believe, the corn is at the roasting-ear stage. The squash and cucumbers are a bit small, but a good size for pickling. You want to help me pick a few? We can do a little canning later today, if you have the time and the desire."

"I think that's a wonderful idea." She poured out the remaining coffee in her mug. "I'll go back to the house and get my straw hat. I'll be right back."

When Cary walked through the patio French doors into her house, she heard the distinctive ringtone of her cell phone. It lay in the kitchen a few steps from where her favorite broad-brimmed gardening hat was hanging. She snatched it off the wall peg and whirled around and picked up her phone from the countertop. The name in the display shocked her. *William? Really?*

It made not one iota what the man had to say, it would destroy her good mood. She punched the icon to send it to voicemail. She sought only to spend the day with Cletus.

***

She and Cletus filled three large grocery sacks with squash, cucumbers, and green beans by mid-day.

"Let's take the veggies to my house," Cary told him. "Our kitchen is larger and would be easier to set up a makeshift assembly line."

"Sounds good," he replied. "Rita, rest her soul, may not have been the easiest woman to get along with, but she sure knew how to cook. I have her pickling recipes. While you're doing the prep work, I'll run into Brownfield and pick up vinegar, salt, sugar, and the spices we'll need. How's that for a plan?"

"I can't think of a better one," she said, offering the broadest smile she could. Cletus left.

Cary began the busy work of setting things up. After about fifteen minutes, while humming a tune, she washed and trimmed squash and cucumbers, and was in the midst of snapping green beans when the throaty bongs of the doorbell sounded. She snatched up a small towel and dried her hands as she hurried toward the front door.

"For heaven's sake, Cletus," she called out, "you don't need to be ringing the doorbell." She yanked the door open. "Just come on—"

It wasn't Cletus. William stood smiling on the porch.

Cary drew a shocked breath. "William? What are you doing here?" She didn't attempt to hide displeasure at his sudden appearance.

"I needed to talk to you, and over the phone was not the way to do it."

"You *did* get the divorce papers, right?"

"Yes. That's what I want to talk to you about."

"There's nothing to discuss. All I want is for you to sign the papers, so both of us can get on with our lives."

"Please, let me apologize for my behavior. It was abominable. I know. But, I'm clean now. No alcohol has passed these lips in weeks. It made me realize how much I love you and how I screwed it up. Will you forgive me?"

She sighed and relaxed. "Of course. I already have." His words of contrition touched her. She smiled. "Look, I know you've traveled a great distance for this. Why don't you come on in for a few minutes? I'll fix a fresh pot of coffee."

William followed her into the house and down the hall into the kitchen. She gestured toward a stool on the opposite side of the island where she had been snapping green beans. "Have a seat."

He looked around. "I had forgotten how big this place is."

"Yeah. There's plenty of room for the girls and me. Room enough so that everyone can have complete privacy." Cary poured water through the top of the coffee maker and turned it on.

"How are Missy and Kyra?"

"Doing great. Missy has a practitioner's position at a clinic in Lubbock and Kyra works at a dress shop in Brownfield. I think Kyra may be offered a chance to buy into the shop. I'll help her if it's offered. We've settled in nicely. I love it here."

William's face turned pensive. He dropped his head and stared at his hands flat upon the counter top. "Cary?"

"Yeah?"

"I haven't signed those divorce papers."

"What? Why not?"

"I was hoping you and I could work things out and give our marriage another chance."

Cary stiffened, now that she knew William's visit went deeper than apologizing and getting forgiveness. "William, we can never go back. I'm sorry," she replied, as gently as her nervous voice allowed.

William slid off the back of the stool. "I understand your hesitance," he said, coming to her side of the island.

As he came to a stop in front of her, the proximity intimidated her. She began back-stepping.

As she did, he quickened his approach. "Look, sweetheart, I know I can make you happy." He reached for her hand. "Now that I've got my life in order."

She put both hands out of reach behind her back. "Please, William, don't come any closer. You're scaring me."

"Oh, baby, it can be good again." He got a hand on the crook of her elbow, bringing her to a standstill. "I'll be better."

Cary attempted to wrench her arm from of his grasp. It only encouraged him to grab her other arm and pull her in close. "Please, William, stop it," she begged. "If our marriage was destined to work, it would have long before your temper ruined everything. It didn't."

"I'll make it work," he whispered, leaning in to kiss her.

A whine escaped from deep in her throat. She tried again to back away from his hold on her. The genesis of her struggle encouraged him to squeeze her arms to a painful degree. "You're hurting me."

"Just let it happen, sweetheart." He squeezed tighter and pulled her closer.

Cary panicked. She now fought to be free of his grasp.

William had no choice but to release her or wrench her arms from their sockets. Once free of his hold, Cary slapped him across the face. The act was born of fear not thought. Her own visceral reaction shocked her. She froze.

William was no less shocked, but quickly metamorphosed into anger. He shoved her hard.

She stumbled backwards, hitting the back of her head on the kitchen counter as she went down. Although conscious, she was dazed. She moaned.

***

Cletus parked his old pickup in front of the Dane mansion behind a car he didn't recognize, a spiffy looking, late model, blue Ford Fusion bearing the emblem of a rental company on its rear bumper. He figured it belonged to a salesman of some kind and gave it no further attention. He carried a sack full of canning supplies in one arm and a gallon jug of vinegar in the other.

After fumbling with the doorknob, he shouldered the door open and went in. "Okay, Cary, I think I have everything we'll need to get started," he called out. He turned the corner into the kitchen and saw William standing over Cary.

She lay sprawled on the floor and terrified, covering her head with both hands. "What the hell...?"

"Get out of here!" William bellowed. "This has nothing to do with you."

Cletus disregarded William's demand and continued advancing. "That's where you're wrong, you crazy bastard. Everything that happens inside *this* house has nothing to do *with you*."

Cletus dropped the sack and lunged at William, swinging the gallon plastic jug of vinegar. It connected with the side of the bigger man's head, blowing the cap off and drenching William with the sour smelling, acidic liquid.

William spun away but caught himself on the countertop.

Cletus was already on him before William could regain his balance. He swung a packed right fist into William's jaw and immediately countered with a left to the other side of his face.

Cary regained her wits and snatched her cell phone from atop the center island and dialed, just as Cletus drove a strong uppercut into William's stomach with such power it forced William high on his toes.

William violently exhaled all the air from his lungs with an agonized groan and wheeze. Doubled and dazed, William held the countertop to maintain balance while recouping his wind.

Cletus stalked him, fully intent on delivering as much damage as he could. Once he saw Cary lying helpless and frightened on the floor, he lost all reason. Blind rage ruled.

William saw the chef's knife Cary had been trimming and slicing squash with. He snatched it from the countertop. Vinegar impairing his vision, he blindly swung it in a wide arc at Cletus. It connected, slicing open his abdomen.

Cletus discontinued his attack and stumbled backward, but not fast enough.

On the backswing, William plunged the blade into the soft tissue below Cletus's ribcage, stabbing deeply.

Cletus looked down and realized his hand pressing against the slash across his belly was all that held the viscera in. Suddenly dazed, he backed up to the counter and slid down to sit on the floor, wide-eyed and scared. Blood from the stab wound spread quickly across his shirt.

Still dazed from Cletus's vicious beating, William looked at the large knife in his hand. He tossed it onto the center island of the kitchen and vigorously rubbed flattened palms on the sides of his legs, as if attempting to wipe away complicity. "Oh shit," he mumbled and ran stumbling from the house.

With the phone against her ear, Cary hurried over and dropped to her knees beside Cletus, getting her first look at the wounds. She whimpered. "Oh no, no, no."

Dwayne answered her call. "What's up, Cary?"

"Get to my house as quickly as you can! Your father has been stabbed." She began to cry. "It's bad, really bad." She wept.

***

Not taking time for an explanation of circumstances, Dwayne ended the call and dialed 911. "What's your emergency?" came the quick response.

"My dad has been stabbed and we need emergency medical attention and the Sheriff's department at the Dane mansion northeast of Meadow as quickly as possible."

We have two sheriff's deputies on another call in Meadow. It may take up to twenty minutes for EMTs. But the deputies can be there in a couple of minutes."

Dwayne snapped the flip phone closed and shoved it into his pocket. Simultaneously, he engaged the hydraulic powerlift on the big John Deere tractor and lifted the plows from the ground.

He had been cultivating a patch of cotton at the farthest corner of the farm. There was no alternative on the route he must take to get back quickly. Dwayne steered the behemoth tractor around and aimed it at the Dane mansion in a straight line across the cotton rows, crushing the growing plants beneath the massive tires.

Approaching the big house, he saw a man running awkwardly toward a blue car parked in front of his old truck.

Dwayne adjusted his course and drove straight for the front of the house and onto the driveway fronting the mansion. He stopped less than a foot in front of the car and blocked it between the truck and the tractor. He flung open the tractor cab door and dropped to the ground, racing for the driver's side door of the Ford.

Apparently, the man took a few seconds too long to determine he couldn't make his getaway, not in that car.

Dwayne jerked open the door and grabbed two fists full of his windbreaker jacket and yanked him out of the car onto his butt on the asphalt of the paved driveway. He was stunned to see who the guy was. William Blakely was barely recognizable when sober. "I don't know what you're doin' here, but it's obvious you're the reason for the mayhem."

"Get your damn hands off me!" Blakely growled through clenched teeth. He had a bloody nose and red streaking from the corner of his mouth. Whatever happened inside the house, this guy didn't get away unscathed. Blakely had taken hard shots to the face. "You have no right to keep me from leaving," he added, quickly coming to his feet.

"Oh, but that's where you're wrong, buddy."

The bigger man lunged at Dwayne and took a swing at him.

Dwayne didn't allow the follow-through of Blakely's fist to complete before plowing his own clenched fist directly into the guy's already bloody nose.

Blakely stumbled backwards into the side of the car, blinking his eyes wildly. He was dazed.

"Dadgummit, man! You have a skull like granite," Dwayne said, shaking the pain from his knuckles.

Dwayne grabbed Blakely's windbreaker front with one hand, holding the other fist tightly clenched, fully prepared to punch him again. "Friend, it makes no difference if you're conscious or not. Although, it'd be easier on me if you weren't, and I know it'd be easier on you, because I'm a hair-breadth away from re-arranging your facial bone structure, definitely softening it some. Which will it be?"

Dwayne glanced up at the road and noticed the rooster tail of dust coming from beneath two rapidly approaching black and white SUVs—Terry County sheriff's vehicles.

Unfortunately, William saw them, too. He panicked and tried to run.

Dwayne hooked his toe in front of the man's foot, tripping Blakely onto his belly on the asphalt surface. He dropped onto Blakely holding a knee into his back before he had a chance to lift himself up, just as the lead sheriff's unit came to a stop.

"Get off me!" Blakely shouted.

"Not gonna happen," Dwayne replied.

Deputy Dale Burns leaped out and ran toward them.

"Hey, Dale. Hold this guy, would you? I have to get inside and check on Dad. I think this yahoo stabbed him."

"Go on, Dwayne. I've got this," the deputy replied as he removed a set of handcuffs from his belt.

Once Deputy Burns had control of Blakely, Dwayne leaped up and ran through the open front door into, the house. "Cary," he shouted, "Where are y'all?"

"Kitchen," came the shouted reply.

As Dwayne rounded into the kitchen, he saw his dad sitting on the floor leaning back against the cabinet below the sink. He was tipping sideways, legs splayed wide. Cary held a blood-soaked towel against his abdomen.

"We've got to get him to a hospital," Cary screeched, sobbing.

Dwayne took a knee on the other side of the elder Logan and lifted the edge of the towel. "Crap, this is a whole lot worse than I thought it'd be."

"Harley Danvers, the deputy from the other vehicle rushed into the kitchen and stood over the three of them. "It doesn't look like we have time to wait on the EMTs," he told them. "Come on, Dwayne. Let's get Cletus into the back of my Explorer. We have to get him to the hospital as quickly as possible. From what I can see, we'd better not waste any time. He's already lost a dangerous amount of blood."

With great care, Dwayne and Harley moved Cletus's around so they could carry him, Cletus lost consciousness and went limp.

Dwayne noticed blood on the back of Cary's head. "How about you, Cary? Are you okay?"

"Don't worry about me," she replied, whimpering. "I just hit my head on the counter when William shoved me and I fell backwards. It's a little bloody. That's all. I'm okay. Get your dad some help. Oh, God, please hurry," she rattled as fast as her lips could form the words.

As Harley took Cletus's shoulders, he backed toward the front door while Dwayne held his dad's feet. Cary followed along beside them, continuing to hold a towel against the wounds.

As they made their way down the sidewalk in front of the house toward Danvers's unit, Deputy Burns was shoving Blakely, hands cuffed at his back, into the backseat of his black and white SUV.

Blakely craned his head around Burns to see Cary holding a bloody towel against Cletus's belly. "Cary," Blakely called out, "I'm sorry. I didn't mean for any of this to happen."

"Missy should have *never* brought you back. You should have stayed dead to this world," she snarled, and then shouted, "Go straight to hell, William! Stay out of my life!"

Dwayne captured Cary's attention. He frowned and gave her a fast negative shake of the head.

Deputy Danvers looked curiously at Cary and then to Dwayne. "Back from where?" he asked.

"Oh, he...uh...may be sober now, but William Blakely was a violent alcoholic. It appears he is just as volatile when he's sober. She was talking about his stint in rehab. Right, Cary?"

Cary stared into Cletus's unconscious face. "Yeah. That's right," she mumbled.

Dwayne followed her gaze to his dad's lolling head. *You're too young to be checking out on me, old man. Hang in there.*

Chapter Twenty-Six

Unfinished Business

"**K**yra?"

"What's up, Missy?"

"Mom called a few minutes ago and said the Sheriff's Department took Cletus Logan to the emergency room in Brownfield. She told me he sustained a severe knife wound in the abdomen." Melissa resisted the strain in her voice as she spoke to her sister on the phone. She raced southward on her way to the hospital in Brownfield from the clinic where she worked in Lubbock.

"Knife wound? Was it an accident?"

"You're not going to believe this, but William showed up on Mom's doorstep this morning and tried to convince her to come back to him. When she refused, it angered him and shoved her stumbling backwards. She fell and banged her head on the edge of the counter on her way down, just as Cletus walked in on them. Cletus and Dwayne are alike in that neither of them walk away from a fight. When Cletus saw Mom go down, all hell broke loose."

"Oh, crap…"

"'Oh, crap' is right."

"What about Dad?"

"Arrested. I'm sure he'll be charged with assault and battery at least. According to what Mom told me about the severity of the wound, it might be upgraded to manslaughter. William, the bastard, will do prison time for this, possibly many years if Cletus doesn't make it. Cletus went right into emergency surgery to repair lacerations in his bowel and stomach. But the doctors are not even attempting to suture his open belly wound. They're certain they'll have to go back in and do a thorough cleaning of the area. He lost too much blood, and they don't want to do such an extensive mop-up of the cavity in his weakened condition. It's not looking good, Kyra…not at all. Cletus is in extremely critical condition."

"I'll meet you at the hospital," Kyra said.

"I'm only about five minutes out. I'll see you in a few."

When Melissa steered into the parking lot of the Brownfield Regional Medical Center, she noticed Kyra's white Ford Taurus and drove to the open parking spot next to it, and then noticed her sister's long strawberry blond hair flagging in the breeze as she hurried toward the front of the building. Melissa got out of her SUV and followed. She caught up to her sister at the reception desk.

"Come on, Missy. It's this way."

They hurried past a series of glass walls with glass doors, some with curtains drawn, others open. Emergency electronics were beeping and dinging in most of the rooms. Gravely ill patients wired to machines with tubes down noses and throats were in rooms they had a view of. They came upon one with the curtains drawn open. Dwayne stood on one side of a bed where Cletus lay. The elder Logan was clearly unconscious. Cary sat on the other side. Their mother held Cletus's hand, pressing the back of it to her forehead. She seemed to be massaging her forehead with his hand. She was crying. It appeared to Melissa as though her mother attempted imparting thoughts by touch directly into Cletus's mind.

Melissa's manic rush ceased. She slowed, introducing a level of respectful solemnity to her stride, not wanting to disturb anyone unnecessarily. She held Kyra's hand and they eased into the room together.

Melissa quietly moved in next to Dwayne. "How is he?"

Dwayne stood staring down at his dad and did not answer, expressionless. After a time, he responded with a negative head shake. His face unchanging. "The doctor said all we can do is wait. Dad lost a dangerous amount of blood, plus his abdominal cavity has been highly contaminated with bile and fecal matter. He is so weak that the doctors want to wait for his strength to improve before they go back in to fix the contamination problem. Serious infection has now become equal to his current problems. They gave him a large transfusion and are going to observe him for a time. The gash across his belly was only temporarily stapled."

Dwayne finally turned toward her and pulled her into an embrace, whispering, "We were told to be expecting the worst. He may never regain consciousness."

"It was my fault," Cary blurted and sobbed, as she slid off the bed and sat in a chair next to it, her forehead remaining against the back of Cletus's hand.

"Don't say that," Kyra told her. "It was *all* dad's fault. We knew his temper would get him into trouble someday." She knelt beside her mother's chair and leaned her head onto Cary's shoulder, adding, "I just never thought he'd be so quick to anger while sober."

"I—I don't understand why I couldn't foresee this," Melissa muttered. "I don't understand at all. It's as though what I see is selected for me by a force greater than me. Why not this? What made this event so different?" Although spoken aloud, Melissa expected no answer.

Cary lifted her head slowly and focused on her older daughter, "Missy, do you think Cletus is in that place right now? You know, the place between life and death?"

"I don't know," Melissa replied.

Cary animated and stood. She gazed down at Cletus's ashen face. "What if he's passing over right now? If he is, I have to say goodbye." She looked at her oldest daughter with laser-like intensity. "Missy, you have to take me. You *must* take me there. You just have to. I have to know," she begged.

"Mom, I'm not so sure that's a good idea."

"I'm not losing someone else I love without the chance of saying goodbye, if I know it's possible. It's simply too much to bear in a single lifetime," Cary said, reflecting on the violent death of her first husband and the girls' biological father, Kyle, to a mentally deranged foster father. Melissa was only four and Cary was pregnant with Kyra at the time. Cary's face distorted in anguish.

Melissa glanced at Dwayne and then over to Kyra. Neither argued for or against Cary's wishes. Everyone in the room knew it was possible.

"If you want to try it," Dwayne said, "I'd like to go along, too."

Melissa silently considered it. Finally, "I suppose it is a blessing afforded to a precious few on this planet. I just happen to be one of them." She drew a breath and sighed. "Okay, I'll do it."

"I have a question," Kyra said. "If you take Cletus to that dimension, won't he still be unconscious and uncommunicative there as well?"

"The way Uncle Jack described the passing of our father, his physical body never left Mom's arms but, even in that moment, he was swimming that lake to paradise on the other side. So, it would seem, if Cletus is nearing death, his body will still be here in this bed, but his essence, life force, soul...whatever you wish to call it will be there already. So, I'll just be taking the four of us. We, of course, will be in that place as a physical presence, nothing ethereal about our bodies. We'll have to find out the rest when we get there." She turned to her younger sister. "Kyra, do you want to go, too."

"No, that's okay. You three go on. I'll stay here." She hinted a smile. "I know you won't be gone long."

"True enough. We will literally be back in the time span of a single eye-blink...your eye, not ours." As she spoke, Melissa took Dwayne's hand and they moved to the other side of Cletus's bed, Melissa in the center, Dwayne on the right, her mother on the left. She draped her arms over their shoulders. "Okay, Mom...Dwayne...are you guys ready for this?"

Cary continued to cry and simply nodded affirmation.

"Let's do it," Dwayne replied.

Melissa closed her eyes, chin sinking to near her chest as she developed the necessary mental image of their destination. The place she wanted to end up was the cliff overlooking the valley separating life from death.

Even with her eyes closed, she felt the instant the radiant heart began to work. But, there was a stark difference when she saw the glow through her closed eyelids. The trademark chill that usually washed over her was absent. What she felt was warmth—comforting warmth. Although never having felt it before, she knew her radiant heart had unlocked a deep sense of love that cloaked them.

With her arms around her mother and Dwayne, she coaxed them to take a single forward step. This time there was no nausea flash, but a full body tingle as she opened her eyes to the reality of the dimension where she had transported them. As desired, they stood at the precipice of the cliff looking across a valley to a ridge on the other side that despite the distance was, not only visible, but perfectly detailed—brilliant and colorful.

God's light streamed in fanning rays from between high clouds, spotlighting innumerable points of beauty. Trees swayed gently to breezes she could not feel. Beautiful birds soared high in the sky and from treetop to treetop. Beneath the canopies lay animals—many animals—predator and prey lying together, clearly content. People mingled among them.

In contrast, they stood in a near colorless and seemingly lifeless place—warm and uncomfortably humid. There was no sunlight, only dusk-like dimness that made the stale air feel even more intense. A distant odor of things decaying was all around them.

After gazing and gawking for a time, Cary disengaged from Melissa's embrace and began a serious search for Cletus. "Where is he, Missy? I don't see him," she said, while turning a full circle.

Melissa scanned the valley, then along the ridge, looking to see if Cletus might be making his way across or, possibly, already there. Suddenly, she caught sight of a human form standing on the ridge on the other side. She had visually swept that area several times without seeing it, but now it seemed to have suddenly appeared. After a brief time, she recognized it as a man coming into sharper focus. "Oh no," she muttered.

Cary spun around to face the same direction. "What is it?" What do you see?"

Melissa slowly lifted her arm and extended a limp finger, pointing. "I think we're too late."

Melissa felt Dwayne's arm around her flinch involuntarily when he caught sight of the figure she pointed toward.

Cary drew a ragged breath and bit into her knuckles, trying not to scream out in anguish.

Dwayne released his hold on Melissa and took a step forward, craning his neck, staring at the image. "Wait a minute. That's not Dad. I don't recognize that man."

Cary slapped tears from her eyes to clear her vision. Her jaw fell slack. "Oh...my...God." She looked to Dwayne and said, "That's Kyle—my first husband—Melissa's and Kyra's father."

Melissa gasped as the image of the man suddenly became larger and clearer. She had not seen her biological father since she was four years old. "Dad?"

"Kyle? Is that really you?" Cary said.

"Go back," he replied. "The one you seek is not here. It is not his time and will not be for many years. I was allowed to tell you this, but these next words are from my own radiant heart; the balance of your life on earth will be shared with him. Love one another always. There will come a day I will see you again. For now, there is a happy life waiting. There will be difficulties, but it will work, and will be worth every effort. Cherish one another. Go back." He began to recede backwards.

"Kyle, wait. Don't go," Cary implored, as she extended a desperate hand.

Kyle only smiled, as his form shrank into obscurity and then disappeared altogether.

Melissa stepped closer to her mother and put her arm around her waist. "How do you feel? Are you okay?"

"I—I don't know. I'm numb. I can't process the different emotions running through me right now."

Melissa turned to Dwayne. "How about you?"

Dwayne continued staring across the valley. He glanced at Melissa, but right back at the valley and beyond. He ran a hand over his hair. "The man said what I wanted to hear." Dwayne was quiet for a moment. "Humph." He scratched his temple and tilted his head. "This was certainly an interesting experience."

As Melissa pulled her mom and Dwayne back into line and held them, she said, "There's nothing left to see. I hope none of us have cause to be here again for many, many years."

The return was sudden. Once again, they stood next to Cletus's bed.

"Wow," Kyra said. "The white glow developed around you guys, and your images seemed to wiggle, but you never disappeared from my sight, or even faded, for that matter. How long were you there?"

"What does your watch show?" Melissa asked.

"Eleven-twenty-one."

Melissa checked her own watch. Hers showed eleven-thirty-two. "We were there a little over ten minutes."

"I'll never get used to that," Kyra said. "Don't keep me in suspense. What did you discover?"

"Most importantly, we were told that Cletus is going to make it out of this crisis."

"You were told? Who spoke to you?"

Melissa glanced at her mother and then over to Dwayne. "Well, dear sister, this may be difficult for you to believe but it was Dad."

Kyra's head snapped back. "Wait. What? How can that be? He's not dead."

A brilliant smile stretched Melissa's face. "Not William. Our biological father."

Kyra looked to her mother. "Mom? What's Missy talking about?"

"It was Kyle, honey. He looked just as I remember the last day of his life on earth. We may never know why, but he was granted an appearance before us and allowed to tell us Cletus would be okay."

"Oh." Kyra backed up to a chair and unsteadily sat. "Wow."

Six weeks passed. It was the third week of August. Life returned to a semblance of normalcy on the farm. Cletus's wounds continued to heal. He was now capable of moving around on his own. He had difficulty standing straight, walking slowly and stooped, like a much older man, but he was improving. Cary had been taking care of him in the spare upstairs bedroom of the mansion. As yet, there had been no mention of moving back into the stucco house up the road with Dwayne.

Consequently, Dwayne spent an inordinate amount of time at the mansion as well. But, on occasion, he and Melissa quietly disappeared for a time and Cary never wondered where they were or what they were doing. Once she realized they were gone, she would only smile, fully aware they were sneaking to the stucco house for alone time. And those times seemed to be increasing.

The time Cary spent taking care of Cletus drew them closer. The relationship moved beyond mutual infatuation and respect, to something deeper. The love lives of the Dane women traveled the same track, going the same direction and at the same speed.

As happy and contented as she was, Cary had dreaded this day for weeks. Now, it had arrived. She and Cletus must testify for the prosecution at William's trial for the assault on her and the attempted murder of Cletus. Although not upset at the strong possibility of prison time for William, her heart was breaking for her boys, Charlie and Johnny. William was their father after all.

"Do you need any help getting dressed, Cletus?" she called out from where she stood at the bathroom vanity, leaning over it, putting final touches on her makeup while watching her reflection in the mirror. "We're supposed to be at the courthouse in thirty minutes."

"Need help? Nah. Appreciate your presence while you help? Always. Shoot, I might even say I need it so we have a reason to be near one another. I can't get enough of ya, girl," he replied from just beyond the bathroom door in the bedroom.

She positioned and re-positioned a misbehaving bang angling across her forehead. She smiled, and then giggled. "You know, you're very good at reducing my stress. You've been cracking jokes from the moment you woke up in the hospital. I was a wreck and you were barely conscious. Still, you tried making *me* feel better."

Cletus's head appeared around the door jamb. "Is it still working?"

"I wish I had the words to tell you just how much it's working." She checked the watch she wore as a pendant around her neck. She eyed him up and down as he came to stand in front of her. She ran her hand over his freshly shaved face and smoothed down the hair over his ear. "It looks as though we're ready for our appearance. Are we? It's about time to head to the courthouse."

Cletus draped his hands over her shoulders. "Piece o' cake, darling...piece o' cake." He kissed her lightly on the lips. "All we have to do is tell the truth and let the justice system take care of the rest."

She sighed. "You're right. Let's go get this done."

***

As Cary and Cletus stepped through the door of the Terry County Courthouse, they were met by Cary's four children, plus Dwayne, and Kyra's boyfriend, Robert. All six had oddly satisfied smiles plastered across their faces. Surprised by the looks, Cary's lips parted in surprise, as she glanced from face to face around the semi-circle. "What are those expressions for? This is not a happy day."

Melissa put a hand on her mother's forearm. "There won't be a trial."

"What? What are you talking about?"

"Mom, Johnny and I talked to Dad yesterday," older brother Charlie said. "He told us his lawyer advised him that the prosecution's case was solid. If Dad lost the trial and convicted, which appeared likely, he could get anywhere from two to twenty years for the second-degree felony of aggravated assault with a deadly weapon. Dad didn't argue the point. A short time ago Dad's lawyer worked a deal with the prosecuting attorney for the minimum sentence of two years in exchange for a guilty plea. Dad agreed to it, figuring he'd need a couple of years to get his head straight and stay off the booze. The way Dad looked at it was as if his stint in rehab had been extended a couple of years, but now mandatory. He was okay with it."

Although smiling, Johnny's eyes glazed with tears. "The judge has already released the jury. It's going to be okay, Mom." He pulled his mother into an embrace.

For the sake of the boys, Cletus had been standing away a respectful distance from Cary. She saw and understood his motivation but took the initiative and put her arm around his waist. She sighed. "It's over. It's finally over. Let's go home."

Chapter Twenty-Seven

Love and Loss

The remainder of the summer and all of autumn was blissfully tragedy free and calm. It was two weeks until Christmas. The first time the Dane women had experienced harvest season on the South Plains. The sight of large mechanical cotton pickers were everywhere, as were huge piles of unprocessed cotton compressed and ricked into rectangular modules, lined up and ready to be loaded on flatbed trucks, and then transported to a cotton gin. When the breezes came from the south, the smell of the gin a few miles down the highway perfumed the air. Melissa loved the aroma. Dwayne told her that, to him, it smelled like money. It was the best crop he had experienced since taking over the farming operation of the old Endicott place they lived on. "Has to be your presence in my life," he told her with a smile. "What else could it be?"

Although Melissa understood not getting to spend as much time with him, that knowledge was not sufficient to ward off loneliness. She had seen little of Dwayne once harvest began. In fact, it had been over a week since they were last together.

Cletus moved out of the mansion and back to the stucco house near the end of September. Dwayne needed support during harvest. Melissa missed them both, hoping the crop would be taken care of quickly. She missed the slower pace with Dwayne around often. Her mother had been helping by spending the afternoons and early evenings at the Logan house cooking for them. Dwayne and Cletus worked long hours and were always dirty, tired, and hungry, but far too exhausted to cook their own meals. Life for her mother had developed purpose. That purpose placed Cletus at its center. Melissa was thankful for the elder Logan's attentive and easy manner.

Melissa's week had been typical at the clinic—nothing special, just busy. It was Friday. Melissa was exhausted. She took a glass of chardonnay to the library in the mansion, sat in the wingback chair, kicked off her shoes, and put her feet up on an ottoman. As she relaxed, allowing her mind to roam, her eyes fell on Uncle Jack's unpublished manuscript of The Last Radiant Heart. It lay centered on the long conference-room-style reading table a few feet away. The comfort his writing provided over the past year was immeasurable, bringing to mind the conversation she had with him on the final day of his life and shortly before he completed it. That day was much like this one—blustery, gray, and cold outside. The only difference was the lack of snowflakes today. She smiled at the memory.

But there was indeed one larger difference. Melissa, Kyra and their mother were in blissfully romantic situations. Whereas Jack had struggled mournfully through to the end of The Last Radiant Heart, just to get the story told. And, then to the end of his life. He had lost his two greatest loves, Nikki Endicott and Arthur Wainwright, years before. He never got over losing them. Their absence took the color from his world. It was so hard on him to relive his experiences, but he had no choice if he was to finish the book. Jack Dane's radiant heart brought them together, but love kept them together. She took solace when she remembered her biological father, Kyle Dane appeared before them across the valley at the gate of paradise. Melissa had no concern; Jack, Nikki, Arthur and her father, Kyle were together there, along with everyone who she loved and passed on before her. It brought an easy, warm feeling to her thoughts.

I made the promise, she thought. I have to get that manuscript published before something happens to it. As far as I know, it's the only one in existence. It had been touched and handled so many times that the pages were curled and discolored. Melissa figured it was only a matter of time until it disappeared or would somehow be damaged or destroyed.

She inclined her head and frowned. 'A matter of time'? The concept abruptly felt odd. "Humph." She sipped her wine.

As the phrase reverberated, she wondered about things in the past she knew little or nothing about. Nikki Endicott was a great, possibly the best, example of that. Melissa realized she had no idea what the woman had been like or even looked like. Now, curiosity gripped her. She turned up her glass of wine and finished it.

Pressing her head into the soft back of the wingback chair, she wondered. What kind of woman would steal your heart, Uncle? And then retain control of it so long after her death, mourning her passing every day for the remainder of your own life. And, what about Wainwright? He was supposed to have been eccentric. He must have been a colorful character.

Melissa opened her eyes. Her entire body glowed white. She was not concerned or frightened, realizing curiosity set it in motion. She went with it, again closing her eyes. Okay. Nikki Endicott, I want to know more about you—you too, Arthur Wainwright. Let me into your world for a brief time.

A chill washed over her. The light bloomed. Without opening her eyes, she stood and stepped forward. When the white light faded, the air was fresh and mild—the light was still bright but obviously produced by the sun. She found herself standing on a turn-row just west of the stucco house. The stucco house was a different color. The season had to be early spring, judging by the occasional gentle, cool breeze. Yet the radiance of the sun warmed her skin. And, clearly, she had arrived at some point in the past.

She turned away from the house and looked farther down the rutted path, noticing a thunderstorm in the not-too-distant western sky rising to meet the sun. She dropped her eyes to see a man and a woman strolling side-by-side engaged in quiet conversation. Melissa called out, "Excuse me."

They stopped and turned.

Obviously surprised, "Where did you come from?" the woman asked.

As Melissa trotted to close the gap between them, she took note of the man first. He was in his fifties with a shock of mussed silver-white hair. It could have been no one other than Wainwright. "Are you Arthur Wainwright," she asked.

"Why, yes I am." He bowed slightly. "At your service." He grinned oddly, almost like a kid caught holding forbidden candy.

If she had not been forewarned by Jack's book about this man's eccentricities, Melissa would have figured him for a mental case. As that thought crossed her mind, another struck. Wait a minute. Jack always wondered the same thing and never mentioned anywhere in his book if he had concluded Wainwright was totally sane or not. Maybe he wasn't quite right in the head. Still, Melissa liked him already.

She turned to the woman. "That must mean you're Nikki Endicott."

"Uh...yeah. That's right. Have we met?"

Melissa was somewhat taken aback by Nikki's beauty. Interestingly, she thought that if she described Nikki's appearance to someone it would be as though she described herself—dark hair, high cheekbones, tall, and slender with a natural sun-kissed complexion. She wore beltless jeans with an untucked white shirt over them. She also wore large, gold hoop earrings that peeked out from that long, dark hair cascading down over shoulders. That's when it occurred to her that, although distant, she and Nikki were related through Jack's side of the family. "No, this is the first time I've had the privilege. I know of you through Uncle Jack. Where is he?"

"We left him to his thoughts and writing back at the house. He's sitting in an Adirondack chair in the front yard," Nikki replied. She turned to Arthur. "I thought Jack only had one niece, that little girl of Kyle's in Coos Bay."

Melissa saw the instant Arthur realized the truth of it. He guffawed and danced in a circle, clapping. She saw no need to say a thing. He knew the answer, even if Nikki had yet to see it. So, she simply smiled.

Nikki looked confused. "What do you know that I don't, Arthur?"

"Nikki, Nikki, Nikki. Don't you see? Don't you understand? You're looking at that little girl from Coos Bay. She's a radiant heart, just like Jack. She's come back to visit us from some point in the future." He clapped his hands again and laughed like a child.

Melissa was suddenly smacked with a sad realization. She remembered this part of her uncle's book. It would only be a short time until they found Nikki's mother having committed suicide by carbon monoxide poisoning, closed up in a running car inside a garage. The joy of the moment drained away. But she held a smile, to soothe Nikki's surprise by the lesser revelation of her sudden presence. "He's right, Nikki. I am that little girl. I'm Melissa Dane-Blakely."

"Remember, Nikki," Arthur said, "Melissa is from the future so you and I will have no memory of her ever having been here, once she returns to her time." He paused for a moment and then added, "Come on. Let's take you back to see Jack. He'll be ecstatic to see you." He grabbed Melissa's hand and took a step toward the house.

"No, no. Not this time," she blurted, pulling Wainwright to a standstill.

"'This time?'"

"I've visited Jack many times since the radiant heart awakened in me, but never you and Nikki. I wanted to see you and to know you...both of you." She chuckled. "I don't know if you guys realize it, but there were no pictures of you found among Jack's things. I had no idea what you two even looked like, only descriptions from his book. Of course, I did develop pre-conceived notions." Melissa noticed a somber expression pull Nikki's face down. "I'm sorry. Did I say something to upset you?"

Nikki shrugged her shoulders. "Not really. It's sad to think that all three of us will be gone before you have a chance to meet us as an adult."

Melissa placed a hand over her heart. "I am so sorry. I know you won't remember this conversation. I had no intention of causing you anguish even for the short time that I'll be here. I just can't help speaking from an historical perspective."

"It's okay," Nikki said. "Come on. Let's continue our stroll. I needed to clear my head anyhow." She bounced a shy smile. "I'm dealing with a few family issues."

Melissa nodded, fully aware of Nikki's problems with her parents. Arthur chose not to speak.

Over the course of the next half hour, the conversation lightened, becoming salted with laughter and smiles. It didn't take long for Melissa to understand Jack's deep love for these two people. Arthur was truly the aging hippy, expressing child-like joy with the simple act of living. Nikki and Arthur were clearly deeply devoted to one another and to Jack. Nikki spoke of Jack with the look of love in her eyes and mannerisms. Melissa became so deeply drawn to them it was difficult to find a point to say good bye. She didn't have to. It was Nikki that indirectly forced the issue.

"Well," Nikki said, "we'd better get back to the house and check on Jack. You coming, Melissa?"

Melissa knew what was about to happen and did not want to be around when they found Nikki's mother dead. "Thanks guys, but no. I need to get back to my own time. But this visit has been wonderful beyond words." She embraced Nikki and whispered, "I so admire the love I've seen and heard about today. You are such a special person, Nikki Endicott."

Melissa turned to Arthur and held out a friendly hand.

"Oh, no, young lady. Arthur Wainwright does not do handshakes. Get over here." He hugged her so tightly that her feet came off the ground and he spun her half-way around.

The moment was so beautiful that Melissa could not prevent tears of joy from filling her eyes. She looked at one, then the other. "I will miss the two of you so much." Standing between them, Melissa wrapped each arm around their waists and pulled them in tight to her sides. "I've got to go before I start bawling like a baby." Before another word was spoken she closed her eyes and envisioned the library in the mansion. She released her hold on them and took a fast step forward into the blooming light. Once again, she was home.

Chapter Twenty-Eight

The Radiant Heart

"I took my cue from Uncle Jack on the use of the radiant heart," Melissa told her sister. "He was always frightened of it and what he might accidentally do to hurt himself or his friends. But, Kyra, it goes deeper for me, much deeper. Fear of the unknown is only a small part of it. Too frequently, there are negative emotions attached to these jumps."

Kyra sat in awe of the story Melissa had shared about meeting Nikki and Arthur. "After what you told me, I can understand it," she said.

"I've decided to never knowingly use the ability unless necessary. I realize there will be times I lose control and it'll happen, regardless. Still…" Her voice trailed off, as she slipped into a deeply contemplative frame.

Kyra did not interrupt.

After a moment, "I can't express the beauty of meeting those two, followed by unimaginable sadness that hummed inside me like a hive full of angry bees when I realized the eventual outcome of their lives and, like those bees, it swarmed me and made me physically ill to think about it. It's more than I'm emotionally equipped to handle. I don't want to go through that again if I can help it."

Kyra nodded and said in soothing tone, "I understand. It must have been equally disturbing to see Dad again after all these years for that short time and the tension of preventing a rape by Ricky Castillo that would have been inevitable, had you not intervened. And, of course, we can't forget the first time it happened when you got into that fight with our stepfather."

"You do understand. Don't you?"

"Yeah. It seems to only bring some form of heartache."

"It would seem so."

"More wine?" Kyra asked, as she got up and headed out of the library to retrieve the bottle from the kitchen.

Melissa smiled and nodded. "Sure. Fill 'er up. I need it." As her eyes followed Kyra stepping out of the library, where they regularly congregated after work, she appreciated her sister's ready acceptance of a decision to avoid using the radiant heart whenever possible.

She stood and moseyed over to the table and retrieved the unpublished manuscript that served her well as a guidebook. She smiled and affectionately ran a hand over the title page, as if making a connection over time with her uncle. She never had the chance to know him in life but quickly learned to love him later. *It's time to keep my promise and get this book published.*

"There ya go," Kyra said.

Startled, Melissa spun around. "Oh, thanks," she said, retrieving the over-filled glass of Chardonnay. She patted the manuscript. "Time has come for me to keep a promise I made to Jack and get this thing published before something happens to it."

"How do you go about finding a publisher?"

She returned to her chair and sat. "Good question." Melissa straightened and scanned the room. "A good place to start would be the company that published Jack's other book about that distant Comanche cousin of ours, Brave Child." She set her wine glass on the side table and stood. She, again, looked around the library. "I don't see it. Do you know where it is?"

"I think it's in the drawer of that desk in your bedroom."

"That's right. I never shelved it in the library. Stay put. I'll be right back." Melissa hurried out of the library, up the stairs, and retrieved the book. She began speaking before passing back over the library threshold. "It's a San Antonio publisher, Haskins-Pruitt and Associates."

"I wonder if they're still in business. It has been over twenty years since that book was published."

Melissa sauntered to the long reading table where a laptop computer lay. "I'll see if they have a website." She typed in the name, Haskins-Pruitt and there was indeed a site. She clicked on it. "Whaddaya know? It appears they not only are still in business but thrived. Besides the home office in San Antonio, they have a location in LA and another in Boston. I'll call San Antonio."

***

Luck was with Melissa. The company acquisitions editor in Jack's day was a lady by the name of Marybeth Wilkins. She was still with Haskins-Pruitt as chief operating officer for the entire company, and still worked in San Antonio. But she was nearing retirement. Ms. Wilkins remembered Jack Dane well.

Jack died before renewing his contract with the company. It was not an automatically renewing instrument. The book, *A Truly Brave Child*, had lain dormant since shortly after his death. So, Ms. Wilkins invited Melissa to San Antonio to discuss renewing it and, possibly, publishing the novel.

Opting to drive, Melissa took off from work and was on her way south. It seemed like a good way to mix business and pleasure. Take a day and see some of the sites. Maybe, take in the Riverwalk and see the Alamo. She had never been to San Antonio. She wanted Dwayne to join her, but it was a busy time on the farm—too busy for a pleasure trip. He reluctantly chose to stay and tend to the many farm duties at home.

As distance from home increased, she began feeling carefree. She turned off the air conditioning, let down her window, and cranked up the volume on the radio, singing along.

A few miles south of the small town of Post, as she drove down the hill leaving the Caprock behind, an older model Buick Roadmaster passed her at extremely high speed. It had to have been traveling at ninety miles an hour, maybe faster. Melissa checked her speedometer. She held steady at seventy-five when the car went around her. *Not smart. Not smart at all*, she thought as the car disappeared around a curve about a quarter mile ahead.

When Melissa cleared the same curve a few seconds later, she saw the car upright in a cloud of dust with the roof partially crushed and the driver's side door sprung open and bent backwards. It obviously had rolled a number of times and came to a rest upright on its tires. There was no driver in the seat, or anyone else in the car that she could see. Her first thought was that if that car had been any smaller, the roof would have been entirely collapsed.

Melissa quickly pulled in behind the car and stopped. Stirred dust had not had time to clear the area. Melissa drove into a brown cloud. That's when she noticed someone lying unmoving on the ground about thirty feet from where the vehicle came to rest.

She leaped out of her vehicle and retrieved a first aid kit from the rear of her SUV and hurried to the person on the ground.

It was a young woman, Latina, lying sprawled on her back—one leg grotesquely twisted from a compound fracture, as was her arm on the same side of her body. She had long dark hair splayed across her face. She couldn't have been over twenty-five. The woman's eyes were fixed and staring at the sky through bloody pools. The young woman had no pulse.

Melissa tightly pursed her lips. Her face sank to a sad slant—now obvious the woman was beyond help. She needed to find something to cover the body with. People slowed on the highway and rubber-necked the scene, gawking.

A guy driving a bob-tail dump truck with a Texas Highway Department insignia on the door pulled in behind Melissa's SUV. As he approached her standing over the body, "Need help?" he asked.

"Yeah. Thanks. Call 911. Tell 'em there has been a fatal accident and give them the location."

The guy pulled a cell phone from his jeans and dialed.

While he went about the business of phoning for help, Melissa went in search of something to cover the young woman with. She noticed a colorfully striped sarape in the backseat of the wrecked car. She leaned through the broken window and retrieved it. Blanket in hand, she backed away from the car. Movement in the front seat caught her eye. She saw a young girl still restrained by a lap belt but no shoulder harness. The youngster had fallen sideways on the old-style bench seat. She appeared to be regaining consciousness.

Melissa raced back to where the body lay and covered the dead woman with the fringed blanket. The guy was still on the phone with the emergency operator. "Tell them to send an ambulance, too. There's a young girl still inside the car. When you get off the phone, give me a hand."

She heard a moan coming from the battered vehicle.

She hurried to the passenger side. The young girl began to squirm.

Fear jolted Melissa that the car might catch fire. The smell of gasoline was strong.

The windows shattered when the roof pushed in. She attempted first to open the door. But a couple of tugs later, she realized it was mangled too badly and jammed.

No choice, she had to remove the girl through the shattered window. But how?

She reached in and worked the button of the seat belt coupler, but it had been rendered inoperable. It would not release the belt hasp, damaged during the rollover.

Then it occurred to her she had a box cutter in the center console of her SUV, left there when she moved to Texas.

The guy from the truck had ended his call to the emergency operator and approached.

"Would you open the glove compartment in my car and bring me the box cutter? I'll have to cut the seatbelt," she told him.

"No need," he replied. "I have a sharp pocketknife."

When he pulled it from his pocket, she noticed it was more than a simple pocketknife. It was a folding hunting knife. She almost smiled. *Gotta love these Texas good ol' boys*, she thought. She turned her attention back to the girl.

The youngster, appearing no more than eight years old, moaned and muttered, "Mama." This time accompanied by a grimace of pain. It was a good thing that the girl was slow to regain full consciousness. It would be a crushing blow when she discovered her mother was dead. With considerable effort, Melissa swallowed the growing lump in her throat. "Hang on, sweetie. I'll get you out of there. I promise." Melissa sent up a quick prayer that she could keep that promise.

Time abruptly became the enemy as gasoline continued pooling beneath the car and wetting a wider circle. "Please hurry," she implored, as the guy reached through the shattered window and cut the webbed belt. "I'm afraid this car is going to catch fire—worse yet, explode."

A mixture of smoke and steam boiled from around the mangled hood but, also, from beneath the car.

Fear knotted Melissa's stomach.

The burly guy had big square hands, and a large belly that kept his jeans riding low, exposing his butt-crack while he struggled to free the girl through the window of the car. It was obvious he'd been working. His hands were grimy. Sweat streaked his shirt. But Melissa thought of him as an angel. She was certain it would have been a daunting chore had he not been here, maybe impossible.

On his massive arms liberally painted with tatoos, he cradled the girl, lifting the partially conscious youngster. He gently brought her through and out the mangled car window.

Melissa was awed by the gentleness of this hulking and awkward appearing highway maintenance worker. She quickly scanned the area and spotted an isolated patch of grass farther off the highway. She pointed to it. "Take her over there and lay her gently on her back. Please take it slow. She may have broken ribs, pelvis, or even internal injuries from being whipped around inside that lap belt."

As he followed through with her request, Melissa ran back to where she left her first aid kit next to the girl's dead mother and retrieved it. She jogged back to the young girl and dropped to her knees. The man stood over her casting his shadow across Melissa and the youngster, providing shade from harsh sunlight. He pulled a red bandanna from his pocket and mopped sweat from his face.

Melissa dropped to her knees and pulled the girl's shirt up. Bruising was evident and would only get darker with time. But her concern was for problems she could not see. She gently danced fingertips over the girl's lower ribs and felt nothing out of the ordinary and the girl did not flinch when touched there, providing a level of assurance that the ribs were intact. Melissa then repeated the process around the girl's pelvic area. All seemed solid.

"Where's Mama?" the girl asked, still dazed, eyes closed.

Melissa necessarily ignored the question. "Where do you hurt, sweetie?"

"My stomach hurts, and my head, too."

From her quick superficial examination, the only issues Melissa could be certain of was that the young girl had a concussion, severe abdominal bruises and a profusely bleeding cut above her left eyebrow. But it was clear the cut was shallow. Melissa pulled a gauze pad from her kit and drenched it in peroxide. She gently mopped the blood away from the cut and then dabbed the cut itself. She squeezed the cut together and applied a butterfly bandage over it.

The man, still serving as shade for them both watched. "You sure seem to know what you're doin' ma'am."

She smiled for the first time since the ordeal began and looked up at the guy. "Nurse practitioner. Nine years. I work at a Lubbock clinic."

"Well, that little girl is lucky you came along."

Melissa looked over at the sarape covered corpse of the girl's mother. Her smile wilted away. "Maybe. But my presence made no difference to her."

Sirens became audible and grew louder.

Melissa stood and shook the man's hand. "I could not have done this without your help. Thank you."

He touched the bill of his grimy cap. "My pleasure, ma'am. It sounds like help is on the way."

"I'll wait for them. Why don't you go and get on with your day. What's your name?"

"Stanley. Stanley Kiminski."

"I'll make a point to tell them what you did, Stanley, and thanks again."

Stanley got back in his truck and pulled out into traffic.

Melissa watched him drive away. *The world needs more Stanley Kiminskis,* she thought. *And I'll do more than tell emergency personnel what he did. I'll call the highway department and see if there is some commendation they can offer.*

The girl whimpered. "I want my mama."

"Shh, sweet baby. Lie still. You'll aggravate that headache. Help is coming.

Sirens screamed louder and she saw the lead car, a county sheriff's vehicle come around the curve followed closely by a red EMT van. They hurriedly wheeled off the highway. The patrol car parked behind Melissa's SUV. The EMT van drove right up beside where she and the girl were.

Melissa looked into the child's face. She was beautiful. Even through the girl's pain, innocent and angelic beauty shined. Her black hair was long and thick, eyebrows to match—features delicate. Her skin was smooth—the color of creamed coffee. *I can't leave her. It's up to me to tell her that her mother didn't make it. It's going to be so hard on her. But not yet. Not until she has been seen by doctors.*

As if on cue, the wrecked car burst into flames.

***

The emergency medical service van had been dispatched from the town of Post, but the youngster was transported to Lynn County Hospital located in the town of Tahoka approximately twenty-five miles away. Melissa followed it. The girl was x-rayed. No broken bones. She also had an MRI done. There appeared to be no internal injuries. Pain medication had the youngster's concussion induced headache under control. Once they returned her to a room, Melissa joined her and sat on the edge of the child's bed.

Melissa pushed strands of the child's hair away from her face. "Hey, sweetie. How are you feeling now?"

"Okay, I guess."

"What's your name?"

"Leti."

"Leti? That's a beautiful name. What's your last name?"

"De Leon."

Well, Leti De Leon, my name is Melissa." She stroked the girl's arm lovingly. "It's nice to meet you. Where do you live?"

"Brownfield."

"Where were you going in such a rush?"

"I don't know. I don't think Mama knew either. We were just getting away from Mama's boyfriend."

"'Getting away'? What do you mean?"

"He started yelling at Mama and then started hitting her." Leti whimpered. "I tried to stop him, but he hit me, too. He's mean." She cried.

"Shh." Melissa went cheek to cheek with the girl and whispered, "You're safe now. He can't hurt you anymore." As she straightened, "Do you have a daddy or other family... grandparents, aunts, uncles, or anyone else?"

She wallowed tiny fists in her tear-filled eyes. "Uh-uh. It's just me and Mama now."

Upon hearing those words, Melissa's heart ached, as if a stone had been dropped on it, knowing the next thing she must do—tell Leti her mama had not survived the accident.

Chapter Twenty-Nine

Moving Forward

Melissa nervously walked through Dane Mansion waiting for Dwayne to finish his farming chores for the day, for Kyra to get home from work, and for her mother to get back from the errands she was running in town. She wanted them together in the house at the same time. She even called Cletus, inviting him as well. The more opinions she could gather, the stronger her final decision would be. Although nervous, she was also excited.

The doorbell sounded its throaty bongs. As she hurried to answer it, she noticed the antique clock hanging below the balusters of the mezzanine would be striking seven o'clock in the next minute or so. Opening the door, she saw Dwayne and his dad waiting. "I hope I didn't interrupt anything important that still needed attention," she said.

"Nah," Cletus replied. "We were about to shut it down for the day anyhow."

"Please come in."

As Dwayne hung his cap on the ornate coat tree next to the door, "Did I detect urgency in your voice when you called?"

"Possibly. I have an idea that I want everyone's opinion on. So, I won't get into it until Mom and Kyra get here. They should be home any minute. I called Mom and asked her to stop and pick up some barbecue and a couple of six-packs of beer. Is that okay for a fast supper?"

"Aw jeez, I can't think of anything finer," Cletus said. "You already have me drooling."

"Me neither. Sounds great," Dwayne said then paused. "Well, you certainly have my curiosity up. I thought you'd be in San Antonio today."

"So did I. I never made it. But, that's part of the story."

"Let's go sit in the library. It's my favorite room in this big ol' house anyhow."

"We're right behind ya," Dwayne said, as the front door swung open.

Cary and daughter Kyra came in, talking as they did. "What's Missy up to?" Kyra asked.

"I have no idea," Cary replied.

"Hey," Melissa called out. "Did you two have a good day?"

"As good as any, I suppose," Kyra said. "Why all the cloak a dagger secrecy?"

"It's no secret. I just want to lay out a plan and I want everyone to hear it at the same time. I'll get into it in a few minutes. Let's gather in the library." Melissa saw the brown sacks with grease spots on the bottom corners of them that her mother carried and the six-packs Kyra held. "Bring the food and beer. We'll eat first, while the barbecue is still warm."

Collective hunger and, maybe, curiosity dictated the speed of the meal. There was little conversation and when there was, sentences were short and trite. Meat, potato salad, and cole slaw were consumed quickly.

Dwayne ran a napkin across his mouth and dropped it on the table. He pushed his plate back, folded his arms and leaned onto his elbows on the table-top. "I, for one, am ready for the big reveal, Missy. What's this all about?"

Melissa took a second to gather her thoughts. "It's about a precious eight-year-old girl by the name of Leti De Leon.

She spoke mostly uninterrupted for fifteen minutes, explaining the accident and then came the plan. "Here's my thinking. This girl's only family was her mother and, now that she's gone, the child has no one. I desperately want to foster her in our home with an eventual goal of full adoption." She went around the table and made eye contact with each one. No one said a thing, only exchanged glances among themselves. It almost appeared to be a game of chicken. Who would speak first? "Come on guys. I need input. What do you think?"

"Well, dear," her mother said, but then paused. "You just caught us all by surprise. It's not at all what I was expecting. I thought it might have something to do with your job or career."

"It does…in a way."

"Or some kind of party or celebration you were planning," Kyra quickly added.

"It would be…sort of."

The table fell silent again.

"What about you, Dwayne?" Melissa asked. "I need your thoughts on the idea."

Dwayne looked down at his hands atop the table, clearly mulling a response. He sighed, looked up at Melissa, and smiled. "I'll start by saying that you're the smartest and most beautiful woman in the world and no matter what you decide, I'll be here to back that decision all the way. One little question though; isn't this a bit sudden? You just met the little girl. Would she even want to live with you? And would Texas Child Protective Services even allow you to foster her? I've heard their rules are pretty darn restrictive."

Melissa smirked. "That's three little questions. But all good ones and things that would have to be worked out. Plus, although she told me she had no other family, there may be aunts or uncles somewhere who would love her and take her in. These are all considerations."

"If you want to follow through, I'll help any way I can," Kyra said.

Cletus, who had been sitting quietly finally spoke. "I think I can safely say we all will pitch in and help whenever, and wherever, we can."

"I have no full-time job, other than taking care of this house and cooking. I could watch her while you're at work," her mother offered. "I think it'd be fun to have a child in the house again."

Melissa relaxed and leaned back in her chair, smiling. Curious questions had rapidly metamorphosed into a planning session on how to bring Leti into their home as one of the family. Her eyes glossed with happy tears when the full impact of the word "family" tingled up her spine. Discussion eventually subsided. She saw fatigued faces—a day of work catching up with everyone.

"Look," she said, "how about I begin the process and I'll keep everyone informed on my progress?"

Dwayne yawned. "Sounds like a plan."

"I agree with Dwayne's yawn," Kyra said. "I'm going up to my room. Good night everyone."

"Yeah, I'd better get Dwayne home. The boy's a might too large for me to carry and tuck into bed," Cletus said with a silly grin.

Melissa joined the laughter that Cletus's comment caused. "Okay. But, Dwayne, could you hang around a few more minutes? I'd like to ask you something privately." She looked at Cletus. "It won't take long."

"In that case, I'll wait in that front living room," Cletus said.

Dwayne nodded. "I'm all yours, Missy."

"That's what I'm hoping," she replied.

"Huh?"

Everyone else took the cue and filed out of the library.

Melissa trailed them and closed the door.

"Are you okay, Missy?"

"I'm fine," she replied as she returned and knelt beside his chair.

"You're worrying me a bit."

"Well, what I'm going to say is important, but it shouldn't be worrisome."

"Well...," he said than went silent, holding a smile as big as the Lone Star state. Finally, after only a few seconds, "Okay. Enough of this. What'n the world's on your mind?"

"Dwayne Logan, will you marry me?"

"Dwayne's sleepy eyes suddenly brightened and sparkled. Beyond all physical limitations, the smile stretched his deeply tanned face even more.

Chapter Thirty

Christmas Hope

Christmas was less than two weeks away as eight-year-old Leti De Leon sat on the cheaply made iron bed with her knees pulled up, surrounded by her arms. She had been sent to this children's home east of Lubbock following her mother's violent death in that car accident. The people seemed nice enough and all the other children tried to make her feel welcome. But the wound of loss was too raw—too fresh. For now, she simply wanted to be left alone. Her juvenile mind could not comprehend the future. All she knew with certainty was that she had no family, no real friends, and dependent on the kindness of strangers. Through watery eyes that seemed to blur the world perpetually, she looked around her bedroom. There were no frills, no stuffed animals, no toys—nothing. It was furnished with the basics—a bed, a small chest of drawers, a sink, and an ugly mirror bolted to the wall.

Beyond her closed bedroom door, she heard chatter and laughter from other children who lived in this cottage. They were playing chase in the long hallway that ended at the kitchen/dining area at one end and full-time house parents' quarters at the other end. Leti had reached a stage where she did not openly weep all the time, but her eyes were hardly ever without tears. She wondered if she would ever smile or laugh again.

Amidst the noise of the children, the sound of adult voices conversing grew stronger and stopped just on the other side of her door. As she swung her legs off the bed, her door opened. There stood her house mother, Bonnie Ray, with a taller woman. The woman was dressed in clothes like they wore in hospitals. She was beautiful and very familiar. When she first regained consciousness after the accident that took her mother from her, she remembered seeing an angel, wings made of light hovering over her. Leti wondered if the angel had come back. She certainly remembered this woman from somewhere. But a much less desirable memory came to mind. The youngster whimpered and asked, "You're not here to give me more shots, are ya?"

The lady drew a broad grin. "No sweetheart. No shots." She held a hand over her heart. "I promise."

"This is Melissa Dane-Blakely," Bonnie said. "She came directly from where she works at a clinic on the other side of town. That's the reason for the scrubs she's wearing."

"Oh," Leti said, mumbling, as she swiped her forearm across a drippy nose. She resumed allowing her head to hang loosely while staring at the floor.

"I would like to talk to you," Melissa said, "if that's okay with you."

"Sure."

"I'll leave you two to talk," Bonnie said as she backed out of the bedroom and closed the door.

Melissa sat next to Leti. "Do you remember who I am?"

"I remember your face."

"I'm the one that helped you after the accident."

No simple glance this time. The child studied Melissa's face. "Oh yeah." The girl's head again sagged as she continued watching her wiggling toes.

"You've been on my mind a lot since I met you."

"Really?" Leti smiled and again wondering if this black-haired, tall, very attractive woman was indeed her angel. It felt weird to think so. She shivered at the possibility. Although she didn't yet have the wherewithal to look up again into the lady's eyes.

"Really." Melissa stroked the youngster's long, gleaming black hair. She leaned down, attempting to get the child to look her in the eyes.

Leti believed the solid wall in front of her was tantamount to her future and that none existed beyond it—for her.

The lady finally asked, "Leti, how would you like to come home with me to meet my family and friends, and then stay through Christmas? Maybe longer."

Leti whipped her head up and looked directly into the nice lady's eyes, lip beginning to quiver. Leti reached and wrapped her tiny arms are the lady's neck and whispered in Melissa's ear, you *are* my angel after all. She refused to let go. Fresh tears tumbled. But unlike tears shed over the loss of her mother, these did not come from a sad place.

Chapter Thirty-One

A New Dawn

"Where'd Leti go?" Melissa asked Dwayne, as she closed the oven door on another batch of Christmas cookies.

With cookie crumbs decorating the corners of his mouth, he swallowed and looked one way then the other. He swiped away residue of a cookie eaten too quickly. "Not sure. I saw her take a couple of cookies and walk out of the kitchen. That's the last time I saw her."

Melissa tossed the oven mitts on the counter and stepped to the kitchen door and looked one way then the other. "I'm probably beginning to hover and be overly protective like an old mother hen, but…" She left the kitchen, Dwayne at her heels. She looked across the hall into the library and saw Kyra and Robert in quiet conversation, but Leti wasn't with them. She walked on toward the front door and turned right into the formal living room at the front of the house. She stopped and drew a broad smile.

There Leti was crouched, sitting on her heels while chewing a cookie bite. Her upturned head and sparkling eyes told the undeniable story of an eight-year-old girl in rapt awe of the brilliantly lit, nine-foot Christmas tree centered in front of a large bay window. Twinkling multi-colored lights reflected off scrubbed shiny little cheeks.

Melissa moved back a step and threaded her arm around his. She leaned her head against his upper arm. He held tightly to the hand on his forearm.

She leaned away momentarily, looking up into his smiling eyes. "This is what Christmas is all about."

"Norman Rockwell could not have drawn this view of that child any better."

"Oh Dwayne. She's only been with us a little more than a week and I can't help but see that sweet child as anything other than part of our family. I'm falling so deeply in love with the child, I...well, I just don't have enough words to describe how much."

"I know what you mean. Now that you've said it, do you remember those pigs you made fun of me talking to a few months back?"

"Yeah," she said hesitatingly. "Where are you going with this?"

He stuck two fingers in his shirt pocket and plucked out a check. "Well, those little porkers kindly provided me with this payment of a thousand-and-eight dollars."

"Are you telling me that you received a good price them?"

"Yep. But that's not my point. With your permission, I'd like to spend the entire amount on Leti. New clothes, toys and, heck, maybe even a bicycle."

Melissa put a hand behind his head and pulled him in so her lips met his. The kiss was long and sweet, perfect for Christmas Eve. "You don't need my permission." She kissed him again. "You're a special man, Dwayne Logan."

***

January and most of February across the South Plains of Texas were quiet. Between crop seasons was great family and social gathering time. If crops had been good, which they had this past season, smiles and laughter were easy to come by in this farming community. For Cary and the Dane girls, it was a great time to become closer to Leti.

Cletus and Dwayne had always pitched in to help the Dane women. Regardless of how busy they happened to be, if Leti was involved, they found the time.

Dwayne had extra incentive. If all went according to plan, sweet Leti would become a permanent member of the Mister and Missus Dwayne Logan family at some point in the future. The near future, he hoped. Or so he'd told her on several occasions. She and Dwayne had numerous conversations about fully adopting Leti. And all monitoring reports by Child Protective Services during the fostering process, appeared as though full adoption had gone from possibility to probability, if they cared to follow through on completing the process. They did.

Melissa thought back over her first romanticized dreams of love, marriage, and Texas—a dream born in her hometown of Coos Bay, Oregon while still living there. *Wow! What a ride this has been. At the time, I'd never have dreamed that a violent confrontation with my stepfather would be the catalyst that would catapult me across the country to a beautiful existence only dreamt of.*

Dwayne surreptitiously slipped in beside her, as her imagination soared. She was leaning back against the kitchen island. "I don't know where your mind is takin' you, but do you mind if I tag along?"

"There's my good-lookin' farmer dude." She faced him and poked fingers in belt loops on both sides of his waist and pulled him close. She gave him a peck on the mouth. "Here's the deal, Stud; I'll be going nowhere without you, even if it's only in my imagination."

"Great answer. Can I drive?"

"No." She laughed.

"So, what *were* you thinking about?"

"A little of this and a little of that. But seriously, my thoughts were leading me to take action to finalize the adoption process for Leti."

"Are ya feelin' pressure to get it done according to some timeline?"

"That question deserves another one: When are we getting married?"

Chapter Thirty-Two

Wedding Bells

Winter weather refused to release its grasp on the Plains. Most mornings continued with frost glistening on the ground in the morning brilliance of the rising sun. But this Sunday morning offered more winter than expected—low gray clouds and snow flurries.

Melissa rocked slowly side to side to music only she could hear holding a steaming mug of coffee. She stood gazing, almost mesmerized, across the barren field through the bay window at the front of the mansion to the field beyond—overcome by the simple fact that she was six feet away from shivers, goosebumps and huffing white clouds of frosty air. Yet here she stood, cozy and warm.

Leti squealed with laughter.

Melissa sauntered toward the archway that opened onto the hall extending from the front door to the back door in a straight line. "Hey, whatcha doin', sweet cheeks?" She took a sip of coffee.

Leti was holding an inflatable rubber ball about half the size of a soccer ball and laughing, dancing in a circle. "I finally kicked it all the way to the back door in a straight line without hitting the wall."

"Can you do it again?"

"I bet I can."

"Then do it."

Leti laughed. "Watch me."

"I'm watching. Go for it." Melissa sipped again from her mug and leaned her head against the moulding around the pass-through archway. She deeply felt warmth radiate through her at the simplicity of such a beautiful sight.

As Leti ran toward the ball on the floor, preparing to kick it, Melissa heard something from where she had just come from in the living room. She turned and saw a woman standing a few feet behind her. Melissa flinched, startled by the woman's presence—a drop or two of coffee splashing out of her mug to the floor.

The young lady seemed oddly familiar. Yet Melissa knew she'd never seen her before. She turned to fully face her. "Who are you and how did you get in the house?"

The young woman put a finger to her lips. "Shh. Watch Leti make her kick. Make no more reference about me or to me."

Like a sudden bolt of enlightenment, Melissa developed a fast inkling what this was about, but not who the woman was. She nodded in a knowing way then whispered, "I'll have Leti go play upstairs after she makes the kick, then you and I can talk in the library."

The woman held a thumb's up, leaning in and speaking low directly into Melissa's ear, "Leti won't remember any of this even if she does catch us talking, but she's so inquisitive, she'll take all our time together asking questions that she won't remember asking or the answers to anyhow. I hate being so selfish with our time but I'm going to be. I think you can understand."

Melissa smiled. "I do." Once Leti was sent upstairs to play, the woman and Melissa hurried down the hallway to the library.

Melissa closed the door behind them. "You're from my future, aren't you?"

"I am."

"You must be a blood relative. Who are you?"

"Allow me to introduce myself again..." she smiled broadly, "...My name is Nikki Marie Logan, the namesake of Nikki Endicott. I am your daughter."

Melissa became weak in the knees and slightly stumbled sideways.

Nikki held her mother's shoulders and guided her backwards to sit on one of the library chairs. "I must apologize. I know better than to introduce myself while you're standing. It's always a shock for you."

"Always? How many times *have* you traveled through time to see me?"

"Let me think. I suppose this makes six times."

"Six! Good heavens. Why so many times?"

Nikki sighed. "Sometimes a girl just wants to talk things over with someone their own age who knows exactly what they're going through. You have and are still going through it. But your views on the radiant heart and world view in general have changed over the years."

"I hope I didn't become difficult to be around."

"Oh no. Nothing like that. You just hold onto fears of what *might* happen if the radiant heart is used too often in an unforeseen way that may turn dangerous. Only slightly less than Great Uncle Jack's fear of it. Even now, in your late sixties, you still induce it occasionally but only for perceived emergencies. I, on the other hand, have come to embrace it and use it for reasons that aren't emergencies."

"Give me an example."

"Well...I enjoy ancient history and have been the proverbial fly on the wall at major historical events. For example, I have a loose grasp on Latin and have heard some of the wisdom of Marcus Aurelias and understood most of a speech he delivered to the Roman Senate. Of course, I stood out of sight in the shadows, of which there are many in a large room like the Roman senate chamber without electric lights. I witnessed Samson bring down the Philistine Temple of Dagon. I can verify that Delilah did, indeed, place his hands upon the supporting temple columns. She was sobbing and did not leave, even knowing what he was about to do. I didn't hear anything, yet I could tell she was grief-stricken, presumably by her own betrayal of him to the Philistines and remained nearby to die with him. I didn't step into that one. I watched through the portal. I didn't want to be crushed by falling debris in the temple. Secondly, I don't speak Hebrew. So, why hear their last words to one another? I've done numerous such investigations—Greek, Roman, Viking, Aztec, Egyptian—you name it, I've joined or viewed many such ancient events of note within these cultures. And listen to this; I've seen tyrannosaurus rex, brontosaurus, velociraptors, triceratops, and many others *in the wild*, in their natural environment. Some of which have not yet been discovered to have existed."

"Nikki, that's fascinating beyond words."

"You can do it, if you want. Just be careful what you step through the portal into." She snickered at the double entendre.

"Oh no. Not me. It'd be my luck I would surprise a serial murderer."

"Don't forget; no matter what we say to one another, You will not remember any of this conversation. Your world will instantly be exactly where you were before you noticed my presence. But I will remember it all."

"You're right. It's that this seems so real...so...now."

Nikki snickered. "It *is*, for me."

"Okay. Sit. Although I won't remember anything, I still want to know some things."

Nikki pulled a chair close and sat facing her mother, knees touching. What would you like to know for this short time together?"

Your grandmother, I assume, has been gone for quite a while."

"She passed away when I was fourteen, but her final years were happy with Grand Dad, Cletus. He passed way not long before I was born."

"Are you and Leti my only children?"

Nikki laughed aloud.

"What's so funny?"

"I think we are, but Jacky Dale may have something to say about it. He'll be turning thirty in a couple of months in my timeline." She snickered. "Okay. I concede. You have three children."

"Jacky Dale is his name?"

"Yeah. Named after Uncle Jack and his middle name was also Grand Dad's. You started calling him Jacky when he was a toddler and it stuck. He even introduces himself as Jacky. So, it looks as though he's stuck with it the rest of his life."

"And Dwayne?"

"Best Daddy in the whole-wide world. He's healthy and both you guys are as happy as you were before you married."

"Is Leti okay?"

Oh yeah. For sure. She has four children and is a blissfully happy homemaker. She lives in Seminole with her husband, Max."

"That is so great. Now to you, what is it you wanted to talk about?"

"I just have one simple question. How did you know Dad was the man for you?"

"As odd as this may sound, I knew when he was eight years old, the first time I met him as a youngster. I was a little younger than you are now. It was the first time I had used the radiant heart and came to this very house. I had no clue where I was but, somehow, knew this was the Texas house Uncle Jack built and ended up talking to him just like you're talking to me right now. Dwayne's mother was Jack's housekeeper. Dwayne knows this part. What he still does *not* know is I fell in love with him that very day, as a dirty-faced little boy with holes worn in both knees of his jeans and playing with his dog. Years later when I officially met him, and he had grown to my age, my love for him took off and never looked back, except for that fond memory of that happy kid and his dog. And there you have it, in a nutshell."

"Wow. That's fascinating—to know that from the very beginning of your radiant heart travels."

"Is there a guy you're growing close to?"

"Yeah. And it's getting serious."

"Melissa sighed. "Well...from my perspective it would be advisable to enjoy what you have currently. Because it's my opinion that if you need outside confirmation if you love him or not, you may not be ready for a permanent commitment. Just enjoy the ride. If love is destined, it'll come in its own time. And believe me sweet girl, when that happens it will come from deep within your soul and then explode from that beautiful radiant heart. On that day, you'll know."

Nikki smiled broadly. "Now you know why I'm here; for that sage advice I wouldn't dream of asking anyone else."

"Nikki honey, I so wish I could remember this visit and am looking forward to a *whole* life with you."

"We'll do it again. You just won't remember we've visited seven times before." Nikki took a deep breath and looked around the library. I suppose I'd better let us both get on with our day."

Melissa stood and hugged her daughter, marveling a final time at the miracle of seeing her adult daughter, knowing she would not be born for another couple of years. It pained her to come to grips with not having the continuing joy of such a sweet moment to live on in her memory. For the first time she believed that not remembering this, or the other visits, may not be such a bad thing after all.

Chapter Thirty-Three

Reflections

D wayne what I'm about to say has a lot to do with a strong intuitive feeling," she grinned mischievously, "and a wee bit about farming."

He shoved the bill of his John Deere cap up and back on his head, as he filled his mouth with a big bite of ham sandwich and pushed it into his cheek. "Feelin' antsy about somethin', are ya?"

"Remember my Uncle Jack's eccentric friend, Arthur Wainwright?"

"Sure do." He took another bite of his sandwich, which served as a quick lunch break between chores. "He was that old hippy guy. Right?" A few bread-crumbs escaped his mouth onto the countertop when he spoke.

"Yeah. That's him. And something he told Jack many years ago has been rolling around in my mind all morning. Arthur told Jack to *never* ignore intu-itive feelings about anything. He went on to explain, 'Because a radiant heart's intuition will always be more than a simple gut feeling about something. Gut feelings are for normal people. You, dear boy, are not normal. Intuition for you is a subconscious prompt to act on whatever issue you happen to be, or should be, dealing with.'"

As a gesture of offering full attention, Dwayne pushed his plate back and set his cap on the kitchen's central island where he had been standing and scarfing down a ham sandwich. He sat on a stool and placed folded arms and elbows on the counter. "Somethin' on your mind that you need to deal with? Somethin' I can help with, maybe?"

"There is no alternative. I *must* have your help with it. No one else on earth will do. Only you and me, Babe."

"This is gettin' good. Go on."

"I realized a few things that all seem to be coming together over a very short period. One of which is obvious; you'll be getting very busy on the farm. That's already showing signs of coming to its annual fruition. The natural order of farm life is all that is."

"Yep. That's a given. But not all unusual." He pushed spread fingers through his hair. "There must be more to cause such concern."

"There is. No one thing is overwhelming unto itself. But add them up and getting it all done in a timely fashion becomes somewhat intimidating."

"Mybe it's best I just shut-up and listen."

"Now that's the country wisdom I love you so much for...among many other reasons."

Dwayne smiled and sighed, clearly appreciating the comment. "Ya know kiddo, ya just bought yourself a kiss when you're done with this. Now, lay the rest of the story on me."

"As you know, I've been working on adopting Leti. And it's heading in a straight line towards a successful conclusion. I'm now quite positive I could adopt without a spouse. And, babe, it appears as though Leti and I are heading toward that conclusion at a rapidly accelerating speed. Here's the kicker; I don't want to start her permanent family life with any other surname than Logan." Melissa drew a big cleansing breath. "Now, do you see where I'm going with this?"

Dwayne backed off the stool, took Melissa's hand and guided her to a more open area in the kitchen. He dropped down onto one knee and took both her hands. "Melissa Dane-Blakey, once you get paperwork I need to sign for joint adoptive custody of one, Leti Deleon, and once it's finalized, would you marry me that same week and become Missus Dwayne Logan?"

Happy tears tumbled down Melissa's cheeks. "You've had my heart for many months. Now you have my answer. Yes!"

Dwayne stood. He wrapped both arms around her almost desperately and kissed her long and deep. "Till death do us part, Sweetheart." In much softer fashion, he repeated, "Till death do us part." He kissed her again.

Chapter Thirty-Four

Full Circle

Kyra helped customers at the cash register in the dress shop, A Matter of Style, in the Texas South Plains town of Brownfield. She had become a full partner with Lisa Rivera, the original owner and creator. Kyra had done this type of work her entire adult life and the obligatory, "Thank you for shopping with us. Come back soon," after ringing up the purchase required no concentration whatsoever. It left her mind to wander and plenty of time to think.

It still blows my mind that Missy, Dwayne and Leti will become an instant family. I've got to get busy helping Mom get the patio decorated, get the cake made and plan hor d'euvre selections. She sighed. *Fortunately, the ceremony and reception will be at the house and that patio is huge. It'll comfortably seat fifty to seventy-five people. Of course, hope for a sunny, mild and calm Saturday and, of course, no rain. That might be too much to hope for early in April.*

She squeezed her eyes shut and shook her head. *Now that's a negative I need to banish from my head. Positive thoughts. Only positive.*

"Kyra?"

She abruptly turned. "Sorry, Lisa. Lost in thought."

Lisa chuckled. "I could tell. I had to say your name three times to get you back to planet earth."

"Three times! I only heard you call my name once."

"Point made."

"What's up?"

"Same-old, same-old. Could you wheel that rack of sleeveless blouses out onto the showroom floor while I continue putting winter wear on the sale rack?"

"I'll get right on it."

Have Melissa and Dwayne set a date for the wedding yet?" Lisa asked as she followed Kyra toward the storeroom.

"Yeah. It'll be the first Saturday in April. We're praying for pretty weather so we can do the ceremony and reception on the patio. It's huge and should accommodate fifty or sixty guests with space to spare."

Is Melissa still working toward adopting Leti?"

"She is and getting nervous about having it finalized before the wedding." She laughed. "Speaking of nervous; she asked Dwayne what she should do about invitations—while chewing on a fingernail, no doubt. His response was simple and very country. He said all they needed to do is stand on the front porch and yell out the time and date real loud and. The neighborhood network will take care of the rest."

"Dwayne may have been making fun but he's not wrong. You take care of friends and family on the west coast and the rest will just happen. Guaranteed."

———

"Missy, you need to calm down," Dwayne told her. "Whatever happens doesn't matter as much as being married by the end of that Saturday."

Melissa had been standing in the front yard, pencil in one hand, tablet in the other, thinking, attempting to be certain that all the lingering issues would be resolved by the day of the wedding. She sighed deeply and exhaled in a huff. "I'm sorry. You're right...as usual." She smiled and then scanned the skies. "But it sure would be great if the weather that day is as wonderful as it is today."

Dwayne leaned close behind her and spoke in a whisper directly into her ear. "Are you still plannin' on that special part of the ceremony just for Leti?"

"By then all the paperwork for the adoption will be complete. And, although Leti knows I've been working on it, please don't slip up and tell her. I want it to be a nice surprise at our wedding. So that means, with your blessing...yes. I still plan on it."

"With my blessin'? Are you kiddin'? I'd have to possess the emotional capacity of a cabbage not to love the idea. Of course it's okay. In fact, I've been so darn giddy about it, I've had a hard time not spilling the beans to Dad about it."

Melissa suddenly became quite serious. She spun around to look him square in the eyes. "You're not tempted to tell him the whole plan, are you?"

He laughed. "Missy, Dad has always thought that I'm crazy. Why would I attempt to remove all doubt? Heck no. I'm not gonna say a word about it...any part of it. I'm strugglin' not to say a word about the normal part. Why would I attempt to explain *that* part."

"Whew! You had me worried."

"Tell ya what; I'll knock off work the rest of the afternoon and then you and I will make a wine run to Lubbock and pick up a couple of cases for the reception. That'll accomplish two things, wine for the reception and a bottle for tonight. Looks like you're gonna need a glass...or six." Dwayne laughed so hard he grabbed his stomach.

A broad smile stretched Melissa's face. "You're on, Stud."

————

Dwayne and Melissa chatted about alcoholic beverages as he held the door of the liquor store open for her. "Okay, okay," she said in answer to his question, "it is a country wedding, so go ahead and order a keg or two of beer."

"I'll make a country girl outa you yet."

She playfully slapped him on the arm. "Go on, talk to the guy behind the checkout counter about the beer. I see a guy stocking bottles onto a shelf back there. I'll ask him about helping take the wine cases to the truck."

The man at the back of the store agreed to get the wine. He disappeared through a nearby door into the stockroom.

Dwayne, having placed the beer order, sauntered back to meet Melissa to wait for the wine to be loaded in the pickup truck together. Melissa picked up a fifth of vodka off a shelf. "If we really wanted a rowdy reception, we could buy a case of this stuff."

Before they could share a laugh, a commotion commenced at the checkout counter.

A shabbily dressed man, unshaven and ratty hair confront the clerk with a machete.

The clerk stumbled backwards into a tall shelf of pint and half-pint bottles, knocking a few to the floor, shattering at his feet. As if already begging for his life, he squealed, "What do you want? Money? Are you after cash? What?"

Dwayne rattled in a rapid whispering rush, "That man has crazy, dead eyes. And with a machete in his hand, it's clear that he plans on takin' whatever he wants at any cost. And that cost might include the life of the guy behind the register. Missy." He put a firm hand on her shoulder and shoved her toward the farthest end of the store. Get back there and don't move. Don't draw any more attention than necessary."

Still holding the bottle of vodka, she took a stutter step backwards but then froze.

"Go now," he growled. "Hurry!"

She knew without needing an analysis of the situation that regardless how tough and courageous she knew Dwayne to be, he would not be able to control a crazy man with a machete—especially being on the same side of the counter facing a blade of that length. The clerk was protected somewhat by the counter. Dwayne had nothing between him and that guy except the machete. That might be a short-lived melee and she feared that it was about to happen in two seconds, and not end in Dwayne's favor.

As soon as Dwayne was within arm's reach, the ratty man swung the big knife at him.

Dwayne jumped back.

Melissa saw that Dwayne would not be able to avoid it twice in the same way.

The man caught himself from stumbling sideways and was already preparing for a backswing aimed at Dwayne's midsection.

No thought necessary. Holding the vodka bottle high, she shouted like a banshee and began running toward the man, yelling hysterically, "Get that blade away from him, you sonofabitch! He's my goddamn fiancé!"

He turned the machete toward her and swung it but was off-balance. It clanged against the vodka bottle in her hand with very little power. She was close enough to get a whiff of his foul breath and body odor.

Dwayne grabbed the would-be robber by the shoulder and spun the guy to face him, hoping to refocus his attention away from Melissa. He simultaneously drove the point of his elbow into the bridge of the guy's nose.

Dazed, the man fell forward and attempted one final downward slash, blade coming up unsteadily over Dwayne's head.

He didn't get the chance to complete that last downward swing.

Melissa had already begun her own swing with the vodka bottle at the back of the crazy guy's head.

It broke, coating all three with clear liquor.

Dwayne fell onto his butt then sagged backwards to lie flat beneath the unconscious man. Melissa tripped and fell on top of the man, completing a crazy-man-sandwich.

She rolled right and Dwayne shoved the man off him to the left.

"Well," he said breathing hard, "I see two upsides here; neither of us will have bandages on our faces at the wedding and the vodka masks the god-awful stench of this fella."

Melissa slapped him on the chest. "That's not funny! You could have been seriously injured, or even killed!"

"Ouch, Girl, that stings." He rubbed a circle on his chest where the slap landed. "Aw heck, Darlin'. I was never in serious trouble with this yahoo. In fact, I haven't had this much fun since that drunken free-for-all at a rodeo in Clovis,

New Mexico a few years back. Calm down a little, wouldja. This isn't my first rodeo." He chuckled. "And, of course, I mean that in the most literal sense."

The clerk behind the counter, next to the cash register, rose slowly. He looked like Kilroy peeking over a fence. "Uh...no charge for the keg o' beer and those cases of wine. Consider them a wedding present. And...thanks."

Still breathing hard, Dwayne grinned. "Thankya, right back, pal."

"No. *Thank you*. I have a strong feeling you saved my ass just now."

"Dang, Missy. Ya know what this means, don'tcha?"

Still lying on the floor next to Dwayne. "I have a feeling you're going to tell me."

"I'll have to wear my best corduroy jacket and put an extra-special sparklin' shine on that ol' bolo tie o' mine for the wedding."

"Okay. But if you do, I'm wearing the tightest boot-cut Wranglers I can squeeze my ass in to, full-quill ostrich boots, a white western shirt with pearl snaps, and the biggest belt buckle I can find. If you're going to play the rodeo dude, then I'll dress like it too. We can look like giant bookends on each end of a series of Louis L'Amour, Zane Grey, and Elmore Leonard novels."

He quickly wiped sweat from his palm on his shirt and held his hand open for a deal-securing handshake.

She took his hand, squeezed it and then kissed his knuckles.

"Now, Darlin', you are truly my country queen."

Chapter Thirty-Five

A Heart's Revelation

As strange as it might sound to an outsider, the episode a few days ago at the liquor store in Lubbock invigorated Melissa spiritually, emotionally, and provided motivation to not sweat the small stuff, which was almost everything that seemed of paramount importance just last week. Dwayne, of course, went about his merry way as if nothing had ever happened except for getting free beer and wine.

She boldly dropped everything in the way of wedding planning squarely in the laps of her sister, Kyra and her mother, Cary. And, from that very moment, gave all those details no more mind, whatsoever—save for one.

She still had lingering thoughts about the use of the radiant heart for pleasure and not just to correct or cure a problem, as Jack Dane, her uncle always did. From the time the radiant heart ability manifested in Jack, he remained reserved and somewhat fearful of using it frivolously.

Melissa did not consider her planned use of it frivolous—unnecessary maybe, but not at all frivolous. Although she harbored a kernel of doubt. She must steel her resolve to follow-through. Not a scintilla of hesitance could be allowed to remain that might hamper such a blessed event and the plan to make it memorable for sweet Leti. Even the tiniest bit of doubt must be banished and made to drift away, like smoke in a breeze.

She figured that she needed to talk to someone who might not agree but would understand her dilemma. And that would be a favorite uncle she never had a chance to know in his lifetime. But was given the divine blessing of a way to know him personally many decades after his passing, Jack Dane.

With some hesitation, she made her way to her favorite room in the mansion, the library. As she closed the door behind her, the first thing she noticed was unimpeded light from the still-rising sun in the east. It was brilliant, streaming at an extreme angle as westerly beams discovered the northerly facing window down to the floor through the large arched window—dust motes floating in the brilliant rays of morning sunshine—occasionally dancing in unison within the hard-edged beam, like tiny butterflies dancing just for Melissa's enjoyment. She smiled and enjoyed the simple beauty of the miniature show for a while. Through the window out on the patio, the light was so bright it created near-black shadows on the western side of the various statues decorating the area. Inside the library, it was as if God had shone a spotlight on the maroon tapestry rug. The rich-looking rug covered most of the library floor. But it seemed as though a very specific area was chosen to spotlight.

Wouldn't it be great if I could focus my own radiant heart at the very spot that the most intense light hits the floor, causing a convergence of God's light and my own at the same spot? And then, maybe, Uncle Jack might appear at that precise point. She chuckled at such a notion. *Now this would be the correct usage of the word 'frivolous',* she thought.

Suddenly, her entire body was engulfed in a misty glow. A beam of light shot from the left side of her chest toward that spot of sunlight on the floor. A billowy circle of light rapidly formed around the radiant heart beam and began to widen at its center, revealing Jack Dane standing in that exact spot holding an open book. *Oh, my God! She thought. It worked.*

There was no hesitation. She immediately stepped through into the decade's old version of the same room she had been in seconds ago, only now, many years in the past. The flash of nausea came and went quickly.

Jack flinched and drew a quick breath. "Who are you? I didn't notice that you came in. Did Rita show you back here? He marked the page of the book in his hand and dropped it on the table.

"Please, allow me to reintroduce myself..."

"Reintroduce? Do I know you? Have we met before?"

"Yes...yes...and yes."

"I don't understand."

"Jack, you are my uncle, Kyle Dane's brother was my father."

"But he was killed... Wait a minute! Are you a radiant heart?"

"I sure am. Just like you. I'm Melissa, your niece."

Jack pulled a chair around and dropped onto it, as if sudden exhaustion had overtaken him. "Wow," he muttered.

"I knew you'd be shocked again. I had to go through this scenario once before."

"So, you've visited before. Is that right?"

"Yes. Once. During that visit, I promised to get your novel, The Last Radiant Heart, published. It never had been. And, although you can't remember that visit and will have no memory of this one, a promise is a promise. I will keep that vow. I swear it."

"The 'Last Radiant Heart'. So, that's what I'll title it."

"Little did you know at the time, this time...your time, that you weren't the last."

He pulled his shoulders up in little more than a suggestion of a shrug, "Obviously not."

The reason I bring this up is because I had an appointment in Austin to meet with a publisher about your manuscript. On the drive, I came upon a car accident where the mother was killed leaving a small child orphaned. I have completed the adoption process and plan on announcing it publicly at the wedding in a couple of weeks."

"Who are you marrying? Anyone I know?"

"As a matter of fact, you do know him. It's Dwayne Logan, Rita's son."

"Even for a radiant heart, this is difficult to fathom. He's just a little kid."

She laughed. "Take my word for it; he still acts like a little kid sometimes. But, Jack, Dwayne grew into the sweetest, most gentle and courageous man in the world. And, of course, country to the bone."

She paused, collecting her thoughts. "I need your advice."

"I'll try. Tell me your problem."

"It's not a problem...per se. It's just that I know by your book that you were always a bit fearful of using the power of the radiant heart, unless necessary."

"True. It always worried me, and still does, about unintended consequences. If it had not been for the guidance of a man by the name of Arthur Wainwright, I would have inadvertently left Nikki Endicott, the love of my life, in a time she did not belong."

"I have met Nikki and Arthur right up the road. She pointed west toward the old Endicott house where Dwayne and his father, Cletus, now live. Apparently, you were in the front yard doing some work while Nikki and Arthur sauntered down a turnrow in a cotton field, allowing you some alone time. It was easy to see in that short visit how you came to love them so much. I know, deep in my gut, I could have, and likely would have, loved them too."

"Thanks for saying that."

"Okay. That said, down to the issue at hand. I want to do something requiring the use of the radiant heart, that would be a glorious thing for Dwayne, Leti, and me during the wedding ceremony. But I also do not, at all, want to abuse the power for the same reason you just outlined."

Melissa spent the next few minutes explaining the desire to her uncle. He did not interrupt a single time. "So, Jack, what do you think?"

"When you consider the power of the radiant heart, the key word is 'heart'. A way to connect over time—past, future and dimension—all for the sake of love in one form or another. My advice is simple; follow your heart. If it feels right deep in your soul, then it is. That is something Arthur told me early in our relationship. And that is never to disregard intuition. It's much different for you and I."

A smile grew and spread across her face. "Yeah. That's what you said in your book."

"Ah, great. So long as you understand that our power goes beyond time and dimension traveling. I'm not at all certain just how far that extends though. Therein lies my personal fear. But my feelings are my cross to bear, not yours. Do what you feel is right, especially if it is for the sake of love. I really cannot envision something done out of love going wrong. I say do it."

The sage counsel struck Melissa with such profound clarity that tears welled in her eyes. She approached Jack and reached for both his hands that lay relaxed upon the arm rests of the chair and gently pulled him to his feet. He did not resist in the slightest. She wrapped her arms around him and pressed her lips to his cheek. The kiss was long and firm. She finally and reluctantly tilted her head back without letting go, while examining every facet of his face.

Jack kissed her gently on the forehead.

She leaned in and quickly kissed his cheek one more time. She backed away and squeezed his hands. "Jack Dane, sweet uncle, I love you so much."

"I love you too. I only wish I could retain a memory of this precise moment."

She kissed the backs of both hands before letting him go. She took a big step backwards. "I'll see you again sweet uncle." She closed her eyes, drew a deep breath. Brilliant light filtered through her closed eyelids then faded. Once again, she was in her own time and Jack was gone. Now, presumably standing with Nikki Endicott and Arthur Wainwright for eternity. Her eyes shifted upward toward the ceiling. She tapped her heart and blew a kiss skyward.

Chapter 36

After a period of eager anticipation, the wedding day had finally arrived. Word had gotten around that it would have a western theme. Wine for the country cultured and plenty of beer for all the good ol' boys. The setting and decorations were simple and inviting, creating more of a party atmosphere than that of a traditional wedding, just the way Dwayne and Melissa wanted it.

Melissa, Kyra, and their mother, Cary stood together on the patio next to the open French doors into the house. Melissa marveled at how well the weather turned out on this first Saturday in April. The breeze was light, the sun shone brightly and the temperature mild.

Kyra elbowed her sister, "Missy, if you had any more love and happiness in you, you'd be like a tightly inflated balloon full of glitter ready to pop. And those tight Wranglers you're wearing might speed up the popping."

Melissa chuckled and shoved her sister with her hip. "Oh, hush."

"And where did you find that belt buckle? It's huge. That beauty reaches from crotch to belly button."

"I did have to do serious shopping to find it. That's for sure. I spent most of the day in Lubbock searching for it."

Kyra grinned big. "I bet your panties having bucking broncs on them."

Melissa laughed loud enough to draw attention. "She whispered to her sister, "That's none of your business."

"Aha! I think you just confirmed it."

"Oh, shut up." Melissa laughed again. She went quiet for a moment and then looked toward the altar without comment or expression.

Finally, "When Dwayne and I agreed on a western theme, I was thinking more along the line of neon beer signs and barstools, but the neighbors went far beyond the call to build something so beautiful out of such rugged materials."

The construction lumber was left entirely unfinished and rough. The cedar latticed arch went over and surrounded a low platform for the minister and Dwayne and Melissa. Placed on each end of the arch were large, shiny Mexican clay pots holding live prickly pear cactus displaying spring cactus roses and young red prickly pears. Additionally, the arch was covered with a multitude of those same cactus roses.

Melissa shifted her attention to the crowd that gathered around Dwayne as he told humorous tales of farming, livestock, and his rodeo days. Until now, she had not truly realized how popular he was in the community. She felt blessed to live in an area where everyone had everyone else's back and were always ready to help with just about anything—including putting together a patio wedding.

She took a moment to watch Leti with her school chums. The little girl looked quite the young lady; long, coal-black hair that draped her shoulders. Her dark skin glistened with radiance and sweet beauty in a smile that none of her friends could even approach equaling. She assimilated at school quickly, developing a circle of friends while doing so. Melissa did feel a pang of regret that Leti's biological mother could not be with her today. She sighed deeply, then shifted her thoughts. *Leti, dear heart, you have no clue what I have planned for you. This is your day too.*

Almost simultaneously, Robert Rivera came to stand next to Kyra. He threaded an arm through hers. Meanwhile, Cletus Logan moved in next to Cary and put an arm around her waist pulling her in a bit closer. He leaned across Cary and spoke to Melissa. "Are ya ready? It's about that time."

Melissa nodded nervously fast.

Robert tilted his head sideways toward Kyra. "Whaddaya think? Could this ever be us?"

"In your dreams." Kyra snickered.

Melissa nudged Kyra without looking at her. "Never say never, because never is a very long, lonely time."

They laughed together. "Touché, Missy...touché."

———

Time had come.

The minister, Joseph Bell, stepped up onto the altar and faced a crowd that had grown to over seventy, according to Melissa's best estimate. Kyra and Cary had planned for up to a hundred. It might best be described as a comfortable size and easily accommodated.

Minister Bell clapped his hands and in raised voice announced, "Friends, neighbors, and relatives, please take your seats. The ceremony is about to begin."

Charlie and Johnny Blakely, the half-brothers of Melissa and Kyra, hurried over to give Melissa big, family-sized hugs. Charlie, the oldest brother whispered, "You deserve all the happiness in the world after the way our father treated you over the years."

Melissa smiled and glanced at Charlie. She grinned and thought, *I gave as good as I got, dear brother*. "Thank you, Charlie. I love you for saying that." A violin had been playing various western tunes, keeping with the western theme.

Melissa walked up the aisle toward the minister flanked by Charlie and Cary on one side and Johnny and Kyra on the other. The brothers and the minister were the only three men in the crowd wearing suits and ties. Once they stepped up onto the altar and took their places, the violin player stopped the playlist he'd been working through, paused, and then began an upbeat country version of the wedding march with a joyous cowboy fiddle beat and volume.

Melissa felt quite comfortable in her snug, boot-cut Wrangler jeans over full-quill ostrich boots, a white western shirt buttoned to the neck with a red rose yoke across the back and, of course, pearl snaps. Her big oval belt buckle of brightly shined silver caught the afternoon sun just right and appeared to produce its own light. She grinned when she thought about bucking broncs on her panties. There weren't.

Dwayne's father, Cletus, walked beside him as they approached the altar, front and center. As promised, he wore his best of two corduroy jackets. This one sported a suede collar focusing attention on a turquoise and silver bolo tie pulled tight around his neck.

Melissa could not help but be amused that as wonderful as he was dressed and looked, it seemed odd for him to be outdoors without that dirty green John Deere cap on. Dwayne was her country-to-the-bone Adonis and she his newly minted, countrified Aphrodite.

Melissa looked to make certain Leti was in her seat in the front row. For her plan to go off without a hitch, the youngster had to be ready to react, although the child remained totally unaware of how she was about to be included in the ceremony.

Dwayne and Melissa faced the minister. With an appropriate amount of piety, he read a couple of scriptures from the bible in his hand. After the recitation, he began the standard wedding spiel. When he was about to finalize the ceremony, Dwayne looked toward Melissa.

She smiled and nodded.

"Uh, excuse me, Reverend Bell, before we get down to the 'I do's', Missy and I have something we'd like to share with everyone here today that is quite appropriate and fits nicely in this ceremony."

Murmuring across the crowd hummed like a docile hive of bees, everyone appearing bewildered by the unorthodox interruption.

Melissa gestured, full extension of the arm, palm up. "Leti, please join us up here."

The youngster made two false starts, looking side to side, seemingly for approval or further confirmation of having heard Melissa correctly.

"Come on, sweetheart, take my hand," Melissa said in the gentlest tone possible. She dropped down onto one knee. Dwayne mimicked her, sinking down onto one knee.

Reverend Bell clearly had no idea what was happening or about to happen, so he simply clutched the bible to his chest and crossed his arms over it. At the same time, he shrugged and smiled at the audience.

Once Leti's hand was in Melissa's, she was pulled in closer still. Dwayne lightly touched the child on the shoulder. Although the touch was truly a loving gesture, it served a dual purpose.

"Dearest Leti," Melissa said loud enough for all to hear, "the adoption has been approved and, if you wish it so, this wedding will not be for two people, but for three: Dwayne, your father...Melissa, your mother...and for you as well, Leti Deleon Logan. Would you like to be a permanent member of our family?"

Leti nodded deeply and fast. She smashed her little body into Melissa almost knocking her over. The child began to sob while tears flowed freely. She screeched, "Yes...yes...yes!"

The audience erupted with applause. Many of the women began to cry, the men hooped and hollered approval.

While still clapping, Melissa nodded at Dwayne.

He returned a knowing look.

Melissa pulled the three nearer to one another.

A white glow surrounded all three of them and a sudden brilliant beam shot from Melissa's chest. A roiling white cloud parted at the center surrounding the beam to reveal a postcard worthy scene. Melissa whispered, "Let's go."

They stood. Dwayne lifted Leti and held her close. Melissa guided them through the portal.

Upon arrival a second later, Leti said, "I think I'm going to be sick."

Melissa assured her that it would pass quickly.

Once the nausea flash passed, Leti wiped away residual happy tears from her cheeks and finally looked around. "Where are we? Where's the house and the farm? Where are all the people?"

"I wanted you to see where we'd be flying to in a couple more days. It's an island over five thousand miles from where you were standing just seconds ago. A place called Bora Bora. It'll be a honeymoon for three people. That means you are included."

Leti looked out and was clearly awed by the whitest sand and the bluest water she had ever seen. Melissa knew it was the first and only beach the little girl had ever seen. "But I don't understand how—"

"Hi, guys," came a male voice wafting to them carried on the stiff sea breeze.

Melissa and Dwayne snapped their heads around at the same time and looked down the beach to see a young couple walking in their direction from some distance away. They were dressed more appropriately for an afternoon at the beach. The girl wore a barely-there white bikini. The young man had on red knee-length swim trunks. "We decided to walk to that monstrous palm tree a little farther down," said the man, "and suddenly, I mean *instantly*, you appeared in front of us."

Melissa looked around nervously fast. "Uh, we walked here from the other direction."

"Honey," the girl asked her companion, "I didn't know there was a place to walk farther down."

Looking bewildered, "There's not. It's all boulders and thick undergrowth all the way to the water's edge." He looked at the three of them from head to toe. "It doesn't appear you're here for the beach anyhow." He laughed and added, "It looks like you're dressed for a hoedown or a rodeo. "Did you get there, I mean farther down the beach, by boat?"

"Oh, we didn't—"

Melissa interrupted Leti, "No, we don't have a boat." She glanced at Dwayne, took Leti by the hand, and pulled the child along as they walked past the couple in the same direction from where the two had come from. "Well, we have to go, but y'all have a great time today."

Leti looked back at the pair and all around, as if her head was on a swivel, still very confused by everything. Now, she was obviously not understanding why Melissa had been so rude.

Dwayne looked back at them as well, just as the young woman said loud enough to hear clearly, "Well, that was weird."

Melissa quickened her pace. "We've got to get somewhere that they can't see us for a few seconds."

"Before ya get ta zappin', you need to quickly explain to Leti what to expect and not be tellin' anyone what happened."

"You're right. This may take a few extra minutes to get us by so we can finish the wedding. A longer talk can, hopefully, wait until everyone has gone home."

The sun had moved to the setting side of the sky. "I suppose there's no need to be rushin', now that we have no one else to contend with."

"Again, you're right." They slowed their pace and Melissa began talking directly to Leti, explaining how to deal with everything she had just witnessed and what would happen when they returned.

Dwayne took an exaggerated deep breath as he looked out across the water that was reflecting sunlight off the ripples in the water and made it appear to sparkle like a blue diamond. "Dang, that's pretty."

Melissa nodded in affirmation but her mind had gone to a different place. She dwelt on that conversation with her long-deceased uncle, Jack Dane. She looked back a final time at the young couple getting very small in the distance behind them. She wondered what they were talking about, as the girl pointed in their direction a couple of times.

Jack had used the word 'frivolous' and the phrase, 'unintended consequences' in the use of the radiant heart when it wasn't necessary. She had summarily disregarded frivolous as a way of describing her plan to him. Yet, he was afraid of dangerous situations that could possibly be set in motion inadvertently.

She didn't alter her pace along the beach but continued looking back. A personal vow had begun to form that she would never again use the power of the radiant heart so casually ever again. All the while, the phrase 'unintended consequences' played in an endless loop in her mind. Could that couple, somehow, be damaged or even set off a tsunami of events, simply by her presence in this time and place? It would be impossible if this was a past event, but this was the present and the couple would, in fact, remember what they witnessed. She wondered.

Chapter Thirty-Six

A Wedding and a Promise

After a period of eager anticipation, the wedding day had finally arrived. Word had gotten around that it would have a western theme. Wine for the country cultured and plenty of beer for all the good ol' boys. The setting and decorations were simple and inviting, creating more of a party atmosphere than that of a traditional wedding, just the way Dwayne and Melissa wanted it.

Melissa, Kyra, and their mother, Cary stood together on the patio next to the open French doors into the house. Melissa marveled at how well the weather turned out on this first Saturday in April. The breeze was light, the sun shone brightly and the temperature mild.

Kyra elbowed her sister, "Missy, if you had any more love and happiness in you, you'd be like a tightly inflated balloon full of glitter ready to pop. And those tight Wranglers you're wearing might speed up the popping."

Melissa chuckled and shoved her sister with her hip. "Oh, hush."

"And where did you find that belt buckle? It's huge. That beauty reaches from crotch to belly button."

"I did have to do serious shopping to find it. That's for sure. I spent most of the day in Lubbock searching for it."

Kyra grinned big. "I bet your panties having bucking broncs on them."

Melissa laughed loud enough to draw attention. "She whispered to her sister, "That's none of your business."

"Aha! I think you just confirmed it."

"Oh, shut up." Melissa laughed again. She went quiet for a moment and then looked toward the altar without comment or expression.

Finally, "When Dwayne and I agreed on a western theme, I was thinking more along the line of neon beer signs and barstools, but the neighbors went far beyond the call to build something so beautiful out of such rugged materials."

The construction lumber was left entirely unfinished and rough. The cedar latticed arch went over and surrounded a low platform for the minister and Dwayne and Melissa. Placed on each end of the arch were large, shiny Mexican clay pots holding live prickly pear cactus displaying spring cactus roses and young red prickly pears. Additionally, the arch was covered with a multitude of those same cactus roses.

Melissa shifted her attention to the crowd that gathered around Dwayne as he told humorous tales of farming, livestock, and his rodeo days. Until now, she had not truly realized how popular he was in the community. She felt blessed to live in an area where everyone had everyone else's back and were always ready to help with just about anything—including putting together a patio wedding.

She took a moment to watch Leti with her school chums. The little girl looked quite the young lady; long, coal-black hair that draped her shoulders. Her dark skin glistened with radiance and sweet beauty in a smile that none of her friends could even approach equaling. She assimilated at school quickly, developing a circle of friends while doing so. Melissa did feel a pang of regret that Leti's biological mother could not be with her today. She sighed deeply, then shifted her thoughts. *Leti, dear heart, you have no clue what I have planned for you. This is your day too.*

Almost simultaneously, Robert Rivera came to stand next to Kyra. He threaded an arm through hers. Meanwhile, Cletus Logan moved in next to Cary and put an arm around her waist pulling her in a bit closer. He leaned across Cary and spoke to Melissa. "Are ya ready? It's about that time."

Melissa nodded nervously fast.

Robert tilted his head sideways toward Kyra. "Whaddaya think? Could this ever be us?"

"In your dreams." Kyra snickered.

Melissa nudged Kyra without looking at her. "Never say never, because never is a very long, lonely time."

They laughed together. "Touché, Missy...touché."

***

Time had come.

The minister, Joseph Bell, stepped up onto the altar and faced a crowd that had grown to over seventy, according to Melissa's best estimate. Kyra and Cary had planned for up to a hundred. It might best be described as a comfortable size and easily accommodated.

Minister Bell clapped his hands and in raised voice announced, "Friends, neighbors, and relatives, please take your seats. The ceremony is about to begin."

Charlie and Johnny Blakely, the half-brothers of Melissa and Kyra, hurried over to give Melissa big, family-sized hugs. Charlie, the oldest brother whispered, "You deserve all the happiness in the world after the way our father treated you over the years."

Melissa smiled and glanced at Charlie. She grinned and thought, I gave as good as I got, dear brother. "Thank you, Charlie. I love you for saying that." A violin had been playing various western tunes, keeping with the western theme.

Melissa walked up the aisle toward the minister flanked by Charlie and Cary on one side and Johnny and Kyra on the other. The brothers and the minister were the only three men in the crowd wearing suits and ties. Once they stepped up onto the altar and took their places, the violin player stopped the playlist he'd been working through, paused, and then began an upbeat country version of the wedding march with a joyous cowboy fiddle beat and volume.

293

Melissa felt quite comfortable in her snug, boot-cut Wrangler jeans over full-quill ostrich boots, a white western shirt buttoned to the neck with a red rose yoke across the back and, of course, pearl snaps. Her big oval belt buckle of brightly shined silver caught the afternoon sun just right and appeared to produce its own light. She grinned when she thought about bucking broncs on her panties. There weren't.

Dwayne's father, Cletus, walked beside him as they approached the altar, front and center. As promised, he wore his best of two corduroy jackets. This one sported a suede collar focusing attention on a turquoise and silver bolo tie pulled tight around his neck.

Melissa could not help but be amused that as wonderful as he was dressed and looked, it seemed odd for him to be outdoors without that dirty green John Deere cap on. Dwayne was her country-to-the-bone Adonis and she his newly minted, countrified Aphrodite.

Melissa looked to make certain Leti was in her seat in the front row. For her plan to go off without a hitch, the youngster had to be ready to react, although the child remained totally unaware of how she was about to be included in the ceremony.

Dwayne and Melissa faced the minister. With an appropriate amount of piety, he read a couple of scriptures from the bible in his hand. After the recitation, he began the standard wedding spiel. When he was about to finalize the ceremony, Dwayne looked toward Melissa.

She smiled and nodded.

"Uh, excuse me, Reverend Bell, before we get down to the 'I do's', Missy and I have something we'd like to share with everyone here today that is quite appropriate and fits nicely in this ceremony."

Murmuring across the crowd hummed like a docile hive of bees, everyone appearing bewildered by the unorthodox interruption.

Melissa gestured, full extension of the arm, palm up. "Leti, please join us up here."

The youngster made two false starts, looking side to side, seemingly for approval or further confirmation of having heard Melissa correctly.

"Come on, sweetheart, take my hand," Melissa said in the gentlest tone possible. She dropped down onto one knee. Dwayne mimicked her, sinking down onto one knee.

Reverend Bell clearly had no idea what was happening or about to happen, so he simply clutched the bible to his chest and crossed his arms over it. At the same time, he shrugged and smiled at the audience.

Once Leti's hand was in Melissa's, she was pulled in closer still. Dwayne lightly touched the child on the shoulder. Although the touch was truly a loving gesture, it served a dual purpose.

"Dearest Leti," Melissa said loud enough for all to hear, "the adoption has been approved and, if you wish it so, this wedding will not be for two people, but for three: Dwayne, your father...Melissa, your mother...and for you as well, Leti Deleon Logan. Would you like to be a permanent member of our family?"

Leti nodded deeply and fast. She smashed her little body into Melissa almost knocking her over. The child began to sob while tears flowed freely. She screeched, "Yes...yes...yes!"

The audience erupted with applause. Many of the women began to cry, the men hooped and hollered approval.

While still clapping, Melissa nodded at Dwayne.

He returned a knowing look.

Melissa pulled the three nearer to one another.

A white glow surrounded all three of them and a sudden brilliant beam shot from Melissa's chest. A roiling white cloud parted at the center surrounding the beam to reveal a postcard worthy scene. Melissa whispered, "Let's go."

They stood. Dwayne lifted Leti and held her close. Melissa guided them through the portal.

Upon arrival a second later, Leti said, "I think I'm going to be sick."

Melissa assured her that it would pass quickly.

Once the nausea flash passed, Leti wiped away residual happy tears from her cheeks and finally looked around. "Where are we? Where's the house and the farm? Where are all the people?"

"I wanted you to see where we'd be flying to in a couple more days. It's an island over five thousand miles from where you were standing just seconds ago. A place called Bora Bora. It'll be a honeymoon for three people. That means you are included."

Leti looked out and was clearly awed by the whitest sand and the bluest water she had ever seen. Melissa knew it was the first and only beach the little girl had ever seen. "But I don't understand how—"

"Hi, guys," came a male voice wafting to them carried on the stiff sea breeze.

Melissa and Dwayne snapped their heads around at the same time and looked down the beach to see a young couple walking in their direction from some distance away. They were dressed more appropriately for an afternoon at the beach. The girl wore a barely-there white bikini. The young man had on red knee-length swim trunks. "We decided to walk to that monstrous palm tree a little farther down," said the man, "and suddenly, I mean instantly, you appeared in front of us."

Melissa looked around nervously fast. "Uh, we walked here from the other direction."

"Honey," the girl asked her companion, "I didn't know there was a place to walk farther down."

Looking bewildered, "There's not. It's all boulders and thick undergrowth all the way to the water's edge." He looked at the three of them from head to toe. "It doesn't appear you're here for the beach anyhow." He laughed and added, "It looks like you're dressed for a hoedown or a rodeo. "Did you get there, I mean farther down the beach, by boat?"

"Oh, we didn't—"

Melissa interrupted Leti, "No, we don't have a boat." She glanced at Dwayne, took Leti by the hand, and pulled the child along as they walked past the couple in the same direction from where the two had come from. "Well, we have to go, but y'all have a great time today."

Leti looked back at the pair and all around, as if her head was on a swivel, still very confused by everything. Now, she was obviously not understanding why Melissa had been so rude.

Dwayne looked back at them as well, just as the young woman said loud enough to hear clearly, "Well, that was weird."

Melissa quickened her pace. "We've got to get somewhere that they can't see us for a few seconds."

"Before ya get ta zappin', you need to quickly explain to Leti what to expect and not be tellin' anyone what happened."

"You're right. This may take a few extra minutes to get us by so we can finish the wedding. A longer talk can, hopefully, wait until everyone has gone home."

The sun had moved to the setting side of the sky. "I suppose there's no need to be rushin', now that we have no one else to contend with."

"Again, you're right." They slowed their pace and Melissa began talking directly to Leti, explaining how to deal with everything she had just witnessed and what would happen when they returned.

Dwayne took an exaggerated deep breath as he looked out across the water that was reflecting sunlight off the ripples in the water and made it appear to sparkle like a blue diamond. "Dang, that's pretty."

Melissa nodded in affirmation but her mind had gone to a different place. She dwelt on that conversation with her long-deceased uncle, Jack Dane. She looked back a final time at the young couple getting very small in the distance behind them. She wondered what they were talking about, as the girl pointed in their direction a couple of times.

Jack had used the word 'frivolous' and the phrase, 'unintended consequences' in the use of the radiant heart when it wasn't necessary. She had summarily disregarded frivolous as a way of describing her plan to him. Yet, he was afraid of dangerous situations that could possibly be set in motion inadvertently.

She didn't alter her pace along the beach but continued looking back. A personal vow had begun to form that she would never again use the power of the radiant heart so casually ever again. All the while, the phrase 'unintended consequences' played in an endless loop in her mind. Could that couple, some-how, be damaged or even set off a tsunami of events, simply by her presence in this time and place? It would be impossible if this was a past event, but this was the present and the couple would, in fact, remember what they witnessed. She wondered.

Also by

Daniel Lance Wright

The Last Radiant Heart

Annie's World: Jake's Legacy

Annie's World 2: New Beginnings

Call Me Mikki

Six Years' Worth

Where Are You, Anne Bonny?

Trouble

Dancing Away

Defining Family

Helping Hand For Ethan